True Promise

A novel by Margie Janes

eBook ISBN: 979–8–9927481–2–3
Paperback ISBN: 979–8–9927481–3–0
Hardcover ISBN: 979–8–9927481–4–7

Cover design by Sooraj Mathew

Cover photo by Jean Lachat Photography

Edited by Hilary Jastram, www.bookmarkpub.com

Dedication

This book is dedicated to my beloved mom and to all who grieve the loss of a loved one.

(Except for the *spicy* scenes. Those are for you, "Amy.")

Get in Touch with Margie!

www.margiejanesauthor.com

FB: @margie.janes.author

Insta: @margie.janes.author

Table of Contents

Prologue

Beck

I shifted my weight side to side, standing at TJ's front door in Charleston, taking slow breaths. A nauseating worry filled my chest, making me anxious. A year ago, on this January date, I ran down my street in Naperville, thinking of TJ. Of that first moment nearly crashing into him at four years old when I fled my grieving mother and how he fixed everything in my world. Now, I was running toward him. After missing him for a decade, we reconnected last spring and promised to always be each other's everything. I needed TJ. He could ease me like no one else, but even TJ couldn't make *this* right.

Inhaling a deep breath, I knocked on TJ's front door. I wasn't planning to be here, at Eastern, this early for the second semester of senior year. He wasn't expecting me.

I was supposed to be home spending the last few days of break with my best friend, Lindsay, and my parents. TJ had planned to stay back at campus as a last reprieve before student teaching in Carlyle mid-week. TJ's roommates were noisy inside. Their muffled but booming voices made it sound like a battle was raging. I was sure it was some kind of game and not a physical altercation. A gust of wind blew strands of my hair around my face, and I tucked a piece behind my ear. It was unseasonably warm for a January night in Illinois. Another unexpected reality.

I knocked again. A little louder, a little more firmly this time, like I was trying my knuckles at being persistent, when inside, I felt like crumbling. We had made so many gains over the past few months. We had strategized so many plans about how this semester would play out.

We had come so far. And now …

The door before me flung wide, and TJ appeared suddenly in the open space. His lips parted, "Beck! What are you doing here?" he exclaimed and pulled me into him, smothering me with his muscular frame. He backed up, warm surprise curling his lip. He leaned down and kissed me. As he pulled away, his genuine smile almost had me thinking this would be a carefree visit. In the next second, his expression turned quizzical with furrowed eyebrows as he scanned my face for an explanation. "Are you okay?"

That was where I had to lie. I had to pretend I was fine. Otherwise, I would just flounder in a pathetic cry and end up sobbing for hours instead of relishing being with him.

"Yeah, I just … needed to see you." I looked down and then up at him, hoping I was giving him an enticing look. I couldn't tell if it worked completely. TJ's sexy smile seemed guarded. I amped up my play, took hold of his hand, and leaned up to him, kissing his bottom lip slowly.

After a few moments of deep kisses, our breaths becoming more rapid, TJ held my shoulders and whispered urgently, "Come on."

He guided me into his house, past his roommates, who were all playing some war video game.

"Hi, guys," I called out quietly.

"Hi, Beck," Trevor said, bobbing with laughter at something on the screen.

"Beck," Mason, TJ's cousin, acknowledged, barely moving his head to look at me. He was fully into his game.

Brandon was whining loudly, "Come on! Fire! Damn it!" He threw the remote down on the carpet, causing it to bounce with a clunk. "Hey, Beck. God damn it!" he yelled, although we were past the living room and moving into TJ's bedroom. I could hear Trevor laughing and Mason's low Southern drawl, most likely poking fun at Brandon.

Once TJ closed the door behind him, I let the world fall away and thought only of him. I rounded on him and kissed him hard. When I tugged on the waistband of his joggers, he sensed my urgency and pulled my leggings down. I climbed out of them as TJ pulled at the back of his T-shirt, balled it up, and tossed it on the corner of his bed. Then TJ lifted my shirt over my head, throwing it aside as I unclasped my bra and let it drop to the floor. We broke for kisses in between shedding articles of clothing. When I finally had him undressed, I pushed against him until he fell onto his bed with a shocked look of want in his eyes. I climbed on him and tried not to think of when I would be back here in this way. If I ever would.

We became a fireball of passion. Sudden, unyielding, charged desire filled the room like an electric current. My hands pushed into his shoulders as I balanced on top of him, my body moving over him as he held my hips steady. TJ pulled himself up to meet my lips with his. He drew long, rough kisses, never backing off the rhythm we created. Only when it felt I would burst into flames did I pull away from him and arch my back, allowing us both to fall to pieces together.

After, he held me closely as I remained straddled over him. His mouth huffed warm breaths onto my chest. My lips were pressed to his forehead as I breathed him in. I almost felt relieved. I would've. He had unnerved me in this way so easily so many times before. But now that the passion had subsided, I was left with nothing but the truth of my early visit. I kept my eyes closed, not wanting to see what I was about to do to the both of us.

"I guess you really did miss me," he panted into my neck, kissing the curve of my shoulder and the base of my collarbone.

Then I couldn't hide it. He pulled back to look at me, most likely surprised that I didn't even muster a chuckle at his humor. I was having trouble looking him in the eyes. I saw his chest rise in a long, deep breath. He gently moved me to the side and grabbed his shirt then pulled it over my head. I slipped my arms in the armholes. How did he know this kind of thing? That I loved the scent of him. That it calmed me. That I needed all the comfort he could give me. This was why I loved him more than anything. TJ shifted to dress himself. I gave him a hopeless but grateful look.

"What's going on, Beck?" All the humor drained from his voice. "I know it's bad, just not sure how bad."

I let that sink in, then breathed in again, not meeting his incredible blue eyes but feeling them drilling into me. I wanted to pretend this was normal. That I just wanted him. Not admit the dire situation I was about to divulge.

My chin quivered uncontrollably. I didn't have all the answers, but I had some.

"It's my mom," I said finally, fidgeting with my nails. Then I looked into his eyes while holding back my tears. He scrutinized my face, considering my words, calculating what I'd say next. "She's sick. Really sick. And I'm staying home to take care of her."

Suzanne

The diagnosis came like a prayer fulfilled and taken away all at once. How long have I prayed for death? How much of my life have I been afraid to live? It's so fitting.

My whole family is taking this hard. Robert, my darling husband, is crumbling after decades of holding me up. Ryan, my middle child, who barely communicates with me, is texting me constantly. Colleen, my sweet and loving sister, might be taking this news the hardest. But Rebecca. My darling Rebecca is determined to fix me. I can see it in her eyes. She has outright refused to continue living away at college if I begin treatment back home. I have never seen such will from her. It's awe-inspiring.

I don't know how much time I have left. There is a battle now between the death I have craved day after day amid shadows of grief since my oldest, Rachel, left us. Either way, I am leaving this journal as a piece of myself. For all the questions I couldn't answer. I hope they will see this as an act of reconciliation, not simply cowardice.

Maybe when I'm gone, you'll understand. I love you all, and I'm so sorry I've let you down.

Test Drive

SEVEN MONTHS EARLIER

In late May, after TJ and I fell madly in love but before summer classes started, I finally, finally, finally bought my own car. I still couldn't believe I'd convinced my parents. But I guess the prospect of being able to come home on my own won out over whatever reservations my mother had. To me, it was an easy yes. I had the money and the skills and was an official adult. I wasn't backing down.

And it didn't matter that my dad was too busy again on business trips and extended work hours to go car shopping. I had TJ to help me.

TJ was a real adult about the car-buying experience. He sent me Google searches for used cars near me but thought it best to go outside Naperville to get better deals. He emailed me pages and pages of cars to consider, like Fords, Chevys, Kias, and Hondas. I had never seen him work so hard on research and was tickled by his great effort.

Our next step was TJ's most anticipated one. He was driving up from his small hometown down south to help me car shop in person and had already made reservations at two dealerships.

The first one was at a Kia dealer in Willowbrook. But after I spoke with the sales rep for twenty minutes, TJ gave a subtle shake of his head, and I took the hint to end our meeting.

"Thank you for your time. We have some other appointments to get to, but we'll get back to you if we're still interested," I said, reaching out to shake the rep's hand.

As we walked to the parking lot, TJ explained, "There was something off about that dealership, right?"

I just rolled my eyes, laughing at him, "Ar-right, TJ."

Next up was a dealership in Aurora to look at a three-year-old Honda Civic with about 40,000 miles. TJ let me know on the way that this one looked promising. It had passed all the safety inspections, was reasonably priced, and the dealership had good ratings for customer service. Again, I was in awe of the little adult he was becoming. The man couldn't make himself an edible meal, but he tracked vehicles with the intensity of a CSI investigator.

TJ asked that dealer a lot of questions and negotiated the price down about nine hundred. It seemed like something my ex-boyfriend Jason would've done. Although TJ was more charismatic and playful about it. He had schooled me beforehand in how to ask about payment options, credit checks, and services I would need in the future. He wanted me to speak up and put myself out there. It was to be my car, after all. All these soft nudges helped me see where I needed to step up and be more independent. Ironic that at this time in my life, when I was wholly attached to my person, I felt the most liberated and self-confident.

TJ and I were having a great time chatting with our sales rep, Samir. I asked Samir if the three of us could take the Honda for a test drive. TJ prepped Samir that I was on the same playing field as the Indy 500 star, Danica Patrick.

"That sounds exciting," Samir responded with a grin.

"Not accurate," I said over my shoulder as we headed out of the showroom and into the lot.

Samir led us through the vehicle lot and guided us toward a sleek, royal blue Honda Civic. TJ opened the door for me. I sat in the driver's seat with Samir next to me and TJ in the back seat. Just sitting in the driver's seat gave me a burst of excitement. I steered out of our spot, and once we were clear of other cars and people, I pushed on the accelerator and coasted down the dealership lanes. We drove onto a main route, then TJ complained about being hungry. He said I needed a more practical experience with the car and got permission from Samir to drive to a McDonald's drive-thru.

"The drive-thru experience will give us a lot more feedback instead of just cruising around an empty lot. You know?" TJ cajoled.

"Of course, Mr. Lawson. I agree," Samir said with a grin.

As we pulled up to the drive-thru speaker, TJ introduced himself to the attendant. "Hello, ma'am, I'm Tommy; my beautiful girl Beck is the driver, and we are pleased to have Samir, our favorite sales rep in Aurora, along for the ride. Beck would like a … "

"Six-piece chicken nugget. That's it," I called into the order board, shaking my head at TJ's formality.

"Samir will have … " TJ gestured to Samir, who waved him off. "Hold on, ma'am," he announced to the attendant. "Samir, we are not buying this car if you don't order something," he said directly, but his eyes shone brightly like he'd just told a joke.

"A Number 2 (Quarter Pounder with cheese) and a Coke, please," Samir almost yelled across my body into the ordering window.

We laughed at how quickly he changed his mind to order once the threat of a lost sale became real.

"And I'll have a Number 1, Big Mac with a 10-piece nugget, large fry, one of those apple pie things, and a large Cherry Coke," TJ called out. Why was he always starving?

"Where exactly do you put it, Mr. Lawson?" Samir asked, eyes wide on TJ's trim frame.

"He expends a lot of calories talking," I laughed.

"I'm a pretty active guy, Samir. I'll slow down when I'm dead."

As we waited a few minutes for our order, TJ explained to Samir that this was the epitome of the test drive. He drilled Samir: "Do the windows operate?" "Can you turn down the volume easily to hear the attendant?" "Can you maneuver a tight drive-thru spot?" "Does the car have enough space for a mini trash can and a spot to put a lot of snacks and drink cups?"

TJ generously paid for the order; the cashier handed us our food and wished us a good day.

Instead of pulling over and eating, TJ suggested we keep going with the test drive. "Let's face it," he said. "It'll tell a lot about our comfort in the vehicle if we can easily enjoy some fast food while driving."

At this, Samir grinned and stuck a handful of fries in his mouth.

"That's a good point, TJ. We are going to be down south a lot." I pulled out of the drive-thru and headed back toward the dealership.

"See, Samir, Beck really needs a reliable vehicle. She's going to be driving to see me a lot during breaks and next spring when I'm student teaching. And I want to make sure she can eat and drive in this car, so we don't waste time having dinner when I finally get to see her." I could hear his smug grin.

"Thomas John Lawson. Not every comment in your head is a conversation piece," I scolded, eyeing him in the rearview mirror.

Samir said that TJ and I were the coolest and most entertaining customers he had ever worked with.

Back at the dealership, Samir cut another eight hundred dollars off the price. We shook hands; I signed papers, and he wished us well on my new car.

Once the car was mine, TJ took great care to make sure I was ready for anything out on the road. He showed me how to jump the battery and which cables connected to what and where. Positive red cable onto the positive red cable and negative from the good battery onto the strut tower of the dead battery. TJ made me practice twice on my new car and then asked a complete stranger in a Gas City parking lot if I could pretend to jump my battery using her SUV. The older woman giggled and obliged.

Once he trusted my practice of jumping the battery, he took off one of my tires and walked me through replacing it. First, finding the spare and pulling it out from the bottom of the trunk. Then, cranking the jack, unscrewing the bolts, fitting on the new tire, and replacing the bolts. We went over locating the recommended air pressure for tires and topping off coolant and windshield wiper fluid.

"I feel like I've just signed up for a mechanics course," I teased him, leaning over his bent shoulder under the hood.

"Oh, this is way better than a mechanics course," he admitted, standing up and away from the hood and turning to look down at me. His eyes softened, and he put his hands on the back of my jean shorts, pulling me closer and planting a sweet kiss on my lips.

"I might get in trouble for sleeping with my mechanics professor." I kissed him back.

"Um, you might get in trouble for *not* sleeping with your mechanics professor." He smiled and moved his hands up to my shoulders, giving me another kiss. Then he pulled away and explained, "My grandpa had me driving as soon as we moved to Carlyle. The tractor, his pickup, the four-wheeler, and his old motorcycle that now belongs to Mason."

"Really?" I said in awe.

"Yeah," he turned and leaned onto the bumper. "He put me through the wringer before I was allowed to get my license. My family had enough car worries to last a lifetime, and he just wanted me to be prepared and safe," TJ stared at a section of concrete on the driveway as if his mind had taken him to the crash that had changed his life forever and eventually moved him away from me. It caused a tender halt in my heart.

"That's very meaningful." I peered up at him. "Do you know how it happened?" I wasn't sure he wanted to talk about it. How could I just bring up the death of TJ's dad and his cousin's parents?

"It was a semi. Just plowed into them. It wasn't Luke's fault. That's Mason's dad. The semi-driver fell asleep, the police said. Of course, *the driver* was fine. It was everybody else who had to deal with losing the three of them." He studied the concrete again for a beat then shook himself out of it.

"Anyway ... " TJ stood up and moved in front of me. He put

his hands on my waist. "Low tires, flat tire, dead battery, engine overheating … I'm not letting anything stop you from getting to me, Beck."

Journal Entry #1 ~ Therapy

FIFTEEN YEARS EARLIER

So, here it is. This journal's purpose is to keep me alive and be my lifeline now. I have been instructed to write in it often, especially at low moments. I am ordered to bring it with me to the doctor's office, but he won't read it unless I ask him to. It is meant only to prove that I have an outlet for my grief, along with medication and check-ups. The options are: journal, weekly therapy, a psychiatric facility, or a divorce. Robert needs this. I need Rachel back.

That is unfair.

Robert needs her, too. Maybe he's better at coping with his grief by throwing himself into work. I know he didn't mean he wanted a divorce when he explained what he was going through. That's never been an option for him. Robert told me ages ago, "Consider when you are building a house, and each room has an escape route: a door or a window. Only our marriage is just one room. No windows. No doors. No way out. Only together." Robert fully believes this.

Sometimes, I wonder if he regrets that promise. What have I become? What a lie I was living, and what a fool I was to wish for happiness.

I've lost my daughter, and my world will never be healed. What does that mean for my other children? How can I pretend to be their mother when I am shattered?

Other than the weeks surrounding Rachel's death, the past week was as bad as it's been. It's been a year and a half, yet it feels like a lifetime. I can barely remember any content of the weeks that followed losing Rachel.

Every moment was filled with horrendous, nauseating, all-consuming grief.

The doctor told me to write what I could remember from my childhood. I didn't get into specifics with him; I just admitted I had a traumatic childhood. Because of that, the doctor seems sure some of my current behaviors are directly linked to my childhood. He asked me to dig back a-ways and see if I could find healing through writing down some memories to release them from my mind. I remembered many situations from my past. I had locked many of those images away because I felt they would never help me. But to move me forward and for Robert, I agreed to do it.

I wanted to die and for the pain to be over. I still do. How can I continue like she isn't here? Acknowledging that she's gone is worse. At first, I wanted to forget her, which made me sick. What a horrible mother I was to wish I could just forget her.

Robert wanted to talk about Rachel and celebrate her by putting up every photo of her. I couldn't do it. I couldn't see her baby face. I refused to look at the photo of Rachel and my baby Rebecca sitting in the grass, facing each other, sticking yellow dandelions in their hair. The ache was too strong. I couldn't bear the family photo of us in a field of green, wearing matching outfits, smiling at each other near the bridge by the nature preserve. Rachel had lost her eye teeth and Ryan his bottom two teeth. He smiled exaggeratedly, extending his bottom jaw unnaturally to show off the wide space there. Rebecca just clung to my skirt with a soft expression of a smile. I couldn't look at the photo my sister Colleen took of Rachel and Ryan at her house in their sleeping bags, snuggled close with Capri Sun pouches in their hands and thin red straws in their mouths.

How could I allow these images showing Rachel connected to Ryan and Rebecca to be here, knowing she is gone? There is only one photo I allowed Robert to keep up. He was so drained when he begged for this.

He never would've threatened to leave me but was so adamant that one photo be left up. I knew Robert wouldn't leave me. He is my savior,

12

even if I don't want him to save me all the time and even if I don't deserve him. He demanded one frozen moment of time, capturing Rachel. He won't pretend she wasn't his first child. His Disney princess. His ballerina. So, the fourth-grade photo that preserves her, as old as she'll ever be, and all alone in the photo, that was the one. Just the dimples to match her dad and my deep brown eyes to remind me daily of what I've lost. My punishment will be one image illustrating how she will be trapped at that age forever, even as we all grow older.

CHAPTER 2

Playing House

TJ and I played "married couple" for a few weeks during our summer intercession. Being alone in his house with him was such a stroke of luck. I told my parents that TJ's roommates were all staying in the house with us for summer classes. But that was not true. We got the gift of being alone at TJ's house for weeks. It was beyond amazing.

Mason, of course, stayed at home to be with his girlfriend, Jenna, and their three-year-old daughter, Tana. Trevor, TJ's sweet and responsible roommate, was back at home working two different jobs for the summer. Brandon came around sometimes when he wasn't traveling with his family. For the most part, TJ and I were alone.

Initially, I felt a little weird being at their campus house—like I lived there. Normally, I was just a guest. TJ's house was a typical bachelor pad. It wasn't a pig sty, but it was not really clean. Since my first visit after TJ and I had reconnected in dance class months ago, TJ and his roomies had turned the newspapers on the windows into waffle paper blinds, at least. But some were crooked. Some were ripped, and a few were missing.

The shag carpet made me never want to sit or lay on it. Who knew what that carpet had seen in its time? The couch was surprisingly great. Definitely lived on, slept on, spilled on, and maybe other things, but as far as I could tell, it was clean and comfortable. Besides TJ's bed, it was my favorite spot.

Once the newness of living there wore off, I felt comfortable. TJ was beyond happy that I was with him. We fell into a routine of classes, homework, exercise, or strength training at the Rec Center and being together. I was quite the little housewife, cooking and cleaning and showing TJ how to do both.

I knew TJ didn't have kitchen skills, but I wasn't fully aware of how awful he was at cooking. The meals he made himself were barely edible. I showed him how to look up recipes with limited ingredients that wouldn't take long. He was a good sport about it although he laughed too easily when I suggested he was pretending to be bad at cooking just to have someone else do it.

TJ and I worked to get this beer-infested, party-center house cleaned and conducive to completing schoolwork. I should've expected it, but I was still shocked that TJ didn't know how to properly clean pretty much anything. I sat him down at his place that first weekend for a heart-to-heart.

"TJ, you do know of my affection for you. Yes?"

"Uh oh. Why do I feel like I'm in trouble?" He grinned at me, sitting backward on a chair in the kitchen, his baseball cap backward, too.

"Could we do something together this weekend?" My eyes flitted around the kitchen, taking in the state of the area. There was no chance these cabinets, with their cloudy film and streaks of grease catching the light, had ever been wiped down. The edges of the floor had crumbs and dust, maybe dirt? I couldn't tell. A brown and sticky stain clung to the bottom and sides of their kitchen sink. I glanced toward the bathroom, knowing the shower was covered in (thankfully) only a light coat of mildew.

My mother's personality was coming through. My longing to clean this space, which had been shared by so many college guys who just didn't care or notice, was breaking my enjoyment of being there with TJ.

TJ was smiling bigger now. "This weekend? What did you have in mind?" he teased.

I raised an eyebrow at him, then winced as I squinted and scanned the room.

"Cleaning," he presumed, nodding his head.

"Yes, but real cleaning. Like a team effort?" I asked. I didn't want to insult him, but I needed him to understand that I couldn't be at home in a space that was probably hazardous to my health.

TJ shot up and slapped his hands together, then rubbed them back and forth vigorously. "Let's do this!" he yelled. "I will become a lean, mean cleaning machine. You watch, Beck."

I nodded at him, fighting a lurking smile. TJ's intentions were sweet, but he was not going to get a personality transplant. I just wanted to show him how to thoroughly clean one space. Or the whole space. So, in our future, he could help me.

Our weekend looked like this: two trips to Wal-Mart for supplies, three buckets of soapy water to scrub the cabinets and floors, two cans of Scrubbing Bubbles, one bottle of Windex, one roll of paper towels, one angled broom, and a dustpan. (How did these boys not have these common household items?) One bottle of bleach, one spray bottle, and four Magic Erasers.

I showed TJ how everything should be scrubbed down, and he was a great sport about it. At the end of the cleaning cycle, TJ looked around with an air of satisfaction. I could finally breathe easy in his place which was now pure and inviting.

He gave me a smug grin as we stood side by side, leaning against his kitchen counter.

"So?" he eyed me.

"So," I said. "Isn't this way better now?"

"It is way better," he agreed. "You definitely get this from your mom." He glanced sidelong at me with an honest grin.

I must've looked startled because he pushed off the cabinet to stand in front of me. Being compared to my mother wasn't usually a good sign.

"You know I didn't mean that in a bad way."

"Yeah," I said quickly, trying to ignore the mom comment. "Thank you," I said, fitting my arms loosely to the sides of his T-shirt. "Honestly, thank you for putting in this work."

"Anything for you." His eyes grew suggestive. "Um, these counters are clean now." He puckered his lips and raised his eyebrows, glancing back at the counter, taunting me.

I laughed and tried to break away, but he only wrapped his arms tighter around me.

Journal Entry #2 ~ Abandoned

How is my therapy going in the form of this notebook?
Terribly.
Why bother writing this if I'm not going to share it?
Will it make any difference?
Maybe it will.
Maybe I want to be found out.
I have always been too weak to handle my struggles and too timid to voice them. Is that something I learned from my mother, to just take it and not speak up? Is that why she left us?

I had promised Colleen that I would be a mom to her. How ridiculous. We were just two years apart, but I did take on the role of her mom. When I promised myself I'd be better than my mom and marry the perfect man, did I know then that I was jinxing myself? Maybe I was just being punished for hating them both. Mom, for leaving, and Dad, for not.

Every time he yelled, he shattered us like a wall crashing down until all that was left was debris.

My thoughts are so scattered on this page. My doctor said there is no right way to let go of your memories. Just let them out.

I am feeling regret.
It must be my fault.

I learned that from my mother. It was always her fault. You learned that when you were raised by an alcoholic father and a shell of a mother—until she finally ran off and left you and your younger sister behind. My father blamed my mother for everything. I didn't see it as clearly then, but here, stewing in this grief and loss, I feel it.

I can look back at all the times my mother turned her head away and ignored my father's vulgarity and insults. Just a slight shift in her posture, and she believed whatever he said and that everything wrong was her fault.

It didn't matter what it was. If the faucet dripped steadily into the kitchen sink, he'd blow up, insisting she hadn't turned it off properly, screaming in her face that he paid for that water and wasn't made of money. If a stack of mail was moved or shuffled to the corner of the countertop, he thrashed his arm over the pile, cursing and sending envelopes and papers cascading to the floor. Then: "Why do you always move my god damn papers?"

He never hit her. It was just as rough hearing his words rip her to pieces. My mother became small. She was afraid and panicked about everything as she made excuses for my father: "He's had a hard day." "Work's been tough on him lately." "I shouldn't have moved that. I know better."

Sometimes, I could see the light in his eyes. The father he was supposed to be would come through on the rare occasion that he wasn't drinking. Most Sunday nights, he would sizzle steaks in the frying pan and whistle. He was always whistling. Dad had a toothy grin that he said was just for me and Colleen because we were his smile, and if he didn't have us, he would lose his smile.

Colleen always loved being spoiled, which Dad did sometimes. More so Colleen than me. She was charismatic while I was quiet. She would put on these theatrical performances for Dad, and when he applauded, she would ask for a new skirt or costume prop so that the next performance would be better. I hated the look in my mother's eyes when Colleen went right to my dad, acting as if mom's permission didn't matter. My mother worked a few hours part-time at the convenience store a couple of blocks over. So, she did contribute to our family's income, but Colleen had learned that my mother was weak and couldn't make decisions. She knew she needed to check with our dad first if she would have a shot at getting what she wanted.

I remember my thirteenth birthday. It was supposed to be a celebration, but my mother and father were fighting again. He was so rough with his voice. The way he talked to Mom was incredibly arrogant, so belittling.

I wanted a bike for my birthday. We didn't have much money, so my mom bought a bike from a neighbor whose daughter had graduated high school. My mom took the bike and asked my dad to fix it up for me, as the chain was off, and the handlebars were loose. He said he would get to it. She asked two days later, and he snapped at her. "I said I would get to it, Claire!" She flinched but saw me in the next room, scared and disappointed. More disappointed than scared. I needed the bike to get around, and go hang out with friends. So, my mother gave me the bike on my birthday, but it did me no good. I couldn't ride it. I didn't think it would take much to fix it, though. My mother and I knew Dad could fix it quickly, so she pressed him again.

The next time he made an excuse, Mom squared her shoulders and replied, "This is her birthday gift. What's she going to have for her birthday if she can't ride it?"

"How about the god damned cake and dinner and a roof over her head and a father who works his ass off? How about that?" Then he stormed away, but not before grabbing a six-pack from the fridge and slamming the door.

My mother just stared at the door. Her shoulders rose and fell in exasperation. I walked away before she could turn and try to justify his behavior again, certain she felt small. I could see her getting smaller.

Later, she stopped by my room to check in before bed. Her eyes were all puffy from crying. I hated that I saw her this way more often now. I hated how sad she became. She'd mastered the art of making excuses for him, yet she couldn't hide her red eyes from me.

"He'll work on your bike soon, baby girl," she said with an even voice.

"It's okay, Mom. Thanks," I replied without emotion.

"Goodnight, my Suzanne." She kissed the top of my head.

Mom only lasted a few more months with us. Then, one day, while Colleen and I were at school and Dad was at work, she packed up her few belongings and left. Dad didn't even seem to react to her being gone. He just held that bottle to his lips as if it were the only thing he had left.

I didn't know why he drank. What was the attraction to alcohol? It smelled foul and made you vomit and yell at your wife. Why would anyone want that? But it was his vice, and he couldn't shake it.

I didn't know how a buzz could make you feel. I didn't know how a few too many drinks could turn you into someone you didn't recognize. Someone who made mistakes.

I know that now.

Maybe I forgive him. Maybe I don't. But I lost my mother because of him, and I lost my father because of him, too. Now, I've lost my daughter because I wasn't being the mother I should've been. I should've paid more attention. I should've looked at the signs of distress. How could I have been so blind?

I think my father is still out there. It's been years, but he may be holed up in his little apartment, still hanging onto that bottle like a lifeline. That's all he had. Colleen doesn't have anything to do with him, either. We are two sides of a broken heart that came out of that union and house.

When I turned eighteen, I moved out and got an apartment, taking what little money I had saved from summer jobs. I took Colleen with me. She didn't need to worry about our family. I tried to shelter her from our brutal history as much as I could. She didn't need to know all of it. She moved in with me easily, as if she'd expected it, as if she knew I would take her from him and into a safe space where we could lean on each other.

Picking up the pieces of our broken family, Colleen and I worked it out and didn't regret losing our parents. I didn't invite my father to my wedding. I didn't tell him when I was pregnant with Rachel. Or Ryan. Or Rebecca. I didn't tell him that Rachel died. What would he do? Blame me? Like I blame myself for so much? Robert thought we should check in with my dad, but I couldn't do it. I didn't want my beautiful children to be subjected to this despicable man who couldn't fight his disease enough for us. He never went for help. For a year and a half after Rachel passed, I didn't seek help, either. Maybe I was more like him than I thought. Maybe I was like both of them—living a lie and refusing help. Maybe I deserve to be tortured with the loss of my baby girl and the disconnect I feel toward my other two.

I only have Colleen and Robert; Colleen, my sweet, reliable sister, who can read me like no one else and razz me when I need a kick in the behind. My compassionate and sturdy Robert, who I don't deserve, who would give his whole life for me. How did I earn this man?

CHAPTER 3

Stolen Season

We were knee-deep in summer classes. I was doing really well with my three classes and had made friends with Penelope, a girl from one of my art classes. She and I spent some time together, even outside of my classes. TJ only needed to take two courses. He was not motivated in an academic sense, but as I pointed out, he could suck it up and do a good job to get those few credits.

One ordinary Saturday, after TJ got back from a quick trip to Carlyle and I had spent some time with some friends, TJ told me he had a surprise for me. From the back of his truck, he took down two bikes. One was his from home. The other was a gift for me for my birthday, which wasn't until the end of the summer.

"Ar-right, Beck. This is an AGT Aggressor Pro," he explained. The white and silver mountain bike looked beyond his price range.

"Wait a second, TJ. This seems really expensive."

"Not when it comes to you." His eyes glimmered, locking onto mine.

I set my hand on his shoulder and pulled him into a kiss. He was a gift in itself.

"And," he said, turning me toward the bike again, "It's sturdy and easy to handle. You need this bike. We need to recapture our riding experiences—except maybe not *all* of them, like when you broke your ankle." TJ motioned with his hand toward my left ankle.

"Good point."

"I've missed out on way too many birthdays and rides with you. So, instead of waiting for your birthday, let's do this now. What do you think?"

"I think you are the sweetest," I said, examining the bike and sliding my fingertips over the handlebars and seat. "And I'd love to ride around with you."

We spent the next two hours riding bikes around campus. The Charleston sky was light, the full sun burning our shoulders. The wind streaming around us made the day ideal.

I was swimming in nostalgia, transported back to our trail in the old neighborhood on a gorgeous summer day, with the biggest piece of my heart. Like I'd traveled back to TJ's block when we were kids. I could almost see the forest ahead of us and the trail that led to the pond where we'd spent our days. God, I was so lucky to still have him. And lucky that he'd been mine almost forever.

I let TJ lead, if only so I could watch the muscles in his legs and back, which were damp with sweat under his shirt, as he moved with the strides of the bike. His golden hair danced in the wind before me. I breathed in a long breath, so thankful for this day.

We rode all the way to Lake Katherine, where we dismounted and set the bikes aside to walk about the lake holding hands. I almost laughed, glancing down at our folded hands. His were sticky and warm like they'd always been in the summer when we were younger. TJ, of course, chatted non-stop, and I threw in uh-huhs and yeses. As he pointed out turtles and herons, I thought of that summer when I was nine, and he was ten, and our nest of turtles we'd kept watch over before he'd moved away. I remembered his sweet, elderly neighbor, Auntie Helen, and our summers long ago when we would live at the pond and camp in his wooded backyard.

After lapping the lake, we walked over to the camping section, and I tugged his arm to stop him.

He turned back toward me, but my eyes were straining to find the exact spot. Then … *I found it!* Our campsite from weeks before, right after spring break. I smiled, thinking about how I'd literally bumped into Lindsay getting out of the car. It was that crashing moment when

I'd found TJ's beautiful eyes on me as he sat across the fire. That was when I finally realized I loved him.

"This is the exact place when I knew I was in love with you."

His eyes searched the area briefly before coming back to me. He smirked.

"What?" I asked.

TJ pinched off his smile and shook his head. "Nothing."

"What?"

He was quiet for a breath, then: "I knew way earlier than that." His smile was too shy and sweet to be real.

"When?" I patted his shoulders. His T-shirt was warm and damp with sweat.

TJ paused for a second, eyeing me. His eyes were a fantastic shade of blue in this brilliant sun—truly stunning. Staring up at him and how intensely he was focused on me took my breath away.

"The moment I knew it was you in Mrs. Mac's gym." He moved closer to me and circled his arms around my waist.

"Uh," I exhaled in disbelief.

But I could tell from his expression that he meant it. I crushed my lips to his and fell in love with him all over again.

***

The days with TJ were a dream, but the nights were a fantasy. I was transforming into someone who hadn't a care in the world. Only he could make me feel like that. We took full advantage of being love-drunk college students on our own, with no roommates around and a whole house to explore.

I didn't understand how I could have this hunger for TJ. I was like an addict. I thought of him and his body all day, every day, in any class, at any time, even though I got to see so much of him. We became so comfortable with each other—never wearing a stitch of clothing to bed.

TJ was morphing into this very calm, very sexy version of himself. I lie beside him, uncovered in the summer heat, while he curled on his side, head on his hand, balanced on his elbow, exquisitely tracing his fingertips over my whole body. Leaning down and gently pulling my ear lobe into his mouth. Kissing the tender part of my neck. Or lapping his tongue on every part of me. I could see the passion in his stunning eyes. Passion that was fire just for me. It was so intimate and perfect. We cuddled together every night, and I felt total bliss.

It was a stolen season. We knew in time that the boys would literally be back in town, and I would be living in the apartment on the back side of campus with Amy and Lindsay again.

I could envision our life together in Carlyle. Just like this. Walking beside him on a path. Riding bikes on the weekend. Learning to live with him, his clutter, and his complete lack of awareness of the messes he made day in and day out. I could laugh at him over his attempts at making food to share. That was sure to be a hurdle for us both. Above all, we could have this incredible life together.

Journal Entry #3 ~ Getting By

It had only been four months since I dropped out of community college. I had given it a good effort and completed a whole year while working part-time at a grocery store near the college. I didn't mind the classes. I just couldn't pay the rent. Colleen was a senior busy with homework, poms, parties, and boys. She didn't have the time to get a job and pay her way. That's why I insisted that I would drop out to work more. A 4-year school wasn't in the cards for me. I didn't have a true career in mind. I just wanted to prove to my father that I could support Colleen and myself. We didn't need him, just like Mom didn't need any of us.

I always appreciated Colleen's attitude about our situation. She went along with me and never complained. Not when we were shopping at the consignment store or Goodwill for jeans and sweatshirts. She knew how dire our situation was. That's why she borrowed dresses from friends for big dances and had me fix her hair and makeup instead of joining the girls at the salon. She never commented on the peanut butter and jelly sandwiches for dinner or frozen waffles with bananas for breakfast. I could sense her satisfaction that we were doing it. We were working this plan out with each other. The bigger picture was that she and I felt safe together without our father.

When I confirmed Colleen's suspicions about me quitting school to work more, she just nodded and said we should celebrate my transformation from dropout to working girl. Then, she broke open an old piggy bank, took the sixty-eight dollars, and treated me to dinner at Texas Roadhouse. She told them it was my birthday, so I could get a free dessert, but more importantly, so that I could ride on the saddle they pulled out for customers celebrating milestones. Colleen hooted and hollered along with the staff when I secured the cowboy hat onto my head and climbed up on the saddle situated on a rolling, wooden horse. I waved my arm around like I had an invisible lasso, and Colleen shouted joyfully. Then, workers sang "Happy Birthday" to me, and Colleen held up her Sprite to cheer me on.

I applied to several stores at the mall just ten minutes from our apartment and received an offer from a kids' hair accessories and jewelry store. I worked there for two months until I got an offer from Julian's, a posh jewelry store on the upstairs level. That was my place. I loved everything about that job. The people were helpful, not condescending or standoffish. The rich leather smell was so inviting, and the brilliance of the jewelry was mesmerizing. Maybe it was because I couldn't have any of the pieces ... but I was obsessed with them all. Gorgeous sapphires, delicate golden chains, exquisite diamonds. I could only dream of decorating my wrists, fingers, and neck with their beauty.

One of my favorite co-workers, Pearl, was a middle-aged woman with a braided updo and the longest gold and scarlet fingernails I'd ever *seen. Pearl teased that she was always meant to work in a jewelry store with a name like hers. She had the best stories.*

"Lord, I need to get me a fine man to buy me that new gold bracelet."

Pearl teased me all the time about men. "Sweet lil' thing like you, girl. You must be pullin' these men." She would tell me, "I'm scoutin' for you, Suzy Q. Gotta be a ripe young man waiting for you."

It normally makes me uneasy to be the target of other people's comments and taunting, but Pearl was on my side. She helped me get so many commissions. I started to creep out of my quiet shell and be a true salesperson. I soon became a company favorite and got a promotion to work evenings and weekends. The money was a nice bonus and helped Colleen and I stay afloat. Before long, I started buying clothes for us at the trendy shops and truly appeared as if I could adorn myself with any piece of jewelry at Julian's.

CHAPTER 4

This Is Me, Trying

One Friday evening, after a muscle-tearing workout at the Rec, TJ and I bathed each other in the shower. We were becoming so disgustingly attached in the house together, never spending a moment alone. Not even for showering. I challenged him to see if he could last one shower without breaking down and taking me right there.

We started strong and simply gave each other space to turn under the showerhead and move out of the way for the other to wash and rinse. TJ finished first, and he had nothing to do but stand at the edge of the tub, staring at me as I lathered my hair and scrubbed my scalp while clumps of shampoo slid down my body.

TJ sang with his eyes shut as a distraction. He must've been too tempted, though. Another minute later, with his legs and feet splashed from my rinsing, he stared at me with hunger-filled eyes, slack-jawed.

"What happens if I lose and can't resist you?" TJ breathed in a low voice, his hands tented over his pelvis, trying to hold back what was building inside him.

I batted my wet lashes. "Then, I own you for the night."

"That sounds like a win," TJ exhaled, his eyes smoldering.

In an instant, his mouth was on mine, tongue wild, hands slick, sliding up and down my back, over my thighs, and threading through my wet hair to the back of my neck.

I let out a gasp of pleasure and gratitude that he had failed this attempt to keep his hands off me for one shower.

His mouth dragged on my chin, then lower, on my collarbone, as the showerhead poured over us. I tried to push myself closer to him, but I was already close enough. Then, he squatted down a bit, hitched up my right leg, and, cupping the bend of my knee with the underside of his elbow, slid inside me. His groan washed out my moan of pleasure. I braced my left hand behind me on the shower wall and arched my back further, letting the water splash over my chest as TJ curled over me. Holding me tightly, TJ slid in and out of me with perfect pressure. I kept my eyes down on him, watching his gorgeous body strain and flex with each push. He didn't waver for a second, securing me to him and giving me everything I ached for. Only once we both spiraled through ecstasy did he carefully loosen his hold on my leg and let me ease off him. He kissed me softly, sucking on my pouty bottom lip as he pulled himself back into normalcy.

"You are so weak," I teased, kissing his neck.

He shook with laughter.

"Absolutely Beck. You're like a little sorcerer. I can't break out of your spell. It's too much." He pressed his lips on mine again and wrapped his arms around my back.

I turned off the nozzle, reached for our towels, and handed him one. We started drying off. Then, I stepped out of the shower onto the bathmat. My phone buzzed at that exact moment. I picked it up to move it off my T-shirt and panties, accidentally answering my mother's call.

My eyes grew wide at TJ, who was still standing in the drained tub, revived and gorgeous, freshly showered, his towel held loosely at his hips, every muscle in his chest rippling. His cut arms moved as his hands rubbed the towel on his washboard abs.

"Mom, hey," I said with what I hoped was cheerfulness and not, "Can you tell I just had hot, breathless shower sex with my boyfriend?"

TJ's eyes widened, and he grimaced apologetically.

"Hello, I thought you were calling me back?" My mom didn't sound mad. Just motherly.

"Yes, sorry. I was." I stumbled, trying to pull on my underwear with one hand and hold the phone with the other. She had called while we were working out, and I had swiped my finger up with a quick: "I'll call you back" instant message. I just forgot. In my defense, TJ could be very distracting.

"Where are you? It sounds echoey."

"Nowhere," I replied, which didn't make any sense. After being with TJ in the shower, I still couldn't formulate a rational thought. "I mean, I was just in the bathroom. Sorry. How are you? What's up?" I moved out of the bathroom and into the hall to escape the echo and the steam.

"Fine, thank you. I—" she paused, and I felt my stomach tighten. My mother rarely paused. Only when she was mad, upset, or had bad news. She usually just let fly whatever comment she was thinking up. Especially if it were a nagging one directed at me; she wouldn't usually care if she didn't put her statements delicately.

"I want you to come home this weekend," she said, sounding uneasy.

My mouth went dry, "Why? What's wrong?" I hadn't anticipated this. I flashed my eyes back to the bathroom at TJ, who was now dressed, his hand scratching through his wet, messy hair. He shot me a sobering look.

"Nothing's wrong," she said more confidently.

"Oh, good," I replied.

"I just want you to come home. Did you have plans?" she asked.

"No, we're not doing much." I snuck a glance at TJ who gave me a devilish grin I had to turn from. "I think ... " I started.

"Rebecca, I was speaking of you. Not the both of you. I'm assuming your 'we' includes Tommy," she said flatly.

And here it was again. Although this time, her icy tone made my cheeks hot with anger. She was purposely excluding him. The way she said "Tommy," like it was some foul taste on her tongue, was bad enough, let alone not putting any subtlety in the matter. She wanted to see me *without* him. This was such a difference from Jason, who my mother practically begged me to go out with. At first, when TJ and I got together, I thought her feelings had more to do with Jason being my ex instead of my person. But as time passed, I realized something about TJ did not sit right with her. It had been that way for as long as I could remember. Even when we were younger, she had never warmed to him.

I walked into the kitchen to pace around a little, holding the phone directly up to my ear to block TJ from hearing any further insults if I were too close.

"Okay, I get it. You don't want him around. You don't have to be rude about it," I said, my voice lowered to shield TJ from her opinion. I sounded as immature as a child. I should've phrased what I meant better. She was calling for me. Just to see me.

"Rebecca, I'm certain you are already spending a lot of time together." She took a breath to let that comment settle. I swallowed, thinking, *yes, we are seeing a lot of each other. Every day, actually. Multiple times a day, in fact.* Coming back to my senses, I rolled my eyes at her angle on it and resumed walking the kitchen floor.

"I would like you to come home, so we can spend some time together," she said.

"Fine," I answered, my heart clearly not in it.

My mother huffed a little. "You do realize this is me, trying," she said evenly, very unlike herself. It jarred me a little. She never spoke like that. Wasn't that what I wanted? To be her daughter? To be close to her? The way I'd always hoped we could be? It couldn't have been easy for her to try and start over when she'd been so standoffish with me.

"Sure, Mom," I replied, trying to sound better than I felt about it. "I'll come home."

"Great. Dad's out of town, so it'll be the two of us." I couldn't help feeling disappointed about that, too. *Dad isn't even going to be there.*

"Okay, I'll leave in the morning, and be there by noon."

"Please be careful driving,"

"I will. See you then."

I hung up with her amid mixed emotions. On the one hand, I was annoyed that she had almost demanded that TJ not attend this little date day. On the other, my mother had just taken a big step. She never asked me to spend time with her. Our tense conversation as we walked around the lake a few weeks ago must've resonated with her to try and be vulnerable and open with me.

TJ was so sweet about my new plans for Saturday. He said it was a sign that he should head home and see what was happening. It was only an hour and forty-minute drive from Eastern to Carlyle, so TJ was completely fine with it. He said he'd miss me, but it was good that my mom was reaching out. I don't know how he didn't talk badly about her or make a few comments, but he didn't. He took her insults like a champ.

Journal Entry #4 ~ Robert

Working at Julian's was such a positive experience. I felt confident and in control. It was fitting that this place of dazzling jewels and beauty would become the spot for a love connection.

One particular evening at work, I wore my new black pencil skirt and red, short-sleeved silk blouse with the satin trim around the neckline. I was finishing up at the register when I heard Pearl say, "Oh, my apologies. I'm about to go on break, but Suzanne would be happy to help you. Just a minute." Pearl walked past me, her face a portrait of the cat who ate the canary, eyes bulging, mouth biting back a huge grin. She went into the break room for the second time in less than an hour.

"Uh," I scoffed and moved over to one of the display cases, where I saw the reason she had excused herself.

The man was on the taller side but not towering and looked to be in his

32

early to mid-twenties. He had an average build and somewhat muscular arms accented by a light blue, long-sleeved, collared shirt unbuttoned at the top and complemented by dark brown dress pants. His hair was a peculiar mix of sandy brown and auburn catching the lights over the jewelry case as he bent slightly, hands in his pockets, browsing some pieces in the front.

"I can take you over here," I called out in a clear, confident voice.

"Ah." He nodded and came closer to me.

And then he did a double-take as he walked over to the case I was positioned behind. I'd heard of the expression "love at first sight." Of course, it's all over in movies, books, fairy tales, and love stories. I'd just never believed in it until that moment. Not for me, but for Robert. He fell for me in a second.

It was beautifully adorable.

One moment, he was a customer, perusing our shop with its trinkets. The next second, he was in love with a stranger: me.

The man with the blue button-down shirt, auburn hair, and beautiful hazel-green eyes stared at me wide awake, mouth slightly parted. I stared back, trying to think of how long I could allow this silent dance to last without it being too bizarre. But there he stood, still looking at me, unmoving, unblinking, for what seemed like forever. A smug smile played at the corner of my mouth, which broke whatever dream state he'd fallen into. "Can I help you?" I asked, a flirtatious turn to my lips.

A smile crept across his face, revealing adorable dimples on both cheeks. "Yes." He nodded slightly. "That would be great." As his grin grew, his eyes seemed to twinkle.

"What can I do for you?" I asked.

He let out a quick breath as his eyes bored into mine.

What was I doing? I didn't know this man. He was shopping for jewelry and, most likely, not for himself. What game was I playing at? But I couldn't stop myself as he intrigued me.

"I, um," he stammered without breaking eye contact. "I'm looking for

something," he stated with a grin forming on his charming face.

I let out a quick laugh and gave him a real smile. "Well, you've come to the right place," I almost whispered. I surprised myself at the emotion I felt in that moment. I suddenly wanted this man here; I needed to keep him talking to me, engrossed in me. It was a thrilling game.

His mouth parted, and a more serious expression darkened his face. It registered on me to pull back into my salesperson persona because he was here for someone else.

"Yes, I'm. I'm looking for a necklace." He finally broke our eye contact, glancing first at the case below us, then darting his eyes back to mine, seeking permission somehow.

"Of course," I said courteously, using my wristband key to unlock the case, "Gold, silver, white gold?" I moved a few chains around in the display to grab some cases in the back row. When I glanced up, his eyes were still focused on me instead of the necklaces I indicated. He righted himself and took a deep breath as I stood and set the velvet tray of necklaces on the counter. I scrutinized his face as he looked me up and down.

"So, who are we shopping for?" I nudged, more or less making him feel a little ridiculous. He had just openly scanned my whole body.

His face lost all color as he stood there like he'd been caught in bed with a mistress.

"Your mother?" I teased, eying him.

A slow grin pulled at his lips, but he pressed it into a thin line. I selected a few more cases and set them on the display case.

"No," he said finally.

I whipped my face up to meet his and gave him a warning look, "Your wife?" I asked, annoyed, my eyes flicking to his left hand to find it, thankfully bare.

"No. No wife, or fiancée." A pause, and then we locked eyes again. For the first time, I felt heat seep into my cheeks. "It's for my girlfriend." His eyes dropped to the case, and I swear, defeat loomed in them.

I pursed my lips and nodded. "Okay, well, let's get started." Now, I was in full business mode. Our few minutes of flirting were over. I was now pulling rank to get back in charge and lead this encounter. He was the one in love with me, after all, not the other way around. "So, how much are you looking to spend?"

"I'm not sure. Maybe ..." he trailed off, fixated on my lips. "Around three hundred."

When he met my eyes, I saw something that seemed like regret.

"Well, that's a fair amount. We can certainly pick out something nice for her. What does she like? Diamonds? Emeralds? We have some beautiful sapphire stones."

He looked lost now. "I ... have no idea." He paused. "We've only been dating for a month. What do you like?" he asked earnestly.

I almost gave him a pitying look, but I could see he was in over his head and had no idea what to do.

"I like the white gold and this diamond pendant. It's a classic beauty." I held up the necklace and let it dangle from my fingers. It was one of my favorites.

"Yes, it is. Classic beauty," he breathed, his eyes still burning on mine.

Now, my lips parted as I stared at him. Suddenly, he shifted his body and blinked.

"Right," he said quickly. "Suzanne, is it?" He glanced at my nametag.

I nodded.

"I greatly appreciate your time and assistance. I've changed my mind on the necklace." He stood taller.

"Oh, well. We have bracelets and earr—"

"Could you excuse me for a minute? I just want to double-check something. Please."

"Of course," I said.

He tapped the display case with his fingertips, turned around, and walked down the mall hallway, out of sight.

I pivoted to see Pearl raise her head from where she was sitting, her eyebrows knotted. She was obviously straining to see where he went.

It was irrational, but I was drawn toward this man. I wanted him to come back.

"Where'd he go?" Pearl yelled in a whisper.

"I don't know," I said more to myself, dissecting the huddle of people moving in all directions through the mall. "Have you been watching me this whole time?" I asked, whipping around to glare at Pearl with shock and embarrassment.

She made a face as if the answer were obvious.

Minutes ticked by in slow motion. I busied myself rearranging pieces in the case for a half-hour. I took care of another sale and an order for a ring adjustment. Just when I thought I would never lay eyes on this man again, there he was, standing before me.

"Hi again. I apologize." He was nearly breathless, his hair sticking up a little in the front as if he'd been running.

"Oh. No problem," I replied. "Still shopping? I intended to ask if you wanted to see a bracelet or some earrings instead?"

"No, I won't be purchasing anything today." He searched my eyes and smiled. "When you get off work, would you like to have dinner with me?"

A soft giggle burst from my lips.

"Actually, Miss Suzanne is off the clock right now," Pearl cut in unexpectedly, hustling over, my purse already in her hands.

Stunned embarrassment burned my face. "Pearl," I started, flashing her a look as she grabbed the key ring off my arm.

"Oh, you are an angel. Look at you trying to cover Yasmin's shift. We are good, right, Yasmin?" She sent a warning expression in the other clerk's direction.

"All good. Thanks anyway, Suzanne." Yasmin waved from the register.

I chuckled, seeing that she was in on this, too.

"Now, what was your name, young man?" Pearl asked, handing me my purse and shoving me toward the mall entrance.

"I'm Robert."

"Yes, Robert. That's it. You two go on and have a nice time. See you tomorrow, Suzanne." Pearl blew kisses to us and turned away, smiling.

CHAPTER 5

A Beautiful Step

That Saturday, when I pulled up to our house in Naperville and walked to the door, my mom opened it and rubbed my arm in a welcome.

She had a whole agenda for us. First, we had lunch at a little café not far from the house. Our next stop was a nursery to buy some annuals for the garden and flowerpots to place along the patio.

I had been to that nursery before, but this was the first time my mother consulted with me about her purchases.

Mom needed some zinnias, cosmos, and impatiens. I didn't know much about gardening, so she taught me. We strolled through so many aisles of flowers, checking out annuals, perennials, and flowers needing more shade, more sun, and more space. I learned which required a lot of care and which seemed invincible. She explained the areas in the yard where she wanted particular species planted and asked my opinion throughout.

I stopped and stared at her profile at one point, feeling as if I didn't know her at all. *Is this what it could've been like all these years?* A tear sneaked up and almost ruined the day, but I turned my head in time for her not to notice.

Later, Mom told me she had planned a paint-and-sip night for us. She had tracked down a fun event where we could drink, eat appetizers, and paint under the instruction of a real artist. I was taken aback at the time she had put into planning to help keep me occupied and enjoy our weekend together.

On painting night, we pulled up to an Italian bistro and entered to find a private party room with paint-and-sip signs. Once we checked in, we were ushered to the back, where exposed venting and rustic pendant lighting decorated the space. I took in the small collection of stools and easels and felt a zing of playful delight.

"Mom, this is so great!" I proclaimed.

She gave me a quick smile and squeezed my shoulder.

We found a small table and sat down beside each other. A waiter came by offering drink specials and menus. We ordered waters and tangy bruschetta with a balsamic sauce and a summer salad of Mandarin oranges mixed with greens, cranberries, and sugared pecans. The waiter pressed us about having an actual drink. I was just weeks away from twenty-one, and my mother didn't drink often—something I never really asked her about.

After the meal, the artist came out and explained the scene we would all paint: a redheaded girl with her back toward us, swinging from the branch of a wide oak in front of a lake. Wildflowers scattered the space around the field in the distance and under the feet of the swinging girl.

Initially, it seemed complicated, but once I looked more closely at the model before us, I knew I could do it. And I had an idea to make it more meaningful.

"What do you think?" my mother asked, indicating the painting displayed for the group.

I smiled. "Piece of cake."

She smiled back.

My mother was a quick learner. After the instructor dismissed me from needing any help, she gave my mom a few pointers and let her create. The conversation in the room grew quiet because everyone was concentrating on their projects—except for a rowdy group in the back who kept cackling and chiding each other every few minutes.

After a while, my mom had a stunning recreation of the artist's creative work. I drank in her artwork, wondering how long she'd had this ability. *How long has she been drawing or painting? Why have I not seen this before?*

I showed my depiction to my mom, who took an audible breath. My girl on the swing had long, brown hair and loose curls hanging over her shoulders. After staring at it for a few minutes, Mom's eyes filled with emotion. Was it regret? She fumbled, trying to speak, and squeezed my hand.

"It's Rachel," I said carefully, hoping she would take my spin on the assignment well.

She attempted a smile but shook her head. "It's you." As she nodded her head at my painting, her eyes grew nostalgic in a way I hadn't ever seen.

The instructor came forward at the end and complimented each individual, pointing out a unique feature in each piece.

When she came to mine, she pulled her head back and turned to me. "This is masterful," she said, examining my painting.

"Thank you," I replied.

"Where do you study?"

"I just started. Eastern Illinois University."

"Impressive. You should be proud."

And I was. It was a fun day and a successful evening. My mom got to see a side of me she hadn't noticed before. I got to see the same thing in her.

***

By Sunday morning, I thought we would be done relating to each other, but my mom wanted to plant the flowers we picked out. It would take a while. She asked if that was okay.

"Of course," I said, although my heart was pulled in two different directions. I missed TJ. How silly. I had just seen him yesterday morning, but I always wanted him by my side. Yet, I was glad my mom wanted more time with me.

Mom and I busied ourselves with gardening. I dug into the edges of the patio, my nose filling with the scent of earth and summer. I planted sections of pink and purple cosmos, then moved on to the zinnias. She took care of planting the potted flowers. It took some time, but after about two hours, we were far enough along to take a break on the comfy patio couch under the shade of the umbrella.

"I haven't gotten used to you being gone all the time, especially now for summer," my mom said, taking in the refreshed yard while purposely avoiding eye contact.

I didn't say anything back. I didn't miss being home. Not really. So, I let that comment fall into nothing, thinking that was the end of it. She wasn't used to expressing emotion, and I didn't anticipate she'd follow it up with another sensitive comment.

"I miss you when you're not here." Her jaw worked, and she blinked a couple of times.

I couldn't believe it. Something swelled inside me. At once, I moved closer to her on the sofa and gave her a hug. Then I just held onto her.

Her skin was softer than I remembered and more delicate, too. *How does she smell so good after working in the garden for hours?* Like lavender and coconut. I held onto her, and she held me right back. We just sat like that, my eyes welling up and spilling onto my cheeks. "I'll be home more often, Mom," I said into her shoulder.

After a long while, I pulled away and saw that we looked exactly the same: glassy eyes, rosy cheeks, and trembling lips. Gazing at each other, we laughed in the same way, wiping at our faces, neither of us explaining the hurt or the heart, yet understanding it.

Journal Entry #5 ~ Classic Beauty

Dinner with Robert should've been awkward. I didn't know this man at all. He had a girlfriend, and those were just two of my main concerns. Instead, it was an easy time. I felt lighter than air. He so desperately wanted to know about me. Robert asked me question after question, ensuring I had his undivided attention. "Is there a certain time you're expected at home?" "Where did you grow up?" "Do you live with anyone?" "How long have you worked at Julian's?"

I asked him if he lived with someone. He said no. I didn't ask about his month-long girlfriend. I didn't want to know about her, and truthfully, I hoped she wouldn't be his girlfriend much longer.

Near the end of dinner, Robert raised his glass of cabernet sauvignon and toasted me: "Cheers to meeting you, Suzanne."

I could only beam back as his eyes sparkled behind his wine glass.

Robert drove me home and walked me to my door. He had his hands in his pockets like he was holding himself back from something.

"This has been …" I fumbled for the words. "Nice." I smiled genuinely at him. His smile matched mine, and he took my hand, pulling it close to him and kissing the back of it.

"This has been …" He clasped my hand. "Wonderful." Robert gave me a dimpled smile. "Thank you, Suzanne. I hope to see you again soon." With that, he dropped my hand and turned around to walk back to his car.

I watched him get into his car and drive away, my head swimming with questions and hopes. I couldn't contain my grin as I headed up to my apartment, opened the door, and gushed to Colleen, who was beside herself with glee.

The next night at Julian's, I buzzed with delight to my co-workers while discussing my evening. Pearl went on and on about how I should be so grateful to her for the setup. I smirked and patted her arm in thanks. Yasmin asked how we ended the evening, and I couldn't quite explain the next step. He didn't have my number. I didn't have his. He hadn't even told me his last name. Just Robert, this sweet man with dimples and earnest hazel eyes.

After about an hour at work, Robert appeared, walking down the hallway, toward the shop, past the sunglasses kiosk. I instantly smiled, watching him move closer to the store. He, however, had a serious, almost defensive expression on his face. My stomach turned, and my shoulders sank.

Robert strode up to my jewelry case and gave a barely-there smile.

"Hi," I said, trying to hide my disappointment at his expression, hoping his hazel eyes would reveal his thoughts.

"Hi, Suzanne," he said warmly yet directly.

I let a silent moment pass, wondering what was coming.

"I was actually hoping to look at that necklace again. If that's okay." He probed my reaction. I took a silent breath, my disappointment a shaken bottle of soda, fizzing up from my toes to my throat, where it foamed over into bitterness. I glared at him for a second, but he didn't falter, seeming to have a hidden emotion behind his eyes.

"Of course," I said, my tone clipped and cold. I unlocked the case and set the necklace on the foam bodice to the side of the display. "If that will be all, I'll have it wrapped, and you can pick it up at the register."

"Wait." He reached for my hand, a confused twist to his lips. "I want to see it on you first."

I just stared at him icily, hoping he felt the stupidity of his request.

"I want to make sure you really like it. If so, there's no reason to wrap it." His eyes were bright. I furrowed my brow at him.

"You are purchasing this for your girlfriend, correct?" I asked, leaning closer to him, annoyance evident in my voice.

"Well, my new girlfriend, yes. I broke up with my previous girlfriend on the pay phone around the corner yesterday. Before I asked you out." Now, he was sheepish, his dimples on full display.

I just gaped at him. My mind stumbled like tires on a curb. He broke up with her before our date? Of course, when he excused himself and came back a while later.

"May I?" He indicated the necklace, and I slowly broke free from the stunned look on my face to place the necklace between his fingers. Then I grinned up at him, still in a cloud of mixed emotions.

Robert carefully fastened the necklace around my neck and adjusted the diamond pendant. His hands smelled like vanilla and leather, sweet and protective. His warm eyes rested on the pendant now hanging from my neck.

"Classic beauty," he whispered smoothly, moving his gaze to me.

Then I leaned in and kissed him.

CHAPTER 6

Heads Up!

One summer night in July, before intercession ended, TJ and I had the whole gang back for a camping party at Lake Katherine. Lindsay, Amy, her friend Tony from home, and some of TJ's friends were meeting us. Mason, Jenna, Freddie, Trevor, and his new girlfriend would all be there, too.

We staked out spots on the shoreline and set up tents. Of course, TJ had his old but trusty blue tent with the clear plastic dome on top. Amy and her best "friend," Tony, set up their own tent.

Freddie was a new addition to the crew. He had been a good friend to TJ and me over the summer. We typically ran into him at the Rec. He brought a case of beer to share.

Jenna was so happy to see me again. She kept hugging me and talking about how elated she was that Tommy and I were together. She swore that Tommy had never been happier in his life! Jenna gushed about seeing TJ at the campout because "Mason's been missing his cousin this summer." Mason had been working construction just outside Carlyle, so his hours were long. He was so tan that he almost matched Jenna's olive skin.

Once the group set up tents, Lindsay started whining about not having a space to sleep like last time, but TJ said she could just share ours.

"Um, no thanks. I don't need to complete your threesome fantasy. Let Amy do that."

"You know I'd be game for that, but I've got my own plans tonight. Right, Tony?"

45

"Whatever you say, McCafferty," Tony replied.

A little while later, Trevor arrived with his girlfriend, Cassie. She was petite with light blonde hair and blue-framed glasses. Trevor looked so adorable, showing her off. I instantly beamed for him.

Everyone started drinking. Amy told us that if we behaved, or better yet if we didn't, she'd show us all her nipple ring. She'd gotten it as a birthday present for herself two weeks ago.

Lindsay was flabbergasted. She couldn't understand why Amy would want a nipple ring. "Ouch," Lindsay said, crossing her arms over her chest.

"It doesn't even hurt anymore. Want to pull on it and see?" Amy stuck out her tongue at Lindsay.

"No. Ew. Wait. Won't that, like, mess up your breast later on when you have kids and nurse them?"

"What part of me says I want kids?" Amy stared at her, eyes wide. "And especially that I would want them sucking on my boobs? The only mouth I want on these girls is a dude's. Like Tony's. Right, Tony?" Amy jabbed an elbow at him.

Tony was kneeling down to push in the stakes and holding the tent steady. "That's right."

I covered my forehead with my hand and cringed.

"Now I have that image in my head ... " Lindsay flailed her arms toward Amy with a grimace. "Along with your nipple ring. Just rotating around in my brain's image inbox," she circled her finger around her head.

"You're welcome," Amy said, taking a drag on a cigarette then passing it to Tony.

"But y'all aren't dating?" Jenna asked Amy, eyeballing Tony.

The two instantly shared an awkward look and busted out laughing.

"Okay. So, no," Jenna laughed awkwardly, too.

"Amy and Tony are just," I paused as they smirked at me. "Special friends." I knew firsthand from my crash course last spring break in

Amy's hometown about her relationships with her guy friends.

"Amy is special herself, anyway," TJ laughed.

"You got that right, Tommy boy!"

After making camp, we pulled up chairs around the fire Mason had started for us.

"Rebecca, I miss you so much," Lindsay whined. "It is so boring this summer. There are still *no* men, and the only action I've gotten is this little annoying redhead at the daycare who pats my butt every time he needs to ask me something."

We all instantly cracked up.

"I like this kid," Mason slurred.

"I've completely messed up my future." Lindsay finished her can of hard seltzer and set it down. She slunk down in her seat, elbows on her knees, fists holding up her cheeks, and sighed, "I don't like kids anymore."

I literally spit out my drink with laughter.

"You're gonna be a teacher," TJ laughed. "That sounds like a complication."

"I'm serious," Lindsay pouted and sat up, close to tears.

I wiped my mouth with the back of my hand and finally managed to ask, "How much have you had to drink?" Linds always got mopey when she drank.

"Not enough to convince me that I actually like children," she complained, reaching into her cooler bag near her spot and popping open another hard seltzer.

"What are you talking about? You love all those little shits!" Amy yelled.

"Kids. They suck. They're awful, and I think I'm making a big mistake."

"So, you hate kids now," Amy said.

"Yes." Lindsay deflated.

"Why all of a sudden, Linds?" TJ asked.

"Because I'm working at this God-awful daycare this summer, and they're horrendous." We all started laughing again.

"Most of them are dirty and sticky and so badly behaved. This one kid just keeps throwing stuff at me, like, the whole time I'm there."

Amy died laughing at this.

"It's not funny!"

"Just deck the little turd," Tony said, and Mason held out his hand for Tony to high-five him.

"Yeah, easy for you to say. I have to deal with the director and this kid's parents who are both doctors or lawyers or something. They said it's my fault for not giving him choices, and he's just expressing himself."

"Yikes," Trevor said.

"I would pay money to see this," Amy said, making Lindsay even more reproachful.

"Well, let's play a game to cheer you up," Jenna said.

We decided to play the phone game Heads Up! The timer starts when you hold your phone, displaying a word you can't see up to your forehead. When your teammates give you clues to the word, and you guess right, you tilt the phone down. You tilt the phone up to pass. We played in teams of two. Naturally, Amy demanded that we choose the X-rated word list.

I teamed up with Jenna who was so funny and could barely get the clues out. She passed on several words and laughed through the rest. We managed all right, getting three answers correct. TJ partnered with Freddie and gave clues in fast, crazy succession. They came in second place. Trevor and his new girlfriend were a pair. She was so embarrassed and quiet the whole time that they only scored a point. Trevor held her on his lap after that, telling her it was his fault. She looked so sweet, and Trevor was so happy.

The most hysterical team of the night was Mason and Tony. Mason guessed the words, and Tony gave the clues. Mason held the phone on his forehead above his barely open eyes.

The first secret word was "mistress."

"Okay, so this is like a girl you have on the side," Tony hurried.

"Uh oh," Mason said, eyeing Jenna.

"It's the name for a chick. You're married, and she's … "

"Skank," Mason blurted.

"No, it's like a proper word for the cheater girl … "

"High-end skank."

TJ roared. He always laughed the hardest when Mason was in the spotlight.

"Mason, don't be dumb," Jenna snapped.

"Pass," Tony swiped his hand toward Mason.

The screen lit up the secret word "foreplay," and Tony said, "Going down on your girl before sex."

"Christmas present," Mason shouted, his eyes unfocused.

"Pass," Tony laughed along with our group.

The next word was "streaking."

"Okay," Tony said, "taking off all your clothes and running around in a public place."

"Saturday," Mason replied immediately.

"Ahh! Stop it!" Jenna yelled through laughter.

The whole circle, even Trevor's girlfriend, was in hysterics. "I got that one right," Mason argued, his eyes scanning all of us. Then he tilted the phone down for a point.

The next word was "lap dance."

"Um, this is where you kind of slide on someone when they're at a club performing for you …"

"Hookers," Mason called out.

"That's not a club, bro," TJ laughed, wiping his eyes.

"Strippers," Mason tried again.

"But they're, like, performing," Tony blurted, trying to beat the one-minute timer.

"Acrobats," Mason slurred.

Tony shook his head, croaking with laughter. "It's like ... ," then Tony lunged toward Mason and gave him a lap dance.

"Woody," Mason yelped with wide eyes fixated on his lap. Tony fell over laughing, and the rest of us couldn't breathe.

Mason and Tony came in last place, not getting a single word right.

Last, it was Amy and Lindsay's turn. Amy did a little dance of enthusiastic anticipation while handing Lindsay the phone. Amy gave the best clues, and she and Lindsay, of all people, came up with the most points in one round. Amy gave Lindsay severe directions to get her head in the gutter and not screw up, or they wouldn't win.

The first word, miraculously, was "nipple," and Amy yelled, "Me!" pointing to her boob.

"Nipple, nipple ring!" Lindsay called, her concentration on point. "Next!" Lindsay ordered nervously.

"Watching sex movies," Amy hinted.

"Uh ... " Lindsay squeezed her fist to her mouth as she tried to recall the answer.

"Internet sex movies!" Amy nearly screamed at her.

"Oh, porn!"

"Yes! Flip. Okay ... giving head," Amy spat out.

"Blow job, oral sex," Lindsay said and tilted the phone down.

"When you fake this with a guy and then go home and give yourself one." Amy smiled and proceeded to grab her crotch.

"Oh God!" Lindsay cringed, shutting her eyes tight.

"Say it, bitch!"

"Orgasm," Lindsay mouthed almost silently, and we all howled again.

"Next!" Amy commanded. They were down to seconds.

"When a guy's thing is hard. Technical term!" Amy barked.

"Uhh, erection."

"Time!" Freddie called out, but too late. They had won.

Lindsay glowed as Amy told her there was hope for her yet.

"Giddy up!" Amy bellowed.

"Wow! I'm so proud of me." Lindsay's eyes were wide with delight.

"And me!" Amy shouted.

"Years of training, Linds," I snorted, indicating Amy.

After snacks and Mason passing out in his chair, we talked casually for a little longer.

"So, Tommy, how's the summer been?" Trevor asked.

"It's been awesome. Right, Beck?"

"Yeah, great," I smiled back at him. It was an incredible summer. I couldn't remember being happier. Having that time to experiment—like playing a married couple without the actual terms. It was heaven. I was spoiling myself; I knew. In a week, intercession would be over, and we would both be back home until fall semester started.

At the thought of that, I grabbed TJ's hand and squeezed it, foolishly thinking I could keep him with me.

"That's awesome," Trevor smiled and clung to Cassie even more.

"Best summer ever," TJ declared.

He looked at me with such care and love. Then he leaned over and kissed me softly. I so adored that about him. He never got embarrassed. Ever. When it came to me, he wanted the world to know about us and how much he loved me.

"Aww," Lindsay cooed.

"So, Tommy boy, have you cracked the family code yet?" Amy asked slyly.

"What's that?"

"The Mrs. Winslow code." Amy eyed him. "Or are you still locked out? I will say Miss Linds is a solid in."

"Yes, I'm a good apple, so she likes me."

"I'm on the fence," Amy continued.

"A rotten apple," Lindsay chided, but her smile was warm.

They were not wrong. My parents loved Lindsay. Everyone loved Lindsay. Her parents were dignified people who had a way of earning the respect of others and had raised a generous, sweet, and compassionate daughter.

My dad didn't have any issues with Amy. I wasn't sure how my mom felt about her. She didn't see her as much, but I felt like my mom distanced herself from Amy, too, just like she did with TJ.

"So, where are you at, Tommy boy?" Amy challenged.

TJ attempted a smile, but when he sought my eyes, I dropped them to the ground, knowing he had not yet won my mother's approval.

"I'm working on it." I heard him answer.

When we cuddled up in his tent hours later, Lindsay to my left, her long, silky black hair laid out in front of me like a river of night, TJ to my right, his soft breath tickling the back of my neck, I wondered when he would get my mother's blessing.

Journal Entry #6 ~ I Do

Robert and I fell quickly in love. My heart took to him immediately, whereas my head needed more time to catch up to his warm personality. I'd had a boyfriend and a first time in high school, but that was fleeting. He was nothing like Robert. Robert made every other man seem like a child. He was mature and special. He made me feel important. He complimented me often, supported my career, and never made it seem beneath him. Robert was empathetic. I wasn't aware that men could be that way, putting your feelings first in all situations. In my heart, I knew one solid reason I loved him so deeply was that he was not like my father. I could tell by his eyes that he would never be like that man.

After dating for two years, Robert and I were married. Before the proposal, he had asked me if there was some way he could speak with my father. He wanted to go the traditional route and ask for my hand. What should've been a sweet gesture turned into a tense conversation and me explaining some of my past, but I put my foot down about my father. In the end, I told Robert he should ask Colleen for my hand, as she was the only family member whose praise and permission I would accept.

In the months before the wedding, I worked extra shifts at Julian's, and Robert moved up the ranks at his new sales job in record time. He was even going on business trips here and there. The long hours at work kept him busy and allowed me to work more. I earned enough to make sure Colleen was set for six months of rent. She was already scoping out roommates, but I still felt responsible for her well-being and wanted to give her a cushion.

I spent my days off researching wedding ideas, surveying flower shops, and touring venues. I explored catalogs for favors and table settings. With costs at the front of my mind, I saved money by renting a hall and decorating it myself, including the tablecloths, cloth napkins, candles, and centerpieces. I researched catering companies and had Colleen come with me to taste-test entrees. We looked at cakes together, as well. She was busy with college, so she didn't have as much time as I did. But, whatever the help, I appreciated it.

I was not in favor of a big celebration. Who would be there for us anyway? Robert had family all over the US, but some wouldn't make it in for the ceremony. His older sisters, their families, and his parents were coming and planned to pay for half the wedding. I wasn't sure how much information Robert had given them about my parents not attending, but gratefully, they didn't inquire. I was pleased that they were only paying half. It was just enough of a gift and would help us financially.

I had never worked so hard on a project before and was elated to show Robert once the wedding finally came into view. I knew he would love it.

The day of the wedding, I was a jittery mess. I hadn't gotten much sleep with last-minute plans and decorations. I was proud, though. I didn't need anyone else's help aside from Colleen's. I was enough in that moment.

My gown was to die for—bright white and sleeveless, with a heart-shaped neckline and tight-fitting bodice over a bell skirt. The bottom half beheld tiny pearls stitched in meticulously.

Robert and I said, "I do," in a beautiful church built in the 1960s. Astounding stained glass hung in the window frames. Crisp blues, wild reds, pearly whites, golden hues, it was ideal. Robert had never looked more handsome in his sleek black tux and vest, with his hair cut short and dimples exposing his glee. His face, seeing me down the aisle, was all I needed as confirmation of our love. His expression mirrored that moment when he saw me at Julian's for the first time.

When, at last, it was time to recite our vows, I stumbled in my resolve. A shaky breath slipped past my lips, but Robert grabbed my hands tightly and gave me the strength to read my intentions. He has always believed in me.

"I will choose you. All my life. No matter what challenges come our way. I will choose you."

CHAPTER 7

Rollercoaster

Summer session let out, and fall classes were about to start up. I was adjusting once again to this new relationship with my mother while being at home with her for the few weeks between school sessions. We were talking more, running errands with each other, and making meals together.

But TJ and I were so in love that we wanted to see each other as much as possible. TJ wanted to do something different and take me to Six Flags for my birthday. I told my mom about it and explained that he would need to stay overnight afterward and maybe into the next night, too.

She shot me an unimpressed look, "I don't think that's a good idea."

"Why not?" My pulse spiked as my heart knew she would still fight me on TJ.

Her face was sour like she wanted to spit something out but kept it down.

"What do you expect TJ to do? Drive back to Carlyle after being in Gurnee all day?" I hoped my exasperated expression was working.

She just bit at the inside of her cheek and contemplated the choices.

"You know, when we decided to work on things together, I thought my choices would be better accepted."

"Haven't I allowed that?" she snapped. "You've had a whole summer to live with him." Now, she was judging me. I just shook my head, so tired of her unacceptance.

"You know, he's the *only one* who's been there for me wholeheartedly," I bit back, although the words died on my tongue. I hadn't felt so much hurt from her in so long; suddenly, I was back in time, and she wasn't accepting me or seeing who I was again. "Let me go break it to him that he'll need to find a hotel room." I stalked off.

My mother attempted to say something, but I had already turned and crossed the room away from her.

I picked up my phone and clicked on his number.

"Beck, hey babe," he sounded out of breath.

"What are you doing?" I tried to sound upbeat. He didn't need to hear my anguish about my mother.

"Shooting hoops with Mason."

"Okay, well, call me later."

"No, I'm good. We can take a break."

"K. Well, I'm not sure about you coming up here for Six Flags."

"You don't want to go?"

I paused, not having thought this through entirely. "No, I do. I just ... " I took a moment, trying to lie, but decided against it. "I don't think I have the go-ahead to have you stay over here later that night. I'm sorry. I'm frustrated."

"It's okay," he said calmly, like he expected this.

"It's not."

"You know what? I'm sure I can stay with Taylor," TJ said. Taylor had been in ballroom dance with us. She'd dropped Lindsay and me off for spring break. I knew her apartment was on the way.

"You think?" I asked.

"Yeah, Taylor and her girlfriend live pretty close to you, right? So, I can crash there. Taylor's easy."

"But she's still like twenty-five minutes from me."

"You don't think I can do twenty-five minutes to see more of you? On your birthday?" he challenged.

Now, he had me smiling.

***

56

Taylor came to our rescue and allowed TJ to stay the night at her place.

TJ was so pumped to spend the entire day at Six Flags. We had gone there once before. Katie, TJ's little sister, was maybe four or five and had whined most of the day. My mother wasn't told about the trip until afterward. She was with Aunt Colleen for her birthday weekend. I was so excited to spend the day with the Lawsons.

I don't remember every detail of the trip when we were younger, but I do recall the color in TJ's face turning to a pale green after a spinning ride. Mrs. Lawson fanned him in the shade to cool him off and recover, and he pulled through. We went to the caravan for lunch and popped open the back. Mrs. Lawson put down a blanket, and we ate turkey sandwiches and green grapes. When we finished lunch, we grabbed our sweatshirts for later when the sun set, and the breeze picked up. Mrs. Lawson said we still needed to hit the log ride, and we couldn't leave until the park closed down for the night.

While we were on the log ride, I sat in the very front with TJ behind me, then Katie behind the divider, and Mrs. Lawson at the back. My long hair kept whipping TJ in the face, but he just ducked lower and wrapped his tan arms around my waist, refusing to admit that he was scared. "Look up!" I yelled. "You're going to miss it!"

As we rounded the last curve on top of the ride, inching closer to the final drop, TJ's mom called from behind us, "Count to three, and we all yell cow-a-bunga, okay? One. Two. Three!"

Mrs. Lawson, TJ, and I called, "Cow-a-bunga!" as Katie screamed. The drop was so intense! My eyes bulged, but TJ just hid behind me, his warm forehead tucked into my back, waiting for the splash at the bottom. A giant wall of water crashed over us—soaking every inch of our clothes. Katie was still screaming, then crying because she was drenched. TJ made her feel better by giving her a piggyback ride as we made our way around the park. Later on, Katie changed her mind and said she loved the log ride and wanted to go again.

We stayed all day until my shoulders were sunburned and my feet ached from walking. TJ and I slumped onto each other in the back seat then slept the whole ride home.

Midway through the day at Six Flags, TJ and I found ourselves reliving our past and stepping onto the log ride again. We had the whole log to ourselves. TJ took up the very back of the long-padded seat dripping with water, which wet my shorts as soon as I sat down between his legs. As we idled in the circular gate, waiting to get to the incline, I leaned into him and rested the back of my head in the space between his shoulder and neck. TJ tilted his head forward and nuzzled my ear. "Happy birthday, Beck," he mumbled through kisses all over my neck. Once we moved out onto the rail, his warm hands slid up and down my thighs. I turned my head toward him, and his eyes narrowed. He kissed me slowly and deeply until we felt a dip in the ride. Then, we flung our arms out to the side handlebars and cried as a tiny splash hit us.

"Whoa!" TJ yelled, shaking out his arms from the splash. We giggled for the next part of the ride as TJ smacked the standing water on the side of the log, teasing me. As we approached the big drop, he reminded me to call out cow-a-bunga just like the old days. I could barely manage the cheer as we sped down the drop. My cow-a-bunga caught in my throat as gravity pulled me down and stunned me in delight. TJ screamed and, once again, ducked behind me for the giant splash, his arms a vice around my middle. I took on the entire wave myself but happily hugged him shortly after to share my drenched self.

Since we were already soaking wet, we went on the roaring rapids, a water ride that held twelve people in a circular raft. The group we were paired with in the raft was the same group of chatting guys and girls who had stood just ahead of us in line. TJ became instant besties with them. He joked with one of the guys, Juan, that his seat would be the cursed one, and he would get the brunt of the water.

TJ was in his glory on the pirate battle water ride. Our new buddies Juan, Karina, and their friends went head-to-head with us as we readied to fight. The ride was constructed of small pirate ships and benches on either side of the centerpiece and masts. Four people could sit together on each side facing cranks. The cranks pulled up water from the small lagoon surrounding the ride and shot it out at the surrounding boats once the ride got moving. Our boat crept around the corner into the maze of the waterway. Suddenly, water pelted us from every direction. Even bystanders squirted water at our ship from the plankway ramp.

"Oh, here we go!" TJ called, trying to dodge the blasts of water.

We worked on the water cranks, aiming and splashing people in the other ships. I was off to a slow start, but TJ's arm moved at an insane rate, cranking water several feet toward the other ships and onlookers. He annihilated the competition, who were all crouched and screaming on their pirate ships, cowering and soaking wet.

Juan's group forced us to go on the Eagle next. It was a massive wooden rollercoaster as old as the park itself, with an intimidating, steep first drop. Both TJ and I had never been on the Eagle before.

TJ's pale face and wide eyes were comical as we approached the ride. He gaped up at the intricate and daunting interwoven planks of white wood then got unusually quiet as we waited in line. I was thrilled as nervous excitement bubbled in my belly. I practically had to drag TJ toward the loading station, which was a definite reversal of roles. He uttered a nervous laugh, shifting his weight back and forth. We snaked left and right around and under the loading station, then curved around again and up a set of stairs as TJ let out a shallow breath.

"You good?"

He clenched his mouth and nodded. I openly giggled at him.

"Hey, Tommy, it's going to be amazing, man. You ain't scared. Come on now!" Juan chided.

"Where's the harness?" TJ asked as we stood next in line, watching the other group of riders sit, buckle up, and take off.

"Oh boy!" I cheered anxiously, grabbing onto his arm. "I'm sure it's fine."

"It's fine, huh?" he asked, looking so *not* TJ. I wished I had a picture of his face to hold over him forever.

Once we were settled on the sticky seats with TJ's long legs crammed into the tiny compartment, we buckled our seatbelts and pulled down the lap bars. Two workers came running along either side, quickly tested our belts then pushed our lap bars to make sure we were secure.

"So, that's it?" TJ asked the woman in disbelief.

"Enjoy your ride!" the teenage announcer in the booth at the front of the ride hollered as we sped away.

"You good?" I asked again, smiling and gripping his right hand as he stared ahead with his mouth open.

We turned sharply and soon headed up an endless lift of clicking rails. It looked like we were going up into the heavens.

"Ar-right!" TJ called, almost hyperventilating. He winced, taunting the ride. "Let's go! Come on!" he edged, pushing his head forward like he was controlling the force of our incline.

I busted up that his new strategy to survive this intense coaster was to taunt or bully the ride itself.

We slowed almost to a stop at 127 feet in the air and looked down at an impossible drop. Then we were zooming below and shrieking. I was knocked around in a turbulent clatter from the tracks, my head ping-ponging left and right, my belly enduring every dip as I screamed and threw my arms high.

As we pulled up to the loading zone after the ride, TJ's eyes were wide as saucers; his hair stood straight up. "That," he paused, his eyes pinned directly ahead. "Was awesome!" He raised his hand to high-five me.

By the end of the night, having gone on nearly every ride and lapped miles around the park, our last stop on TJ's agenda was getting a funnel cake for my birthday celebration. TJ shoved in a partially melted 21 candle he'd had in his drawstring bag the whole day in the center of the fried dough and mound of melty ice cream topped with whipped cream, caramel syrup, and tons of sprinkles. TJ got the employees to light my candle and help sing me "Happy Birthday."

It was such an incredible day of fun with sun-kissed shoulders, aching feet, wind-swept hair, two stuffed prizes from a basketball shooting game, and a handful of new contacts in our phones for Juan, Karina, and their friends. Later, TJ scooped me up on his back and trampled through the parking lot to his truck. I squeezed my arms around his warm chest and thanked him for the best birthday ever. It was only when he dropped me off at my house and pulled away to go stay somewhere else for the night that I felt the coolness inside my heart.

Journal Entry #7 ~ Mexico

For our honeymoon, Robert and I traveled to Riviera Maya, Mexico, and stayed at an all-inclusive resort. I ordered my passport six months before the wedding. I had never been out of the country before.

The resort was beautiful. A long entrance to the hotel wound around a white stucco wall where stunning palm trees lined the way toward the grand entrance. The smell of sea and sand salted the breeze as we exited the shuttle and stepped over to the entrance. As soon as we arrived, we were treated like royalty—a red carnation placed in my left hand and a cool, refreshing mango drink set in my right. Bellhops greeted us warmly and offered anything to make our stay better.

Robert had booked us a villa near the shore. We hopped in a golf cart and were driven to our spot: a pale, yellow villa with a red-tiled roof. The inside was a dream with a wide, stone foyer, large cedar furnishings, a massive king-sized bed that looked like it was floating in the center of the back wall, and the fluffiest, whitest linens topping the bed. A huge picture window displaying the bluest ocean took up the wall opposite our bed. My mouth dropped in adoration for this masterpiece of a location. Once the bellboy had brought in the last of our bags, Robert thanked him with American dollars and locked the door behind him.

Upon hearing the click of the lock, I shifted from stunned tourist to sultry wife. Robert's eyes darkened as we both moved slowly toward each other.

"What do you think?" he asked, placing my hands on his sides.

I pulled them from his grasp and lifted off his shirt. "I think I'm never going to want to leave. Ever," I said, pulling his shirt up over his head.

Robert swept his mouth over mine and untied the strap at the neck of my sundress. "I think I like your thinking, Mrs. Winslow," he panted, gazing at my bare chest and panties as my dress dropped to the stone floor.

Robert and I made every effort to live out our honeymoon to the fullest. We christened every area and space of our villa. We even made love in our own private pool in the early morning hours as the sun rose.

Everything was luxury.

"I could get used to this," I confessed to Robert, running my hand over the plush fabric of the duvet, my eyes enraptured by the waves crashing before us.

"You will," Robert breathed behind me.

We spent the days sightseeing, lounging by the pools, and basking in the sunlight. We shared stories and talked about what our future could look like. I teased him about hitting on me when he had a girlfriend. He admitted feeling guilty about that, even though it wasn't a long relationship. "The moment I looked at you, that was it for me," he confessed.

At our final honeymoon breakfast, Robert wanted to have a more serious conversation. He didn't want to alarm me but thought it necessary to talk about his work and leveled that his job had a lot of opportunity for advancement, which is why he had taken it. There were opportunities to network with larger companies and advance to higher-stakes levels.

That would come at a cost, though. It included business trips and would require many hours, even more than he was working currently.

"I know this will take some adjusting to, but I think it'll work out well for us. It's a lot of hours, but then we'll get to enjoy vacations like this. And your job will give you flexibility, right?"

I nodded.

"So, you can work whenever you want—if you want—doing whatever you want. At Julian's or anywhere else."

Robert was so good about managing his time. I believed him wholeheartedly that we would be fine. He smiled so true with those dimples and a promise in his hazel eyes that we could have everything we wanted for our life together.

I wanted the honeymoon to last; then, I remembered that my parents were newlyweds in the beginning, too. My stomach lurched, thinking of their marriage. I took a breath to steady myself and vowed we would never be like them.

"And one other thing." Robert began. "I know you're worried about Colleen paying for her schooling. So, I have set aside money from my salary to help with her student loans. I imagine she'll feel a little overwhelmed as she's still earning her degree in business and doesn't have a full-time job yet …"

But I had stopped listening fully. All I clung to in my mind was Robert declaring: "I am going to take care of your sister."

I pushed back my wicker chair abruptly and crossed the space between us. I took his face in my hands and kissed him for a long moment.

When I pulled away, there should've been tears in my eyes, but they were so full of love and hope that instead, they just radiated gratitude at my husband—this sweet man that I did not deserve. We left breakfast early and practically ran back to our villa. Robert fumbled at my shorts, and I broke into a soft laugh between kisses, noticing his cloth napkin was still tucked into his waist.

He chuckled along with me and pulled the napkin away.

I pulled him to the bed and climbed on top of him. Wanting to take care of him now, I showed him with every roll of my hips that I was so grateful for his love.

CHAPTER 8

The Guys

September brought the routine of classes, workouts, and TJ's roommates. It took some adjusting to being in their place with all of them around again. I tried to give them enough time without me at the start of the semester, as I also needed a lot of reconnecting time with Amy and Lindsay at our campus apartment.

The second week of school, we all bonded over shopping for and eventually sending Amy's younger brother, Kellen, a care package. He was just starting school at Illinois State University. Amy had us help buy and pack the necessities she couldn't send from home. We included an array of interesting, very Amy-like items attached with little notes:

A clean pair of his underwear and socks she stole from his dresser. "Put these on right now. Don't lie to yourself. Yours are both dirty."

A jar of peanut butter because "You probably slept through breakfast. Again."

A bottle of beer because "I am a practical sister."

A bottle of Tylenol. "For your hangovers and annoying roommates."

A box of protein bars. "Get off your ass and go work out, or you'll start looking like Dad."

A mini fan because: "You're probably sweating right now. So gross. Turn this on, or go grab a shower."

A twenty-dollar bill because: "I am the absolute best sister."

A picture of her friend Megan's cleavage. "In case your internet is down. Megan wants you anyway, but this is the closest you'll get to having her. So, F-off."

A giant box of condoms because: "Babies suck! So, don't be a dumb fuck."

A prerecorded alarm clock set to Amy's voice. "Get up, you lazy shithead. Go to class, or I'll tell Mom you had sex on her bed."

A picture of the two of them: Amy standing on a chair, squeezing his head in glee, and Kellen just standing there, taking it.

It was really cute. And everything else was so inappropriate but so fittingly Amy.

Amy got me thinking about TJ's roommates and how they would've responded to all the redecorating I did at their place. I had cleaned and furnished it with some new things. It was a gift for their courtesy of letting me stay for free and practically taking over the house.

I asked TJ to have me over to make dinner for the guys, as well. I used that as my opportunity to pay it forward a bit. The guys were so accommodating and helpful, allowing me an exceptional summer living with TJ in their house.

I made hot Hawaiian roll sandwiches with shaved ham, Swiss cheese, and buns coated in a gooey mixture of butter, minced onion, poppy seeds, and Dijon mustard. I also made potato salad, which I learned how to make from Grandma Lawson. The whole pan of sandwiches was gone in ten minutes amid a lot of moaning and burping but little talking as they stuffed their faces. It was pretty fun to take care of them.

Mason set up a poker game while Trevor grabbed beers for everyone. I helped to pass them out and handed Mason one.

He shook his head at me.

"You aren't drinking tonight?" I asked in disbelief.

"Nah. It's dry September," Mason proclaimed.

I smiled at him, considering that. Although I couldn't be sure after just an hour or two of really hanging with him, it seemed Mason had a new air of maturity about him. I wondered how much of that was Jenna or Tana influencing him.

"Jesus, are we at AA? Let's go," Brandon complained. "I'm winning this one."

Mason just shook his head slightly.

The game started, and it was so enjoyable to hear these guys bait and dog on each other like they always did. I loved my private time with TJ but got a thrill from listening to their nonsense.

I shot back some good one-liners. After a while, the round was down to Brandon, Mason, and me.

"I like having Beck here," Mason said.

"Me too," TJ laughed.

"What, are we gonna start talking about our feelings?" Brandon barked. "I like having Beck here, too. For food and her money."

Brandon slapped down his hand, showing four of a kind.

"Ohhh!" Shouts reverberated around the table.

I just shook my head, grinning, and gave Brandon a fist bump on his rare, brilliant play. Then I set my pair of queens down and scooted away from the table.

"Damn," Mason said, looking at the cards before Brandon.

"Well, since I'm out, want me to get you anything?" I asked.

"Laid," Brandon said. I instantly shifted my attention to TJ, whose eyes went cold in a flash.

"Uh oh," Mason said, his eyeballs glued to the deck he was shuffling. It was as if Mason could feel TJ's stare. They had that unique connection.

I gave Brandon a "not a chance" face, but he saw TJ's glare and backpedaled.

"It's called humor," Brandon said with an awkward smile.

"Is it, though?" I countered; my head tilted slightly.

TJ leveled him with a look, and I had to admit, seeing him ruthless made me happy.

"Beck, I'll take a beer, please." Trevor, always with the manners, deflecting. I winked at him.

The conversation started again, but TJ remained quiet. I snuck around, wrapped my arms around his neck, and gave him a kiss on the cheek. Then I whispered, "Easy killer," and let go of him to snag a drink for Trevor and me.

Mason got up to grab some snacks and draped an arm around me, giving me a sentimental moment. He looked at me sideways for a long stretch. His hair was shorter now, blonder than the usual sandy brown. His skin still had that summer glow.

"You're really good for my brother. You know that?"

I felt a tug in my heart when he said that. *My brother. How adorable.* TJ had always told me that Mason was more of a brother than a second cousin.

"You're really good for him, too." I snaked my arm under his and hugged him.

That night, I got a sense of what our life would be like, and it made me light up. Having Mason and Jenna close by. The ease of people willing to sit around with us, in their slow style. Saturday night poker games. Mrs. Lawson's emotional attachment to us. Grandma Lawson's delicious feasts. Watching Tana grow older. I wanted to continue to be a part of that. Just one other issue needed resolving: not being close to home, which meant being far from Lindsay and my parents.

Journal Entry #8 ~ Baby Girl

Rachel was born on a glorious September morning. The pregnancy was everything I had hoped for. I glowed and did not gain a significant amount of weight. More importantly, she was here. I labored for twelve hours, and though exhausted, once she was placed in my arms, a new energy came to me. I was someone's mother now.

I couldn't wait to prove myself in being her mother. I promised her in that hospital bed that I would do right by her. I wouldn't run away like my mother had. I would be there for her as the best mom. Robert leaned over my shoulder and kissed our girl on the top of her head. I had the most compassionate husband, a loving sister, and now, my angel, Rachel.

Yet, the first few months with Rachel were challenging. She was this sweet, quiet little bundle of pink until the second week of her life. Then, something changed, and she became cranky. Our pediatrician observed that she wasn't gaining weight fast enough. He advised us to give her formula in addition to nursing her. It helped, but only marginally. She was still irritable. I never lost my patience with her, as Rachel was perfection despite being crabby.

Her sleep schedule was erratic, and her feedings seemed to bother her. She was only calmed when we drove around in the car or when Robert or I held her. Had I known then that my time would be cut short with her, I would have never put her down.

Once we made it through the first rough months, Rachel's personality and intelligence made every day a blessing. I know all parents think this of their children, but Rachel met so many milestones before she should have. Eye contact, grasping, holding her head up, making cooing noises, smiling. She was a treasure.

Robert and I were so overjoyed with our girl. She was trouble for sure with only taking 20-minute naps at random times, not sleeping through the night, and fussing a lot. But she helped us draw even closer together as a couple. I adored the father version of my husband. He was made for it. Robert was so attentive and patient. He helped with everything and looked truly disappointed if Rachel fell asleep without him rocking or holding her. Sometimes, I would be out running an errand or sorting laundry in the basement, and I'd return and walk up to spy Robert holding Rachel and talking to her. He chatted to her about baseball mostly (who just got drafted, the infield fly rule, what hitting the cycle means), but he talked to her about other things, as well, like national monuments, state capitals, the Supreme Court, the best ideas for presents for me, and random thoughts and concepts. It didn't matter what it was, he kept talking in his explanation voice and bopping around the house, bouncing Rachel in his arms.

A few months later, her skills grew even further. Rachel was turning over at three months old, sitting up at four, and crawling at five. She began to love music. She preferred certain colors, loving the brightest ones, like yellows and pinks, most of all. She reached for these colors and smiled at them more so than blues or greens.

The trouble started when Rachel got her first cold. It was just a virus, but it shook us to our core. Her cough was so horrific, causing wheezing like she couldn't get enough oxygen. Twice, I had to take her out at night in the cool February air and sit with her to help her breathe fresh air. She didn't know what was going on but seemed to know it was important. Getting a nebulizer treatment for your baby is a sad reality. Unfortunately, Rachel needed it to help her live and function. It impacted our lives for many years to come.

CHAPTER 9

Parents' Weekend

Since the paint-and-sip night I shared with my mother, I started calling home more often. I also didn't roll my eyes each time my phone buzzed with a call or text from her. It was hard to put an exact emotion to it. We had played this disconnected game for so long; it was like learning to write with my left hand—unpracticed and messy. Sometimes, I even looked forward to her text messages. I thought often of our few weeks together in the summer. Both of us planting flowers and hugging. Later in the summer, after intercession, we connected even more. I was becoming increasingly comfortable breaking down my wall with her.

I found myself staring at a poster advertising parents' weekend in late September while I was on my way to class. For the first time, I wanted my parents to come down to Eastern to experience some aspect of my life before I graduated. Part of it was me wanting to include my mom; part was hoping that if she saw TJ in a different setting, it would help her learn to love him.

It was definitely bizarre to walk around campus with my mom and dad. We started at the football game. My mom smiled and clapped for the Panthers when we scored. My dad and I got louder and had more fun, but she was a good sport. We grabbed some concessions, then headed to the bowling alley on campus to meet up with Linds and Amy.

Lindsay was a riot on the bowling lanes. She kept getting gutter balls and cried with laughter.

Amy went to help her. "Jesus, it's like you've never held balls before, put your finger in a hole, or scored," Amy laughed, her body flush against Lindsay's.

Linds was too shocked to even scold Amy.

"Aim!" I yelped, trying not to laugh.

I glanced quickly at my mom, who pursed her lips in laughter. It made me smile. My dad pretended not to hear anything.

Turns out, Amy didn't help Lindsay at all with her technique.

After bowling, my parents took us all out to dinner. Amy and Lindsay were so sweet and easy to talk with. My dad loved the both of them so much. I could see my mom wasn't as comfortable with Amy, but she managed fine. I knew she'd like Amy better when I mentioned her engineering major and how brilliant she actually was. My mom always took the bait on successful people. Jason, being pre-law, had fed into that. It bothered me that she thought more of people with those types of careers. I'm sure much more than a high school gym teacher.

Amy and Lindsay each did their best to sing TJ's praises, but my mom wasn't playing into their hands.

I should've stopped our evening together before the bar. I pushed my parents to come to Marty's with us. I figured the party bar, Mom's, would be too much for them, but I insisted Marty's would be a good spot for us to hang out. I didn't intentionally ambush my mother. TJ happened to have plans to be there later. Why did she have to be so unfriendly? Why did her face drain when she saw him?

My dad was having a blast at Marty's. We were playing pool while Lindsay entertained my mom. Amy was talking to strangers again, but she wasn't drinking. She didn't want to take a greater chance of offending my mom. She wanted to keep it clean. Commendable.

TJ, Trevor, and Brandon walked up to us by the pool table in the back. God, he was so gorgeous. Turning my legs into taffy every time I laid eyes on him. It didn't matter that I was lining up a shot on the pool table. I set the stick down and made a beeline for TJ. He gave me that adorable smile and threw his arms around my waist, leaning down to kiss me at once. Sweet perfection made my heart dance as I pushed my lips onto his.

Just then, I heard my dad: "Tommy!" A huge smile broke across my dad's face. He'd had a few beers, and it was refreshing to see him loosen up and live a little.

"Mr. Winslow!" TJ cheered back, hugging my dad fiercely. They broke their hug and took turns patting each other's backs.

Then we turned to my mom, who, of course, was stoic, sitting at a high-top, peering down at her plastic cup of ice water.

"Hey, Mrs. Winslow," TJ called out and gave her shoulders a quick squeeze.

"Tommy," she said without emotion.

TJ said hi to Amy and Linds while I introduced Trevor and Brandon to my parents.

Dad and I finished the rest of our game then he and TJ teamed up to play against Trevor and Brandon. My dad wasn't very good, but TJ made up for it. He couldn't miss a shot. Brandon hollered and tried to talk smack, but TJ couldn't be stopped.

"Wow," Dad called out. "Tommy, you're unbelievable."

"Thanks, Mr. Winslow. You're pretty good, too. We make a good team." TJ winked at him.

I grinned beside my mom, who anxiously studied them.

In truth, she was pissing me off. I was having an easy weekend with her and Dad then TJ showed up to bring more fun and joy, yet she just dampened the mood like a gray cloud.

I sighed loudly and jumped down from my seat. "I'm getting a drink."

I met Amy at the bar and complained to her.

"Maybe she just needs to get laid. Or drunk. Both?" Amy hollered above the music blaring from the speakers. The bartender slid my credit card back to me.

"Let's hope for drunk," I answered, pocketing my card and grabbing my beer.

"Here, get her a Truly. Every up-tight mom drinks Trulys."

I nodded, seeing Amy's idea. "She doesn't really drink, though. Maybe wine sometimes, but never … "

"Get her drunk, and she'll loosen up." Amy handed me a drink for my mom.

"Thanks, Aim."

I brought it to my mom.

"What's this?" she asked, glimpsing the drink I held out to her as if she had never seen an aluminum can in her life.

"It's a hard seltzer," I said, my brows knitted.

She shook her head.

"It's called a drink, Mom. Just try it. You need to chill out," I scolded and took a large gulp of my beer.

Her eyes narrowed at me. She simply took the can from my hand and set it on the small tabletop, sitting up even straighter in her seat.

"What's with you?" I snapped.

"With me in what regard, Rebecca?" Her voice was tired and edgy.

"Why don't you just get drunk and have fun for once? Maybe you'd be nicer to my boyfriend then."

She swallowed, which seemed to wash away her angry face.

"I would rather not."

"To which option, Mom?" I glared at her.

I was baiting her for a fight. I was. And I didn't know why, other than just being frustrated and buzzed. Thankfully, she didn't bite. Instead, she slid down from her stool as the game concluded and stood facing my dad, raising her eyebrows at him in a signal.

My dad grinned at her, tilting his head up.

"Robert, let's head back to the hotel. It's late, and we've a long drive tomorrow … ," she called.

"Sure, honey."

Dad shook hands with TJ's friends, hugged TJ, Lindsay, and Amy, and kissed my cheek in a goodbye.

"We'll pick you up for breakfast by nine," my mom told me, all trace of annoyance gone from her face.

I nodded. TJ came over to us.

"Good night, Tommy," she almost smiled.

He shook his head. "Yep, have a good night," he replied, draping his arm around my shoulder.

I watched my mom leave the bar, feeling dizzy and stuck. When I finally turned my head toward TJ, he was grinning down at me or, more like, laughing at me.

"You ar-right Beck?"

I shrugged my shoulders and burrowed my face into his shirt.

"Come home with me," I mumbled onto his chest.

"Ar-right," I could feel the chuckle make its way up his throat.

Always wanting to push me, TJ argued that we should walk back to the apartment. It was a gorgeous September evening with hardly a breeze. I whined that I was too drunk and tired, but then he offered to carry me the last half of the walk. I tried pouting as I felt the urge to whine, but TJ just shut me up with a kiss or sang loudly. Then I would crack up. And he still loved me when I cried for ten seconds, then laughed. He still loved me as I snuck behind a bush to pee. He still loved me when I begged him to be gone in the morning by 8:30 before my parents came over. And he still loved me when I stripped down to my T-shirt and undies for him, teasing him, but then passed out on his outstretched arms.

Journal Entry #9 ~ Big Sister

Rachel was three when Ryan was born. Ryan became her new favorite toy. Rachel called him her "big guy." Ryan was soft and pudgy with sweet, fat cheeks, thick legs, and folds in his arms. He was a very calm baby compared to Rachel. Ryan took to nursing right away. I felt so much joy in that experience. It was miraculous that I was able to provide for him and soothe him. I was everything at that time for my family. Robert was the boat keeping us afloat, but I was the ocean holding all of us.

Rachel doted on her little brother. She wanted to feed him, burp him, rock him, and read to him. She was a bossy little mother. When Ryan didn't roll over, she would scold him. She smacked his chubby hand when he pulled her brown hair. She sang to him and dressed him up. She pushed the stroller down the sidewalk. She reassured him that he was fine if he cried. I melted a little bit each time I witnessed their adorable interactions.

Robert and I were so in love. We never let a moment pass by without acknowledging how lucky we were. We moved to a new home in a quiet neighborhood with an excellent school district. At our new home, we had more space and a fenced-in yard with a pool. We had two beautiful children who lit our very souls. Robert and I showed each other more than ever how much we meant to each other.

And then I found out I was pregnant again.

Rebecca came into the world unfairly, the third child following two who were planned. Robert was delighted about the pregnancy. I was overwhelmed. Ryan was just over a year old. Rachel was four and becoming adorable trouble. She started mouthing off and became more demanding about everything, sensing that these little ones were going to steal my time from her. Robert was gone so often that I felt alone. I was so tired. More tired than I'd ever been.

Even Rebecca's birth was different. She arrived three weeks early. Robert was stuck at the airport, trying to make flight changes to rush home. He was crushed that he missed her birth.

My Rebecca was a beautiful little doll. While sitting alone in the hospital bed with her, I stared at her and stared at her. I counted her little fingers and toes, kissing each tip as I did. I talked to her about how much fun she was about to have with Rachel and Ryan. I cried, telling her how happy her dad would be to meet her in a few hours. I didn't know if the tears were happiness, frustration, or loneliness.

My heart grew heavy right after we brought Rebecca home. Colleen had been over, watching the other two. I believe Colleen could sense the trouble for me before I even could. She eyed me warily and kept asking if I was okay. If I was sure. I thought I was, but I was wrong.

Robert made a doctor's appointment for me, and the doctor confirmed I had postpartum depression, a common condition in many new mothers. My body was trying to regulate my emotions and my physical and emotional well-being, but I was having trouble. I didn't want to do anything. I cried and cried, but I wasn't sure why. I couldn't bond with Rebecca. I couldn't nurse her. I cried even more about that. I had struggled for a while with Rachel and nursed Ryan for months. But with Rebecca, I was just shattered.

Colleen started sleeping over. She went to great lengths to make sure I was taken care of. She checked in with doctors for me, made my appointments, and got Rachel to and from school. She held me as I wept. She was my rock.

Robert was gone so much for work at that point. Every other week. He even worked Saturdays for a few hours. He looked so torn. I didn't know how he could manage all these huge changes. How could he be with us for a few days and then leave for a week? I started thinking more and more about my mother and wondered if she had felt hopeless at times. The goodness of my life sank a little, making everything fade like a sun-stripped painting—vibrant blues turned gray.

After a month at home, Rachel helped me turn a corner. Once again, she became a little momma. Only this time, for Rebecca. I was sleep-deprived, having put Ryan down for a nap, and was attempting to sit with Rebecca. Rachel held out her arms and said, "Mom, I've got this. You go relax." Rachel turned on the television, propped her arm on a pillow, and motioned for me to bring the baby to her. I gave her a near-sleeping Rebecca and laid on the couch beside them.

And for the first time in a while, I felt lifted.

The days got better after that. I fell into a routine to keep myself on track. I started to feel more like myself, as if I had footing beneath me.

CHAPTER 10

Paddling

On the long Indigenous People's Day weekend, TJ wanted us to have a turn with his family. It was homecoming for Katie, and she was one of the girls recognized for senior night. We showed up like a couple of celebrities. TJ, as the catch. A soon-to-be new teacher at their high school, me, the girl on his arm. I really did feel like I was there with someone famous. Everyone knew the Lawsons, and especially TJ. Hundreds of girls in the stands, along the field, and standing at the fence called out his name.

Katie was still in cheerleading, celebrating her final homecoming with her cheer team. I watched in awe as she jumped and kicked and did a handful of twists and backflips in front of the screaming fans. She had come a long way from that sideways cartwheel in TJ's backyard. Here, her voice was used to its full effect. Katie was on the louder side. Whining or singing. Always vocal. This was an ideal spot for her. I noticed her friend Sarah and her hugging and crying during the presentation of flowers. It should've made me feel nostalgic for my high school, but the best part was still with me in the form of Lindsay. And college was mountains better than high school. Especially with the company I had been keeping.

The next day, we drove to the Lawson's for breakfast. As usual, almost all of TJ's family was there. I couldn't get a word in if I had wanted to, but I loved seeing everyone: Mrs. Lawson and Howard, aunts and uncles, Grandma, Mason, Jenna, and Tana. Katie was exhausted and crabby with puffy eyes. It was a joy.

TJ took me out on Mason's motorcycle, and we spent the day at

Carlyle Lake, where we went kayaking and noticed the leaves turning from green to gold and crimson. What a beautiful and peaceful place. No wonder he loved being here.

We were each situated in a kayak, floating on the lake, the water like emerald glass. It was so quiet and calm. I paddled along, following TJ for a long while. He stopped eventually, and I asked him if we were closer now to the opposite shoreline.

"Oh, no chance. Carlyle Lake is about three and a half miles wide. This is probably a good stopping point, though." He paddled closer to me then grabbed the inside of my kayak so we could float together for a bit.

"Yeah, this is great." I leaned back and took in the blue of the sky and the orange leaves in the distance. The green of the lake. Every view in my sight was stunning. TJ's eyes were almost hypnotic, reflecting off the water.

"Thank you for taking me here."

"Absolutely." He lowered his head and surveyed our breathtaking surroundings. "I want to do something for you. You bring out the best in me."

I grinned up at him.

"I'm going to make you a delicious feast for dinner at Howard's."

I gulped back the dread working its way up my throat and just grinned at him, trying to disguise my genuine terror-smile as affection. *Is he serious?* "Yeah?"

"Yeah. I have been taking notes, and I want to cook for you. To prove I'm good enough to keep."

"You're crazy. I couldn't let you go if I wanted to." I let my eyes hang on his. It was true. TJ was the most intense addiction I had ever had.

It would take death itself to pull me away from him.

Later, at Howard's, TJ's very grown-up dinner was roasting in the oven. I tried my best not to get involved. A mess of spices and seasonings littered the counter. A dirty plate of juices on a cutting board mingled with broccoli. He placed some doughy rolls on a pan. I noticed he didn't spray the pan first, and it was all I could do to hold back any advice and hope he wouldn't be disappointed.

TJ wiped down the counter and turned to me, leaning up on the counter.

"Are you not fully moved in?" I asked, scanning the place. "I noticed you don't have many of your things here." TJ had been gifted his stepdad Howard's family home in the spring. I thought by now he would've fully moved in. Between his grandma's place in Carlyle, his house at Eastern on campus, and Howard's place, TJ had a lot of options. I assumed he'd want to completely move into this amazing country home.

He gazed at the living area and up the stairs. "No, I don't want to fully live here unless it's with you." His eyes were so bright and full of fire that it almost knocked the wind out of me.

I had nothing to say. What more was there than that? I let out a breath and approached him, laying my head on his shoulder, my arms circling his neck.

The timer buzzed, and TJ took out the meal.

It was some kind of pork tenderloin. Grayish meat sitting in watery grease.

The rolls he made were moderately burnt and, not surprisingly, completely stuck to the pan. The broccoli was tender but tasteless as he'd forgotten to season it as it simmered in the saucepan.

We sat there at the table, inspecting this meal.

TJ's face was a weird mix of humor and disappointment. Not the face you look to for confirmation that something will be edible.

After further inspection, it appeared the pungent pork had not been cooked long enough. I had my fist against my smile as we assessed his sad meal attempt.

"I'm sorry," TJ said, cringing. "I failed." He slumped in his seat and indicated the grayish blob of pork swimming in oily gravy in front of him.

"No, you didn't fail." I moved from my seat and stood beside him, pulling him to me. "You tried something new. That's the first step to being great."

TJ squeezed my waist. He buried his head in my chest and sighed roughly.

"Thanks, Beck."

"Don't worry about it," I said, ruffling his hair.

Then he laughed and tickled me until I screeched and darted away from him. He stood up and grabbed his keys to the truck.

"Let's go to Hardee's!"

Journal Entry #10 ~ Ballerina

Rachel was such a girly girl. It feels bad to say that, though she did greatly prefer dance and dressing up to sports. What a contrast she was to my Rebecca. Rebecca has amazing athleticism. Robert brags about that all the time. "Suzanne, you should see her balance, her arm, her speed. She's amazing." Such a devoted, bragging father.

He bragged on Rachel, too. I wonder how much of it was influenced by me and my wants for her. That little baby, swaddled and bundled, came home from the hospital dressed in pink. Everything was pink for a long while until she was old enough to prefer color. Then it was yellow. She loved yellow. It's the color of light, so it makes so much sense. She was light in itself.

At four years old, we started Rachel at a community dance venue. She was enrolled in a class called Jazz, Tap, and Tumble. I wasn't sure what my expectations were about this class, but it was very disorganized and greatly lacked instruction. Rachel loved it. She made adorable little friends, and they would hug each other, jumping up and down excitedly. It was one of the first times I let her go off on her own to branch out. I was delighted that this idea I had in mind for Rachel turned into something she actually loved: ballet.

Her first recital was an ordeal: two costume changes, several hours of practice, hair and makeup, photos, group photos, and individual photos, not to mention months of practice. She was electric on that stage, captivating the whole audience.

When Rachel turned eight, Colleen took her to the Nutcracker in downtown Chicago. The moment she came home, she told me all about it. The joy on her face was priceless.

"Mom, holy smokes! You wouldn't believe it! The place was, like, massive. It was so cool. There was this huge, fancy theater, and Aunt Colleen and I had seats in the first row of the balcony! The first row! So, we were, like, up above everything else. Oh my gosh, the ballerinas were so amazing! They just floated across the stage. Their pirouettes were so good. And the stage and the set was so cool. Ahhh! It was magic, Mom!"

I couldn't even get a word in. I just smiled at her and held onto her waist as she recounted the whole evening, her eyes dancing like the ballerinas must've done.

"Darling, I'm so glad you had such an amazing experience! Isn't Aunt Colleen the best?"

"Yeah, she's the coolest," Rachel agreed, pulling away from me.

Rachel twirled around for the rest of the night. I was getting Rebecca settled down for the night, but Rachel roused her so she could spin with her baby sister as she hummed. Rebecca was cozy in soft, pink, footy pajamas. Rachel twirled them around as Rebecca laughed and threw her head back with glee.

CHAPTER 11

Costumes

Fall semester started off as a dream. I loved my unique and thrilling classes. I met so many cool people who I had never crossed paths with before. Artsy people, who were mostly inviting and nonjudgmental. It was pretty refreshing to be in their company. Some of them were so talented, like Nair and Penelope. Nair's sketching was other-worldly. He and I had gotten close in a few classes. Penelope was the best painter I'd ever known.

Some of the courses were difficult due to the amount of required assignments, studying artists, and researching histories behind the work. Looking at different mediums was great, though, and obviously a huge jump from my business and math courses. I was so inspired. My art classes opened up a new dimension outside my usual lecture-style, impersonal, factual classes. In art, we focused on seamless discussions and exploring different ways of thinking. It was so liberating to be immersed in this world.

Somehow, in the midst of these outlandish, free-spirited art lessons, I thought about my mom more and more. *She would've loved this study in school—if she had finished.* She'd really surprised me with our painting session over the summer. The feel of these courses would fit her. She was always decorating, picking out patterns, and redesigning things as she created beauty. Her jewelry line was a prime example, enabling her to coordinate beautiful styles, colors, and textures to make her pieces dazzle.

I sent her pictures of the work I was doing in class, and she would send me back similar images.

"Saw this and thought of you," I'd text. Although she didn't love my change in major when I discussed it with her and my dad months ago, she was coming around to the idea of me being an artist.

***

It was the Saturday of Halloween.

Amy, Lindsay, TJ, his friends, and I planned to go to Mom's for the Halloween festivities. Then, we would most likely hit TJ's house to party afterward.

TJ was brainstorming costume ideas one night while hanging out in my apartment. He wanted us to have fun, matching costumes, like one of those inflatable outfits where your feet look tiny, as if you are riding a horse, but really, your feet are designated to another piece of the costume. I burst out laughing at his suggestion. "Do I strike you as someone who would want an inflatable Halloween costume?" I teased from my spot on the sofa. I went on to explain that the batteries in those inflatable packs wouldn't last; people at the bar would probably jump us and pop the inflatable, and all the blowing breeze inside it would make me freeze.

While I explained these points, TJ stood, leaning up against my wall, amusement alive on his face.

"Wow, you've really thought this through," he said, biting his bottom lip so his grin couldn't sneak out.

I giggled and said, "I just want to make the most of our time and not create something unsustainable."

"Again, that's a lot of specific information, Beck," he laughed and bit his lips harder.

At that, I threw a couch cushion at him. He came at me and grabbed my hands, forcing them behind me.

"Can we go to your room and make the most of our time now?" he asked quietly, all humor practically erased.

I barely nodded as heat warmed my lower half. TJ bent down, tossed me over his shoulder, and took us to my room.

Lying in bed after, TJ had more time to brainstorm. We took turns stroking Scooter, Amy's cat, who purred and leaned her chin into TJ's soft caresses.

"She loves you," I commented, watching Scooter make paths on my bed, walking back and forth, nuzzling into TJ.

"I know," TJ remarked. "She's so soft. I love how her tail is like a paintbrush. Right?" TJ lightly gripped Scooter's tail.

"I've got it!" he said with raw excitement. "That's it! The perfect costume for my artist girlfriend and me."

It was so adorable learning that he loved how I was embracing my artistic side now. He wanted me sketching, drawing, or painting all the time. His pride in me was palpable. He was my biggest cheerleader by a long shot.

Sometimes, we would lie in bed together while he would talk about "our future."

"Wouldn't it be cool, Beck? If you were the art teacher and I was the gym teacher back in Carlyle?" A far-off mix of wonder and love shone in his eyes. I knew he saw this future for us more than I did, and I was torn about it. I didn't know how to tell him that. I loved Carlyle and felt at home there. But I was not interested in being an educator. Some people had that in them, and I was not one of those people. TJ's and Lindsay's innate abilities and desire to teach were evident. They were entertaining and craved attention. Not me. The thought of standing in front of a large group of people and speaking made me nervous. The other part was, *how could I willingly be that far from home?* I was surprised to feel that way since, for so long, I hadn't enjoyed living in Naperville. Although the thought of living permanently away from my dad and mom, and Lindsay, hours south of "home" was a lot to take in.

"I don't think that's me ... " I whispered as if the volume of my words would hurt TJ. I smoothed my hand over his face.

He just studied me softly. "Yeah, I get it." A few long moments settled. "It would be fun, though."

Finally, TJ came up with our winning costume: a paintbrush and palette. It would really highlight my new path as an artist. He insisted on being the paintbrush. We ordered costumes online. TJ found this huge gold hat with copper bristles on the top that he *had to* wear. A chin strap secured it in place. Other than the ridiculous hat, TJ wore all black: a black, fitted T-shirt that clung to every muscle on his chest and black athletic pants. From the neck down, he was hot. From the chin up, hysterical. He even insisted on a fake mustache with the same coloring as his fake bristles. I could hardly look at him without dissolving into laughter. What a goof!

My costume was a simple, long-sleeved, fitted black shirt and black leggings with an oversized painter's palette that fit around my arms and tied loosely in the back. I also included a black French-inspired beret. We were adorable in the best way.

Jenna texted photos from earlier in the day of her family trio in matching M&M costumes. She was a pack of regular M&Ms, Tana was a container of M&M Minis, and Mason was a pack of Peanut M&Ms because, as he put it, he was the one with the nuts.

Lindsay dressed as Ariel from *The Little Mermaid*. She spent way too much money on a costume that didn't allow her legs to move well. Showing a lot of skin was pretty uncharacteristic of Linds. Her purple shell-string bikini top looked too delicate to trust, hovering over her flawless skin. The bottom of Lindsay's costume was a tight-fitted, long skirt formed like a glittering mermaid's tail. The skirt hung low on her waist, showing off her trim stomach. She had donned a red wig of lustrous, long, soft curls. Lindsay announced proudly that since there was an African American Ariel from a recent Disney film, she was breaking the glass ceiling for little fellow Korean mermaids everywhere.

Amy's costume was my favorite: a nun's habit that ripped off with Velcro to reveal barely-there lingerie.

By the end of the night, the Velcro had come undone from so much tearing and reattaching that Amy said she was a nun-turned-stripper.

Many of our usual friends were up at Mom's. Freddie, Brandon, Trevor, and some of my new friends from art classes. Trevor and his girlfriend clung to each other all night. I loved seeing such bliss on his face. He was so deserving of happiness.

Brandon and Amy were keeping their distance from each other. He'd been into blondes for a bit now. That didn't bother Amy. She was having a blast with some guy dressed up as a devil. She said it was destiny that hellfire and brimstone brought them together as she toyed with his plastic, light-up, devil's fork.

Linds had Amy and I busting out laughing way too many times. All Lindsay could do was bend and pivot around on the dance floor. Her costume scarcely allowed any movement.

"Why are you dressed so slutty? That's my department," Amy said, gawking at and manhandling Lindsay's shells. Lindsay screeched and smacked Amy's hand away.

"Um, clearly, I'm desperate." Lindsay threw up her arms in frustration. "I only have a chunk of time left at college, and I need to secure a real relationship."

"And you think this mermaid costume is going to do that?" Amy asked, exasperated.

"Well, yes," Lindsay nodded.

"You look beautiful, Linds." I slid my hand over her curls.

"I do. Now, let's find someone to buy me a drink." Linds threaded her arm through mine and literally hopped to the bar.

Unfortunately, the only fish Lindsay caught that night was this odd guy named Kevin dressed like Zorro, who knew more about Disney movies than Lindsay.

As usual, Lindsay turned a little mopey by the end of the night. She got touchy-feely with Amy and me, talking about how "Things just aren't going to be the same next year for Halloween when we are all in different parts of the state."

Amy tried to get her to shut up by forcing a shot into her hand. I don't think Lindsay even realized she held it.

"I'll be teaching somewhere and hating it."

"Come on, you'll love it," I said.

"No, it's terrible," Linds yelled over the loud music. "Next year, I'll be trading my hot-girl mermaid costume for an Etsy special witch costume with my fellow teachers and preschoolers probably. Rebecca will be here finishing up her art degree. And Amy, where will you be?"

"I'll be drunk," Amy called and threw her shot glass up in the air. I belted out a laugh.

"Right! See?" Lindsay cried, her eyes filling with tears. "And it won't be like this!"

"Throw back your shot and stop crying!" Amy hollered, taking another shot glass from the bartender.

We all clinked our shot glasses and tossed the burning liquor down our throats.

My heart grew heavy, realizing Lindsay was right. It wouldn't be like this for long. Other than the Amy being drunk part.

My eyes strayed to TJ, with his ridiculous copper mustache and giant hat, at the bar with Brandon laughing and so carefree. He wouldn't be here, either. He'd be student teaching in Carlyle for the spring semester, then teaching full-time next fall. We hadn't brought up that so much was changing, not wanting to waste a good thing on future worries.

It would work out.

Somehow.

Journal Entry #11 ~ Saving Rebecca

FIVE MONTHS AFTER LOSING RACHEL

I had come out of a drowning stupor and lifted my eyes, looking for my four-year-old, Rebecca.

She was not there.

Rebecca and I had been alone in the house.

I couldn't breathe.

The silence wrapped around me, choking me.

All I heard was the drumming of my pummeled heart.

Rachel was never quiet. She would've been singing or dancing in tap shoes on my wood floors. She would've hummed while making clothes for her dolls after picking out patterns from Nana Maureen, Robert's mom, who taught her to sew with a needle and thread. In contrast, Rebecca was a quiet child. I would sometimes lose track of where she went in the house.

I couldn't take it. I was so broken already. I couldn't lift my tear-soaked face from the table. That agony. Rebecca needs me, I thought, yet I could do nothing but sob. My heart was shattered in that stillness and quiet. I felt the loss of my beautiful girl, and it overwhelmed everything.

When I came to my senses, I was frantic as I jolted up. I couldn't find Rebecca. I screamed her name again and again until my throat felt coated in shards of glass. I threw off her bed covers, tossed stuffed animals aside, charged to the basement, and searched behind every shelf and corner, calling for her. I bolted back up the stairs, nearly hyperventilating. That's when I noticed the front door more carefully. It wasn't completely shut—not securely. New adrenaline and terror overtook me.

I flung the door wide and rushed out, calling for her. I looked in the yard as an icy dread hit, and my eyes landed on the pool. I flew across the yard and up the deck, searching the depths of the pool and calling her name. Thank God she was not there. I hurried to the garage and looked in every corner. I ran down the street and back, but I could not find her. My body was shutting down. Tunnel vision made me woozy. Then, I blinked and spread my arms out with one thought. Get to the phone and call for help. I made my way up the step and onto the porch. I pushed the door open and stumbled my way through as dizziness clouded my vision.

I moved to the sink in the kitchen and splashed cold water on my face, then wiped my face with the towel from the drying rack and tried to remember how to breathe as I focused on the phone sitting at the table. My hands shook as I scrolled through my recent calls, clicked on Robert's contact tab, and pushed the call button.

After two rings, he answered sweetly but in a hushed tone. I paced over by the front room, and then I lost it. A hysterical cry leaped from inside me, and I collapsed on the floor.

"Suzanne!" He was so frightened in that moment. I heard him rustling, probably hurrying to some empty space.

"Suzanne, what is it? Oh, God."

"I … I …" I was bawling but trying to explain so he could help. I didn't even know how long she'd been gone.

"Breathe, Suzanne. Please. Was there an accident? Should I call 911?" he blurted all at once.

"Rrr … Rrr … Rebecca," I managed. "I … I can't find her," I sobbed and put my head on my knees.

Robert let out a breath. "Okay, tell me when you saw her last." He seemed somewhat relieved.

I lifted up my head, registering different sounds outside the house. Muffled voices. My eyes shot to the door just as it was pushed open.

"Hello? Anyone here?" a woman called out and peeked into my house. She held Rebecca's hand while carrying a baby and was flanked by a little boy.

"Robert. She's here," I cried, dropping the phone, jumping to my feet, and rushing toward them. "Oh, my God!" I grabbed her and lifted Rebecca's warm, little body like she was a rag doll. I crushed her to me. She put her arms around my tangled mess of hair, and I melted in gratefulness. I clung to Rebecca with every piece of myself, pouring tears all over her soft, little shoulders. I slumped down to my knees onto the front room carpet to drink her in. She sadly backed away as if she expected this now. The woman who cries. This weak person was her

91

mother now. Fresh tears fell from my eyes as I pulled her into another hug, wishing I had both daughters in front of me. Wishing I could be more for her.

"Oh, honey. She's okay," the stranger's voice sounded, and I realized I hadn't given an ounce of attention to the family that had brought Rebecca home to me.

A pretty woman with strawberry blond hair and freckles wiped at her eyes and bumped a baby on her hip.

I finally let Rebecca go and slouched onto my heels, completely spent.

"Tommy," the woman started. "Why don't you and Becky go play for a sec? Maybe over there? That looks like a toy bin. Is that okay, sweetheart?"

Rebecca nodded and moved over to the toy bin. Tommy followed her but looked back at me questioningly.

"I was taking these two for a stroll and saw this little darlin' about three blocks away. I don't know; I just saw she didn't have on any shoes and seemed lost," the woman spoke quietly.

I didn't look up at her. I was mesmerized by Rebecca sitting on the floor with this strange little boy.

The woman waited a moment, then said, "I'm Janet Lawson. We live right over on Meadowview." Her baby started fussing then, and I peeked up at her. She shifted her arms, trying to console the whining baby. "I'm so sorry. What can I do for you? Do you need anything?" she asked softly, despite the little girl fidgeting and whimpering in her arms.

I looked up at her, tears still puddling in my eyes. "My ..." I stopped as my throat ached with what I knew my mind had to explain. I hated divulging that part. Hated it. I tried again, "My daughter." I held my throat now as if trying to force the awful words out and explain what in God's name was wrong with me to this woman who had saved my child and couldn't understand what was happening with her mother.

To my surprise, the woman, Janet, she had said, moved closer and rubbed my shoulder with her left hand while crimping her mouth closed.

"My older daughter died," I burst out, covering my face.

"Oh," Janet cried and knelt down in front of me, pulling me into a one-armed hug beside her whimpering baby. Janet smelled like freesia and sunshine. She held my shaking frame and just stayed there like that with me for a minute.

When Janet's baby started wailing, we broke apart with tear-streaked faces. Janet stood up and offered me her hand. She pulled me up and had me sit on the couch while she apologized about her daughter. She proceeded to nurse the baby and cry and hold my hand while I told her everything about Rachel and her passing.

I don't know how long we sat there talking as she comforted me. Her baby, Katie, I learned, slept on Janet's shoulder in a satisfied milk-drunk state.

We dried our tears, then cried again on and off for a long while. Janet discovered I had not told Robert the whole story of Rebecca being lost and found, so she grabbed my phone and called him herself, explaining who she was and what had happened.

Colleen showed up later that afternoon with her very pregnant belly to drop Ryan home from his day camp. It was a lot to take in when Ryan walked into the house.

Tommy and Rebecca ran out of her room with a newly constructed Lego castle then.

He was beaming. "Hey, Mom! Look what me and Beck made."

Rebecca was skipping behind him and grinning. I had never seen her look happier than in that moment. I looked over at Tommy. He was so adorable it was hard to look away from him. Such golden hair and piercing blue eyes.

"Oh, wow! That's great, Tommy! Becky, good job!" Janet smiled at the two of them and then at me.

That was the day Janet Lawson saved my Rebecca and me.

CHAPTER 12

Becoming Family

"Ar-right. You know what I've decided?" TJ asked one November night as we were snuggled up at my apartment in Charleston.

"What's that?" I asked, leaning my head back into his, feeling his warm breath on my shoulder.

"I'm done having holidays without you."

I turned my body to face him. "What do you mean?"

"I mean, I want you to be part of my holidays. From now on." He leaned in and kissed my cheek. "So, what do we do about that?"

"You are adorable. Do you know that?" I put my hand on the side of his face.

"Absolutely."

***

Thanksgiving was approaching, and I was stuck on TJ's proclamation about spending the holidays together. Aunt Colleen always hosted Thanksgiving. I couldn't ask my mother about inviting TJ. That's not true; I could've, but I didn't want to see her face crumble or hear the annoyance in her voice. I texted Ryan to ask if he was bringing his girlfriend, Pilar. He wrote back, "No, she's traveling for a few weeks to see her family, so we can see her after Christmas."

I asked him how I could include TJ.

Ryan didn't hesitate. He said, "Go through Colleen. It's her house, after all. Then it's not Mom's decision."

On Thanksgiving Day, TJ showed up early, arms full, carrying two pots of mums. His smile was brilliant. My heart spun around my chest in sweet joy that he was here with me for a family holiday. I couldn't help myself from hanging around his neck to greet him. His clean, woodsy scent smelled so good. It felt like a month instead of a week had passed since I'd last seen him at school.

"Hi, babe." He kissed me with soft lips.

"Hi." I looked into his eyes. "Thanks for being here." I took one of the plants from him.

"Thanks for inviting me." TJ pulled my waist close with his free hand and kissed me again for a few more moments.

"Are you ready for this?" I glanced sideways toward the kitchen.

He confidently stared back at me. "Absolutely."

TJ and I crossed the foyer into the brightly lit kitchen brimming with activity and mouth-watering aromas.

"Hello!" TJ called out and moved steadily toward my mom and Colleen.

"Hi!" Aunt Colleen said.

"Mums for the mums!" he said cheerily. "Happy Thanksgiving!" TJ handed Aunt Colleen an arrangement of orange and red mums.

"For the mums," Aunt Colleen repeated, smiling and grabbing TJ for a hug. "Thank you. Let me see you," she said, backing away a little. TJ grinned at Aunt Colleen, then slowly turned like a supermodel.

I chuckled along with Aunt Colleen.

"Wow, Rebecca!" she said with wide eyes. Then she pretended to whisper, "He's gorgeous." I nodded my approval and smiled back.

TJ then grabbed the mums I had been holding and turned to present them to my mother. Yellow. I didn't even have to tell him.

"Mrs. Winslow." He handed her the flowers.

She had something else to do with her eyes now. Look at the flowers instead of him.

"Thank you," she said quietly.

"You're welcome," TJ said to my mother's bent head. I saw the tiniest clench of his jaw at that moment. "Aunt Colleen, thank you for having me," TJ said, turning her way again and grinning.

"Thank you, TJ," Colleen said. It was weird to hear someone else call him that. But I liked it. How else would she refer to him? I talked about him as TJ. Colleen wouldn't know him any other way.

I gave him a smile that I hoped he knew was filled with a "thank you for being so thoughtful."

Colleen and my mom set the planters down in the center of the island.

"What are we doing?" TJ peeked around, examining the kitchen. "Need any help with the bird?"

I couldn't help it. A laugh slipped out of me. "I don't think that's a good idea."

"Oh no?" Colleen asked.

"TJ is not the best in the kitchen. No offense," I faked the apology.

"I can't believe I'm hearing this, Beck. What about the pork tenderloin I made for you?" TJ replied with an open smile and fake surprise on his face.

I covered my mouth with my hand, muffling the next outburst.

"Do tell," Colleen said, shifting around the kitchen and then stirring a pot of mashed potatoes.

"Oh, my God. It was awful. We threw it right into the trash." I glanced at my mom to try and include her, but she was busying herself, getting platters and bowls out of the cabinets, being weird and standoffish. I gritted my teeth.

"That's not good," Colleen continued.

"No, it was not good," I laughed off my annoyance. "TJ won't be taking on the cooking duties, that's for sure."

96

"So, are we making future plans?" Colleen asked me with excited alarm on her face.

All at once, a crash stunned the room into silence, and my heart stopped. We all turned to see my mother's face flash from white to red. Shards of a ceramic serving bowl were scattered around her shoes.

"I'm so sorry," she said breathlessly, horrified embarrassment staining her face.

"Save the pieces!" Jim, Colleen's husband, joked loudly from the other room.

"Are you okay?" TJ asked, dashing to her side and taking her arm to get her out of the way.

He missed my mother's reaction at the mention of TJ and I making future plans. Or maybe he was just too clever to let on. I didn't. Mom locked eyes with me, and it was all over her face. Colleen and TJ swooped over to clean up while my dad appeared to help lead my mom carefully away from the broken pieces.

A while later, after Jim swept the floor, Ryan arrived, and we all sat together for the meal.

TJ folded his hands expectantly like we were going to say grace. We didn't, and I could see in that moment it bothered him.

I quickly grabbed my glass and stood up, holding it out to the table. "I'd like to toast everyone. Happy Thanksgiving to all of you whom I love. Thanks, Mom and Colleen, for this impressive meal."

A chorus of "Happy Thanksgiving" resounded as glasses clinked. TJ had a sweet smile on his face. When I sat down, he squeezed my leg.

After the meal, everyone retreated to themselves or their screens.

My dad cleared the table and offered to do the dishes, but Colleen shooed him away, so he joined Jim to watch the football game in the living room. Mom helped Colleen. Ryan was on his phone at the end of the table. My cousin Carly sat on the couch, head bent, texting or scrolling through her feed.

TJ looked confused that my family didn't sit around talking after the meal or engage in a game of some kind like his family did. It struck me then that we always did that with TJ's family. They were present with each other, playful. I loved that about them.

"You guys want to play some cards or anything?" TJ called out. Carly didn't respond. Jim hollered that the game was on. I gave him a pitying look.

"Jer," TJ said to my 12-year-old cousin, Jeremy, slunk low over his phone, still at the dining room table. He looked up at TJ. "Want to play something? What you got?"

Jeremy shrugged, "Uh, I don't know."

"Yeah, Jeremy, go play TJ in ping pong," Aunt Colleen chimed in, turning her head to him.

"Ping pong?! You've been holding out on me." TJ made a mocking face at Jeremy, who smiled a little. "Let's go, man!" TJ scooted out from his chair and headed for the basement steps, waving for Jeremy to join him.

I popped over to the kitchen to relieve my mom from cleaning up. She had been washing pans in the sink but then sank onto an island stool, claiming to be overtired. I didn't prod her about it too much, not wanting her reason for being spent having to do with TJ's presence and trying to become part of our family.

My hands in suds, I heard TJ's outbursts from the basement and some higher-pitch laughter, which I assumed was Jeremy, destroying TJ at ping-pong.

By the time I finished the dishes and crept downstairs to check on the game, TJ was sweating.

"He's killing me." His eyes flared competitively, but a smile brooded in the corner of his mouth.

Jeremy hooted with laughter at each frustrating, lost point TJ collected.

Later, TJ got Carly to put on her Just Dance game on the Xbox. Then he bragged about us and our dancing. TJ had Carly find a swing song, and we showed my family what we had learned last spring. We weren't nearly as fluid as we had been at Janet's wedding, but we were entertaining. Aunt Colleen loved it.

Then the whole family was down there. TJ attempted to teach Aunt Colleen how to swing, but she couldn't get the steps right.

Holding onto me, slow dancing, much later, TJ leaned down and kissed me so softly, as if showing me this life I wanted so badly. As if he could fix everything with my family in one evening.

I moved my eyes to the side and noticed my mom staring at us with her hand over her mouth and tears in her eyes. She ducked her head and disappeared back upstairs, gripping the railing.

After the pumpkin pie, cookies, and fruit were served, at the end of the evening, we followed Ryan and my parents back to the house in TJ's truck.

TJ was sleeping over at my parents' house for the first time in our history. I knew I shouldn't risk any consequences of sneaking into the guest room later, but I also knew my mother wouldn't lurk around to catch us. If anything, she'd be camped out in her bedroom for the next twenty-four hours just to avoid him.

Once I was certain everyone was asleep, I crept out of my room and tiptoed to the guest room. I slowly opened the door and spied TJ, arms folded, gazing out the window of all things.

"Hey," I whispered.

TJ turned toward the door. "Hey." His face was unreadable for once.

We moved across the space lit with shadows and laced our hands together. I hoped I conveyed with one look how much I loved him and that he was just perfect with my family. I think I did. TJ's eyes moved to my lips, and they parted unconsciously, like whenever he got that fire in his eyes.

Then he folded me into an exquisite kiss. Slow and passionate. The night went exactly like that. Nothing rushed. Every touch purposeful.

We didn't speak at all the whole time. Almost silent, we smothered out each other's moans with our tongues and lips on our shoulders and necks. It was quiet, pure bliss, topped by TJ's breathless, intense: "You're everything" afterward.

In the morning, my dad was up, showered, and watching the news when I came out of the guest room. I decided I didn't care. TJ had not slept in my room. I hadn't broken their rules.

"Morning, Dad." I wore TJ's T-shirt and a pair of boxer shorts I'd found in the dresser. My hair was tied in a high bun, and I had instructed TJ to go shower in the guest bathroom while I handled the walk of shame solo.

My dad looked at me like he wanted to smile but decided against it.

"Want me to make breakfast?" I crossed the kitchen to the fridge and pulled the door open, searching for ingredients.

"Thank you, but how about we go out to breakfast?"

"Is Mom still sleeping?" I turned my head toward their wing of the house.

"No, she's just not feeling well."

I challenged him with an eyebrow raised, and bless my father; he gave nothing away.

TJ, my dad, Ryan, and I grabbed breakfast at the Nook a few blocks north of our subdivision. We left my mother out of our conversations as we dug into omelets, bacon, and sourdough toast, pretending that her not being there to approve or support us was normal. Our breakfast together went well. TJ was charming, winning Ryan over; I could see it. My dad had loved him all along. Like me.

As everyone bantered on, my mind drifted to Colleen's comment about making future plans. Of course, I was planning ahead. I couldn't see a future without TJ in it. After yesterday, it was more solidified. He was here with my family, getting most of their approvals. I wanted him in this life with me. More than anything else.

Journal Entry #12 ~ Mornings

Every morning was a struggle. A gut-punching reality that Rachel was gone. I had no light in those moments.

A buzzing sound came from my phone. It was a text from Janet, despite the early hour.

"Want to go for a run? John's watching the kids. Send Ryan and Becky over."

I didn't respond. I barely knew her. I certainly didn't know her husband. I set the phone down and turned over onto my pillow. Feet pounded up and down the hallway. I couldn't get up and go parent the kids. I knew I should've been getting Ryan ready for camp, but I just lay there.

Robert wanted to be home, but he had taken so much time off work for Rachel's death. He couldn't be with me to monitor my moods and be both a father and mother to our children.

"Mom, Rebecca took all my Legos, and she's not giving them back," Ryan whined at my door. I turned back over, ignoring them. "Give it!" Ryan yelled, and Rebecca yelped. The thud of feet rushing down the hall resumed.

My phone buzzed, and I picked it up. It was Janet texting again.

"I don't want to bother you. But this will be good for you. And I'd love some company with my run. What do you say?"

I stared at her message and then typed a simple. "K." I didn't have the energy or desire to explain that Ryan wouldn't be home today, and I would just be bringing Rebecca. It would be good to get away from this house where Rachel was everywhere and nowhere.

I went through the motions of changing, washing up, combing my hair, and wiping my eyes of fresh tears again. Crying was as much a part of my morning routine as brushing my teeth.

As was her new habit, Colleen had come by to take Ryan to camp for me. She shouldn't have been doing that since she was close to popping with her pregnant belly, yet she insisted. She would ramble on about errands to run or wanting to squeeze in some time at work, and this was on the way, or she wanted to pretend she was already a soccer mom. I love my sister.

I got Rebecca washed up, dressed, and ready to go. I told her we were going over to Tommy's house. She looked confused, and I explained, "Oh, what did you call him? TJ. That boy from the other day."

At this, she gave me a loud "Yes!"

Rebecca ate a granola bar in the car on the way to Janet's house. I pulled up to the address she texted me and felt a twinge of unease. They lived in the older section of the neighborhood. Their house was modest and unimpressive, a white A-frame with black trim. I felt badly thinking that. A tiny front stoop of four stairs with a black, chipped wrought iron railing looked ancient and presided in a well-kept yard. Still, the house seemed little and insufficient.

I parked along the street and got out of the car, followed by Rebecca. I didn't see anyone in the front yard but heard noises from the back. An open gate by the side of the house led into the backyard. The first thing I noticed was the baby, Katie, sitting on the grass, chewing on plastic dolls.

"Suzanne!" Janet called, and I moved my eyes to her. She was sitting on a picnic table bench, tying her shoes. Suddenly, the side screen door burst open, and a flash of golden hair rushed past me, screaming. The door opened again, and a tall man ran out, hollering just as loud, chasing Tommy and brandishing a large foam ball.

"I'm so glad you took me up on this. It's going to be great," Janet said, moving closer to me, oblivious to what was going on around her. I stood very still beside Rebecca, who I could tell didn't quite know what to make of the situation.

"Um, huh," I managed to reply.

"Hello, Suzanne, and hello, Becky. I was just so happy to meet you that I wanted to see you and your momma right away again!" Janet cheered to Rebecca, who smiled at her. "How's that sound?"

Rebecca nodded.

"You are gonna have so much fun with Tommy and Katie, but mostly Tommy," Janet laughed. Katie threw down her doll and grunted, a string of drool hanging from her mouth. She gurgled, picked up another doll, and banged it on the grass. "John! Come here!" Janet waved him over.

"Ahh," he yelled trying to grab Tommy in the far side of the yard, but Tommy dodged him and sped away laughing.

John straightened up and nodded his head in a hello. Then he wiped his forehead with the back of his arm and wiped his hands on his shorts as he jogged our way.

"This is Suzanne," Janet explained.

"Hi Suzanne, John Lawson, great to meet you," John said in a Southern drawl. He took my hand in his calloused palm and shook it vigorously. He was tall and confident. A towhead with a tan face and crooked nose— that clearly had been broken at least once. He wore a damp gray T-shirt and green basketball shorts with no shoes or socks. But his eyes were what shot through me: blue-green and captivating. I looked at Tommy, who had just come running up beside his dad. Now I knew where Tommy got those eyes.

"Beck! Come on, help me get him!" Tommy patted Rebecca's arm.

"Oh no!" John yelled and bolted from our space to the back of their massive yard. Tommy ran full force after his dad and threw the sponge ball that narrowly missed John. "Beck, come on!" Tommy yelled again, and Rebecca scurried away to retrieve the ball. She ran after Tommy, handing him the ball, and he launched it again, striking John in the chest. John let out a fake groan and proceeded to fall over like a dead weight in the grass. Tommy let out a howl of laughter then jumped on top of him, laughing hysterically.

"They'll be fine," Janet said, clapping my shoulder and starting toward the gate; I followed her. "Just a bunch of kids, playing around." She closed and locked the gate behind her, joking that at least the gate would help corral them all.

Janet walked ahead of me to the front yard, then bent low, grabbing at her ankles and twirling her hips. As she stretched, I saw she had an athletic build except for some weight along her midsection.

I stood, feeling foolish and out of place with the sudden urge to fake an upset stomach and pull myself back into my car. I fidgeted with my hands as Janet rambled about the weather and how sunny it had been the last few days. I felt so dizzy, I must've missed a question because Janet stopped stretching and stood up.

"What?" I breathed. "Sorry."

Her face took on a sympathetic frown. Then she was hugging me. She didn't say anything. Just wrapped her freckled arms around me and kept holding on.

It should've been so awkward. I didn't know the first thing about Janet or her family. I hadn't wanted to be touched within the last five months. Not since Rachel. But I felt myself crumpling. I cried quiet tears on Janet's shoulder for a few minutes.

After some time, she pulled away, and her face was as wet as mine.

She pulled up the front of her shirt to wipe at her tears. "Maybe let's just walk and not run."

For whatever reason, this made me laugh. She laughed, too. All at once, we were in a fit of hysterics. Janet held onto my arm, steadying herself as she jerked with laughter. I hadn't laughed in so long. It felt foreign. But necessary.

We walked down a trail that she always took the kids on. I hadn't ever been in this part of the neighborhood, so it was new to me. Janet wasn't squeamish about divulging information about herself.

She explained that she knew loss. Her parents both had died, and her in-laws had become parents to her, but they didn't get to see them as much as they lived farther away. Carlyle was in southern Illinois, just an hour east of St. Louis. "You'd think John was raised deep in Kentucky with his Southern lilt, but no, that's just Carlyle. Great people in Carlyle, though, especially my mother-in-law, Noreen. God, I love that woman.

She's something else," she chortled.

I remained quiet as Janet went on and on about memories of her childhood, her brother, and her in-laws. She spoke so freely that it gave me something else to focus on.

We were nearing the end of the looping trail when she paused for a minute and looked at me.

"When is it the hardest?"

I didn't answer.

"Missing your daughter. What time of day is the hardest?" she asked earnestly.

I shook my head and managed, "Every moment is hard. But mornings are the worst." I swallowed the lump in my throat.

Janet squeezed my hand. "Mornings it is."

CHAPTER 13

From a Distance

Fall semester ended. I scored a 4.0 in all my art classes. Professor Bahnimin was so approachable and helpful. She had become a great source of comfort for me in this new field. She offered to meet with me outside of class to give me insight into choosing my courses for the next semester. I felt good about where I was headed and this new direction I'd chosen.

TJ finished his last actual college classes, with my help, of course. His study habits were really lacking. I assumed it had something to do with his flighty personality. TJ got sidetracked often and normally didn't perform well with deadlines. I did my best to kick him in gear, but his high energy and lack of study structure were exhausting. All he had left was student teaching in the spring.

He was very proud of himself and me for helping with papers and studying for tests. It was a big deal. He and Mason would be the first in their family to graduate from college, something that Mason's grandparents insisted on. They had offered all their love and support to get him there.

TJ wanted me to join him for Christmas at the Lawsons. I loved that idea but thought it would be too much for my mom. We hadn't left things well after Thanksgiving. Something bothered me about that. She sounded different on the phone, too. Lost and resigned. I couldn't make up my mind on what to do. On the one hand, I wanted so badly to be part of TJ's celebration. But then I thought of my mom and how Christmastime and the new year were usually so jarring for her. It would set her back in a funk, thinking of Rachel and the upcoming horrific anniversary of her death in January.

I confessed my mixed emotions to TJ who was naturally sweet and understanding about all of it. He invited me to spend a few days with him and his family before Christmas so I could at least be part of the big Lawson Christmas party. He couldn't wait to show me the grandness of this gathering. Tons of people. Most, I vaguely remembered from his mom's wedding to Howard.

Card games, darts, music, chatting, and eating nonstop—TJ was in his element. The joy bursting out of him was adorable when he was with his family. I wanted to see him like that forever.

Back at my parents' house for Christmas, I invited TJ to come up and stay for a few days.

Right before his arrival, my mother was sick again and really low on energy. I thought she looked older and duller somehow. She made a comment about getting her thyroid checked. I hoped a doctor could put her on a medication to make her perk up. That day, she didn't talk much, and I knew she wasn't happy that TJ would be hanging around her house.

Mom and I were slinking back to that earlier time when we were short with each other and avoided one another.

I asked her if she planned to get TJ a Christmas gift. Her face fell. "Because his parents had gifts for me," I challenged.

"I don't think it's necessary," she dismissed the idea.

"You know what, Mom?" I snapped, making my words daggers of ice. "You're a liar."

Her eyes grew wide, and she swallowed some of her snippy attitude. "A liar?" she asked with a gasp.

"Yes. Because you said you've always wanted what's best for me."

Now, the smugness was back on her face.

"Which is bullshit," I raged on. "TJ is what's best for me. I don't know why you can't see that. He is the best person for me; I know that for certain. You need to accept this, and be honest with yourself."

107

She turned her head slowly like she was watching a shadow move across the floor. It felt in a moment like I'd lost her. She was just eyeing nothing.

"Mom, do you want to be part of my life?" I almost yelled at her, wanting to smack some sense into her. *Am I pushing her away?*

It had only been a handful of months since we'd tried this new relationship. I wasn't in the habit of making space for my mom. But I also never used to push her, maybe because she never really pushed back. We were both uncomfortable with conflict. My mom wasn't a fighter. She would jab from a distance but wouldn't fully engage. I was so sure now that she did want me around that I needed her to push me back on this.

She stood, holding herself up, one palm flat on the dining room table. Her mouth worked at getting something out. I saw sadness and defeat in her eyes.

"Yes. I want to be part of your life, Rebecca," she rasped.

"Well, that life includes TJ."

Journal Entry #13 ~ Auntie Suzanne

One hot and sticky August morning, Colleen called me in a rush of frantic breathing and jumbled words to tell me her water had broken, and she was on her way to the hospital. This was to be her first.

Colleen was a planner. Once it was confirmed the baby was a girl, she had the nursery designed to look like something out of a magazine. The massive room was adorned with light gray wainscoting along the walls and a garden mural of delicate flower blossoms in muted green and gray grasses painted along the crib wall. A gorgeous chiffon, sheer fabric tied loosely from a hook in the ceiling, crowned a reading nook with a white oak rocker. Colleen had carefully picked out overstuffed chairs, plush beige, white, and gray stuffed animals, and all the trendiest baby books and story classics.

She was the picture of prepared.

But her voice on this call sounded only distressed.

"Suzanne, I need you. Please. I'm scared. Jim is out on a call, and I can't get ahold of him. Can you meet me and my neighbor, Kadence, at the hospital?"

Of course, I did.

On my drive there, I battled to keep my tears at bay. Colleen's entire pregnancy was coated in my sorrow of losing Rachel. It was a sick twist of fate that a new life, a baby girl, would be announced just after Rachel passed. It wasn't fair to my sister. I imagined she wanted to bask in the happiness of her first baby. After years of dating and finally finding a man to care for her the way she wanted, she deserved to celebrate this creation of life. Despite that, she was so good to me. She thought of me and my emptiness and muted her joy for me even when I didn't ask her to.

Once I reached Colleen's private room, I relieved Kadence and moved to Colleen's side.

"You can do this," I reassured Colleen, kissing her forehead.

She was battling the pain at that point, but the doctors said it would be a while. The baby had not dropped. Not even with her broken water or uptake in contractions. Colleen looked near panic. I grabbed her hand and squeezed, saying, "You have plenty of time. Don't worry."

Did I sound convincing? It must've worked. She seemed to believe me.

Everything about being in this place killed me. It wasn't the same hospital where Rachel passed, but it might as well have been. The sterile smell burned my nose. The beeping of machines, the racing of nurses, the wailing of family members accepting that their lives were about to become much, much worse. It overwhelmed me. It was a true battle to push the memories away. It had only been seven months since Rachel had died, yet it felt like decades in Hell.

Then, I steadied myself. Colleen was about to become a mom, and she needed me in this moment of joy.

After three more hours of no progress, the doctors worried the baby was in distress. So, they ordered a C-section, which caused Colleen to break down and sob. She didn't want a C-section. She was ready for a natural birth. She had trained and gone through the Lamaze classes. She had worked on her breathing and was an athlete with a killer bikini body. For Christ's sake, she had practiced Kegels, yet the reality was that Colleen was about to be cut open.

After Colleen's epidural, I got a set of scrubs to wear and met her in the surgery room. I checked her phone again to see if Jim had tried to get in touch. He finally replied to her messages with just the word: "SHIT!" I deleted it and only told her he was on his way.

A large blue sheet hung vertically in the OR, separating Colleen's top and bottom half. Her face was a mess of exhaustion and fear under her hair cap. I crouched down, moved as close to her as the nurse would allow, and leaned my head against hers.

The doctors gave instructions and information about the procedure. "You'll feel a lot of pressure. Let us know if you experience any pain, though." It was hard to process, and Colleen was fading from lack of sleep.

"Will she be okay?" Colleen whispered to me, a tear rolling down from the corner of her eye.

I swallowed thinking of all this question implied. Will the baby be born healthy? Will she meet her milestones? Will Colleen's parenting practices help the baby or hurt her? Will Colleen and Jim have expectations for their baby's life before she's lived it? Will she get sick and fragile due to an illness? Will she outlive her mother?

I shoved the thoughts away with a clench of my jaw as I took Colleen's hand and squeezed it.

"Yes," I said finally but firmly. "She will be perfect." I sucked in my quivering lips, determined to be strong for my sister.

A whole team of nurses moved around the doctor. I didn't let my eyes stray beyond the blue curtain. I only wanted to comfort Colleen. At last, we heard the perfection of an ear-splitting cry. Colleen shook with relief and exhaustion; fresh tears streamed down the sides of her face.

"She sounds like you," I said with tears and laughter in my voice. Colleen gave a rueful smile and finally let go of my hand to wipe at her eyes. I braced myself for the emotion to hit me as the nurses cleaned the baby.

Then, a nurse brought the baby around the blue sheet. She was nothing more than a tiny bundle of white cloth surrounding a pink face and swollen eyelids. The nurse stopped and held her close to Colleen's face.

"Oh, you little stinker. I love you already," Colleen said and kissed her tiny, wrinkled head three times as the baby squirmed in displeasure.

And then the most beautiful and emotional moment happened when Colleen touched the baby's face. "Auntie Suzanne is here to meet you, Carly Rachel Frontman." She looked up at me, and we both burst into tears.

CHAPTER 14

Double Date

Winter break and the end of December brought a double date with Ryan and Pilar in downtown Chicago. TJ was urging me to spend more time with my family. Ryan and I had never been super close, and we didn't connect over our feelings. I could count on one hand the number of genuine conversations I'd ever had with my brother.

Unlike most people, TJ didn't have his phone in his hand all hours of the day. He wasn't on social media or scrolling constantly. He used his phone merely for his family. He would call his mom and grandma every few days and text Katie every day, most often sending her a weird picture, like an opened bag of chips or a meme like "Watch out for raccoons stealing hubcaps on the highway." I'm sure Katie loved it. She insulted him, yes. She thought he was annoying, yes. But she adored him.

I knew TJ thought it was odd that my family wasn't as connected. I could tell by the way he would ask me off and on, "Do you ever want to have a stronger connection with Ryan? Have you ever told Ryan how you feel about your mom? Do you and Ryan ever call each other, or is it just texts every once in a while?" He wanted me to think about my responses.

So, in true TJ fashion, he set up a chance for us to be with Ryan over Christmas break.

Ryan and Pilar had a studio apartment in The Loop. At Christmas, TJ had talked to Ryan, who said we should see the city. It had been a long while since TJ had been downtown. Ryan was not usually a very friendly guy, but I suspected that TJ had made him feel comfortable at Thanksgiving, and Ryan decided to give him a chance.

We took the Metra train into the city. TJ wanted to sit up top to have a clear view of Chicago and a chance to people-watch the level below us. He chose names for people we were spying on and made up elaborate circumstances for these people's lives. "Trenton works at Apple but isn't satisfied, so he's quitting today to stay home and start his own organic Chia Pet business. Janice and Angela were college friends until Janice caught Angela with her boyfriend, Devonte. That's why they stopped talking, but destiny brought them back together on this very train." TJ had himself a good ol' time.

After about forty minutes, we pulled into the station. Ryan and Pilar lived only a quick Uber away, so they planned to meet us there. It was a very chilly night, but freezing winters in Chicago are expected.

Pilar wanted to show us her favorite restaurant, Cabra, so we went to dinner first. I noticed Ryan and Pilar had backpacks with them— holding their skates, they explained.

The goat empanadas and steak saltado, a Peruvian stir fry of thinly sliced steak, with onions and tomatoes were otherworldly. TJ couldn't believe that each dish he tasted was even better than the last. He loved all of it. Pilar teased that he needed to get out more.

Pilar was laid back with an air of calm confidence. TJ kept the conversation moving, avoiding pitfalls and dead ends. He was so easy to love. Ryan and Pilar really warmed up to him.

"So, where did you guys meet?" TJ asked, scooping another morsel of empanada into his mouth.

"Pilar used to work with me at Stockworks. Now she's a senior chair of risk at Morgan Stanley just a few blocks from my office."

"Very nice." TJ nodded.

"And you are friends from childhood?" Pilar asked us.

TJ smirked sweetly, his eyes skimming my face. "Yeah. I met Beck when she was four. Been in love with her ever since." He wouldn't take his eyes off me. I nestled into him.

"Wow. That is remarkably sweet," Pilar said.

"But you haven't been together that long," Ryan added, earning a cautious look from TJ. "They moved downstate," he indicated to Pilar. "So, they just met back up at college."

"That's romantic, though. It must be comforting to share some history with your partner," Pilar said.

"Yes, absolutely," I agreed and smiled at TJ.

After our meal, we hopped in an Uber to Navy Pier to ride the Ferris wheel. As cold as it was, the line for the ride was long and winding, giving us a few moments to appreciate the grandness of the space. The black of the waterfront, the dazzling Christmas lights twinkling every which way from the trees, Buckingham Fountain, and the shimmer of the skyline—Chicago was basking in holiday magic.

"Oh, man. I haven't been here in forever," TJ gleefully announced staring up, mouth agape at the 200-foot-tall structure in front of us. The renovations on the newly crowned Centennial Wheel were amazing. Each gondola was heat-controlled and cozy, with comfortable benches on either side, granting gorgeous 360-degree views of downtown and the lakefront. TJ loved it.

Once seated inside the gondola, TJ and I sat beside each other on a bench. "This is awesome, isn't it?" he asked me, squeezing my knee.

"It is." I peered out at the lights, a sense of enchantment overtaking me.

"We're at the top, Beck," TJ whispered, eyeing my lips.

I looked back at him.

"Let me kiss you." He moved in a little.

"In front of my brother?" I quickly checked out what Ryan and Pilar were doing, but they were busy enjoying the view out their side of the gondola.

"I don't care. You're beautiful; this city is beautiful."

I didn't have to deny or approve him. I always wanted to kiss him.

He leaned over and pushed his soft lips on mine, gently pulling at my lower lip. He stayed there kissing me momentarily, and then we broke away.

We arrived late to Millennium Park for ice skating. A crowded and fun group of people sped around the rink. Some in puffy jackets, some in sweaters, most in adorable winter hats and gloves. A few looked like legit skaters, while others were loud, sloppy-skating teens, not nearly dressed appropriately for the ice rink and 30-degree weather.

I should've anticipated Ryan being a skilled skater. He was long ago. His skateboarding days served him well on the ice. He had his skates fastened in no time and walked easily to the rink to start. Pilar was still finishing up her skates but did not look to Ryan to wait. Neither seemed bothered by that. He had grown to be self-sufficient and sometimes hard to know. It seemed Ryan and Pilar were very independent people who happened to live together and be in a committed relationship.

Pilar got on the ice next while I tried on a number of skates before I found ones that fit. Pilar was a smooth skater but slow and cautious. Ryan glided circles around her, then eased up beside her, spraying slush in her direction before smiling and taking her gloved hand.

I didn't think to ask TJ if he had ever skated before we arrived. I didn't have a memory of us skating together. Even rollerblades weren't TJ's thing. Balance wasn't his strong suit. Balance with life was more like it. I was the one with the good balance, and we both knew it since I would surf on his back in my pool as a child. Ice skating was a fun activity with some friends during high school for me, but this was my first time skating with him.

Finally, TJ and I had our skates on, and we trudged our way up to the opening. The comedy was about to begin. TJ had a "let's go!" attitude, but he wiped out immediately upon hitting the ice. I covered my mouth, holding back hysterics, and helped him up.

"Well, glad that's out of the way. Thanks, Beck."

He stood up on shaky legs and wobbled, trying to walk on the ice.

I put one foot on the ice, slid in front of him, then turned around to offer my hands.

"I'm okay," TJ said. "Let me see you!" he cheered excitedly, shuffling forward and almost falling backward, then flapping his arms to regain his balance.

I laughed. "Are you sure? I could help."

"No, please, let me see you skate."

So, I spun around and pushed off with my left, then right, then left, instantly sailing along the ice. The cold evening wind made my cheeks tingle and my eyes glaze with tears. It was lovely, regardless.

I heard a "Whoop! That's my girl!" and turned back, still moving fluidly on the ice, as TJ rushed forward with a huge grin, only to collapse again. He fumbled, knees pressed on the ice, gloved palms pushing up to get back on his feet. I laugh-snorted.

Ryan skated near me.

"Is he gonna be okay?" he asked, nudging his head toward TJ.

"Yes, he is just going to take this as a challenge now." I smiled and glided away from Ryan.

After a few more trials and errors, TJ figured out a slow system of awkwardly shuffling on the ice. He was sweating, so he tossed his coat on the rail and continued to skate in only a thin, gray, thermal long-sleeved shirt.

Soon enough, I saw TJ befriend a cute couple who skated so brilliantly that they could've been professional skaters. I learned their names were Dominic and Teddy. Dominic was long and lean in a tight holiday-green beanie and white sweater, Teddy, slender but more muscular in black, felt earmuffs and a short, brown leather coat.

Dominic took to TJ right away, giving him tips and guiding him on the ice. "Come on, goldie, you can do this, right, push, left, push; you are way too clunky with this footwork. These are skates, not cement blocks, sweetie."

TJ fumbled but took Dominic's outstretched hands. "Yeah, I got it,"

TJ said, screwing up his face in concentration.

"You've got it, alright," Dominic said, swiveling his head toward TJ. "You are a dream. Tell me you're taken. You have to be."

"And you're taken too," Teddy snapped, although playfully.

"Of course, my Teddy Bear," Dominic agreed. Teddy swept away from them and spun in a very impressive, tight whirl. His body twirled like a top before he evened out and pushed off on one skate effortlessly again.

TJ laughed, although a little uncomfortably at Dominic's flirting. I decided to swoop in and save him.

"Definitely taken," I called out, zipping around in a circle to grab his arm. I cuddled up against his side.

TJ's smile was full of charm. He adjusted his arm to squeeze my waist.

"Yes, ma'am. Handcuffed, shackled, and tagged." He kissed the top of my head.

"Oh, and he's straight," Dominic sighed, skating backward, then forward. "But look at you, cutie," Dominic remarked, his eyes lingering on me as he circled his finger around. "If I were straight ..." His head tilted side to side.

TJ and I giggled.

"Onward, Dominic. Let these adorable creatures play on the ice!"

"Thanks for the help, guys," TJ called.

"Keep at it, blue eyes. Step, step, glide," Dominic recited as he smoothly swept past us on the ice.

"I can't take you anywhere without you getting hit on, can I?" I asked.

His smile was devious. "Maybe you just need to stick closer to me." TJ wrapped his arms around my waist. "That way, everyone will know I've been captured already."

Those sweet eyes, rosy cheeks, and muscular arms. He was everything.

"Like, I should up my PDA?" I asked.

He grinned, so I obliged and kissed him. Cold lips parted, giving way to our tongues exploring. Me, keeping him balanced and pressing into him. Even in the dead of winter, on a block of ice, TJ could make my body turn into melting fire. I pulled back and took in every one of his beautiful features, trying to find a way to capture this scene forever. The gorgeous skyline over us and the trees glinting with Christmas lights peppering the snow. This man who had my heart adored me with nothing but devotion in his eyes.

"You ready to head out? Or do you want one more crack at it?" I teased.

"I'll do two more rounds. Without stopping." And then he pushed off.

Ryan motioned me over as Pilar left the ice to change back into her shoes.

"You look really happy," Ryan said, studying me.

"I am." I waited for him to say more. Ryan wasn't smiling. He seemed bothered. "Please don't mention Jason … "

He cut me off with a baffled expression. "I don't care about Jason."

"Then what?"

"I'm trying to see what Mom sees. Or doesn't see."

My eyes snapped into focus with alarm. "What do you mean?" But I knew.

"She doesn't like him. She even makes it obvious. Don't you think it's weird how she's never liked him? Especially when you think about how Mom and Mrs. Lawson used to be friends."

At this, a crease must've appeared between my eyes because Ryan continued, "You knew that, right?"

"Mom and Janet? They were friends?" I tried out the foreign words. *How can this be?* "No. I never knew that at all."

"You were younger, but I thought you'd remember. We were over there a lot," he said as if waiting for me to get it.

I tried to picture my mom with Janet. Or Ryan over by TJ's. It was like that piece of my memory had vanished.

"And then," Ryan went on, "Mom just stopped talking to her. She's wanted nothing to do with Tommy's family ever since."

I gaped up at him, my mind filled with questions.

"Anyway. It's just odd. He's great for you." Ryan waved to Pilar on the bench. "I just don't get her take on it."

We all slid off the ice and changed back into our shoes.

"Good seeing you, sis." Then he hugged me. Like a real hug from my brother. "I mean it," Ryan said warmly with a side grin. He looked exactly like my dad in that second. My eyes welled up. Then TJ was at my side. He hugged Ryan and gave him two quick, hefty pats on the back.

"Thanks so much, guys. Great to see you both," TJ said appreciatively.

"Yes, absolutely," I agreed.

I was so happy with how the night turned out. Still, for some reason, I felt anxious about Ryan's observation. *My mom was friends with Janet?* I couldn't comprehend that; worse, I didn't understand where it all went wrong.

Journal Entry #14 ~ Splash

Janet was becoming a great distraction. She never liked to be idle, nor did John. They were always doing something. Tending their garden, chopping firewood, building a birdhouse, painting the garage.

The Lawsons were different people and very free, with lots of open affection at their house. One night, Robert and I were over there for a barbeque outside. I went in the house to use the bathroom and walked in on John, picking Janet up by the thighs and shoving her on the kitchen countertop as she giggled quietly. He smirked and kissed her deeply. Seeing his forearms flex and witnessing their intimacy made me uneasy.

Of course, they were carefree. They weren't living the day-to-day suffering Robert and I were. Their child hadn't died, leaving them wounded with nothing but despair. I envied their affection.

One warm September evening, we were in our backyard with the Lawsons. I admit I didn't want to host. We'd been spending more time with them. Their house wasn't an ideal space, but it wasn't full of emptiness like mine. I didn't like having people over to see Rachel's photo to talk about or avoid. I didn't want to be here in this house—ever, but especially with others. It was hard enough just being here to be present in all the memories of Rachel. It was easier to manage my grief being lost at the Lawson house, especially in their massive backyard, surrounded by a new space where Rachel hadn't ever been.

Robert insisted, "Suzanne, we are over there often. They're very accommodating, but I think we should have them here. Let the kids swim. We'll hang out on the deck. It'll be great."

So, I said okay.

Janet brought over homemade deli rolls made for little fists. I prepared a pasta salad and lemon garlic shrimp skewers with pineapple, peppers, onions, and mushrooms. Robert did the grilling and John helped him out, as they talked and drank beer by the grill.

After we ate, Janet got in the water with Katie, who was wearing Rebecca's puddle jumper for swimming. Janet lowered herself into the pool in a white one-piece with red flowers.

John didn't waste a minute racing Tommy up the deck and cannonballing into the water. He was long, lean, and muscular, his too-tan body set off by his white-blonde hair.

John didn't put his shirt back on after swimming, not even while we ate dessert or later, as we all sat on the patio talking. He guzzled down a handful of beers. Robert just kept them coming for him. I don't drink often. Drinking reminds me of my father, and I never want that reminder.

Rebecca and Tommy had the best time in the pool together. I was nervous about not being more involved in their swimming. Rebecca had *taken swim lessons and was very comfortable in the water. I was a little surprised to see how proficient Tommy was in the pool. He was fluid and controlled—especially for a five-year-old.*

Regardless, I craned my neck often to see what they were doing. Robert caught my gaze and nodded, reassuring me that the kids were fine.

In the water, Robert took turns catching Ryan, Tommy, and Rebecca from the deck as they squealed and leaped at him. Robert laughed but got winded after a while.

Tommy stood on John's shoulders and dove off him. Then John grabbed Tommy's hands and pulled him forward into a somersault before he could hit the water. In that moment, they looked so alike. Then, John started throwing all the kids in the water. He tossed them higher and higher. Ryan got out of the pool, giving John a sideways glance. He didn't want John to throw him around. Rebecca laughed wildly, a sound I couldn't remember ever hearing from her. I moved closer to the pool deck, my eyes wide with fear, but John stopped and looked me over.

"We're okay, Sue. Right, Beck?" He held Rebecca up with his muscular forearms, so she was facing him. His hands were wedged under her arms. Her soaked suit dripped water all over him.

"More!" Rebecca shouted.

John launched her up and away from him. She rocketed through the air screaming and splashed down.

I looked over to make sure she was okay, but she barely breached the surface before she was already swimming frantically back for another go. Her smile was all the confirmation I needed that she was enjoying it. I reasoned with myself to let her be.

CHAPTER 15

Diagnosis

I t was the date I lost my sister and, in a fateful twist, the day I found out I could lose my mother.

I had just come back from the mall with Linds. We had grabbed some new outfits and essentials with Christmas cash. The spring semester, when Lindsay would be student teaching, was nearly here. She was so anxious with nervous excitement. Lindsay would have a whole class to herself to stretch her wings and begin her dream career.

I had some reservations about the upcoming semester since TJ would be a glaring missing piece. He was set to student teach in Carlyle, while I finished school at Eastern. We wouldn't get to see each other every day, but he was certain the weekends would be great. Eastern wasn't far from Carlyle. "Completely doable," TJ said. "Now that you have a car, and I have my truck. We'll just take turns driving." Or we'd take some weekends off so that I could spend more time with the girls. He knew Lindsay would need time with me as a break from her student teaching. No matter, we would easily make it work.

My parents were going to check out a potential rental property, so I had the morning to myself. TJ had gone back to Eastern for the weekend with his friends. He wouldn't leave for his long-term student teaching spot at Carlyle High School until Tuesday. I was so happy for him. He was starting this important step–exactly where he wanted to be. From there, it would be a seamless transition to picking up a PE teaching position in the fall since he would have already been there for a semester for student teaching.

Then, my parents came home.

I knew something was off from the moment they walked into the house through the garage access. They came in at the same time. Unusually quietly. A grimace and mournful eyes had replaced my dad's signature grin. My mom was stoic.

"How'd it go?" I asked. Mom eased out of her coat and held it, her eyes on the floor.

Dad stood there, hands playing with his key fob. "We need to talk."

My stomach dropped as I peered at my mom. She had just finished lifting her coat onto the hanger and hanging it in the closet. Then she let out a tired sigh and moved carefully to the sofa in the great room as though each step was an arduous effort.

I glanced back at my dad to get a sense of what was going on. I couldn't tell, but my heart was hammering beneath my ribs.

Dad gestured to the sofa near Mom, and I moved over to it while he, coat and shoes still on, walked over and sat near my mom. His expression reflected that he was still processing the information he was about to share.

"We didn't go to the rental property," he said in a controlled voice. "We had an appointment at Northwestern Hospital."

Then he unloaded.

The doctors sat my parents in cold leather seats and delivered a diagnosis: metastatic breast cancer. Now, in her lungs.

My head swirled with questions, but I tried to focus on what they were telling me. I couldn't stop the questions I badly wanted to ask, so I only heard pieces. "Aggressive." "Options." "Treatment immediately." "Not sure."

My mind reeled. *What were her symptoms before? Didn't she feel anything?* This must've been why she had had such low energy over the past few weeks. It had nothing to do with her mental health, as I had wondered about. She had been on pills for depression for years.

I remembered sneaking into her bathroom and looking under the cabinet for Band-Aids. That's when I found the prescriptions in orange containers with white childproof caps. "Suzanne Winslow. Take once daily." I found the paperwork accompanying the pills: "For anxiety, depression, and mood swings." Of course, I understood then why she had to take them. She'd been unhappy for so long. I had internalized forever ago that it must've been me. My fault. Or Rachel.

But those pill bottles were prescribed. *Wasn't she seeing a doctor frequently? Hadn't she been going for mammograms? Wouldn't Colleen have demanded her to be seen? Or my dad?*

I didn't understand how it could be this bad. *It's bad.* The cancer had ravaged her breasts and moved onto her lungs. She had four nodules in her left lung and three in her right. It was inoperable. My parents disclosed more information while my head swam, but I had to keep paddling. I couldn't miss this information. *If she had caught it early, or it hadn't grown so quickly, she could've maybe prevented all of this.* But ...

I didn't know how to respond. I just gulped and clenched my jaw to keep from crying. I couldn't break down. Could not. For some reason, instead of being present, I drifted into the past with my mother. We hadn't been connected. I didn't have a full sense of adoration for her. At any other time in our history, this news may not have affected me this way, but now, when we'd been steadily getting closer, it nearly knocked the wind out of me.

I absorbed all the information, nodded a few times, and took deep breaths.

"I am going to call Ryan. Let's all try to attend the appointment with the new oncologist later this week," my dad said.

I thought of my schedule for the semester; then I hit on a resolution.

My mom had her fingertips to her mouth. "Mom," I said, sounding braver than I felt. I waited until she looked at me before continuing: "We're gonna work on this. Together. Do you understand?"

She gave me a tremulous smile, and tears streamed down her face.

I couldn't fully explain to TJ all the details of what I had learned about my mom while sitting on his bed with him in Charleston. He was stunned but understanding and comforting. I could see pain in his expression, like he was having an internal battle with himself and wondering if he should try to keep me at school or come up north with me. Ultimately, I had to manage this on my own. Of course, I needed TJ, but I needed to help my mom more.

***

Since returning to Naperville, I had been clinging to the phone like a life source, calling TJ often. I told him everything pressing on my heart, including the tears Lindsay and I shared, while Amy was quiet as I explained the situation. I told TJ how the girls were so supportive.

I shared what I'd noticed about my mom getting thinner and rundown. She didn't have as much of an appetite, but she never did. She had always been thin and put together, but with a lifetime of depression from Rachel's death, it was a lot to overcome. My mother just seemed on edge, except when it came to her jewelry line. That was a true light in her life.

She would make excuses for her thin frame and lack of eating when I dared to bring it up. "I already had lunch," or "Colleen and I are grabbing a bite later." I wondered if she'd known all along that she was sick. If this was what she wanted deep down. A way out.

With TJ, I could let out all my questions and frustrations.

"You can't think about the what-ifs, Beck. That's something Howard told me. You've got to keep moving forward and not look back. I get it. I've thought about those what-ifs before. What if my dad hadn't gone on that trip with his cousin? What if they had left a few minutes later? What if that semi had been going slower? What if that driver hadn't fallen asleep? What if my mom had gone down with them, too? You don't get anywhere with those what-ifs. Trust me."

Of course, he was right. I broke down then and started crying. Really crying. My parents were not talking timelines with me. Googling didn't make me feel any better.

"Yeah, I wouldn't recommend Google," TJ said gently. Then: "Can you do something for me?" he asked when I was quiet for too long. "Can you first really imagine I've got you in my arms right now? Really. And I just showered, so I smell pretty good. Get there. Can you do that?"

I closed my eyes and fought to feel every sensation, inhaling slowly.

"I've got you on my lap, but I swear, I'm keeping my mind PG. I've got my hand up at the back of your neck, and I'm holding you. Can you feel that?"

"Yes," I told him, wiping tears from my eyes. Yes, I could feel it. Because I desperately wanted that embrace to be real.

"Second thing, I want you to use this as fuel for a better outcome. You know? Just try that."

"Ar-right," I said, wiping the last tear from my eye. "I'm gonna get to work."

Journal Entry #15 ~ Trick-or-Treating

The first Halloween with the Lawsons was the best it could've been.

Rebecca and Tommy were in their karate phase by mid-October. They had watched The Karate Kid over at the Lawsons about a hundred times. That family seemed to spend only two hours a day inside their actual house (aside from sleeping), and those two hours were apparently reserved for movies. After seeing the movie a few times, Tommy went around the neighborhood karate chopping everything. Tommy only had two speeds: full or off. He was like John in that regard. The man barely sat.

Janet had the idea of getting the kids matching karate uniforms for costumes. My initial reaction was disappointment that Rebecca wouldn't be dressed as Cinderella, a cute pumpkin, or a good witch. She was into sports and always getting dirty—so very different from Rachel.

Rachel had dressed as a rock star on her last Halloween. I'd bought her a bedazzled turquoise skirt and tank top. She had a side ponytail and a sparkling black top hat. I'd painted her nails hot pink and let her wear a load of makeup. She took an old karaoke microphone from a toy she had gotten from Colleen and sang "Trick or Treat" into it around the neighborhood. It pained me again to think of her in the past. Her last Halloween, her last time Trick or Treating, her last self-starring concert, her last school day, her last Christmas, her last night at home, her last breath.

Once I conceded to the costume for Rebecca, I knew she would be thrilled. As a bonus, she would match Tommy. Janet and I stood side by side in their yard two weeks prior to Halloween, and I started to ask the kids if they wanted to dress up in karate outfits. Tommy hollered an ear-splitting "YEAH!" before I could get the question out. Rebecca chimed in with an equally loud "Hi-ya!" chop. Then they were once again running around the yard, hi-ya'ing everything in sight. Janet clapped her hands in happiness and cheered, laughing right along with them.

The grown-ups sat on lawn chairs around John's new fire pit, and the kids played pretend in the yard. Ryan was always encouraged to play with Tommy and Rebecca, but even at seven, he seemed too put out to play with them and, instead, just sat at the picnic table focused on a game on his tablet. I worried sometimes that he was on it too much. Was he learning social skills? He didn't seem to want to do much. Although I would've preferred him to play with Rebecca and Tommy, I was grateful he had a distraction—even if it was in tablet form. It did allow the adults to take a breath together around the warm glow of the fire. Janet asked Ryan if he wanted a karate costume so he could match Rebecca and Tommy. He just shook his head and went back to his game without even picking up his head or acknowledging her.

"Ryan?" Robert chided gently. "It's 'no, thank you.' Right?"

"No, thank you," Ryan parroted back, barely audible.

"Of course, honey," Janet said. "I'd hate to leave him out. Do you know what he wants to dress as?" she asked, turning back to the adults.

"He wants to be some Mario character," Robert said, waving a hand at Ryan and giving him a dismissive smile. "I don't get it. I never sat on a screen when I was young."

I knew Ryan being on the tablet bothered Robert. He was sliding away from us and was so quiet. Since he wasn't interested in sports, Robert felt out of touch with him.

"Same, Bob. Hell, I wouldn't know the first thing about any of those devices," John said, popping the tab off a beer can and sitting with a hefty sigh on a lawn chair. "Kids need to be outside catching snakes."

My eyes went wide at this. John chuckled at my expression.

"Well, maybe not snakes, but catching a baseball, at least," Robert added, smiling.

"One hundred percent," John said.

"What about all of us?" Janet asked. "What should we do to dress up? I'm certain the kids will want to Trick or Treat together. We should get a theme for costumes for us." Her eyes were bright as they panned side to side, gauging our reactions. "Wouldn't that be great?" She patted my knee.

"That would be fun," I said, making myself sound more convinced than I felt. In the end, we didn't decide on anything, and I was relieved I wouldn't have to fake enthusiasm for the group costume.

On the day of Halloween, I was so thankful for Janet with her kind smile and ready attitude. Every day was easier because of Janet. She made Halloween so enchanting for the kids. Their costumes were adorable. Janet crafted Katie a puffy red strawberry costume with the cutest stem hat over her soft, blonde curls. Rebecca and Tommy had little white guis with bonsai tree patches and black belts. She gave them matching headbands that didn't stay put, so their hair was scrunched up in plumes, which made them look even cuter. Janet and John also set up a whole karate obstacle area in their backyard with perforated cardboard pieces the kids could easily break when snapping their arms down on them. Janet even invented a game where they had to take turns squeezing chopsticks and picking up little plastic spiders.

Once John had stoked the fire to a steady burn, Katie slumped over, fast asleep on Janet's lap. The kids finally grew tired of the themed games, so they took turns balancing one-legged on the tree stumps John had cut weeks beforehand. The kids whipped their legs, kicking outward like Mr. Miyagi—John included. Shortly after, though, Tommy and Rebecca began roughhousing with John. John had Tommy throw punches at his stomach. Tommy let out an arsenal of grunts and shrieks while throwing fists into John's hard stomach. He stood unmoved, his stomach clenched, hissing through each blow. Rebecca didn't punch John, but she did help to "push" him down and crawl over him, attacking him with "karate cooties." She was having the time of her life.

Robert tried to get Ryan involved, but Ryan just sat on a tree stump and filled his cheeks with packs of Goldfish crackers, KitKats, and Sour Patch Kids. Robert eventually got Ryan to play some catch with him, but it was short-lived when Ryan dropped the ball for the tenth time and pouted that he couldn't see anything because it was so dark.

Aside from Ryan's complaining, the evening was truly special, and I felt blessed to have been there. I hadn't felt that way in a while. My thoughts didn't stay in that free space for very long, though. Soon enough, I was walking back inside my house with only two, not three, children. I dreaded setting my head down for the night, thinking of all the fun Rachel had missed and would continue to miss. How she had missed seeing her little sister twinning with her boy bestie. How she had missed spending quiet time with her brother, who maybe missed Rachel the most.

No matter, I couldn't let another sweet day end in tears and disappointment. I couldn't do that to Robert again. That I might have one day when I was not sobbing in front of him, Robert, helpless to stop it—I couldn't put him through that again. So, I practiced my breathing until I felt almost okay. Then I curled up to Robert's side of the bed, put my hands on him, and let him help me forget my thoughts.

CHAPTER 16

New Information

The oncologist's office jarred everything into a painful reality.

Dr. Ahmed, my mother's new oncologist, sat with my mom and dad and discussed the next course of action after reviewing my mom's health history. Ryan and I positioned ourselves in chairs beside each other along the wall, stealing glances at our parents.

Dr. Ahmed started with a line of questions: "Were you ever hospitalized?"

My mom suddenly became rigid. My dad snapped his head toward her, his expression unreadable.

"Yes," she whispered.

"And what was that hospitalization for?" Dr. Ahmed asked.

She had gone sheet-white.

"Depression," my dad admitted, his elbows on his knees, hands folded. "For about a week, a year and a half after our daughter passed."

The room grew silent, and my mind filled with questions. I couldn't look at Ryan, who I could feel staring at me. I don't think the hospitalization surprised me as much as the lapse in time. *A year and a half after Rachel died?* It was confusing.

The doctor continued with questions and went over my mom's current medications as I tried to wrap my brain around what my mother had just revealed about her past.

"Is there a history of cancer in your family?" Dr. Ahmed asked. My mom stared through the doctor, her mind taking her somewhere else.

"Your father ... ?" Dr. Ahmed coaxed.

After a few moments, Mom's mouth moved. "I'm not certain. I

don't think so." She twisted her fingers together, looking down at them instead of at the doctor.

"Did your mother have any cancer diagnosis?"

Again, it took her an extra moment to answer. "I wouldn't know." My mother swallowed. "She left us when I was fourteen."

I shifted in my chair. I'd never known this detail. She'd never told us anything. I stared at my mom as if noticing she was someone else. Then Ryan and I locked eyes in a silent conversation that included, "Nope, she has never mentioned that to me, either."

The doctor said that although her lung tumors were inoperable, a double mastectomy was necessary to prolong my mother's life. As she pulled her sweater tighter around herself, I could see her already struggling with this fight.

The treatment her oncology team recommended involved a double mastectomy, which was scheduled in three days. Three weeks after the mastectomy, three weeks of radiation, five days a week, would follow.

Every number the doctor threw at us added a treatment, a test, and a hypothesis while subtracting time, comfort, and hope.

Journal Entry #16 ~ Snow Day

The first week of December without Rachel we were pelted with snow. A massive cold front collided with a low-pressure system, creating a perfect storm that dropped two feet of snow. School was canceled for the day, and Janet phoned to ask if she could come over with the kids.

I didn't mind having them over. Janet and the kids were always fun. I had been keeping to myself a little more, though. The holidays were looming, and I couldn't figure out what to do about it. I didn't feel capable of being in our house and decorating for our first Christmas without Rachel.

I wanted to leave the country, to go somewhere else, but I couldn't or wouldn't go somewhere by myself, and Robert couldn't take the time off work. He was traveling even more than usual and taking trips to New York about every two weeks to catch up for all the time he had taken off. When he wasn't flying into New York, he was in Philadelphia or Sacramento. I knew he felt guilty. I wondered if he had called Janet to have her check in on me. It seemed the type of thing he would do. He was always so sweet and sensitive to my needs.

Janet showed up, pulling a bright orange sled holding Tommy and Katie. Her cheeks were flushed, and the kids were covered in huge flakes. Katie was crying, having been knocked sideways in the sled, while Tommy was cheering and yelling with his tongue stretched out, trying to snag every snowflake.

Rebecca and Ryan were bundled up and ready for the snow, but I was not. I thought Janet would come in, put Katie down for a nap, and warm up while the kids played around in the front or backyard. Janet yelled to me through the door: "Go grab your snow gear, and meet us outside." I didn't want to go play in the snow. I wanted to melt right into it and be taken away. I wanted an easy day where it didn't hurt to look at all Rachel was missing.

Once I found my snow boots and waterproof gloves, I opened the front door and stepped onto our snowcapped porch. Janet was shoveling a path on the sidewalk up to our front door.

"Oh, thank you," I said. "You don't have to do that. Let me."

"I'm fine. I'm fine. I actually have so much energy right now! It'll just take a sec."

Tommy and Rebecca took turns pulling each other on the sled. They ran up and down the snow-covered walk and threw themselves into the air, landing on soft, white pillows of snow.

Katie sat on her bottom and stared at the world turned white, trying to figure it all out.

After a bit, Tommy ambled over to Janet as she had just about finished shoveling the driveway.

"Mom, will you help us make a fort?" Tommy asked.

"That sounds like a super idea!"

Janet secured a flat space in the yard and showed the kids how to make snow bricks. She patted the snow into blocks and made a curved structure in the yard, working on the base first and putting in one brick at a time. Then, the kids helped. I started making bricks as well. Rebecca looked at me in surprise, as if she didn't know I was capable of play.

"Is it okay if I help, too?" I hated the pathetic sound of my voice.

Rebecca answered me with a quick hug around the middle.

Later, in the house, Tommy, Rebecca, and Ryan sipped hot cups of cocoa. I brought out the whipped cream to delightful yelps. Janet kept me busy with conversation while the kids finished their mugs, then ran to Rebecca's room to play dress-up.

When they came down, they were both wearing layers of mismatched clothes. Rebecca giggled at Tommy, who was jumping around and falling over in too many layers of Robert's shirts. Ryan wasn't in on the fun. He was, I guessed, in his room on his video games.

The next run down the stairs had Rebecca and Tommy in white sheets like ghosts, oohing and ahhing. Katie laughed at them instead of getting scared, and Janet and I chuckled at her unexpected reaction.

The final beauty show consisted of actual costumes. They must've dug out the bin of Rachel's and Ryan's dress-up clothes. I didn't even remember where I'd stored it. No one had touched those items in years. Rachel was the only one who had loved playing dress-up. Tommy wore a Batman costume that had once fit Ryan. It was tight on Tommy, although he fit the part well, leaping and pretending to swing on wires.

Then, Rebecca came floating down the stairs wearing a painfully familiar dress. All shades of pink with fine lace, glittering tulle, and satin bows. My heart suddenly stopped beating as I gaped at Rachel's favorite Sleeping Beauty dress.

Rebecca must've seen the horror on my face because she stopped gliding through the room and regarded me with sadness. She ran back upstairs *and came down sometime later wearing her usual sweatpants and sweatshirt. I never saw her dress up like that again.*

CHAPTER 17

Caretaker

Despite the news, the surgery, medications, and the overall feeling of dread, I was steadfast for my mom. I developed a routine when I was home that kept me organized, as well.

I would get up and go for a run before my mom was awake. The trail by the house was ideal. The paved surface was wide and smooth as it stretched around the lake. I hadn't given much thought to how beautiful this place could be. All I used to see was my sweet golden retriever, Buddy's absence, along with TJ's. Now, I saw tall river birch trees, pines, and bare-bone maple trees covered in frost. It was peaceful and usually quiet, with faint mumblings of geese flying over. I saw the back patio where my mom and I had held each other last summer and connected over gardening.

When my mom woke, I helped her get ready. She would insist she was fine, but she did let me give her a hand. She had to change how she shifted in bed to avoid pain from the surgery. I had to help her lightly hug onto pillows before pulling her forward. She didn't complain much. I'm sure it was painful, but she didn't let on about it.

I learned how to do her hair the way she liked. Some days, she was too tired and didn't want to go through the motions. We would just tie it up in a bun, then. But, most days, I helped her shower, then had her sit while I blew dry her hair and curled it a little. It was stupid to go through these steps for her to just sit on the couch and stay home. To have no visitors but, me, my dad, Ryan, or Aunt Colleen. But these quiet moments with her were so wonderful. She sometimes grabbed onto my wrist as a thank you.

I felt like she saw me as someone new. I did feel new. I was newly determined and organized. I was not a grumpy teen or an adolescent crawling beside a pond, covered in mud, or throwing a football with a neighborhood of boys. I was Suzanne's careful and artistic daughter, Rebecca. I caught her looking at me often like she was trying to take a mental picture she could bring into eternity.

I couldn't stop thinking of what had been revealed about my mom at the oncologist's office. I wanted to know more about her. Was it my fault for never inquiring before? Or was it her fault for never being open with me? I tried a few times to get some information from her. To learn about her past. To learn about Rachel, but she shut down. I learned the signs of when to push and when not to. Overall, my mom had been really good about complying with most of my requests. And it was the first time, in her delicate condition, that I saw her real strength coming through.

Journal Entry #17 ~ Bubbles

I had never had a friend quite like Janet Lawson. Even Colleen, who knew me better than anyone and was the best sister I could've ever had, didn't have all the qualities I had found in this unusual neighbor-turned-friend.

Janet knew certain triggers for me and my grief. I don't know how she knew, but it felt like she had a whole other set of empathy that normal people did not have. She was sensitive. Too sensitive at times. She teared up easily. It could've been a commercial, the sunset, or a story about someone's family member. Her eyes would water just looking at her kids. But then, in the next breath, a laugh would roll out, and she'd let the wind take her worries away.

One spring day, she came over to my door with two bottles of bubbles and the plastic wands that little kids use.

She rang the bell, and I saw her standing outside our door with Tommy at her side and Katie on her hip. It was early spring and a nice, dry day for a change. Katie was absolutely adorable in tiny blonde pigtails and a purple polka-dotted jacket. Her eyes were more ice blue than Tommy's. Tommy had on a gray windbreaker and shorts above scabbed-up knees. I never saw that child without a cut or bruise. He played hard and ran wild all the time. Janet's hair was wind-blown, a pile of frizzy, strawberry-blonde curls. She said that since I hadn't responded to her message, she wanted to see if she could help me with my troubles.

I furrowed my brow at her, but by then, Rebecca had heard guests at the front door and came bounding down from her room.

"Hi, Tommy," I barely got in before a barefooted Rebecca and he ran to the chalk bin in the backyard and grabbed pieces, talking excitedly about a plan.

"Don't you love seeing them together?" Janet asked, dreamily gazing at Rebecca and Tommy in the yard.

I shifted my eyes to them. I knew what she meant. Something about the way they played together was so sweet. They had this constant attraction to each other. I didn't respond to Janet's comment, so Janet turned to me.

"Are you ready?" she asked, shifting Katie to her other hip.

"Ready?" I asked, confused.

Katie whined and leaned down toward the ground, her arms dangling. A clear indication she wanted to get down.

"Okay, Katie. Just a minute," Janet pleaded, then turned to me. "Yes, are you ready? We are gonna take some of our worries away. Let's go."

Janet moved toward the front of my house. She plopped Katie on the grass and pulled off a backpack I hadn't realized she'd been carrying. She bent over the backpack and brought out dolls and plastic cars for Katie.

Then, she sat down and motioned to me as she folded her legs. "Come on, Suzanne."

There, we sat on the grass in the middle of my front yard.

I must've indicated my unease by looking around at the few cars driving up and down the street.

"Yes, we are gonna sit here where all the cars can see us, and what does it matter? They may just come over and join us because we are fun," she said. "Here's what we're gonna do," Janet declared, handing me a container of bubbles.

I stared at the bubbles and then at her blankly.

"We are using these bubbles to blow our worries away."

I looked again at the container of bubbles and felt foolish. It was a low day out of the blue; I was lost in my head and quiet. I wanted to stay in my bed, try to sleep, not dream about anything at all, and not wake with this instant panic and dread that, yes, Rachel was still gone and had been for over a year. Yet, I was still here, missing her.

I looked around, wondering how Janet would let me get out of this.

"Come on now. Don't worry about anyone else. This is so fun and rewarding. You'll see."

Janet unscrewed her bubble cap and took out the thin orange wand. She dipped it in the solution and then put the wand up to her lips. A drop of soap hit her leg as she paused a second, closing her eyes. Then she opened her eyes and blew.

Tiny iridescent bubbles zoomed out of her wand and floated in the air above us. Katie jerked back and let out a happy yelp, waving her arms around, trying to grab the floating bubbles.

"Just think of something hanging on your heart, and close your eyes, then blow."

Janet did it again and again.

"It might make you feel a little better," she said. Then, for emphasis, she leaned over and squeezed my ankle. "You can say the worries out loud if you'd like. Or just say them in your head. I'll give you one of mine."

Janet closed her eyes again. "I worry that we won't be able to afford this campground. That we've bitten off more than we can chew." She blew into the wand and watched the bubbles float away.

I was supposed to dunk the wand in the watery bubble mixture, pull it up to my lips, and blow into the air. "This," she said, "is to acknowledge that there is a true worry. But then, watch as it disappears. Light as nothing." She told me to use the whole bottle. I felt so foolish about it but finally gave in and felt the sun on my face and the breeze in my hair.

I took that 4-inch plastic wand and dunked it again and again, filling it with troubles one by one: my heart never healing, Robert being gone so much, never having energy, never smiling, not getting close to Ryan and Rebecca, worrying that Ryan wouldn't make friends, that Rebecca would have nothing in common with me, that she wouldn't need me. I imagined blowing all those worries away. It was pretty magical. Each time I complied, she told me, "Now, watch the bubbles shine."

Although the one worry that wouldn't quite disappear was the only one I needed to release. That worry would never leave me. It would stick to me forever like a haunting shadow.

I tried to explain this as my throat closed up in agony. Janet stopped me.

"Hang on. With a worry like that one ..." She nudged her head toward me, tears in her eyes. "I think we're gonna need more solution and a bigger wand, darlin'."

Then she leaned over and squeezed me. Whereas Janet was quite affectionate, I was not. But I got that about her, and I hope she got that about me.

CHAPTER 18

Our Space

My new job was taking my mom to and from radiation appointments. It wasn't far from our house. One advantage was that her treatments were given at the cancer center and not the hospital, which was farther and a less convenient drive. And, though she wouldn't tell me, I knew the hospital was part of her nightmares. The place where Rachel died.

My mom was always quiet when we drove home. She stared blankly out the window. Her hands looked thin and frail, folded loosely on top of each other. Her body was almost motionless, tucked into her long, fleece-lined winter coat.

The timing was rough. The Chicago area was unforgiving this time of year. Winters were harsh, laden with dull skies. Lifeless. The promise of spring was so far away. I had to snap her out of this funk.

At home, my mom wanted to lie around in her bed. She was already having a rough time after her surgery and was in so much pain that she moved as if every cell in her body were breaking down. I had to take advantage of any day she felt slightly okay. I did let her lie in bed for a spell—just for a few hours then I would wake her up and force her to eat.

I had reached out to everyone I could think of, watched every YouTube video on cooking for those with chronic illnesses, and learned that food needed to be healthy, good, and filling, all while being gentle on your stomach. I never thought I'd get the hang of this type of cooking, but I was feeling more and more confident about the meals each day.

One of my parents' conditions for me to stay and care for Mom was that I take a class online—at least one—as a promise to myself and my family that I'd come back to my degree no matter what. I talked with my advisor, and she and I figured out I could take Art in My World—a course I had already signed up for that semester. It was an interesting class and easy to manage, allowing me to work at my own pace.

After checking in with Professor Bahnimin for the online class, I mentioned how I was caring for my mother. She asked me if my mother was an artist.

I said, "No, but I can see potential in her."

"You should get her involved in your art. If your mom and you have a good experience with it, maybe look into becoming an art therapist."

It would tack on more schooling because I would have to get a master's, but Professor Bahnimin said it might be worth pursuing, especially if I didn't have the clearest idea of what I wanted to do with my art degree.

"Consider it," she said. "You have some great qualities that could lead to a successful career in art therapy."

Professor Bahnimin sent me some printouts and other resources, which lit a fire under me. Feeling inspired by my art and what TJ had said about moving forward and being a positive force, I made over the spare room into an art studio.

I thought back to the jewelry concept, the flowers, the decorating habits, the curtains my mom had put up in my dorm room. She had always loved art and design. Of course, she had. I wanted to use this to springboard a motivational purpose for her.

First, I called my Aunt Colleen.

"I just want to ask you some things about my mom."

"Uh oh. What happened?" she teased.

It wasn't unusual for me to call or text Aunt Colleen now. We were constantly checking in with each other about my mom. We would be the ones to pull her through, and my dad, of course.

"How did the jewelry business start?"

She paused for a second. "That was my idea."

"It was?"

"Yeah, your mom was going through a hard time. You might've been around six or so, and I suggested she help me with it. She loved jewelry. Rachel loved jewelry. I thought it could at least give her something to do. Get her out of that house. You know how much she hated being in that house."

"I think so." I wondered how much of that rested on the Lawsons being so close, so involved.

"So, I just got on board with another rep and introduced Suzanne, and here we are. Is there a reason you're asking?"

"I just want her to still be part of that. Maybe in a different way. I could make some pieces with her instead of just selling things to other people?"

Silence echoed from the phone, which I wasn't sure how to take. Was this a good thing?

"I think," Aunt Colleen said, her voice suddenly thick. "That would be perfect, Rebecca."

I spent my evenings doing coursework and searching for ideas on how to start the art studio. I wanted it to be a space for both of us. I looked at different websites for beads, implements, and accessories of all kinds: glass beads, metals, chains, wires, clasps, round nose pliers, chain nose pliers, wire cutters, crimping tools, bead caps, head pins, and beading wire. I became a design student and found boxes and organizers to keep it all together.

I bought a table, a couple of easels, movable shelving, and all kinds of supplies.

In the late evenings, my dad helped me put the room together. We bought a soft, yellow paint and transformed the room. My dad did the roller, and I worked on the trim. Afterward, Dad and I put together the table, shelves, and storage bins. Ryan came by one day and added track lighting in the center of the room above where the table would be.

We had the room ready in just under two weeks and finally allowed my mom to come in.

My dad and I stood back and let her walk in first. She pressed her hand to her mouth, turning her head in awe at everything we had done. Then, she moved over to the large table in the middle, where all the organizers were open and ready, showcasing beads of every color, texture, pattern, and design waiting to be set into something beautiful.

"You did all of this?" she asked me and my dad.

"Dad and I did it together, and Ryan did the lighting," I said, hoping for a good reaction from her. "Do you like it?"

She took a minute to survey the space then reached out her hand and touched the table. With a warm smile gracing her wan face, she said, "I love it."

This space would become our space. I didn't know it at the time, but it would help both of us in so many ways.

Journal Entry #18 ~ Precious Wonder

Today, Janet had to take Katie to the doctor for her two-year check-up. I offered to watch Tommy. John was working part-time at a gas station. He always had some odd job, trying to get by. When he wasn't plowing driveways or roads, landscaping here and there, working construction, or at the gas station, he was trying to set up the campground permits and site. He was as outdoorsy as they came. He even periodically took my Rebecca and Tommy fishing at a nearby retention pond. When John was home, he was outside in the yard.

But all wasn't as easy as the Lawsons made it look. Janet confided in me that John was in and out of work often. His dream was to own a campground. He and his cousin, Luke, back home, had spent their lives camping and living outdoors. He wanted to share that with his kids.

Janet worried a little about the money. They had even taken out a loan on the house to pay for the permits, land, equipment, and facilities. But John's excitement was contagious. He was all in on their new endeavor and delirious with joy.

Since it was pouring rain outside, I watched Tommy and Rebecca play with race cars and a track they were setting up in the front room. Tommy really was an adorable kid. His messy blonde hair was more golden than ash, and he had the most beautiful, impossibly blue eyes.

Tommy was so natural with Rebecca that they sometimes seemed like twins, considering the way they connected and communicated. They played well together, just the two of them, lost in their own little world. You could tell from how he looked at her and longed to be with her that Tommy adored Rebecca.

Janet was in love with their friendship. She talked all the time about how, "Sure, now we're watching them play with blocks and cars, but soon we'll be watching them march down the aisle." She nudged me, grinning. I didn't know how to feel about that. It was a joke or sentiment, but I saw what she meant. They had an undeniable connection.

I was so happy that Rebecca had Tommy as a friend. He made her days more enjoyable.

They were building a race track around and underneath my dining room table, winding the curved plastic pieces through the chair and table legs. They'd taken the big cushions off the couch and propped them against the underside of the table, so the space under there was dark and mysterious. Tommy said it was so the track could be "lost in a different dimension!" Rebecca was giddy about this. Some pillows didn't reach the top, so light filtered through the narrow space. They had used all the pillows and still didn't have enough to surround the table. I was folding laundry and purposely dropped one red linen tablecloth and one bronze satin tablecloth on the carpet near the kids.

"Yeah, look, Beck!" Tommy called out, spying them.

"Thanks, Mom!" Rebecca piped.

They both positioned the tablecloths over the table so that one blocked out the light from the tops of the pillows, and the other acted like a door to their racetrack cave. They used Ryan's old track and remote controls. Ryan was at the point where he would rather watch TV on my bed or play in his room on his Xbox than play with Tommy and Rebecca.

For their lunch, I made homemade mac and cheese in little bowls alongside a plate of veggies that I cut into artwork with varying themes for each of them. Rebecca had ants on a log and a ladder of carrots over a pool of ranch.

I made Ryan a skateboard of celery and black olives with a carrot bench and Teddy Grahams on top.

Tommy had a golden sun with yellow and orange peppers. I laid out broccoli stalks and celery sticks for the trees.

Once I placed the meals in front of the kids, Tommy was beside himself with awe. He stared at his plate with precious wonder without saying a word. I covered my mouth and held back my smile. In the end, Tommy couldn't eat it. He said he wanted to keep it. I gave him a plate with other veggies to eat instead so he could save his veggie art. For dessert, the kids had little fruit and yogurt parfaits with cinnamon granola on top.

Tommy said everything was "So, so, so, so very good!" and ate more than Ryan and Rebecca combined.

Out of habit, I turned to Rachel's empty chair at the dining room table. I meant to include her in this cute moment, but I had forgotten for a moment that she was gone. In the next second, I turned and half expected her to grin with me at Tommy's cuteness and Rebecca's loving smile directed toward him. My heart stopped cold as I saw only her empty chair. Rachel would've adored Tommy. Absolutely adored him.

CHAPTER 19

Getting Muddy

Picasso said, "Art washes away from the soul the dust of everyday life."

That's what I wanted for my mother. A place to wash away what she'd been through. So, we would come into the art studio together on days after radiation and her nap. Sometimes, I drew or sketched whatever I could see out the window or in my mind. I didn't pester my mom to participate. I simply set a blank canvas in front of her with brushes and palettes of oil pastels and sharpened pencils in arm's reach. She could paint if she wanted to.

More than anything, I was soothed as we spent this special time together. Sketching, drawing, or painting regulated my heart rate and brought me peace. I thought back to my initial love of art I'd found that summer the world fell apart when TJ moved away. I thought about Ryan showing me his drawing books to keep me occupied. I drew all the time after that. It healed me when I thought I'd never be whole again. I hoped my mom felt the same now and that my presence bringing to life a beautiful work could be enough to heal her.

She took to painting often, but her heart was always drawn to the jewelry. Because of that, I experimented with the boxes of beads and crystals, and together, we arranged artful pieces.

It was early February, and we were both bowed over the table, working our hands in beads and crystals. My mom was doing most of the creating, and I was finalizing the pieces for her. I had learned to use the beading wire and how to clamp everything. It was taxing on my hands, but I wanted to get used to it.

TJ's face lit up my screen with a call while I was closing a complicated loop on a bracelet that was taking all my concentration. "Mom, could you get that?" I asked.

"Sure," she said, but then I heard the ring again. I lifted my head to see her, wide-eyeing the call and not answering.

For a second, I was angry. She didn't want to answer my phone because TJ was calling. I inhaled loudly so she could hear it.

"Just answer for me. Please," I snapped.

Out of my peripheral vision, I noticed she lifted the phone to her cheek and murmured a shaky hello.

I moved the pliers and tried to bend the last piece down and fit it in the loop before I had to start all over again. My pulse rose in irritation that my mom still wanted nothing to do with TJ.

I heard TJ's loud voice come through the phone, "Hey, Mrs. Winslow!"

"Tommy," she said with careful effort. Not snippy, but not friendly. Tired.

"It's great to hear your voice. How's your day been today?"

"Fine, thank you. Here's Rebecca."

She set the phone beside me and backed away from the table, her face pale.

I wanted to snap at her again but stopped when she fumbled for the back of the chair to hold onto. I looked at my phone and realized it was later than I anticipated. She hadn't gotten enough rest today.

"Mom? Are you okay?"

She waved a hand at me as if swatting a gnat and slowly walked out of the room.

I set the bracelet down and watched her as I picked up the phone.

"Hi," I breathed into the receiver.

"Hey, babe. What's going on over there?"

"I don't know. I had my mom working here in the art room for too long, I think." I was still staring after her as she made her way down the hall. Still embarrassed at how she had responded to TJ's call and still annoyed that, once again, we had taken two steps forward and one right back.

***

TJ treated me to a spa day with him for Valentine's weekend. He wanted to go big on this one since we had never officially been Valentines before.

He booked us Saturday reservations at Stone and Soul in Naperville, which meant he had to come up to see me for the weekend.

TJ did warn me that we weren't relaxing in the typical way—secluded in a dark room with soft hands and oils caressing our scalps. He had something more interesting planned.

The receptionist, Kyra, was easily one of the most beautiful women I had ever seen in real life. She had smooth, chocolate skin, high cheekbones, and intricate braids draped over her shoulders like streamers of black pearls. Her lashes were obvious extensions but stunning in how they fanned out from her gorgeous light brown, honey eyes. She wore a black work suit with a high collar, her name etched in gold lettering.

"Good morning. How may I be of service?" Kyra spoke in a regal whisper.

"Hi, Kyra. We have an appointment at ten for Lawson," TJ said.

Kyra tapped on the screen in front of her. "Of course, Mr. Lawson." She gave him a practiced smile.

After she explained about the towels, flip-flops, and carafes of tangerine hibiscus tea, we were told to change into our robes and wait.

"Beck, it's unreal how good this is! Come here and try it!" TJ's exuberant voice cut through the zen space like a car horn on a quiet street.

I laughed quietly, shushing him as I walked over.

"Oh, shoot," TJ whispered and looked around apologetically.

Another attendant then brought us to a surprisingly bright room with exotic plants, bamboo chairs, and two spa tables draped with thick, folded white linens. In the center of the room, I spied a cart with drawers and a large ceramic bowl of what looked like melted fudge.

"What exactly is this idea of yours?" I studied the collection of smooth fudge.

"We are going to get painted in mud. You know, to relax you." He winked.

The two care technicians excused themselves so we could undress and prepare for the services. Once they were out the door, I untied my soft, terrycloth robe and pulled it off my shoulders. I walked over to the side of the room and hung it on a hook. Turning back around, I saw TJ focused on me. His eyes roved up and down my body as I stood there wearing only my panties.

"Don't get any ideas," I teased, walking back to the table.

The slightly raised corners of his mouth told me he was indeed getting ideas. "Nope. None," he admitted while taking off his robe and hanging it beside mine. "Completely blank." He turned back toward the table to reveal his trim, muscular form and boxer briefs clinging too tightly over a sudden display of arousal.

"Hey!" I accused in a whisper yell. "You can't have that." I flashed my eyes to his boxer briefs and then frantically toward the door.

"I have no idea what you're talking about, Beck. Totally blank." He grinned.

"Oh my God, TJ. Stop it," I scolded while climbing on top of my massage table.

The massage table felt divine. Soft, warm cotton sheets cushioned every bit of me. TJ and I lay on our bellies with our heads turned toward each other. He had the sweetest smile on his face.

"This is fun." He smiled bigger, which made me smile bigger, too.

I chuckled. "Nothing's happened yet."

"But I'm anticipating fun. Aren't you?" He looked so much like his younger self in that moment. Wide eyes, goofy grin, child-like excitement written all over his face.

"You're fun," I said just as the two massage technicians entered the room.

Soon, we were treated to the amazing pressure of trained hands working our shoulders and necks. Our faces were set in the hollowed-out space in the headrest. Soft foam encapsulated our cheeks. The masseuse took my hand and threaded her fingers through mine, pushing, pulling, and rattling my hands wonderfully. We turned onto our backs for a bit as they worked our foreheads and feet.

It was luxury as I tried to just focus on the push and pull of the massage and not think about my mother: weak, cut apart, and fighting at home under blankets and sorrow. It would help me be better for her if I got a chance to unwind. When her image crept back into my mind, I pictured TJ's face and took another breath.

After a while, the technicians smeared globs of smooth, warm mud on our backs. Our mud-covered skin was then wrapped in clear plastic wrap, and the techs finished by massaging our arms, legs, and heads. My muscles loosened up, and calm resurfaced.

The massage ended after the techs wiped our backs clean with steaming towels. I was invigorated but spent.

TJ hopped off the table first, drunken happiness on his slack face as he approached me.

"That was nice, right?" he asked.

"Mmm," I moaned, stretching beneath the sheets.

"This day is amazing. Thanks." I grinned up at him.

"I agree." TJ raised his eyebrows. "And after we get cleaned up … " he leaned down and kissed me softly. "We're getting sandwiches!"

Journal Entry #21 ~ Buddy

A YEAR AND A HALF AFTER RACHEL PASSED

Buddy came into our family to fill the holes left behind by my beloved girl. Robert had asked me one night after making love if we could please get my tubal ligation reversed. I flew off the bed and away from him with a startled gasp, clutching at my heart as if he had just jabbed a white-hot poker through it.

He apologized, then cried with me and held me for a while.

A few days later, though, Robert wanted to talk to me again. With tears in his eyes, he begged that he needed something—someone else, something else to help make our family feel alive again. It didn't mean that he would forget or replace Rachel. He needed to grow another piece of his heart.

"I'm worried about all of us," he said carefully. "I'm worried that the kids need something. Maybe a pet? They need an outlet for their grief."

He studied me intently.

"Suzanne, we could all do with some mending. The kids aren't connecting with each other or with you, honey. You and Janet aren't close anymore. If therapy didn't work for you, we need something else. We've already forgiven each other about so much." Robert took hold of my hand.

I froze as he spoke, fearing my heart would shatter worse if I looked at him. I was so broken. It hurt that I wasn't there for my children or Janet. I was barely there for Robert. I hadn't been able to handle the therapy sessions and had bowed out after two appointments. Robert was so helpful and accommodating. What more could I do?

"How about a cat?" I asked, my eyes drifting to the floor, resignation washing over me that I wasn't enough for our family. That I might never be enough again.

"I'm allergic." Was a grin peeking out of his voice?

I met Robert's warm eyes. He was hopeful.

"Not a puppy, okay? An older dog," I agreed, reading his mind.

Robert smiled widely, dimples on display. I walked closer to him and wrapped my arms around him.

"I love you," I breathed into his neck. It wasn't just an "I love you." It was a plea for continued forgiveness and for him to stay with me. To still choose me.

"I will always love you, Suzanne."

So, we got Buddy.

Buddy was a five-year-old golden retriever who lived with a nice, older gentleman until he'd had a stroke and had to go into assisted living and couldn't care for Buddy anymore. Robert had been calling around to the shelters for a while. The shelter a few miles away called him back one Saturday morning and explained Buddy's story. The shelter manager said that this dog was such a gem; she was thinking of keeping him for herself, but then she thought of our grieving family and how Buddy was grieving, too. She explained that Buddy needed a family, not some old lady running out of yard space because of her four dogs and five cats.

Robert said he took one look at Buddy and fell in love. That is Robert's way, after all. I know it well.

One of the best days was a year and a half after Rachel died when Robert brought Buddy home. Even now, as I write this, I feel guilty having a best day at all without Rachel. How can there be any best day if she is not here?

Ryan and Rebecca were so overjoyed when Buddy hopped out of the backseat of Robert's car and pranced toward them like he'd known them their whole lives. I stood on the edge of the grass, watching them gush over Buddy. Ryan, who had been getting angrier about every little thing, was suddenly calm and gentle. He smoothed Buddy's fur and smiled so genuinely that it hurt me. When was the last time I'd seen him smile? Months? Before Rachel passed?

Rebecca was in love, just like Robert. She kept rubbing a spot on the top of Buddy's head. Buddy had his eyes closed and a big, lazy smile on his face.

"See, he likes that," Rebecca said.

When Rebecca pulled her hand away, Buddy lifted his paw to nudge her for more. Ryan and Rebecca both giggled at that. I made my way over, slowly, admiring this creature who was to bring some light back to our family. Buddy seemed to know how hesitant I was. He just let me come to him. I could've sworn he winked at me when I knelt before him. As if to say, "Don't worry as much. I'm going to make things a little better." He did. He was just perfect.

CHAPTER 20

Bridges

It was alarming how quickly a new routine could take shape, and an old routine could seem so far off. I felt different when I was away from Amy, Linds, and the college crew. So many pieces of my day were altered now. I wasn't lounging around at all hours and then drinking all night at a bar. I wasn't laughing wildly with my roommates in the evenings as we'd go over the guys Amy had "dated" and ranked with her special system.

All of that seemed trivial.

Then Amy called me instead of texting, which was rare for her. As much as we joked and harassed each other, I knew she was loyal. She would never *not* be a friend to me. I can't explain how I knew this; I just did. She said the semester was boring, and Lindsay was bugging the "ever-loving shit out of her." I confessed that it was hard being away from them, and I felt like I was disappearing. Amy was quiet for a beat.

"Miss Rebecca, do not worry about us forgetting you. Our relationship is like a bad STD. Long-term. You may not always see us, but believe me, we are lurking in your sensitive parts for eternity."

She was one of a kind.

Linds came up for a weekend shortly after Amy called me. She missed the heck out of me and wanted me over for dinner.

Lindsay's parents were very formal but loving. Her mom made sticky, sweet, and spicy fried chicken with rice, which was on another level. She'd also dropped off a homemade soup for my mom a couple of weeks ago.

"How are you, Rebecca? Lindsay tells me you have been staying with your mom for a while now," Lindsay's mom said.

"I'm okay. Thank you." I had to swallow to clear my throat. "It's been hard seeing her so weak."

"I'm sure that is very difficult," Lindsay's mom said.

"It is. She started a chemo treatment and has been feeling pretty awful." I looked down at my feet as my stomach twisted in a knot.

"I believe she will get stronger having you to care for her."

I wished what she said was true.

"Thank you," I said. "I'm trying to get her into art with me lately. Just to have something to do. You know?" *Something to do with me. To have my time with her. Before …*

"How wonderful! And how is your mom liking the art?" she asked.

I paused for a beat too long. "We're just starting," I admitted.

The art studio had quickly become a sanctuary for me and my mom. Just being side by side in front of the easels was working to rewire our habits of shutting each other out for so many years. I'd never criticized anything she made or ordered her to try anything. Until the bridge painting.

On Professor Bahnimin's advice, I'd started researching art in a healing capacity and come across an idea to paint a bridge in the center of a canvas. What you paint on the left, you are leaving behind. What you paint on the right is what you are headed toward. I thought of what I wanted to leave behind. It was the gray. The cold and separation. I wanted to walk toward the sunshine. My canvas had quickly filled with a transgression of colors. The blues and austere side had given way to bold orange and warmth.

My mom hadn't been eager to create her picture, but soon, she was intently working on her own canvas. I hadn't looked to see what she was creating, only continued to layer my colors over the canvas, letting the feeling of leaving that blue behind structure a path for me to go forward. At last, she'd put her brush down and taken a step back.

"Mom?" I'd asked.

She'd just shifted her eyes to mine, a lost look on her ashen face. Then she'd turned back toward her work and stared at it for a while.

I hadn't known what to say or how to approach her. She'd seemed out of it, her coloring bad. I had taken her arm and told her she needed to go lie down. Once she was settled in bed, I'd noticed her lashes were wet. She'd turned gingerly onto her side before I could mention it.

Back in the art studio, I'd set my eyes on her painting. It hadn't looked much like a bridge, but it was understandable enough. Brown slats over gray water. The sun going down, casting a shadow on the water. Two girls with brown hair on either end of the bridge. Only I hadn't been able to tell which one was me and which was Rachel.

***

Later, Lindsay and I talked for a while on her bed.

"Tell me how it's going down there," I said, desperate for a different topic.

Lindsay was student teaching a first-grade class at a school near Eastern.

"Well," she started, and her face took on a huge smile. "I mean, I'm not going to toot my own horn, but I'm pretty remarkable with this class. They are a huge step up from the toddler demons at the daycare last summer."

"Good!"

"Literally, every day, I come back to the apartment with a folder filled with cards and pictures the kids drew for me. They freaking love me. Some of the kids are awful and have meltdowns and stuff. But right now, it's good. And, oh, my God. I am like a genius teaching reading. I've been taking this course, The Science of Reading, and it is fascinating. Did you know that you have to introduce all kinds of syllable types, so the kids can learn sounds and phonics? Dude, I'm brilliant now."

"You've always been brilliant. That's wonderful. I'm so happy for you."

Then, the light in Lindsay's eyes dimmed.

"Rebecca, I'm sorry. I shouldn't brag about school stuff. That's so unfair to you … "

"No, it's good."

"It's just that you made this huge sacrifice, and I'm all: oh, my God, my life rules."

"Linds, We're good. Please don't do that. I feel better hearing about you. I promise."

"So, what's going on with your course?" she asked.

"Yeah, I'm just doing the one online right now. I really like it. So, I'll have another requirement done soon," I said.

"That's great," Lindsay said. But I could tell she had more on her mind as she studied me for a minute. "Are you thinking about going back? Soon? Or like summer session?"

I just swallowed and thought about my response.

"Crap. I'm sorry," she blurted.

"No, I just. Don't know yet. I want her to be stable. I feel like …" I fidgeted with my nails, my mind stuck on how to explain the information my mom was forced to tell her doctor in front of us. The fact that Ryan said she and Janet were once close. I swallowed and tried again, "I feel like I've barely known her my whole life, and I'm not going anywhere until I either know her or know she'll be okay."

Lindsay was crying now, and I wiped at the tears simmering around my eyes.

"You are my actual hero." She bent over and kissed my cheek. "We need chocolate. Let's make chocolate-covered strawberries and watch a movie?"

So, we did.

Lindsay's mom helped us melt almond bark in a small glass bowl. Lindsay and I took the most perfect, organic strawberries and rinsed and dried them. We then took turns holding them by their stems and dipping them in the melted chocolate almond bark. We set them on a tray and stuck them in the refrigerator to cool.

Lindsay wanted to watch an epic drama, sure to last three hours, but I pleaded that it was way too long, and I was so tired. We decided on a slapstick rom-com to take our minds off our troubles and have laughing fits.

When I was ready to leave, Lindsay handed me her mom's leftovers for my family and a container of the strawberries. She hugged me for a long time, and it was everything I needed in that moment. My mind cleared of my worries about my mom and the questions about her past. It was just my bestie giving me all her love.

Journal Entry #22 ~ Chop

Knowing how well my plan worked out for Rebecca is so painful. She is so removed from me. I didn't want to be close with Rebecca because of the pain. I couldn't stop seeing Rebecca in all the memories of Rachel at the time. Her first tooth, Rachel's first tooth, Rebecca's first school picture, Rachel's first school picture. God, she looked just like Rachel sometimes. It hurt to touch Rebecca, so I didn't. But then again, it hurt not to touch her.

I'd succeeded in keeping her away from me. She didn't seek me out, nor did she ask for me. She only wanted Robert, TJ, and Buddy. They were the light in her eyes. My light was burned out.

***

The summer when Rebecca was nine years old, she cut her hair. I knew my reaction was not the best, but I didn't know how to stop it. I also knew she didn't like her long, chestnut brown hair. I loved it, though. Her hair was similar to Robert's but a deeper color—a mixture of mine and his. It was chocolate caramel in a sunset, long and bouncy. Everything about my Rebecca was gorgeous. She looked so cute strutting around with her little ripped jean shorts. I wished she'd wear dresses and skirts, but I knew she despised them. She would argue with me about it all the time. Her tan, muscular legs coming out of those tiny shorts were adorable, even if I never told her.

It was a hot June day in the middle of the afternoon when Rebecca came flouncing out of the bathroom with hair up to her shoulders on one side and closer to chin length on the other. I screamed. I actually screamed.

Despite my efforts to stop, I cried all the way to the salon. It was a stupid kid mistake. I took scissors when I was very young and cut my bangs, so I should have handled it better.

She thought I was furious with her, but I wasn't angry with Rebecca. She just didn't come to me about it. It felt like she didn't trust me. I was angry with myself for not paying attention.

She was so sporty that I sometimes wondered where she came from. Robert liked baseball, but he didn't play. Ryan didn't have much interest in sports. He was into skateboarding and handled gymnastics well when he was younger, but Tommy was looking for a playmate, and Rebecca was it. He had her over at his house all the time. I didn't exactly fear that she would become too sporty. It just hurt because Rachel was the opposite of her. She loved playing dress up, curling her hair, and applying a ton of makeup. Rachel always came to me for help or with an idea. Rebecca wasn't like that.

The stylist did what she could to fix Rebecca's horrendous cut. I felt as if Rebecca had snipped me away with the chop of those scissors. I wished I could tell her all the reasons I cried then, but I couldn't find the words.

CHAPTER 21

Pop-Tarts

Standing in the Northwestern Hospital parking garage, I flung open my driver's side door and dropped heavily onto the seat. I had to get my bearings. It had been a long day of uncertainty.

My mom's CT scan showed no improvement. The two larger tumors in her lungs were even more massive, and a new, smaller tumor had appeared. How had the radiation and chemo not worked at all? Was it even worth it at this point? But how do you throw in the towel? *This is it. The fight of your life.* We needed to keep battling.

It was becoming so toxic to my body to keep my emotions in check. I couldn't break down in front of my parents. They needed me to be the strong one. The voice of reason. The one with the questions. My dad sat there at the appointments with his pad of yellow paper, writing frantically. He took careful notes on every update from the doctors and nurses, from blood pressure data to weight fluctuation, from theories and possibilities to medication side effects. I think it was to keep himself busy more than anything. To have a place to look objectively. The notes rarely did him good. He just kept scribbling while I was the one with the questions. "What was the name of the treatment?" "How many rounds would she need?" "How often does she need check-ups?" I was a powerful force at her side.

In the car afterward, on my own. I was drained.

I refused to sit in a cold parking lot outside Chicago, crying in my car. I started the engine, put it in gear, and headed out of the parking garage toward home. Turning onto the main street, I thought of TJ and grabbed my phone. He was the only remedy I needed. I set my phone down as my car picked up the Bluetooth speaker.

TJ answered after only one ring, like he was waiting for me.

"Hey," he said warmly.

"Hi," I clipped the word before my emotions tipped over and drowned us in a long-distance cry.

"You leaving the hospital?"

"Yeah," I swallowed and could say nothing more.

He paused, and I could hear him calculating. Hear his breath and almost see his lips pressed together. I knew his face so well, and he knew me so well, too.

"Anything I can do to help?"

I wiped my eyes with my left palm. Frozen mist sifted down on the cars merging onto the highway under a blanket of gray clouds. It had been that way all day. Cold, miserable, and without hope. TJ knew how to change my skies. "Just tell me about your day," I managed.

"You sure? It was insane. I don't know if you'll be able to handle it."

He paused, waiting for my confirmation, but went ahead anyway.

"So, at school today, there was a big commotion in the girls' bathroom next to the gym because the soap was out. In *both* dispensers. I mean, can you believe that? That's messed up. Right?"

I tucked my lip to keep laughter from sneaking out as tears ran down my face.

"So, after the soap crisis, we had to do the fitness challenges. I bet this hothead senior that he couldn't do more push-ups than me. And you know what?"

TJ waited on me. "What?" I finally asked.

"He could. So, I had to do five laps around the gym."

"Oh no," I giggled, still wiping my eyes.

"Ah, it's good. Keeps them honest, ya know? I did beat this other kid in a burpee contest. So, I made everyone do five laps for that."

"Everyone? Not just that kid?"

"Yep. It's me against them. Team unity building. So, then, the most exciting part of my day. Are you ready for this, Beck?"

I bit back a chuckle, knowing this was bound to be even funnier than the first half of his rant. My heart ached that I couldn't be with him. That just holding onto him could make everything so much easier. I took a long breath in and blew it out slowly.

"I'm ready."

"I made myself dinner."

"No, you didn't," I said in mock disbelief.

TJ was very accustomed to getting meals made for him by family, friends, me, or food chains near him. If it wasn't throwing slices of turkey on a bread roll with some mustard, then he likely didn't make it. He insisted on sharing his absurd food habits with me. TJ would try to make it sound like a success that he'd had a container of Pringles and a scoop of peanut butter for lunch, etc. He said he had good intentions of learning how to cook, but I didn't quite believe him.

"Yes, scout's honor. Want to know what it was?"

"Of course."

A long, dramatic pause. "It was a Pop-Tart. Do you want to know what kind?"

Now, the laughter I held back had me wobbling. "Oh, my goodness. Yes, TJ, tell me what kind of Pop-Tart you had for dinner."

"Ar-right. Strawberry frosted with sprinkles," he announced with an air of satisfaction.

I giggled again and continued wiping my eyes with the front and back of my hand.

"There's really no other acceptable kind. Strawberry frosted is king."

"See? This is just what I needed." I squeezed the wheel with my left hand and sighed.

"I'm sure they're at any local grocery store. Check Wal-Mart. Target has them, for sure. Or I can ship some to you," he continued, playing me.

"Wasn't exactly referring to Pop-Tarts, TJ. But thanks for the offer."

"Anything for you, Beck."

Journal Entry #23 ~ Just a Fight

The last two days have been so trying.

Rebecca was across the street, playing football with Tommy again. I saw Ryan coasting down the street next to Scott on his skateboard. That summer, Ryan and Scott got close. I was glad about that. Ryan had trouble making friends. He was introverted and standoffish. Although Scott was a little rough around the edges, he and Ryan seemed to be hitting it off. Ryan and Rebecca, though, were turning into sworn enemies.

I was on the phone with Colleen, sitting on the couch, as Buddy sat beside me, allowing me to scratch the top of his head the way he loved. Colleen was just getting back from a weekend trip away. In one minute, she was telling me about the upgrade Jim had secured for their hotel room, and in the next, Scott was helping Ryan through the front door— Ryan's face covered in blood.

I panicked. There was so much blood. I didn't know what had happened. Had he fallen into the street and gotten hit by a car? I wasn't sure if he'd hit his head. I was shrieking until Ryan shouted at me, "I'm okay! It was just a fight." He threw himself on one of our dining room chairs, leaned his head back, and closed his eyes. Anger colored his face. I stepped back and tented my hands over my temples, attempting to calm down. I didn't want Ryan to be frustrated with me, but I needed help handling the situation. I hung up with Colleen, called Robert, and told him to get home. Scott excused himself from the situation.

Robert made peanut butter and jelly sandwiches for the kids as he tried to figure out the details. I could only cringe and kneel over Ryan's chair, trying to assess his injuries. Rebecca had come running in to say it wasn't TJ's fault. Shock rattled me that Tommy had hit him; it didn't seem like him. But I was angry. I was so angry with Tommy. I hated the way he made me feel. Every time I looked at him, I felt like less of a mother. All my perception, of course, but awful still. He was too important to Rebecca, and she was losing opportunities because of him. I wasn't being rational, though.

My emotions spilled over, and I was out of control. I had been slowing down my intake of meds because I didn't want to be on them anymore. I thought I had built-in strategies to overcome these moments, and I didn't want to be a zombie or nullified by life. I wanted to feel things again.

I snapped at Robert and Rebecca.

Just like that, I put myself back in that dark place of accusing us, Robert and myself, for not seeing the signs that Rachel was too sick. That it wasn't just something she would get over. I only went back to those moments in the worst times, where I was throwing in all the bad, hoping it would drown me. So, I screamed at Robert in front of my kids and couldn't stop myself.

Then there was the next day, when Rebecca ran away from home. Marilyn Abrams was coming by with her daughter Melanie to visit again. I was so desperate for a new friend for Rebecca and for one of my own. Rebecca didn't seem to enjoy Melanie as a friend yet, but she could with time, I hoped. Melanie was calm and not overly rowdy. I thought that could work with Rebecca, who was so shy when meeting new people.

But Rebecca ran off.

I met Marilyn and Melanie in the driveway and brought them inside. After calling for Rebecca a few times, I heard nothing—no answer, no callback. I opened the door to the basement. "Ryan, is Rebecca down there with you?"

"No," he answered firmly.

My pulse thrummed as I excused myself to Marilyn. I flew upstairs, unable to hide my concern. Was she okay? Stuck somehow? Choking on something? She wasn't in her room or any room. I had to stop searching the house and pause in the hallway, putting one hand on the wall as I gasped for breath. She has to be fine, but where is she? My mind immediately went to that nightmare of a day when she ran off at four years old, and Janet brought her back. Thinking of Janet made it worse. The utter panic swirled in my stomach as a reminder of all I had already endured as a mother. I stood still as my face tingled with heat. I closed my eyes and took two deep breaths, keeping my palm's pressure flat on the wall. Marilyn was talking low to Melanie. "She's just probably worried that she can't find Rebecca. Maybe we should help look for her."

I took another slow breath and smoothed out my hair. I walked back down the stairs and crossed the dining room.

"I apologize, Marilyn and Melanie. Just give me a second. This child ..."

I walked over to the sliding doors and let myself outside, surveying the yard and spying the garage side door open. She wouldn't.

I quickened my pace, stepped over the threshold into the garage, and checked on the side wall for her bike. It was gone.

My mouth dropped in surprised fury. I balled up my fists in frustration. What a little shit! Clenching my jaw, I turned on the spot. I didn't even make a plan to speak with Marilyn and Melanie. I just walked determinedly back into the house and said, "I am so sorry for this, but can we please reschedule? I must've got my wires crossed."

Marilyn gave me a knowing look but played along. "Oh, don't worry, Suzanne. I understand. These summer schedules. So little time to fit everything in, don't you think?"

"Yes. Thank you. I'm sorry, Melanie."

Melanie angled up her chin and gave Marilyn a bored expression. "Mom, can we go to the mall now?"

"Sure, honey," Marilyn laughed a little too easily as if that was their hopeful plan all along. "Well, good luck getting everything in today. Hope Rebecca is having fun summer days. We'll talk soon." She squeezed my arm and turned toward the door.

"Yes, thanks again," I said, unable to give her a goodbye smile.

Once the door clicked closed, my jaws ground together in rage. I tromped over to the table and picked up the phone, steeling myself as I scrolled for Janet's number. I hadn't called her phone in four years. I didn't want to call her. But I had to.

She answered in a startled, unsure voice almost immediately.

"Hello, Suzanne?"

The sound of her voice almost broke me. I gripped the dining room table and let out a silent breath.

"Rebecca snuck out on her bike. Is she there?" I said in what I hoped was an expression of direct boredom.

"Oh, um," Janet was fumbling. "I didn't see her."

I closed my eyes again and held back my frustrated and embarrassed tears.

"But Tommy said he was going for a ride on his bike. I'll check the yard and the street and call you if I see them," she sounded upbeat. Not like I had abandoned her four years ago.

"Fine. Goodbye." I hung up.

I grabbed my purse and keys and rushed to my car. I wanted to find Rebecca safely riding around, so I could yell at her. I couldn't wait for Janet to call. As I drove past their house, I scoured the front yard but didn't see any bikes. So, I drove by the park, although I knew they didn't go there often. After scanning the neighborhood and not seeing either Rebecca or Tommy, I assumed they'd ridden into the woods again. With no other clues as to where she might be, I pulled up before my house again and sat in the driveway, head on the steering wheel, fuming and tired. Why does it have to be this hard? How can she just ride away from me?

Then, my phone rang loudly in my purse. I saw the caller ID as Janet and was relieved.

"Yes," I replied.

"Suzanne, it's Janet. She's here, and she's hurt her ankle badly. I think it may be broken."

I felt the color drain from my face.

"I'm on my way," I choked out.

"Yes, all right," Janet replied, and I hung up on her.

I tossed my phone back inside my purse, stalked to the house, and yanked open the front door. She's hurt. I'm hurt. I'll be spending this day at the hospital now. I almost crumbled into a ball on the driveway. I raced into my house, wiping furious tears aside and calling inside for Ryan. Now that a hospital visit was necessary, I would have him checked, too.

Once I had Ryan in the car with me, I tore down the street again toward the Lawson's house, the house I swore I wouldn't ever set foot in again. My stomach churned seeing the front steps and Rebecca sitting beside Janet. She was crying. Rebecca didn't cry often.

I threw the car into park and flew out the door. In an instant, I was beside Rebecca and unable to look at Janet, but I felt her eyes on me.

"Dear God. Rebecca, what happened?" I knelt before her and took a quick inventory of the damage. Her ankle was purple and swollen. She had a big gash on her elbow as well. But the worst was the look she gave me. Tear-filled and unfavorable. She had run away from me again. But this time, she ran away from me to be with them. She would always choose them.

"She fell off the drop on the trail," Tommy clarified. I hadn't even noticed him sitting there.

Of course, the trail. Her favorite place. Not being at home with me, having a playdate with a cute, normal girl like Melanie, but venturing to the swamp. She preferred the swamp and all those turtles, snakes, minnows, frogs, slime, and mud. That, I couldn't understand. And here she was, broken, like Ryan. Tommy was the common denominator. My eyes suddenly burned. In that moment Tommy was the cause, although I knew there was no way he was at fault for her accident.

I stuck my right hand underneath Rebecca's knees and then quickly pulled her and myself up in the process. "Let's go! Maybe we'll get a two-for-one deal at the emergency room," I barked, charging toward the car.

"I'm so sorry, Suzanne. Please call and let us know how she is," Janet

pleaded. She wanted to help—after everything. She wanted me to phone her to tell her about my daughter when I couldn't give her the shoulder to cry on for losing John. She still wanted to reach out with a kind heart. I couldn't say anything without my voice breaking, so I said nothing.

CHAPTER 22

Gym Class

TJ's birthday was just a week away. I would've loved nothing more than to be with him for the whole weekend, but it seemed out of reach. My dad had a business trip to Boston. Aunt Colleen was planning to stay with my mom until she and her whole family came down with a virus and needed to stay away from my ailing mother. She felt horrible about bailing on my mom and me, but I reassured Aunt Colleen that everything would be okay, and I hoped that she and her family would be well soon.

I didn't feel comfortable leaving my mom without support. I had explained all of this to TJ, who was, as always, incredibly understanding and sympathetic. He had offered to come up my way. Yet, he had to coach a basketball game Friday night, so he would have to leave late and then spend a chunk of his birthday driving up to see me. And my mom. I knew she wouldn't want him here. When I mentioned TJ's birthday, she stiffened up about it and didn't say anything.

Just when I thought we were getting somewhere. I felt more comfortable pushing her, prying to uncover information about who she was, but now, the cancer had stopped all of that. I had to be careful with her, not just with her body but with her feelings. I was selective with my words. I didn't want to hurt her.

In my head, I wished I could drill her about TJ. I wanted to know what it was about him that she was so against—this person so fitting and perfect for me.

Instead of lashing out at her, I turned my anger into a plan. I made sure she was lying down in her bed while I went for a run on the trail in the backyard. I missed having the Rec Center so available and having TJ as my workout partner. I have always craved fitness, sports, activities, and getting my heart rate up. All those activities lighten me and move me forward.

At least the trail behind our house gave me some reprieve. It had become a peaceful place for me. Not long ago, my mother and I had walked along this very path and held hands. That was the beginning. This area was growing on me. The lake out back was beautiful. The expanse of land and stunning homes. All of it was gorgeous, especially during the high points of the seasons. Chicagoans are treated to get the best and worst of it all. Extremes from burning hot, humid summer days to frigid winter winds. In between, we have beautiful blossoming trees in spring, sunshine and blue skies in June, a symphony of colors in fall, and delicate snow-covered views in winter.

I wasn't as unfamiliar with our house now, either. It wasn't as stark and empty as it had felt some time ago when I desperately missed my old house on Foxgrove, Buddy, and the football guys, but mostly TJ. There was hope in this house now. I barely dreamed of Rachel anymore. If anything, Rachel was more of a comfort in my dreams. But I did sometimes have trouble sleeping and woke up in the middle of the night, as the house was too quiet. Too echoey.

I missed my loud roommates. I missed the warmth of TJ's body beside mine. Unbelievably, I missed seeing my mother dolled up for jewelry sales with Aunt Colleen. I missed seeing her obsessively cleaning the house that was already pristine. How odd to miss that. Those were my thoughts pinging around my mind as I jogged.

On my run, I went through options. I needed to see TJ for his birthday. He had been so helpful and accommodating to me. I wanted to be there for him. That's what made me call Ryan.

Ryan and I had been getting closer. Texting often. I never imagined having an actual relationship with him. Not when we were little or teens. Now, it was just like Mrs. Lawson had told me in that Dairy

Queen long ago, shortly before she'd moved herself and her kids down south, probably trying to prepare me to lose TJ: "You'll come to really need your brother someday."

That someday was now.

Ryan was very receptive to my TJ surprise and agreed to my request. Of course, he would come out and stay with Mom for the weekend. He'd disapproved of my choice to stay home with her and put off college at first, but he came around. Especially after hearing I was still taking a class and looking into other areas of study I could at least research while suspended from earning my college degree. When he arrived, he hugged me and sincerely said, "Thank you for being so helpful with Mom."

***

The four-and-a-half-hour car ride to TJ's felt like an eternity. It was overcast and drizzling most of the way. I was a bundle of nerves. When I called Mrs. Lawson and Katie separately, asking if they could help me surprise TJ, Mrs. Lawson gasped with what sounded like the rise of tears but, of course, said yes. She suggested I drive to Howard's; that way, she could drop me at the high school for an even better surprise for TJ. Katie said I should show up at seventh hour, so he would only have one more class to teach, which would be Katie's class for eighth period. She was beyond excited and impatient to show me off and see Tommy "completely freak out."

Thinking about surprising him made me giddy. I wasn't sure how he would react. I did imagine him smiling. He might rush toward me, wrap his arms around me, lift me up, and spin me around. I could also picture a stunned silence, like when I'd surprised him at his house at Eastern at the start of the semester, a look of wonder on his sweet face and a wide, delighted smile.

I knew TJ would love having me there at his school, in his gym. I anticipated him having me take part in whatever exercise or game his class would do. So, I prepared myself to see a class full of high schoolers and young ladies who were probably in love with TJ.

Mrs. Lawson came out onto Howard's drive to meet me with arms extended and a huge grin squeezing her eyes and cheery cheeks. She went on and on about me being there for TJ. She couldn't wait for the big surprise. I set my bag in Howard's house and noticed how spotless it was, side-eyeing her.

"Why is this house so clean?" I asked. She playfully rolled her eyes and smiled.

"Well, I had a feeling things wouldn't be presentable. So, I just got here a little early and picked up some." She winked at me.

"I'm sure it was not presentable at all," I laughed.

"You would know about that by now, wouldn't you?" She patted my arm.

I left my bag, then Mrs. Lawson and I walked out to her SUV and headed to TJ's high school.

My nervous excitement grew as I entered the school. I had been there once before when TJ had taken me for a grand Carlyle tour almost a year ago, so I knew where to find the office. I met Katie there. She told me to follow her toward the gym.

Katie went through the gym door and gestured that I should wait outside. I fought back an overwhelming smile.

"Excuse me, Mr. Lawson!" Katie called in an ear-splitting voice.

I struggled to keep my muffled laughter quiet.

"Go back to class!" TJ scolded. Right then, I saw what teaching at a school where your little sister is a senior could be like. I knew he loved Katie to death, but she could be naggy or bothersome. I got that.

"Your new student is here!" Katie completely ignored his dig on her being out of class.

"Now? Okay, send him in."

Then she held the door open for me, and I moved through, completely aware of the thirty-plus eyes on me in my loose gray sweats, tank, and unzipped hoodie. I was their size, but everyone in Carlyle knew everyone else. A new student didn't happen often.

All eyes were on me amid murmurs and conversation, but my eyes tore straight toward the person opposite me, halfway across the gym.

Typical dark gray joggers, white T-shirt. Golden messy hair on top of impossibly blue eyes. The surprise on his face was one of the greatest moments of my life. His jaw hit the floor, and I swear his eyes instantly filled with tears. Tears, seeing me.

He didn't even say a word, just charged over to me as I moved to him. Then, he fiercely wrapped his body around mine in a heartwarming hug.

TJ was silent. Silent. My TJ! For moments. Finally, a whisper. "Beck," he mumbled into my shoulder, his breathing erratic, like he was holding back a cry.

"Surprise," I whispered into his ear.

His students called, cheered, hooted, and cooed, "Awwww." TJ didn't hear a thing.

He just pulled me closer as the kids made their opinions of us known.

"Omg. I'm going to die of cuteness."

"Damn, Mr. Lawson."

"I can't."

"I told you he was married."

"He's not married."

"He sure looks married."

"I wish I was her right now."

TJ finally pulled back a little, and his eyes were wet. He was beginning to smile. "How are you here?" he asked, his gaze moving from my eyes to my mouth to my hair as if assessing that I was real.

"Ryan." I smiled. This drew a deep breath from TJ.

"I always liked him," he grinned.

I exploded with laughter. "Right."

"How long are you here?" he asked once again, oblivious to the chatter getting louder and more obnoxious by the minute.

"All weekend," I said boldly, staring him down.

Now my TJ was back. He shook his head, picked me up, spun me around, and put me back down. Then he kissed me like we were the only ones in the room.

Ordinarily, I wouldn't care for this type of PDA or stand for this behavior, especially in this place. But I needed it.

The callouts got more ridiculous, and the noise grew so much that I was sure TJ would go off on these kids. He only pulled away, smiled at me softly again, and stepped back, finally addressing his students.

"Excuse me, everyone!" he called loudly but happily. "My apologies for the delay, but this is my Beck, who has just come a very long way to surprise me. Thank you for your patience and discretion."

They all shut up and eyeballed him like they wanted to *be* him. He was *that* good.

That class period was basically a wash. The group wanted to know everything about me. TJ kept his eyes on me as he answered their questions—almost like he thought I would vanish if I were out of his sight.

He had the kids do basic exercises like squats, pushups, and sit-ups. Then the bell rang, and Katie's class tromped in.

She sprinted right up to me and hugged me again. Then she announced that this was her future sister-in-law, and the whole group went nuts. TJ just smiled with an air of confidence.

He gave his students some context about me and said we were going to have a race. "Beck will beat, at minimum, ninety-five percent of you weaklings in a sprint race back and forth across the gym."

I shook my head.

"You beat Beck; you can sit out for the class, and play on your phone."

He got a loud response from that.

If anyone thought they couldn't beat me and didn't want to race, they didn't have to, he explained. "If you race her, though, and she wins, you've got to do one hundred burpees immediately after losing," TJ announced. "But any of you playing in our playoff game tonight, you are not eligible. I need you on the court at seven, not cramping up on your couch at home. Understood?"

A few basketball players groaned. TJ motioned for me to line up in the middle. I stretched for a few seconds and tossed my hoodie in the corner.

Katie called out from the stands, "Come on, Becky! Get 'em!"

A dozen kids were in the running with me. Mostly guys. Very athletic, muscular guys.

TJ shouted, "Ready … "

I planted my back foot, leaned over, and got my game face on.

"Set … "

I squatted lower and narrowed my eyes on the black line on the opposite wall. I didn't care one bit about the outcome. I knew I would do well. I hadn't been doing a lot of exercise except running. A lot. Each day.

"GO!" TJ yelled, and we all took off like a shot.

I burst into a sprint, my arm thrusts short, slicing the air. I pounded the gym floor, screeching up to the line, pivoting expertly, and charged back the whole way. One of TJ's guys tied me. No one beat me.

TJ jumped up and down, whooping as I walked it off and high-fived him.

"Aww, yeah! Beck!" he gave his sprint-tying student the rest of the class off. But the other eleven had one hundred burpees to do.

Journal Entry #24 ~ Good News

My heart is torn in two as one of my prayers has been answered. Robert found out that Janet is moving with the kids down south. Her campground went under, and she's lost their investment. My chest aches for her. She'd been living out John's dream with such high hopes for the last four years. She'd spent so much time there, borrowed loans, and planned the site. It must be devastating.

A good friend would drive over and hug her. A good friend would cry with her and explain that she did all she could've. Or even more, maybe a good friend would loan her the money to pay back the bank. But I am no longer her friend. So, I did nothing. Worse than nothing, actually. I cried tears of relief and joy that they would be gone. For four years, I have been dying to move or get some distance from the Lawsons. Being so close kills me each day. It's my own personal punishment, pummeling me like a fist on a bruise, day after day. I deserve it, though.

I am so relieved this will be over.

At the same time, I am crying for Rebecca. She is losing her best friend, like I lost mine. She really only has Tommy. Her TJ. She would follow him to the ends of the Earth. I am sorry for this pain in her heart. It will take a while for her to recover. She will not be herself, and I am genuinely crestfallen about that.

I wish she could see the opportunities I see for her future. I hope this move will open her up to other friends and new possibilities. Rebecca is such a good girl and so talented at so much. I hope this move won't break her because she appears to be in pieces.

CHAPTER 23

Waterfall

After dismissal, I hoped to grab TJ's hand and high-tail it back to his place. Of course, he introduced me to every single staff member at the school. Some looked familiar. Perhaps I'd met them last spring or seen them at his mom's wedding, but I hadn't met most. TJ gushed about me and told everyone how I'd surprised him and come all this way from the Chicago suburbs to be with him on his birthday weekend. The smile on his face made him glow.

Finally, he made his last flitter of small talk, and we readied ourselves to head out to the parking lot. A storm had moved in, and sheets of rain doused everything in sight.

"Want to wait? I'm not parked close," TJ asked me as he looked out the glass panel in the vestibule.

I stared at the rain. We would be soaked. Completely. Even if we ran to the truck. So soaked, we would certainly need to change. Like strip our clothes off and change. Like *The-Notebook*-passionate-kissing-in-the-rain soaked. I continued staring into the downpour, and then I smiled up at him, saying nothing until he locked eyes with me. TJ matched my grin and nodded.

"Then, after you, my love." He held the door open for me.

"Catch me!" I yelled over my shoulder and dashed to the parking lot. Rain washed over me at once.

"Ohhh ho!" TJ called after me with glee.

Downpour was putting it mildly. Monsoon may have been more like it. Sheets of lukewarm rain pelted my skin as I raced around the parking lot. My sneakers were soaked immediately, but I was still lightning and well ahead of TJ when I decided to make a game of it and hide behind other cars, pulling him off course.

TJ let out a howl, which made me laugh and slowed me down. I slid around a red Toyota Camry and darted for a gray SUV, but I should've realized that TJ was way better at defensive moves in football. He rushed at me from the other side of the SUV and hoisted me up in a bear hug.

"Ahhh!" I screamed, startled by his strong, slick arms. A rumble of thunder sounded over the fields west of the school.

"I win," he panted loudly above the noise of the rain.

I watched his mouth as he breathed heavily, and warmth spread through me. TJ changed his grip on me, sliding me down his body easily. Despite the rain squelching us, his eyes were fire as they settled on mine.

We moved at once and crushed our lips together. Intensity and heat raged in our kiss. His tongue rolled frantically over mine. My arms clasped at his neck and shoulders, bringing him closer to me.

Another shake of thunder crashed in the clouded sky, and we pulled apart for a moment.

TJ's chest rose and fell quickly as his hooded eyes searched my lips. "Let's get home," he breathed onto my mouth then sucked in my bottom lip for one more exquisite kiss.

Next, his hand had mine, and he yanked me toward his truck in the next row.

We rushed to the truck. TJ opened the door for me and hustled to the other side. I threw my soaked body onto the cold front seat, yelping and shivering. TJ swiftly tucked himself into the driver's side, soaking the car from seat to floor.

"Woo!" He shook off like a dog, whipping his head vigorously.

I squinted and leaned away from his spray but settled my eyes back on him as he started the truck. A wide smile filled my face. The warmth of his company settled over me, making every painful moment I'd endured over the last few weeks drip away like the rain from my hair. He was my every remedy.

"Damn, that's a ton of rain," TJ hollered and shifted the gear to roll us through the parking lot and onto the two-lane road.

I wrapped my wet arms around my middle and shook from the cold.

"Here, move closer. You're shaking."

TJ extended his right arm toward me, leaving a space to rest on his collarbone. I scooted closer and pushed my wet head onto his body. He rubbed my right arm up and down with his hand.

I closed my eyes and filled myself back up with TJ. His light, his joy, his love. I tilted my head and scooted closer until I was grazing the right lower part of his neck with my lips, kissing his wet skin.

He made a low sound in his throat like a purr, and I felt him exhale. The rain was still coming down like a waterfall crashing over the truck. The wipers moved frantically from side to side, pushing off waves. I continued to kiss TJ's neck with softer, slower kisses, tracing my way to his chin and mouth. He fixed his left hand tighter on the steering wheel and jabbed his head toward me to kiss me once on the mouth. Then again. And then back to the road.

By now, I was practically facing backward, leaning on him and kissing his chin and the corner of his mouth. I wasn't cold anymore. TJ scooted up in his seat and used his right arm to pull me closer, his grip getting firmer. He was quiet now, apart from his uneven breathing. I kissed his jawline and the corner of his lips, quickly slipping my tongue inside. TJ exhaled, then pulled off to the side of the road and onto an embankment of gravel a few yards away.

The rain cascaded over us. The moment he threw the truck into park and killed the engine, my insides smoldered. In one fluid movement, TJ hoisted me up over the console, so I was straddling him. Our kiss was desperate and hungry, wet and insatiable. I moved over him, feeling him beneath me. He blew out a heavy breath, low and needy. I started on the waistband of his joggers. He pushed off my unzipped sweatshirt, grabbed the back of my soaked tank top, and pulled it over my head, whipping it onto the passenger side. Grabbing me with both hands, he pulled me up higher on top of him and bent his head until his mouth was sucking at my breasts. I let out a pent-up whine and pushed my hand on the roof of his truck. He kissed and sucked at my chest again and again as I moved my legs off his and rested my feet on the floorboard between his legs, then shimmied my pants and panties down.

Once I had them off, TJ arched up and ripped his joggers and boxer briefs down to his ankles. I straddled him again and lowered myself onto him.

Completely naked in his truck, on top of him, on the side of a mostly empty road, the rain coming down in sheets, making the truck invisible, I had never felt so unabashed. So freely exposed of my own will. In that moment, I felt the world open up with TJ moving under me.

Once I lowered myself over him, he filled my insides with the sweetest, perfect pleasure.

"God," I cried out, and TJ grunted low. Slowly, I moved over him, bucking my hips, my weight fully on him. He was panting now, rocking me on top of him, bending down, and kissing my chest, my neck, my lips. I clawed at his damp shoulders and the roof of the truck. His movements hastened, and he grabbed my backside and pushed and pulled me again and again as our breaths became gasps of air, and the windows fogged up completely as we created our own storm. At last, sweet release came for us, and I exhaled onto his shoulder as he relaxed his arms then slowly tickled my back with his fingertips.

I moved my head off his shoulder and peered down at his love-drunk eyes and full, swollen lips. He kissed me for a few moments.

Then TJ looked quickly at the driver's side window, all fogged up, and slowly raked his palm lazily down it, creating an image identical to Kate Winslet's hand in *Titanic*. He smiled at me, and I bubbled a laugh.

Then I pressed my forehead to his and breathed, "Happy early birthday."

TJ shook his head and cupped a hand around the back of my neck.

"Happiest early birthday." He studied me for a long moment, looking straight into my eyes. "I love you."

I ringed my arms around his neck and hugged him tightly, feeling that love.

"I know." I smiled on the top of his head.

Journal Entry #25 ~ Change

It has been two months since the Lawsons left town. I thought it would be a blessing when I could wake up and push past the remembrance of Rachel's passing, when I could see the sun and possibilities. It's still hard. I am grateful that I don't see them each day, but I still see them in my memories.

The school year started, and I anticipated that Rebecca would make new friends. She certainly needed them. However, she hasn't made any. If anything, she's worse. I am truly heartbroken and so upset for her, but I can't pretend that I am sad they are gone.

I knew she would ask to call her TJ or want to go see him by the end of the summer. I had to devise a way to keep him off her mind.

Ryan turned eleven and had been begging me for a phone. His friend, Scott, had had one for months. Ryan pleaded that he would get made fun of if he didn't get one, too. "Everyone my age has a phone," he said.

I gave in and then had an idea. We could add a line. This would be an opportune time to change phone numbers to ensure Janet couldn't contact us again. I had to convince Robert it was for the best. Adding a line, maybe two, for when Rebecca would need a phone in a year or so. "Wouldn't it make sense to have all our numbers just a digit off?" He saw right through that.

Robert was usually quick to accommodate. He spoiled me so much. It was in his nature to please and dote on us. This time, though, he looked me over, defeated.

"It would be easier for all of us to have similar numbers? Or it would be easier to make sure the Lawsons can't contact us?" he asked.

My breath caught for a moment. "I think tha—" I started.

Robert interrupted me, his voice flat, "It's fine. Go ahead." He got up from his chair and walked past me down the hall.

I may have gotten his okay, but I didn't get his approval. I think part of his heart broke for Rebecca at that moment. My guilt ascended to the surface again, reminding me that I was controlling and damaged.

CHAPTER 24

TJ's Church

I t was early. Too early. Like, *way* early. But TJ was already awake. He rarely slept in. Ever. He was cuddling me and pulling me on top of him, then curling up beside me, then crushing me in some sort of wrestling match that I was pretending to sleep through.

Finally, when he stilled for a second, I grabbed his face and kissed him. "Happy birthday!" I kissed him again.

"Thanks, Beck! It is a happy birthday!"

Then TJ's thoughts were insanely random, flitting between "How is your car running?" to "Did you see that viral video about the dog and the rabbit and how they are completely dancing to 'The Humpty Dance'?" to "I think one of my students, Trey, may get a college offer soon, and he's just a junior on the basketball team, but he's insane." Then, his last remark snagged me awake like a fishing hook.

"Marry me."

I blinked a handful of times and tried to straighten myself up. I patted my hair down, sure that it was sticking out in all directions from lying over his bare chest.

By the expression on his face, I could see that TJ was thrilled and too stimulated to lie there, which is why his mouth had been going a mile a minute.

"Right now?" I asked slowly, my eyes rolling up toward my disheveled hair.

His cheeks flushed a light pink.

"Sorry, I mean," he suddenly tried to say a lot without saying the whole thing. "I know I want to ask you. But I'll set it up better. Let's hold off on that, okay?" His eyes softened, his right hand cupping my chin.

"I won't need anything fancy." I winked at him.

TJ smiled sweetly. "Not your style?"

"Not me. That's my mom," I said and then realized what I'd just done. My eyes grew wide, and TJ inhaled, studying me.

He let a few moments pass.

"What's the latest? Is she responding to the treatment at all?"

I shook my head. "I'm sorry. I didn't want to think about that today," I confessed.

"I know," he whispered and took my hand, turning it over softly and intertwining our fingers. "You know what Beck? I want to take you to church. What time is it?"

I was really hoping he'd turned a corner with his sleep nonsense, as I called it, but ... no such luck. I face-planted into a downy pillow. "It's sickeningly early," I muffled. TJ was completely unaffected.

"Perfect. Will you come with me? You have to experience my church."

I flipped over and said wryly, "I thought you didn't go to an actual church."

TJ slid off the bed and reached for his phone on the nightstand. "I don't most of the time." He clicked it on, scrolled for a couple of seconds, then put the phone up to his ear.

"Who are you calling?" I asked in disbelief. "It's barely six a.m."

"Howard," he said into the phone resting on the side of his face. TJ shot me a "duh" expression.

"Hey, Pops!" TJ yelled into the phone, "Thank you, sir. Thank you. Yes, absolutely. Want to take Beck and me to church?"

A bit later, after getting ready and having cereal, TJ had us throw some rain gear on and get ready for "church," which he explained was fishing with Howard and utilizing the Boat Bible. I wasn't sure what to say about any of that, but TJ was steadfast in his resolve to go to "church" with me.

He said we needed "stuff" in the shed, so we headed over to the back of the house, and TJ tapped in a code onto a keypad on the side of the shed. I was surprised there was a code for the shed. It seemed out of place when everything else I'd experienced about Carlyle was warm, welcoming, and open.

As TJ pulled open the door, I was hit with the realization that this space was nothing like I'd imagined. It was clean, roomy, and thoroughly organized, the interior belonging on the cover of *Fisher Magazine*. Rows of poles in all kinds of styles, colors, and sizes were tacked up onto pegboard walls. A folding fish-cleaning table with a sink and a grid rack graced the far wall. Hooks, bait, wire, buckets, knives, and tools were arranged systematically on a pegboard with clips and hooks. The flooring wasn't concrete as I'd imagined, but polyurethane—easy for cleaning.

"Wow," I said in a soft, stunned voice. "I had no idea this was even here."

TJ nodded. "Yeah, this is Howard's lil' shop." Then he grabbed a tackle box and three poles. He must've been deducing something in his mind because he eyed me up and down, squinting while moving his hand over a pole, then another until he seemed satisfied with a medium-length silver and blue pole.

We heard the rumble of tires on gravel and turned toward the driveway. TJ and I moved outside the shed, and he closed the door behind us. We walked back to the front of the house as Howard pulled up in his truck and eased himself out of the front seat. He wore jeans, a red plaid shirt under a puffy brown vest, and a baseball cap framed by his big ears. His eyes were slits of crinkled happiness as he took in the both of us.

TJ adored Howard so much. He physically lit up when he saw Howard. It was so endearing.

"Hello, Beck." Howard squinted at me, holding a thermal tote in one hand and pulling me into a tight, one-armed hug with the other.

"Hi, Howard!" I smiled brightly at him, truly happy to see him.

"Howard!" TJ cheered beside me.

"Happy birthday, Tommy!" Howard hugged him with fierce love. "I hope you're hungry." He extended the tote toward TJ, who took it and unzipped the top.

"Aww, yeah! Grandma's biscuits and gravy!"

Even though we'd already eaten Crunch Berries cereal with zero healthful impact, TJ hurriedly took the bag and leaped up the porch steps.

Howard and I followed him into the house. We all sat at the dining room table and enjoyed deliciously fresh, puffed, doughy biscuits smothered in savory sausage gravy. In another container were roasted, diced potatoes seasoned with salt and pepper.

After scarfing everything down, TJ and I were stuffed and ready to work off some of the calories. We all jumped into Howard's truck and headed to the lake.

When we arrived at their "spot" on the lake, I spied a dock, a long pier of faded brown slats stretching toward the gray-green water before us. The sky was overcast, and the wind blew a cool breeze from the west. Howard stepped out of the truck with his own bulky tackle box and fishing pole. TJ grabbed our fishing poles while I held the smaller tackle box, and we walked over to an unbelievably impressive fishing boat. I had stupidly expected a rowboat. Why hadn't I considered that Howard was established and owned a fishing shop? Of course, he would have an awesome, massive boat. It was at least eighteen feet long, with comfortable leather seats, an expansive console with a steering wheel, a digital display, and a huge motor on the back. It had a steel blue finish with the word "LUND" on the side in white paint. TJ moved to it like he had done so hundreds of times before. "Come on, Beck, you haven't been introduced to *Lady*," which appeared to be the name of Howard's boat.

"Well, *Lady* will do, but I thought you'd like to try yours today,"

Howard interjected.

TJ stared at Howard in sheer confusion until Howard indicated a red fishing boat bobbing in the water a few paces away.

TJ looked truly stunned, his brow furrowed in confusion, but I smiled, darting my eyes from TJ to Howard and back, my mouth in an open, awed smile. I saw the same name on the side of a smaller boat boasting three tan leather seats and a console accented by a giant red bow attached to the steering wheel.

"No way," TJ said, goggling at Howard.

Howard stood there grinning and pulled a set of keys from his vest. He jingled them in his hand a little before extending them toward TJ.

"No," TJ said, barely shaking his head, realizing this was his gift. He moved closer to the boat. "Are you serious?" TJ asked, his voice hinting at a smile.

"Happy birthday, Tommy. And happy early graduation," Howard said, holding the keys out to him. His smile made his eyes crinkle again.

We both moved toward Howard. TJ took the keys from him and wrapped his arms around him.

"This is a Lund." He pulled away, incredulous at Howard. "It's too expensive." TJ shook his head.

"We got it half-off in a giveaway."

"But you can just sell it,"

"We wanted you to have one of your own. You'll take good care of her." Howard nodded toward the boat.

"Damn, this is a sweet boat." TJ's smile was too wide for his face as he checked over his present. "Thank you. And Mom!" He squeezed Howard again, then looked back at me, awestruck.

"That's incredible. What a gift, Howard." I tucked my arm around TJ's middle. TJ kissed the top of my head.

"Well, it's getting late. Let's get aboard your new boat, shall we?" Howard asked, and we all climbed in.

There was a very worn-looking *King James Bible* in Howard's tackle box. Howard had added plastic tabs to several pages. I got the education about them from Howard as TJ steered us into the open water, his smile a mile wide.

Once we found a good, calm spot, Howard explained "church."

"So, Beck, we each pick two verses and the gospel. Then, we end with the 'Fisherman's Prayer.' How's that sound?"

"Great."

TJ chose a psalm of gratitude about treasure and heart. He also chose a passage about joy and praise. I sat in wonder as this wild love of mine calmly recited Bible verses in a fisherman's vest out in the middle of a lake. I never anticipated this side of TJ, but I loved this new piece of him. TJ would always be engaging and full of character, but now I got the chance to see this intimate, religious side of him. It made him stand out even more from basic college guys and pulled me toward him in a new way.

Howard read his psalm aloud to us. It was longer than TJ's and focused on a message of renewal, mercy, and healing. TJ was quiet beside me.

"Beck, we may not know why God's path for us twists. But we know we are not alone." Howard squeezed my hand, and I knew he was indicating my mother.

"Thank you, Howard," I said, putting my other hand on top of his and squeezing back.

Over the course of two hours, I managed to somehow catch a catfish, which made TJ squeal in triumph. I explained that I'd done this before while trying to give him a scornful smirk, but he saw my smile through it.

We ended our time in the boat with TJ and Howard each catching a sunfish and a few largemouth bass. Then Howard led us in the "Fisherman's Prayer."

After Howard dropped us off, TJ and I made our way upstairs to his bedroom. He sat at the foot of the bed, tired, his hands folded in his lap. I took off some of my layers, and he got undressed, too. "How'd you like church, Beck?" he asked, peeling off his socks and tossing them in a corner.

"It was lovely. Very calming. Thanks for bringing me. How exactly did all of that start?"

"Howard's been doing that for years. He and my grandpa would fish at the lake. After my grandpa died, he checked on my grandma and started connecting with us more. I was pretty much an asshole at the end of high school," TJ said, scooting onto the bed and leaning up against the headboard.

"Really?" I asked, eyebrows furrowed. "That's impossible."

"Yeah." He raked his hand through his hair.

I waited a second. "Tell me." I crawled onto the bed and knelt before him.

"My grandpa died. I was angry about my dad. You know? Not having him around to help my mom. My shoulder was bad. I tore my rotator cuff twice, actually. Remember I told you?"

"That was all at once?"

"Yeah. Then Mason and Jenna had their own issues when she got pregnant with the baby. I was really lost." TJ's eyes lowered to his finger as he dug at a cuticle.

I moved closer and sat crisscrossed, facing him.

"I think my mom was really worried about me. I was in a lot of pain because of my shoulder, but then I couldn't quit the Oxy. I started trying other stuff, and I was drinking a lot. She must've told Howard about me. Then he just showed up. And kept showing up."

It occurred to me that I hadn't known all about his Carlyle years. As much as I felt I knew TJ, I'd never heard about this chunk of time in his life.

TJ smiled a little and found my eyes. "We went fishing all the time. But, on Saturday, Howard said it was 'church.'"

"Why Saturday? Why not Sunday?" I asked.

"I think Howard had to work a lot of Sundays. He said so many people prayed on Sundays that he wanted to make sure God could hear our prayers loud and clear. Saturday would be less crowded. For prayers, at least." TJ winked at me.

"That's cute."

"Yeah, and it made a lot of sense. Jesus was a fisherman. The peace on the water, getting your thoughts ... " We let a few quiet moments pass.

"You think I'm super sexy as a fisherman, don't you?" TJ asked, eyes narrowing.

A surprised laugh popped out of me. TJ reached out quickly to pull me on top of him.

"I caught you in my net of charm." His eyes glinted as he flipped me onto my back and hovered over me.

"Is that what that was? Your net of charm?" I laughed.

He leaned down and kissed me once.

"I was very patient, trying to catch you." He searched my eyes as he lowered his hips between my legs. His beautiful blue eyes shone with love for me. Then he slid the backs of his fingers down my cheek. "I let you get away once, but that's it."

"Are you kidding me? You had me hooked from, 'Who are you?' when you were five years old." I beamed up at him.

"Well, I sure am grateful that hook didn't break."

"That hook won't break," I whispered, suddenly feeling emotional. I couldn't count on many parts of my life being set, but at least TJ was secure. I didn't doubt that.

His expression strayed from playful to serious. Then our kiss became an unspoken promise, raw and passion-filled. TJ tugged at my bottom lip with such softness and heat. His tongue slipped skillfully around mine in a slow but somehow urgent build. He moved to my neck and the dip at my collarbone, all the while giving me goosebumps and want. I pulled at the button on his jeans as he scooted my leggings down. We each threw off our bottoms, and TJ settled over me again. He didn't break eye contact with me as I took him in.

I could've cried with love for him. It was everything in that moment. "So. Damn. Grateful," TJ declared with each push of his body into mine.

Journal Entry #26 ~ New Friend

I'd had enough of living in this house with Rachel's ghost. It didn't help that Robert was gone so often with one business trip after the next. I thought things would be better when the Lawsons moved away. I thought Rebecca would flourish and do well in middle school. She hated it. It was worse than hating it. She seemed completely broken.

Rebecca hadn't signed up for any activities despite my suggestions. "Why not get into student council? That might be fun." She'd just glared at me. "You could join cheerleading. Aunt Colleen used to love that." Her head slumped onto the table, and she gave me no response.

She just rode her bike to that damn pond and moped all the time. If she wasn't riding her bike up and down the street in misery, then she was drawing in her room or while sitting on the field across the street. She never let me see what she drew. She didn't smile anymore. She didn't even sass me. I hated Tommy all over again, feeling that he took her soul with him when he left.

I tried to get Colleen involved with Rebecca, but that was tricky, as she had her hands full with the jewelry business, Jim's business, and their kids, Carly, and Jeremy. I knew Rebecca really loved Colleen, though. I was hoping she'd listen to her aunt better than she listened to me. Colleen called her a few times and took her to the movies. Rebecca was polite but not chatty. I didn't think she would be. Even after those attempts to reach out, Rebecca still dragged around. She slept more often, sometimes going to bed three hours earlier than she normally would. It didn't seem healthy, and that behavior, honestly, scared me. After three years, her new normal was barely existing.

Ryan was having a tough time as well. He never opened up to any of us and didn't have many friends. He wasn't invested in junior high. His grades dropped, and he confined himself to his room, playing the Xbox more and more. Ryan had moments of rebellion, not just with us but at school. Once he started puberty, he wanted to be noticed, and suddenly, he was … for all the wrong reasons. Ryan and some boys from his school got in trouble for defacing a playground at the elementary school. He should've known that cameras would pick up what he was doing. Maybe he didn't care. Robert was livid with him. I tried to encourage Robert to spend more time with him, knowing he needed one supportive parent taking an interest in him.

Ultimately, we decided to move, get a fresh start with new scenery, and figure out a new normal. Ryan and Rebecca would be around different people, which we hoped would be a good thing.

Robert encouraged Rebecca to be in sports by the time she hit junior high. I let up about it while she looked at me sidelong. The only thing she enjoyed with our family was playing catch with Robert—nothing with me.

Robert mentioned to Rebecca that she should try out for basketball and rejoin gymnastics and swim. Maybe even try track in the spring at school. She didn't want to do any of it until we gave her an ultimatum that she either do some physical activity, join a club, or start seeing a counselor. At last, she agreed to the sports activities and found her place there.

I was happy to hear that Rebecca had found a junior high friend named Dana. She didn't seem like the sweetest of friends, but she was involved in Rebecca's life from the start. She included her in her activities, too. Dana played soccer and convinced Rebecca to come to some of the practices. She picked it up immediately. Her speed made her a huge asset to the team. She didn't have her footwork down, though, so Robert encouraged Rebecca to get private lessons from the coach, which she did for two nights a week and never looked back. She became so skilled so quickly that she moved up to the elite team at the start of the next season.

Being part of that soccer club was such a boost for Rebecca. She began holding her head up. Coaches complimented her regularly, and her teammates looked up to her. Even coaches on the opposing teams would spend an extra few seconds congratulating Rebecca on her athleticism at the end of the games instead of doling out the quick handshakes and "Good game" we'd hear for everyone else.

Then, in high school, she found Lindsay, who became her closest friend. Lindsay must've made quite an impression because Rebecca came home after the first day of freshman year and truly smiled.

We had just sat down for dinner together, Robert, Ryan, Rebecca, and myself.

"So, how was your first day, guys?" Robert asked as he spooned out some salad into his bowl.

"Okay. I've got a tough schedule, but it'll be fine," Ryan said, biting a chunk of his garlic bread.

"What looks to be your toughest class?" I asked.

"Either Trig or AP Bio." He rolled his head on his shoulders.

"You're going to have to hunker down and study a lot," Robert said to Ryan, who shrugged him off.

"You had a good day, Rebecca?" I asked.

"Yeah. I met this really funny girl named Lindsay. She was so sweet to me," Rebecca said with calm happiness in her voice.

"That's wonderful," I said, smiling at her. My heart flipped momentarily with happiness.

"Great, hon," Robert said, nodding.

"Yeah. She's really friendly. And Lindsay loves soccer, so we already talked about how we should try out together in the spring," Rebecca added, stirring around her angel hair pasta with her fork.

I wished that Lindsay was there in our house at that moment because I would've smothered her in a hug. She made Rebecca happy.

"Yeah? Great start, huh, kiddo?" Robert winked at her.

"It was good. We have three classes together, too. So, that's cool."

"I'm so happy to hear that," I said.

"Is that Erin's sister? Is her last name Kelso?" Ryan asked.

"I think so."

"I think that's Lindsay Kelso. Her sister Erin's in my grade. Erin has a younger sister named Lindsay, who plays soccer."

"Oh really?" Rebecca said.

"Erin's like an actual genius," Ryan said, grabbing his glass of ice water and taking a gulp. "What did you think of Zeker for Freshman Seminar?" Ryan asked with a grin.

Rebecca stifled a laugh. "He's odd."

"He's super weird, but he's really easy."

I found Robert's eyes across the table and sighed, my eyes filling with tears. My sweet Robert gave me his dimpled grin. I felt so grateful at that moment, in our new home, at this easy discussion bouncing around the table from Ryan to Rebecca. It made my heart ache with happiness that we were finally all sitting together with good news and positivity surrounding us.

CHAPTER 25

Karaoke Night

Later that day, TJ and I headed to his mom's for a birthday party. I offered to drive him because his present was already stowed in my trunk. It would be easier to surprise him there. Plus, he would certainly use it at the party. And he would possibly drink too much.

I was happy to see Trevor and Freddie there for TJ. We had seen a lot of each other over the past year. They were both solid guys. Trevor had this never-ending, quiet energy and was so helpful and motivated. He was such a good role model for his younger brothers. Freddie was the last in his family to graduate college.

Of course, the house was packed, as I'd expected. Mrs. Lawson was the first to greet us at the door with her bright smile.

"Happy birthday, my sunshine!" She pulled TJ down and hugged him, rocking him back and forth and back and forth. "Twenty-two! How is my baby twenty-two?"

"Thanks, Ma. And the boat. For real?" He shook his head. "It's too much."

"Never too much for you." Then, of course, she wiped at her eyes.

"How are you, Becky, my sweet angel?" Mrs. Lawson hugged me so tightly.

Tana came charging toward us. She was getting so big now, long and lean, and resembling Jenna more and more every time I saw her. With her olive skin and big brown eyes, she was so beautiful. The moment she saw TJ, she leaped for him, squealing.

"Tana banana! Where's my kiss?" TJ leaned his cheek close to her.

She made a loud mmmuh sound but barely touched his cheek with her lips.

"Happy birthday, Uncle Tommy."

"Thanks, baby cakes."

"Hi, Tana," I called and leaned down to hug her.

I caught up with Katie, Sarah, Jenna, and Mason. Then, I thanked Grandma for the breakfast. She was moving slower and looked a bit thinner, but she had her wit and same no-nonsense personality. TJ's cousins, aunts, and uncles had come over for the party, sure to be entertained.

Once the party got going, I snuck out to grab his gift from the trunk and brought it to the basement. I smiled to myself, knowing TJ would flip out about it. I *knew* he would love it. I could see so far ahead with him that it sent little tremors of nerves up my spine. I suddenly felt I had so much to lose. Would we have long enough? I thought briefly of his dad having his time cut short. Of my sister and now my mother hanging on. I stopped myself and shook out the thought to refocus on the task at hand. It was my gift of entertainment for the entertainer in my life.

I called TJ over, and Grandma whistled to quiet the crowd. Then, I asked him to open my gift. He was smiling big, a red plastic cup in his hand. He put it down on an end table and eyed me.

"What's this, Beck?" He gave me that side grin.

"Something I'm sure to regret," I laughed.

TJ tore at the paper, and someone in the crowd groaned in annoyance, followed immediately by laughter.

"Aww, no shit!" TJ yelled.

A karaoke machine. Equipped with two wireless microphones, portable Bluetooth speakers, remote control, and a QR code to scan for thousands of song choices.

TJ was ecstatic. He grabbed me roughly, spinning me around and kissing me. "Thanks, Beck! Hell yeah! Let's get this bad boy going!"

TJ sang at minimum eight songs in a row. I lost track after the sixth. His voice was nearly gone from screeching, cracking, and shouting into the mic with fervor. Truly a sight. Jenna and I spasmed with laughter for so long that my cheeks hurt. Mason hadn't heard much, as he was concentrating on another poker game—still beer-free.

Katie came up to TJ at one point and complained that he was hogging the karaoke. She slapped him on the shoulder and yelled, "Other people are here, too, you know? Did you ever think to ask them if they want to sing? You're so annoying!"

"Aww, love you, too, Kate."

When it was time for cake, Mrs. Lawson carried a large, store-bought rectangular cake with white icing and blue flowers to a table set up in the basement. "Happy Birthday Tommy" was spelled in thick blue-gel cursive letters. TJ sat at the head of one table, grinning like a lunatic. He looked down at the twenty-two candles Mrs. Lawson had shoved into it. She expertly lit each one as TJ gave a little thank you speech.

"This is all I could wish for. Fishing today, great food, singing with y'all, family and friends by my side, and Beck." He cleared his throat for a second. "Thank you. This has been the greatest day. Love you all."

There was a jumble of cheering and whistling. Then, TJ stared at the flickering candles and up at me—another stare at the cake, and he clenched his jaw, closed his eyes tightly, and made a wish.

My mouth opened slightly, and my pulse skipped a beat. He didn't have to tell me. I knew he'd made this wish for me. For my mother to survive.

The next morning, we headed over to TJ's mom's again to have breakfast and help clean up from the party.

We had just enjoyed a breakfast of blueberry pancakes with fresh fruit. TJ and Howard were busy replacing a window in the basement, a party foul from one of his younger cousins who went red-faced and apologized profusely.

I was sitting with Mrs. Lawson, making conversation. A nagging feeling bothered me as I kept glancing toward the downstairs, wondering how long I might have to talk to her without any interruptions from TJ. It was the first time I'd really seen her since Ryan told me about my mom being friends with her. Also, the first time, my mind wasn't buzzing about surprising TJ with his gift. I wouldn't get another chance. For some reason, I didn't want to bring up what I was about to ask her in front of him, but I couldn't keep the question out of my mind. I needed to know more about her relationship with my mother. I needed to know where it all went wrong.

"Mrs. Lawson, can I ask you something?"

"Of course, Becky," she said. One hand clutched her coffee mug, and the other rested on mine. "But enough of this Mrs. Lawson. I've been Mrs. Roth for a while now, and anyway, please call me Janet."

"I'll try." I scooted in my chair, suddenly anxious that this question wouldn't be easy to ask or answer. She watched me with warm eyes as I thought about how to start.

"I've been wondering if you could tell me anything about my mom."

Mrs. Lawson tilted her head slightly.

"I mean," I stumbled. "About you and her? You were friends?" I asked, and it felt just as foreign on my tongue as it did hearing the words aloud.

And then I realized I hit on something. She stiffened ever so slightly, but it was there. Mrs. Lawson looked at me for a long moment, opened her mouth, then dropped her eyes toward the table.

She took in a breath and hung onto it a little too long. "Your mom and I were very close a long while ago," Mrs. Lawson said, her eyes a haze of memories.

"What happened?" I almost whispered.

Another long pause, and Mrs. Lawson was still engrossed in her cup of dark roast, as if the answer would come swirling up to the surface.

I saw the pain in her eyes as she faltered, "What I can tell you is that your mom, as long as I knew her, always struggled emotionally. There's a lot of hurt there."

I nodded because I didn't know what else to do. I was waiting for more of an explanation. The silence wrapped around me, almost suffocating me.

"I'm not sure this should come from me, sweetie," she said at last with a sympathetic grin. Heartbreak reflected in her eyes, making my confusion more pronounced. She patted my hand and lifted herself from her spot, changing the subject to: "Now, what can you please bring back home? We've got all kinds of leftovers … "

I wanted to stay in that conversation. I wanted to know about their friendship. I wanted to apologize on my mom's behalf for whatever broke them up because I felt more certain that it was my mom's fault. But I didn't say anything at all. I watched Mrs. Lawson flitting around the kitchen, pulling out Tupperware containers and opening the fridge. She was rambling about desserts now, but my mind was fixed on getting home and finding answers.

Journal Entry #27 ~ Afloat

Over the next few months, I encouraged Rebecca to see Lindsay as much as she wanted, and I planned more time for us to be together as a family. Colleen, Jim, and the kids came over more often for dinners. I made a promise to myself to start building a better relationship with my family.

I also felt more comfortable at work. I had built up connections with frequent customers and joined a Facebook group for jewelry lovers. Colleen's business was such a light in my day. I was grateful she had found a way to keep me busy in this productive company.

The next year was harder. Rebecca started dating, and Ryan was about ready to leave for college. In the summer, he started working as a caddy for most of the week and was out with friends constantly in the evenings.

I felt empty thinking of how grown-up he was getting. Sometimes, I pretended to have an issue with my computer just to ask for his help and have him near me without being too obvious.

He always kept me at a distance, though. They both did.

Robert decided to take us all on a cruise for a family vacation late that summer before Ryan left for college.

We went to a few islands in the eastern Caribbean. The weather was gorgeous, and the views were stunning. The kids weren't with us much on the ship. They only joined us at excursions or popped up for dinner.

One night, we were eating with a middle-aged couple at an Italian restaurant on the ship.

Robert and the couple made small talk for a bit, and then the woman commented, "You have a beautiful family."

"Thank you," I said, smiling at Robert. He grinned, exposing his dimples.

"Is it just the two of you?" she indicated to Ryan and Rebecca. "Or do you have any other children?"

All at once, my heart sank. Those questions from polite and inquisitive people were simply good-natured. I got them all the time, yet I never learned how to handle them. One of those questions and heartache like fire burned me from the inside out. Rachel was gone again in an instant, and I grew cold in defeat.

"We have an older daughter as well. How about you?" Robert said directly.

I froze, unable to breathe, and felt Rebecca's eyes on me. Ryan picked at his plate, too embarrassed to look my way.

The next day, I couldn't get it out of my mind.

I was horrible to Ryan and Rebecca; I know I was. I forbade them to go parasailing. I demanded they stick near each other when wandering around the ship. After complaints about wasting a lot of fun opportunities on shore, I finally agreed to let them go snorkeling, but only if we all went together.

It was beautiful under the water. The dancing coral was filled with brilliant species of fish and marine life. Then I accidentally slacked my lips around the mask, and my mouth filled with salt water. I sputtered and scared myself, reaching for the surface. Being calm after that was an impossible task. I grew anxious, scanning the water for Ryan and Rebecca. A few times, I popped up and couldn't find them or couldn't specifically find Rebecca. I panicked and called out her name as my voice echoed my terror.

"Mom, stop it. I'm right here," she whisper-yelled at me, mortified. I was ashamed for ruining her experience.

Robert tried to smooth things over. He made sure he and I spent time alone that evening. We listened to music in the promenade, and he got me up and slow danced with me. I rested my head on his shoulder as we swayed, my eyes welling with tears. Robert pulled back and wiped tears from my eyes. "I will always be here for you. I promise," he whispered and kissed the top of my head.

Despite Robert's efforts, I couldn't get out of my stupor. I hadn't been taking my meds. I thought I had outgrown the grief. How foolish. It was a never-ending ocean of grief. The swells were all that changed. Sometimes, the waves were vast and steady, crushing me constantly. Sometimes, the waves weren't waves at all—just ripples of aching. But then that current would pick up, and the grief would pour over me again and rip my feet out from under me.

I spiraled further and wept when Robert and the kids were all out at a show, and I was alone in the cabin. When I called Colleen, she helped me calm down. She drove to my house, tore through my medicine cabinet, and found my pill bottle. Then she called my doctor who forwarded the prescription to the doctor on call at the medic's office on the ship. They located a pharmacy at Key West where we could stop the next day to acquire my refill.

I hung my head for the rest of the trip. My family's disappointment was evident in their expressions and resigned frowns. It mirrored my own. Robert was tender with me. He tried his best to explain that every emotion I felt was important. He wished he could take the hurt away, but since he couldn't, the best he could do was be there for me.

I held my hands against his soft face and told him with teary eyes how much I loved him.

CHAPTER 26

Searching

When I got home from the Lawson's that Sunday, I was charged with new adrenaline for needing proof that my mom and Janet had been friends before becoming strangers. I didn't want to involve my dad. He was too soft with her and would just make excuses about her behavior.

Obviously, I couldn't ask my mom about this. She would completely shut down. She'd never even told me about her mother, my grandma. She never spoke of Rachel. Of course, she wouldn't open up out of the blue about being great friends with a woman she'd then completely ghosted for over a decade.

I made small talk with my dad at dinner one night. It was just the two of us as my mom lay in her bed, refusing food and wanting to rest. She'd been nauseated all day. The change from the treatment had made her unrecognizable over the past few weeks. Her beautiful, rich, vibrant hair, usually the color of chocolate, was now dull, mousy, and thin, hanging on her shoulders. Her eyes were worn and empty. She refused to wear makeup or have me fix her hair. So not typical of her that it made me feel more urgency than ever to figure out anything more about her life. To know her while she was still alive.

I spent the next three nights digging for any evidence to help me figure out their past. I searched the basement, the crawlspace, and the attic, but I couldn't find a trace linking my mom to Mrs. Lawson. No old videos, no photos. Not even a birthday card.

I almost gave up on it. Maybe they'd had a misunderstanding, or my mom became judgy. I could see her being that way. Yet, from Mrs.

Lawson's quiet answer, I knew there had to be more.

I waited until my dad took my mom out for a ride. He wanted to get her out of the house when she didn't feel too awful. I dug around in the kitchen drawers and the spare rooms. I snuck into their room and tore through everything in their closet, finding more magazines and packets explaining prescription drugs. My mother had shoe boxes of items and envelopes and pictures at the bottom of her closet. Still nothing. I went through all her dresser drawers, digging in between her clothing and under sweaters. I looked under the bed to no avail. I rifled through every drawer of her bedside table, finding face masks, flashlights, pens, little packs of tissues, and an old spring jewelry catalog. The catalog looked thicker than I anticipated, and when I lifted it up, a leather-covered notebook slid out. My heart skipped a beat as I caught it before it fell to the floor. My eyes flitted to the door, but I didn't hear any noises that would indicate they were home.

I opened the cover to see a letter paperclipped onto the first pages of this unfamiliar writing pad, and my eyes grew wide, taking note of my mother's handwriting. The letter was dated this past January, at the time of her diagnosis. Behind that was an entire notebook of my mother's careful cursive handwriting. I had found more than a picture or birthday card. More than a photobook of vacation memories. It was a journal about my mother's life.

Journal Entry #28 ~ Losing Ground

Things are starting to fall apart again.

Rebecca wants to explore colleges on the coast.

Not only that, but she wants to continue playing soccer at college. I didn't think it was the right decision. I know she loves to play. She has skill, agility, and speed—so much speed. However, I can't help but question where her priorities will be if she keeps up the soccer. I can't stand the thought of soccer getting in the way of her schooling. College will be hard enough. I never made it through college, so I am desperate for her to succeed and get a degree. Her future is much more valuable. I need her to flourish in all things.

I didn't directly tell her no, but I made it clear that she shouldn't seek soccer as a distraction from schooling. I wasn't being fair. To say Rebecca was unhappy with me was an understatement.

In the hunt for colleges without soccer as a condition, I tried to get her to visit some reputable universities within driving distance. We visited Michigan, Northwestern, and Purdue, but she balked at those, saying they were too big and intimidating.

Lindsay was going to Eastern because of their education program. She brought up the idea that Rebecca attend Eastern, as well. That was the first time Rebecca had shown interest in a college other than some private schools along the coast known for their soccer programs. I couldn't stand if she were that far away from me. I feared I'd never get her back if she went across the nation to play a sport she loved.

Robert thought Eastern with Lindsay sounded like a good fit for her, and it was very affordable. To sweeten his deal, Robert told Rebecca that we could give her a monthly allowance with no pressure for employment during college since she was attending a far more reasonably priced university. She agreed without enthusiasm.

All of that was just prior to Everett. She met him late in her senior year of high school. As far as I knew, he wasn't in any of her classes. One day, he just latched on to her. Everett gave Rebecca all kinds of attention, and she craved it. He was rail thin with greasy black hair that fell into his eyes, black jeans, black shirts, black boots, earrings, bracelets, rings, you name it. That and he smelled like skunk, which I took to mean he was smoking pot constantly. Everett was quiet, unfriendly, and not even close to the type of man suited for my Rebecca.

I will never forget the first day she brought him over. She stared me down while I raked my eyes over his wormy face and skinny black jeans. I *believe she introduced us by saying, "Mother, this is Everett, and he isn't interested in soccer, either. So, you two have that in common." Rebecca shot me a wry smile.*

She made life hell for a month. Everett came over constantly to pick her up in his black Mustang. He'd speed down the driveway with her and skid away around the corner as if he couldn't wait to get her alone. He disgusted me. I couldn't imagine what they were doing with their time. In truth, I didn't want to imagine that.

Rebecca would stay out late with him; then she'd sleep in late. She was on FaceTime with him all night. She came home, reeking of smoke, skunk, and alcohol. She ignored me and gave me a death glare anytime I looked at her.

"I don't know why you care about who I am hanging out with," she fumed at me one night after being dropped off at home past curfew, stinking of alcohol. "It's not like you really give a shit about me, anyway." Rebecca might as well have struck me across the face. I startled and blinked at her. She did wince a little, like it pained her to say that to me.

I was at my wit's end. I didn't know how I'd get her back. I knew I couldn't fly off the handle, or I would just push her further away. Robert tried to talk some sense into her, but she didn't listen to him, either. I truly thought I was losing her.

It took Lindsay to finally step in and tell Rebecca that Everett was all wrong for her. I know this because I overheard them talking one night when Lindsay was over. I stood outside Rebecca's bedroom and listened to them.

"So, what is the deal with Everett? Are we still considering him long-term? Because ..." Lindsay asked.

"I don't know."

"Well, I know he's not good enough for you. And he ..." Lindsay paused.

"What?"

"He just looks dirty. Like he smells bad."

There was a moment of silence, then they both started laughing.

"He actually does smell a little bad," Rebecca giggled.

"Right?" Lindsay asked. "Come on, dump him already so we can have a hot girl summer before we go away. Please?"

"I don't even think it would be a dumping situation. He's not really into monogamy."

"Monopoly? What the hell does that have to do with …"

Then Rebecca was in hysterics. "Not monopoly," she hooted. "Monogamy."

"Oh," Lindsay wheezed in laughter. "Okay, I have no idea what that is." Then they were in louder hysterics.

I knew what monogamy meant. I was in the hallway balling my hands into fists just thinking about this loser sleeping with my Rebecca and other girls, too. God, I hoped I was wrong. Even so, at that moment, I was so grateful we had already had the talk about protection, and I'd started her on the pill a year before that to help with her cycle.

I tried not to let my mind go there, but it did. I wasn't naive to the fact that she had grown up. She was gorgeous and bound to experiment with boys her age. I myself had fooled around with a few guys before Robert. But this guy? For my Rebecca? It made me sick.

Later that night, as Lindsay was leaving, without Rebecca knowing, I took a second and gently pulled on Lindsay's arm. She turned, surprised, and I said, "Thank you," and jerked my head toward Rebecca's back. "I'm glad she has you for advice," I whispered. Lindsay just grinned at me, nodding—as if she only partly trusted me, too.

CHAPTER 27

Hug Emergency

A night out with Amy and Linds was just what I needed. It was time for a reality check after reading all the unbelievable thoughts my mom had about the Lawsons. It killed me to discover that my mom essentially loved Janet. To read how fun TJ's dad had sounded. And how my mom was so broken from losing Rachel. I kept looking at my mom and trying to figure her out. I tried to understand. She had been happy once, but she had also been so wronged by my grandfather and abandoned by my grandmother. My dad was her hero, and I loved him even more now after reading all about their life together. It was so much to wrap my head around.

The part I hadn't anticipated was that I was connecting with my mom on a bigger level. I felt all her emotions and wished I could confess that I knew her better now despite her trying to keep me away. She loved me fiercely. With each page I read, it broke my heart a little more that she couldn't have shown this to me. And that I had a completely different perception of her when I was younger.

I needed to talk about this journal, but I couldn't tell anyone about it. Not yet. Besides, it still didn't explain anything about her falling out with Janet.

***

Amy made the long way up from Peoria/Dunlap to see me and spend the weekend with Lindsay. We met at a cute little Italian restaurant for dinner. I took my time hugging the girls when they walked in. Lindsay quickly began chastising Amy the second we were guided to a booth. "I'm telling you, Amy, you'd better be on your best behavior while you are staying with us this weekend. My very Korean mother will be horrified if you go for the startle factor."

"That was one time," Amy insisted.

"At orientation, and they haven't forgotten how 'bold' you were," Lindsay retorted.

"Oh, Miss Linds. Have we met? Everyone's parents LOVE me. Get over it."

"Mmm," I hummed a high-pitched note and tilted my head slightly.

After winding our way through the maze of bustling tables and wait staff, we got to our booth. Amy ordered a pitcher of red sangria from the waitress, who gave us a basket of fresh rolls.

Lindsay was bursting to tell us all about her last date. She had been dating a Korean guy named Eun for two weeks. Linds suspected, though, that he was only going out with her because she was part Korean, and she deemed this: "Not cool."

Linds was out to dinner with Eun one night when he commented about going out with a different girl. That's when Linds chirped, "I said, 'What?' He said, 'You thought we were exclusive?' I mean. Oh, hell no. So, I gave him the cold shoulder for the rest of the night. He got the hint and stopped talking to me." Lindsay was a rock star with the cold shoulder. She had amazing endurance in keeping a grudge—which isn't a good thing, but it is a Lindsay thing.

"So, then what?" I asked.

"Well, I continued eating my meal because, HELLO! I was starving."

Amy shook her head, and I grinned.

"Then, I ignored him, and he scrolled through his feed while I ate. When the bill came, I stood up, looked him dead in the eyes, and said, 'Eun, this relation*ship* has sailed.' Then I left him sitting there with the bill."

Lindsay went to high-five me and Amy, who stared at her, mouth agape.

I clapped my hand against Linds' halfheartedly and cupped a smile with my other hand.

"Please tell me you are joking," Amy deadpanned.

"Did you actually say that, Linds?" I asked.

"Um, one hundred percent. I thought it was the perfect line." Lindsay smiled and fist-bumped the air.

"Do you ever wonder why you're still a virgin?" Amy asked with wide eyes, leaning closer to Lindsay.

"Excuse me! You say that like it's a bad thing."

"It's not a bad thing. At all," I interrupted.

"You, Miss Linds, are always the one complaining. 'Why don't I have a man? Why aren't guys into me? How long am I going to be a virgin?' Blah freaking, blah."

That was true. Lindsay enjoyed having high standards and being a good Catholic girl. She didn't like giving in to reckless behavior and every human instinct/desire. At the same time, she so badly wanted to be loved and intimate.

"Well, there are NO men. They all suck. The few that don't suck are just not interested in me."

"No, you just need to use them and stop thinking about boyfriend material to bring home to your parents." Amy raised her glass of sangria to Lindsay and toasted her.

"I can't pull the ones I want," Lindsay insisted.

"Then pull the ones I want. They're fun. Say the word, and I will have five very able-bodied men at the ready." To capitalize on this statement, Amy took out her phone and eyed Lindsay up and down, then did the same to her phone, as if taunting her that she was already texting guys.

I shook my head, watching this volley of wits and insults.

"Ew. No. What? All five at the same time? To lose my virginity or film an orgy?" Linds yelped, her arms flailing.

"Yes, of course, all five at the same time," Amy stated flatly. "Come on, they'll show you a good time. Even if you won't know what you're doing." Amy tried hard to stifle a laugh.

"God, why do you hate me?" Lindsay shouted playfully at Amy and threw a dinner roll at her shoulder.

"I hate you because you're a virgin," Amy said in her serious, sarcastic voice.

It was too much. I leaned back in my seat and rocked up and down in a sudden burst of laughter. The ridiculousness of this conversation and their sarcastic and obnoxious banter, put on like a favorite TV comedy, moved me. These girls. These two crazy friends, who I knew would have me forever. Their eyes snapped to me, and they caught up with my laughter. Then my bright mood turned to sorrow in a flash, with the realization that I'd soon need them much more than at this moment. That even a year ago, losing my mom wouldn't have hurt as badly as it was about to. I'd need these weirdos to help soften the sting.

"Oh, Rebecca." Lindsay instantly teared up. "See Amy? Now she's crying. Oh, gosh. This is awful." Linds scooted closer to me in the booth and grabbed my hand. "We talked about this. About how we wouldn't let you cry, and we made a plan."

"I didn't make any plan about dinner and sitting around talking about sad shit. I said we should go to a crowded bar with loud music, and get you drunk. But Miss Boring here … " Amy trailed off.

"Excuse me!" Lindsay yelped as a tear ran from the corner of her eye.

I wiped at my eyes and nose with my free hand.

"Oh," Lindsay moaned. She couldn't take it. She scooched closer to me and hugged me. I heard her sniffle as she silently squeezed my shoulders.

"Jesus, here we go. Do I have to come over there and hug both of you now? Or just Miss Rebecca?" Amy asked with exaggerated annoyance in her voice.

"Yes, both of us. Hurry, my eye makeup is getting washed out," Lindsay whined.

"Okay, cry-bitches, watch out," Amy called and then climbed up on top of the table.

"Whoa!" I yelled, edging a few inches away from the side of our booth.

"Amy, this is a nice restaurant ... " Lindsay scowled at Amy, eyes teary, and glanced at the other tables of customers ogling and gasping at us.

Amy crawled over our breadbasket, threw her leg around the pitcher of sangria, nearly knocked her head on the ornate golden orange light fixture, and jumped down in the tiny space between me and the wall.

"Sorry, folks! Hug emergency!" She waved her arms at the other guests. Then she pushed her chest up to me and wrapped her arms around me, pulling Lindsay closer, too.

We were all giggling by that point.

"When things with your mom seem really awful," Amy began with not-typical-for-her sincerity, "just remember that you have a freaking hot boyfriend, and *everyone* is jealous of you." Then she blew a raspberry on my cheek.

Journal Entry #29 - Milestone

Robert and I drove Rebecca to college.

My thoughts and emotions were all over the place. I didn't want her to go, but she needed this. I always wanted to go away to school, and I wanted that for Colleen, too. A young person has a need to branch out and earn their independence. It felt different when Ryan went to college. Robert and I still had Rebecca at home. Now, we would have no one. Not Ryan, not Rebecca, not Buddy, and, of course, not Rachel.

I was jealous for Rachel again. She didn't get to experience this part, and I didn't get to see her off on her first year away. What school would she have attended? What would she have studied? She would've gone away for sure, instead of finding a college to commute to from home. She was feisty and determined. It hurt to try and picture all she could've accomplished.

Ryan was in his third year at The University of Chicago. He loved the city and had found his niche. Apparently, he'd found a girlfriend as well.

Rebecca and I didn't have a great summer together. She was busy spreading her wings, and I was trying to cage her. I'd felt that way once, too, trapped by my surroundings, wanting to get away, wanting to prove myself. She probably wanted to get far away from me, too. The tension was growing tighter.

She was still angry with me for not letting her play soccer in college and at an out-of-state school. I couldn't let her go because I knew she wouldn't come back. I just needed her closer, only I never confessed that to her. I knew she didn't need me in the same way that I needed her. Sometimes, it felt as if she never needed me.

Thankfully, Lindsay would be Rebecca's roommate. Her parents, Jack and Seung, were reputable people and wouldn't tolerate any self-deprecating behavior. Lindsay was very sweet and responsible. She would be Rebecca's rock.

As we exited the elevator on Rebecca's new floor, Robert put on a brave face, but he was not okay with sending his baby off to college. He forced a smile and disguised his emotions with unnatural pep in his voice.

Rebecca was calm and confident. She didn't appear hesitant at all. That bothered me. She knew she would be just fine without us, or specifically, without me.

Rebecca's and Lindsay's dorm room was utterly tiny at barely twelve by nineteen feet, with two twin beds parted by a narrow walkway. Two desk stations sat at the foot of the beds, and standing-shower-sized closets with three drawers flanked the entrance with modest space to hang a spring wardrobe and store some folded clothes. That's why Robert brought the rolling dolly loaded with cinder blocks. Four for Rebecca, four for Lindsay to stack their beds on, and double storage under their beds.

"I forgot how small this space would be," I said, inching past Jack's tall frame into the room to look at the window.

Rebecca rolled her eyes at me. "It's fine, Mom. We have plenty of space."

The girls had agreed to arrive at the exact same time. That way, the room would belong to both of them.

"Which side do you want, Rebecca?" Lindsay asked.

"Doesn't matter," Rebecca replied.

"Oh, good! I want the left. Because I sleep on my left, and if I was on the right, I'd just be staring at you all night. You know?"

"Staring while you're sleeping?" Rebecca asked, a smile breaking through her momentary confusion.

"Well, you know …" Lindsay swatted down the thought.

"Okay, over here, Dad," Rebecca said, indicating the right side of the room.

Once the spaces in the room were established, Rebecca, Robert, and Jack mounted the beds on the cinder blocks. Lindsay and her mom argued in Korean about the closet and how to best unpack and organize all the clothing.

I headed for the window with a flat, oversized bag I'd smuggled in without Rebecca noticing.

I pulled a cinch rod from the bag and double-checked the window's width. It would fit nicely. I stood up on a chair, balanced myself on top of the desk, reached up, unclasped the old, burgundy curtains from the titanium rod, and set those aside. Then I unscrewed the rod. I gathered the gray and white diamond pattern fabric and scrunched it onto the ends of the rod. I climbed back up on the desk and balanced the rod with the fabric in front of me. Then, I fastened the tension rod against the walls.

I gathered each bottom section of the curtains in my hands one at a time and tied a blue satin ribbon around each side. The adorable, gathered curtains framed the window nicely, adding texture and a modern touch to this space.

By now, the beds were lifted, the storage containers loaded and stowed beneath them, and the sheets and blankets secured.

Seung and Jack were excusing themselves and preparing to say goodbye.

"Okay, Mom and Dad, Rebecca, and I have to go meet the neighbors now," Lindsay said.

"Studying comes first," her mom reminded her, shaking her finger at Lindsay.

"I know," Lindsay said.

Seung kissed Lindsay's cheeks four times while tearing up.

"Stop it," Lindsay scolded, dabbing her fingers under her eyes. "I look good today; don't ruin my face."

Then Lindsay's dad hugged her with his long arms.

We said goodbye to Jack and Seung as Lindsay walked them into the hallway. Then, I gathered my bags and took a deep breath, trying to steady myself before the emptiness settled in.

I stood, taking in every detail of Rebecca with so much in my heart unsaid.

She finally noticed the window treatments. I hadn't told her I was making them, that I'd investigated the room dimensions, bought fabric, sewed it to fit, and planned to surprise her and Lindsay.

Her mouth parted as she appraised the curtains.

"Mom," she said simply, walking over to them and running her thumb and forefinger down the edge.

I would've normally explained more about them—that you could throw them in the wash and not worry about drying them. That you'd just pull the ribbon at night and for privacy. Instead, I stood rooted, silent. Afraid that any sound I'd utter would make me fall apart.

She looked up at the curtain rod and then at the dusty, folded, worn burgundy curtains on the desk.

She met my eyes with a glimmer in her own.

"Thank you." Her eyes brightened as if seeing me for the first time. She

was so beautiful in that moment. Her cheeks were flushed from carrying and lifting storage cubes, her skin, sun-kissed from summer, her caramel hair, her rosy full lips, and Robert's kind eyes.

I swallowed and nodded, tears edging. Then I reached out and hugged her shoulders. She was my height. When had she become my height? I took in her soft, toned frame. She hugged me back, and it all was perfect and heartbreaking. I suddenly saw her as that little rag doll with warm shoulders the day Janet Lawson brought her to me. How had she grown up so quickly? Why hadn't I been paying attention? Now, here she was, a woman, leaving the nest for school. I had missed so much of it. I bit the inside of my cheek hard to keep from breaking down.

Then Robert was around us, getting in on the hug, too.

We pulled away at last, and Robert leaned in to kiss Rebecca's forehead. "Alright, kiddo. Love you. Work hard. Have fun."

"I will," she said.

My Robert was the perfect father and the most adorable man. After we closed our car doors and pulled away from the campus, we both dissolved into tears. He stopped for lunch at a place three miles down the road, and we sat side by side, eating barbeque on the patio. We didn't say much, just nudged each other and leaned our heads close; this milestone hurt. We would miss seeing our beautiful Rebecca each day.

CHAPTER 28

Hide and Seek

Hospitals are supposed to be a place for healing, but lately, it felt like they were just prisons of invasive tests and more bad news.

My mother had fallen ill with low electrolytes and shortness of breath. They were going to keep her overnight. Aunt Colleen and my cousins came to see my mom at the hospital. It had been a long day of waiting around for the doctors to speak with us as the nurses gave her meds and monitored her IV.

TJ came up for a visit and did his best to sit still and be patient, but I could see it wearing on him. He was barely ever this quiet for this long. After a bit, he paced the floor and tried to get comfortable leaning on different surfaces. Jeremy whined to Aunt Colleen that he was bored, and she gave him a look like she'd kill him, so he merely ducked his head back down mid-eyeroll.

TJ had an idea to give my dad, mom, and Aunt Colleen some space while we waited for news. He invented a game of hide-and-seek with partners. Jeremy smiled widely at this. He and Carly were partners, and TJ and I were partners.

We hid in every small space we could find on that hospital floor: behind chairs in the waiting room and under the nurse's station, which earned TJ a cross look from a nurse, to which he replied a hurried "Sorry" as we sprinted down the hallway. Jeremy took a flight of stairs and popped up on the elevator. He was laughing, his cheeks flushed with glee. Carly got annoyed with Jeremy, so she sat in the waiting room on her phone instead of playing along. But at least TJ and I succeeded in getting Jeremy to engage in some activity while we ran playfully through the hallways, trying to find or be found by him. When we were out of breath with wild eyes and plastered slapstick smiles, we returned to the hallway near my mom's private room.

A team of white coats blocked her doorway. A hushed atmosphere loomed, and I felt like a fool for playing hide and seek. For making a joke of this serious time. I read the regret on TJ's face, too. He inclined his head at me as if to say, "Sneak in there, and listen."

I gave my best, stealthy but professional "Excuse me" as I squeezed through the bodies at the door. One of the interns moved aside to let me pass, and I found my way to a chair beside my dad, whose eyes were round with alarm. TJ didn't follow me in. I glanced at my mom, but she wouldn't meet my eyes.

"Rebecca," Dr. Ahmed addressed me.

"Yes, hi, Dr. Ahmed. I apologize for the intrusion."

"No, not at all," she continued.

"We are discussing the findings of the latest scans. We noted that nodule two has an increase of 2.2 centimeters, and nodule three has an increase of 1.6. At this point, continuing the current treatment plan is not in Suzanne's best interests. Her condition is not stable, but rather, the cancer cells are progressing."

I was spinning. "Not stable." "Cancer cells are progressing." "Not in Suzanne's best interests." These words spiraled through my mind like a tilt-a-whirl. I clenched my fingers onto the sides of the chair to help keep calm while I forced myself to breathe out of my mouth without sounding like I was hyperventilating. Then I leaned over, grabbed the yellow legal pad, and flipped it open to start taking notes. That's what my dad usually did. It made sense to me now. Of course, he did this. He could compartmentalize everything he heard on paper. Objectively. In a document. Just focus on the facts.

"Okay," I said slowly because I wasn't sure what to say.

My dad asked a few questions, and I realized he'd been holding my mom's hand the whole time as she gaped at the doctors.

"I know what I just stated may be alarming, and you will have questions about discontinuing treatment, as this regimen isn't responding. We know there is growth and need to address it with a more crucial treatment. A more aggressive treatment. We have a few options to discuss. These would be other forms of chemotherapy. There are some in-hospital treatments with an IV and a few experimental treatments in pill form that are managed at home. Obviously, there is a great list of possible and probable side effects. We will give you the information and make an appointment to have you come in and sit down with us to discuss the best course of action. We are not going to overwhelm you any further today. The important thing now is for you to rest, Suzanne. Try to ease into a comfortable position and get some sleep. However you can do that, please do. We will keep you here overnight to ensure your levels are in the normal range, make sure you are fully hydrated, and then discharge you in the morning."

Discharge her in the morning.

I couldn't help but feel like they were dismissing her entirely. I heard what the doctor said. I knew I should think about the next options and lend myself to believe in the promise of these new treatments, but I was stuck on the fact that nothing had worked. After all these weeks of having her attention, taking up her time, being there for her, and digging to figure her out, and now, she was an actual step closer to Rachel than she was to me.

Journal Entry #30 ~ First Date

Colleen's jewelry company was bringing so many new opportunities to both of us. Colleen was so clever and organized, with a great understanding of marketing, sales, and acquiring new customers. I was just along for the ride to set up, display, and answer a few questions. I would chime in for the sales, but Colleen was in charge.

I did meet a handful of compatible ladies to connect with, like Brenda. When Colleen started a Facebook page for the company, we had some regular traffic. Brenda always commented on our pieces and asked me to run a party for her. She was an excellent customer and spent hundreds of dollars on jewelry. Some for her and some for her two daughters. After getting to know her at a few parties with the same crowd of people, we chatted about our families. I learned that she had a son Rebecca's age, named Jason, who was also about to start junior year in college. Brenda showed me some pictures on her phone, and I opened up about Rebecca. Jason sounded like an ideal date for her.

Brenda and I staged a meeting for Rebecca and Jason. I didn't want Rebecca to know I was behind the set-up, but Rebecca was too clever and figured it out anyway. Fortunately, almost immediately, Jason won her over on his own.

The evening of their first date went so well. Jason was charming and impressive. He made it a point to be polite to Robert and me. He was a gentleman and on his way to great things, attending the University of Illinois then moving on to law school. Picture perfect.

When Rebecca got home from her date, I was so hopeful. She walked in and made her way to the kitchen, where I was busy reorganizing the cabinets and dishes. I didn't need to do any of that. I just wanted to see her when she got home. Robert had gone to bed hours earlier. He had a trip early the next morning.

"Mom?" Rebecca said cautiously.

"Oh, hi, sweetheart. How was your night?"

"What are you doing?"

"Well, that new platter I bought didn't fit in the other cabinet, and now I've gone and changed it all around." I set the glass dish down on the counter and moved the hair back from my forehead. "How was everything?" I asked casually, hoping she wouldn't see my nervous energy.

Rebecca smiled at me. A real smile.

"It was good." She tried to stop smiling.

I couldn't help it. I opened my mouth with a sharp, happy inhale. We shared a glance and giggled a bit.

"Oh, good! Are you planning to see Jason again?"

"Yeah," she said, gathering her hair with a thin band she'd fished from her pocket and tying it up in a bun. No hesitation in her response.

"That's wonderful. I'm so glad you had a nice time." Then I wished I were the mom she could confide in. I wished she would tell me more at that moment. Where did you go? What did he smell like? What did you have to eat? Did he kiss you good night? I wished again that her sister were here to dish over her date, like Colleen had done with me. My chest ached for an unexpected second. Then, instead of asking for any more details, I smiled at her and lifted the glass dish again.

Rebecca shrank back a little like she, too, thought we were making progress, but then she, too, felt disappointed that we weren't or that I wasn't that mom.

Later, as I climbed into bed, Robert lifted his head off his pillow. "Everything okay?" he asked.

"Yes, Rebecca had a good date tonight," I exhaled, situating myself on the soft sheets and extending my legs.

"Good," he said quietly. "Night, honey," and with that, he turned onto his side and fell back to sleep.

I took it for what it was worth. "Good." It was not another awkward interaction with Rebecca. I tumbled that word around in my mind for a while before dropping off. We could all use some good, and I was glad she was experiencing that now.

CHAPTER 29

Loving Sundays Again

It was too quiet when I woke up the next morning. I could feel the sunlight kissing my eyelids. I stretched and turned over to the warmth of TJ nestled beside me.

He had come home with me late last evening after seeing my mom. My dad refused to leave her there overnight by herself. It wasn't the first time he'd skipped on his luxurious king bed to sleep in a narrow, pleather recliner in my mom's hospital room. My dad was such a devoted husband. He felt better, too, knowing that TJ would be with me at our house, so I wouldn't have to process the new information alone. I was glad for TJ's company. We didn't talk much. Just held onto each other as we snuggled in my bed.

When I blinked awake the next morning, I saw him studying me. I grinned and shifted closer to him. "Good morning," I said softly with a kiss on his lips.

"Good morning," he replied, but not in his usual great-day-to-be-alive tone.

I blinked to get him into full focus. His chest rose and fell in long breaths. I looked at the stillness of his face. "What are you doing?" I said, trying to be playful, although I gathered he wasn't quite himself.

TJ bit his bottom lip as his eyes hovered lazily over my mouth. "Torturing myself."

I looked at his throat and saw it move. Then I looked back at his beautiful eyes, shadowed in sadness.

"What do you mean?"

"Just looking at you." He shook his head and clenched his jaw.

I took in his expression again and caressed the side of his face. He closed his eyes, grabbed my hand, and kissed my palm, his eyes still closed.

"What's the matter?" I asked, propping myself on my elbow.

TJ shook his head once and kept his eyes closed, holding my hand. Then my stomach started turning. He was holding back something heartbreaking. I could see it.

"Tell me," I pleaded carefully.

"Beck, you have a lot going on. I don't want to add to that." When he finally opened his eyes, they were blurred with tears.

"Hey," I whispered, leaning over and kissing his cheek delicately. "I want you. Every bit of you. Add it on. Please. What's wrong? Is it all this illness and stress?"

TJ put his left arm over me and rubbed my back. Closing his eyes again, he said softly, "I just miss you." Then, two fresh tears rolled down his face.

"Oh, babe." I clung to him, feeling his heart cracking. A piece of mine broke right along with his. "I love you so much." I squeezed him.

"I love you," he breathed on my hair. We held each other for a while like that.

When TJ did pull away, he still held back some of his emotions.

"It feels terrible not to be here for you all the time. Yesterday, at the hospital? That was rough. I feel really bad for your dad and you. Your mom looks ... " he didn't continue. "I can't imagine what you're going through." TJ laced his fingers through mine.

He paused for a while, but I didn't want to cut in.

"I don't want you to experience this kind of loss," TJ whispered, his eyes drenched in sadness.

Of course. He was thinking of his dad. I wondered then if he remembered how playful his dad had been. How he'd chased TJ all over the yard, throwing balls at him. How he'd made their backyard into something great. And how he hasn't been here for so long. I swallowed a knot in my throat. He was right. I didn't want that feeling. The loss of a parent. TJ's family had been through that, losing not only his dad but Mason's parents and, later, his grandpa. Grief rippled through me. We didn't bring it up; I should've invited this conversation from him over this year when we'd gotten so close. I should've been a better friend to him and asked about it.

"You miss him," I whispered.

TJ nodded and lightly ran his fingers over my back.

He straightened up, propping his back on the pillows. "It makes me afraid, too. Like I'll be left behind."

We didn't say anything for a while. I searched his face and eyes, waiting for him to open up more. Then, he cleared his throat.

"You know, I used to love Sundays. When I was younger, having the weekend. No school. Just family dinners, running around, fishing. Then in college, going back to Eastern on Sundays. The best."

I kept watching him and held onto his hand.

"Now, it's the day I have to say goodbye to you. Again and again. And leave you here to handle all of this." His jaw worked again, and he took a deep breath.

I looked into his shattered expression amid mixed emotions. What he had just said was truly precious. My heart wanted to cry with him. I hated not being with him. Any chance I would get, any second, I wanted him. But I was feeling proud that I could finally be the strong one. The one comforting him instead of TJ being there for me.

"Thank you for that. For loving me so much," I whispered, nudging my forehead against his. "You're right. It is a lot. But I'm hoping for the best results, and I'm getting good at being here for her," I said with a determination I didn't have before.

"You are. It's impressive." He brushed my hair back from my shoulder.

"Listen, I'm holding onto the future and imagining Sundays being amazing." I wrapped my leg around his.

TJ's mouth bent into a tiny grin. He grabbed my leg and pulled my body closer.

"Imagine all the Sunday mornings we are going to have in Carlyle. Just you and me," I said, slowly flipping on top of him with a glint in my eyes.

Sad TJ was gone. He gave me his full, adorable smile. I raised my eyebrows at him, grinning with confidence.

"You are. Incredible," TJ said.

Journal Entry #31 ~ Gut Punch

ONE WEEK AFTER VALENTINE'S DAY

I tried not to bother Rebecca at school. It was hard because I missed everything about her. I missed seeing her, hearing her voice, and sometimes, just having her take up space in the house. We'd had such a great summer after her sophomore year. She'd opened up with me more. I lit up every time I saw her smiling. I loved seeing Jason hugging her hello or goodbye, even stealing kisses from her.

Rebecca spoke more with me. She laughed with me.

The start of spring semester of her junior year was hard. I felt like she was forgetting me. Last week, it was only brief text messages.

"How are you?"

"Fine. You?"

"Are you getting more work from your professors now?"

"Yes. A lot."

"Did you have a nice Valentine's Day?"

"Yes."

I was surprised at how little I'd heard about Valentine's Day from Rebecca or Jason. It probably wasn't right for me to contact Jason myself. He was just so open with me that I felt as if I could. He even reached out to me from time to time. I knew this bothered Rebecca, but I was willing to be present for them both. We had been getting along so well. I hoped Rebecca saw herself in a new light. She seemed happy with Jason. That gave me joy, which was still hard to come by.

Jason seemed like a great fit for Rebecca. She had a wonderful summer with him, and they made it through being separated in the fall. I could see a sturdiness in him that I wanted for her. I knew his family and hoped we would be involved with them long-term.

Robert had so much on his plate with work. He was gone for hours on end and several weekends in a row. I admired his devotion, but it was hard to have so many quiet days at home. Shortly after Valentine's Day, when I was out helping Colleen with a show, Robert came home to an empty house for once. He was fast asleep by the time I got back, having washed up and crawled into bed.

In the morning, Robert was the first one up. I was groggy, feeling the two glasses of wine from the previous night. I also was holding onto a dream where Rachel was swinging on a swing at the park. She had on a yellow jumper. Her chocolate hair was bouncing on her shoulders. She looked so young, maybe five. I watched her pull back on the ropes and soar, her head dipped back, her dimpled cheeks bursting with happiness from her huge grin. I rushed to her as soon as I realized it was her, but then I woke. That was the bittersweetness of the dream. I could see her and swell in the happiness that she was living in front of me. Smiling, not coughing. Laughing, not wheezing. Life in her eyes, not dullness. It was a gift to see her that way, although it wasn't real. It was a temporary hologram. Of course, she wasn't there. As always, it took a minute to gather myself and let the pain fizzle down.

I heard the water turn off from Robert's shower as I sat on the side of the bed, facing the windows, practicing the meditation Colleen had found for me. Three full minutes of breathing. Two full minutes of gratitude. "I am thankful for this day. I am breathing. I am alive. I am capable. I am grateful for my loved ones. I am grateful for love."

I rose from the bed and gently pushed open the door to the bathroom.

Robert was in his boxers and fixing his freshly showered, thinning, graying hair. He still looked good. His eyes were bright and ready for the day.

"Hi, honey." He smiled at me in the mirror. Then he turned around and gave me a holding hug. His arms were solid and comforting. He smelled like clean citrus mint soap. I closed my eyes for a second and rested my head on his shoulder, breathing in his scent.

"Hi," I muffled.

He pulled back and gave me a quick glance. Then he kissed me swiftly and loosened his grip.

"How'd it go last night?" he asked, taking his wadded towel off the sink counter and stretching it out.

"Good. A nice turn-out. Long night, though," I said to my reflection in the mirror. I tapped underneath my eyes, thinking the puffiness would magically go down with a cool touch of my fingertips. It was a lost cause.

"Nice." Robert hung the towel over the drying bar. He opened his drawer and pulled out a flossing stick. He pivoted it inside his mouth, hitting all angles as I combed through my bedhead.

"Rebecca called yesterday," he expressed, jumbled words mumbling through the flossing stick in his mouth, but we are familiar. I knew all his sounds and understood it all.

"Oh?" I instantly felt like pouting. I hated that I'd missed a real call from her. I'd only spoken to Rebecca a few times that semester.

"You won't believe who Rebecca said she saw at school." Robert sweetly grinned at me. He leaned over to drop the flossing stick into the trash bin at his side. I tried to match his face and conjure up even a small smile, but a hot sensation gripped my stomach unexpectedly. I don't know how I knew this would be bad news; I just did.

Then, the floor dropped from under me.

"Tommy."

I stumbled. Literally stumbled backward as if his name alone sent me reeling into a haunted past. My vision narrowed to a tunnel. I couldn't have heard him right.

"Suzanne? Are you alright?" Robert stepped toward me, and I pushed up on the counter to gain my footing.

"I'm fine. I think my blood sugar is low," I breathed, lowering myself onto the makeup bench. I played at my falsehood, holding my temples and swirling my neck in careful circles.

"Oh, do you want me to get you ..." he offered, but I shook my head and cut him off.

"Rebecca said they have that dance class together, and he was so happy to see her. Tommy." With Robert's dreamy expression, I couldn't even pretend to match his face. "How about that?"

"How about that?" My throat was dry. My heart raced. This couldn't be happening. This could not be happening.

"And Rebecca said Janet is remarrying. Some local fisherman downstate where they're at."

Janet, I said to myself. I hadn't said her name aloud in a long time. A very long time. It conjured up every emotion: joy, sadness, loss, friendship, regret. I was suddenly nauseated. I rose slowly and moved to my sink, pretending to wash up so Robert wouldn't give me any more information. I splashed cold water on my face and took deep breaths.

"I'm happy for her," he said. Robert finished with a spray of deodorant and patted his neck with cologne. I was still hovering over the sink, pretending to wash up. "I've got to run, honey. See you later." He made a kissing sound and hustled out the door.

I picked up my head from the sink and waited until I heard the garage door open and close before I allowed myself to cry.

I waited for this time almost daily—my chance to grieve, my time to myself. If Robert was home, then it was crying in the shower. Yet, when the garage door closed, the floodgates fell. I could let it out.

I don't know how long I sat in my en suite bathroom bawling at this news. A long while. I cried until my head pounded. I did not have the brainpower to figure anything out then. There was no one I could speak with. I had to focus on each moment. First, how do I get up from this seat? Second, how do I make my headache go away? The answer to the first was to push up into a standing position. The answer to the second was to take two migraine relief pills. The rest of my morning was a fog.

Later that day, I called Rebecca. Anxiety flooded through me as I paced the floor, waiting for her to pick up. She sounded annoyed as soon as she answered. This was not unusual, but now it seemed purposeful. How do I make her happy to talk to me? I thought instantly of the necklace I helped Jason pick out. Yes, more talk of Jason. I prayed she wouldn't mention Tommy. It hurt to even think of his name.

"What did Jason give you for Valentine's Day?" I know I tried too hard with my peppy tone. I just wanted her happy. And thinking of Jason should make both of us happy.

"I'm sure you already know that," she mumbled back.

This was not good. She was already irritated and wasn't taking the road I was trying to lead her onto—to think of Jason and sweet gestures. I felt the need to keep batting for Jason and to explain why I got involved. He came to me about the necklace. He wanted my advice and to include me, but how would I put it gently?

"He said he wanted to give you something very special. Isn't he so thoughtful?"

Instead of acknowledging my question, I was hit with a testy, "Did Dad tell you I called yesterday?"

I had to steady myself before speaking, but I could not give her an inch to mention his name or their discussion. I could feel it through the other end of the phone that she wanted me to provide more information about her conversation. I had to keep talking. I wanted her to come home at that moment. I wanted to give her distance from Tommy.

I was careful with my response, "He mentioned it, yes. So, when are you coming home next? Jason said you had a test and couldn't come last weekend."

Rebecca huffed and took a while to give me a real answer. It made me anxious to hear her tone. There was so much hostility in her voice.

"I don't know, Mother. I'm really busy, and there's a lot going on."

We ended the conversation with strained responses, and I didn't feel any better afterward. No, I felt worse. My heart panged a question: Am I going to lose her, too?

CHAPTER 30

Graduation

The second Saturday in May was graduation day for my whole crew at Eastern. I should've been so happy for them all. And I was. But I also felt sorry for myself. I thought about how much I'd missed this past semester, and it nearly broke me. I'd lost my last opportunity to live with Lindsay and Amy. Of course, we would always be close, but this seemed final. And what of TJ's friends? I would see Mason, possibly Trevor, but Brandon and Freddie would probably not be around anymore.

I exited my car and walked up to the pavilion as a visitor—a guest at my college graduation. Then, I was torn about who to sit beside during the ceremony. I was invited by Lindsay's parents and Erin, her sister. But Amy's family believed they'd adopted me. I was a great influence on their daughter, or so I was told during my spring break with them. That couldn't be true, though. Amy was not bent by anyone or anything but her own will.

Yet, how would I not sit by TJ's family? They had always felt like family. Wouldn't they become my family? Now, they were here for TJ and Mason, both the first in their family's history to graduate from college. It was a momentous occasion. I could imagine their conflicted feelings celebrating each other without their fathers clapping them on their backs and grinning at the camera in congratulations. Selfishly, I imagined graduating eventually and only having my dad and Ryan there to take photos with me. A twinge in my chest made it seem more real.

I wouldn't be good company, no matter who I sat beside. I wasn't graduating. I wasn't in a current program. My timeline had so many gaps. The person I had been spending every day with lately didn't approve of the Lawsons for one reason or another. It wasn't just that. Correction: she had approved at one point. I'd read many pages of their closeness in her secret journal. I just didn't know what went wrong, and I had looked everywhere. The only clue I had was some evidence of pages being ripped out of the journal, a gap in the binding from a removed section. And a chunk of time was missing between loving the Lawsons and hating them. *Why? What could've happened?*

The more I wanted to learn about it, the more I did not. Because then what? Whose side would I take? Where would my loyalty lie?

After debating with myself for quite a while, I sat with Lindsay's family. I texted TJ to give an early congrats and an "I'm here." He let me know where to meet up afterward.

Applauding for my friends and watching as they walked up the stage steps, shook hands with the university president then marched across with a diploma was bittersweet. Amy got a piercing whistle in the stands, probably from her brother Kellen, and Lindsay walked properly with her back straight and chin out as she accepted her diploma, having achieved cum laude honors. Tears filled my eyes when Mason nodded thanks to the president, and then my heart broke when TJ smiled his broadest smile, accepting his degree.

After the ceremony, Lindsay had her family take a million pictures of her, Amy, and me. I took the quintessential picture of Amy and Lindsay. Linds with her hands balled into fists at her collarbone, eyes squinted tightly in happiness, and Amy, one arm draped around Lindsay, winking with her tongue out in a sexy grad pose.

My phone kept lighting up with messages from Katie and TJ. I couldn't explain why I didn't answer right away. I just couldn't.

After my goodbyes to Linds and Amy, I finally walked over to TJ's gathering. As expected, I was overwhelmed with emotion as I observed TJ's family celebrating together.

Janet, Howard, TJ, Katie, Grandma, Mason, Jenna, Tana, and Mason's grandparents stood in two rows in the field house, a blend of flowers, dresses, suits, graduation gowns, and caps. Everyone beamed with joy. Then TJ moved aside and took a picture with Mason, just the two of them. TJ was an inch or two taller than Mason, but with their arms around each other, they had never looked more alike. There was something about their chins and statures. Mason, sober and proud. TJ, ever like the big brother, looking out for Mason.

Jenna and Tana took photos with Mason then. Mason draped his cap over Tana's dark brown hair, and she giggled as he held her. Stunningly adorable. It took a lot for him to get this degree. Great sacrifice by his grandparents, and Jenna, supporting him with her time and love for Tana. I could, for once, see his pride and determination to be a college graduate.

Then Katie rushed forward to get a picture of just her and TJ. She angled her face and kissed him on the cheek as TJ grinned.

I'd been watching in the distance for so long that I felt I shouldn't be there or intrude on their family time. I almost turned around and headed out of the way, but I was so proud of TJ and Mason that I wanted to congratulate them. So, I took a few steps forward.

"There's Becky!" Katie called out.

I did my best to grin, but my heart was partly broken.

Several voices called me over and said, "Where've you been?" and "Oh, there she is. Thank goodness. We thought we lost you."

TJ's eyes searched mine, but it was Katie who came rushing out of the huddle and was the first to approach me.

"Becky! Where were you?" She squeezed me.

I made my way through the whole family, saying hello and apologizing for getting lost finding them, although that wasn't true. I teared up a bit, hugging Mason and telling him I was so proud of him.

Then, finally, I reached TJ's side. His eyes softened as he looked me over. He wasn't smiling.

"You ar-right?" he whispered.

I nodded because it was all I could do. Then I reached up to him for a hug to guard my face so I could push down my tears with all my might.

"Congratulations," I snuffled onto his robes, my arms wrapped around him.

"We were all looking for you," he said, pulling away from me. I could hear that I'd disappointed them. They all wanted to include me and make me feel important at this momentous event. I'd let them down.

"I'm sorry. I didn't find you guys until just now," which was only a half-truth. He had told me where they would be. I just hadn't gone there until now.

Then, I was pulled into many different arms and kissed, patted, and smiled at.

We took some more pictures with the "whole" family, as Mrs. Lawson called it, and my heart tore a little more.

Journal Entry #32 ~ Spring Breakdown

I had ruined it again. After spending a truly enjoyable day with Rebecca, it's all forgotten. We had one day of connection while shopping at the mall. I was elated to show her off to acquaintances and walk beside her. We looked at jewelry together. She tried on various articles of clothing and had never looked better, in my opinion. Rebecca has always been fit with a muscular body and defined legs from years of gymnastics and soccer, but she'd matured—come into her own.

We laughed while picking out clothes. Some of the blouses were simply ridiculous: a tan one with no shape that looked and felt like a paper bag. I offered it to her, concealing a smile. She rolled her eyes and giggled, "No, thanks."

I wished I could've bottled up that moment and kept it beside me for when I'd need it from missing her too much. I wanted to spend more time with her and make more happy memories.

Instead, Rebecca and Robert went to a ball game that night, leaving me alone. The next day, Robert attended a golf outing. I tried to welcome Rebecca back home. I tried to be open and friendly, but I didn't know how to reach out to her. I struggled to hide my awkward behavior, sure that her mind was somewhere else. She hadn't mentioned Jason at all. He hadn't phoned. Jason's mom, Brenda, thought the two of them were on a break because of another guy, claiming it was due to an "old southern friend." That equated to my worst fear coming true.

I could not let Jason get away. I believed that if Jason came over to see Rebecca, he would change his mind and apologize for this tiff or disagreement. He could pull her back with his quick wit and charm. I needed his help in winning her back. The alternative was ... not possible.

However, that's where I failed. Rebecca didn't want Jason any longer. I forced my hand, and it backfired. She surged with unrecognizable anger. I deserved it. I needed someone to scold me—besides myself.

What an odd moment, though. On one hand, as she screamed at me, I was proud of seeing my quiet girl fight. Alternately, I was gutted in an instant. Just like that, I had wrecked the last few years I had worked so hard to win her over.

CHAPTER 31

A Special Gift

I heard my mother coughing roughly in the shower. Not a normal-sounding cough, as she had been doing more often. This was worse—a gurgling barking.

I barged into her bathroom, not caring about the privacy she always wanted. She didn't have much of a choice since I'd become her caretaker.

I saw her leaning on the glass door, one hand pushed against it and the other clamped over her mouth.

"Mom!" I called.

She stumbled back. I threw open the shower door, hot water spraying the front of me, stunned shock in her eyes, her palm covered in blood.

I barely comprehended following the ambulance in my car. Or registered the doctors, explaining they would need to cauterize a lesion in my mom's right lung—not an easy procedure, but necessary.

My dad texted non-stop, reassuring me that he would arrive at the hospital late that night. He was cutting his business trip short.

Ryan showed up after a few hours, and Colleen came not long after that, releasing us from duty, so we could get something to eat in the cafeteria.

Ryan and I didn't talk as we picked over our meals. We were stuck in a well of emptiness, our drained faces filled with worry. A long while later, he looked at me with tears in his eyes.

"Listen, I never appreciated you. You know I wasn't ever good to you."

My mouth parted in disbelief.

"Ryan," I choked on his name.

"No, let me get this out." He braced his hands on the table. "I was jealous of you about everything growing up, and I missed Rachel. And Mom wasn't there. Dad was barely there. I should've been there for you." His voice broke, and he dropped his head in his hands. I watched in agony as his back moved up and down with exhausted sobs.

I rose from my spot and put my arms around his shoulders. "You're here for me now."

***

My entire body seemed to shake from exhaustion after the longest day at the hospital. I could still feel the tension from the moment I saw my mom in the shower and the ambulance and Ryan's shuddering shoulders. I somehow managed to drive myself back to our house. Once inside, I slumped down on a kitchen chair and called TJ. I had already texted him the important details.

He picked up immediately.

"Hey, Beck."

I could hear the smile in his voice, and it alone made my eyes close in peace.

"Hi," I sighed, so tired.

"Tell me anything that'll help," he said quietly.

I relived the moments of my day in revolving images. My mom, her frail, naked body, her mouth covered in blood, staggering in the shower. The rush of the ambulance and the flashing lights showing me the path to follow. The doctors scrambling to secure a procedure room, and my mother's gaunt face trying to register it all. The beep of machinery and the door swinging in and out from the nurses. Aunt Colleen's worried expression as they wheeled my mom down to surgery. Ryan breaking down in front of me.

"It was all just pretty awful," I said emotionlessly.

"I hope tomorrow is better," he said.

I loved in that second that he didn't say, "I'm sorry." It's what everyone told me. All the time. Nothing else, just "I'm sorry." I was so sick of it. Had I mentioned this to TJ? How did he know not to say it? My love.

"Well, I have a gift for you that I promise will make you smile," TJ said airily.

"A gift? Where? In Carlyle?"

"Did you come in through your garage?"

"What? Yes."

"Then, go look on your front porch. But it's not me, I swear," he quickly added.

I walked down the hall to our foyer and opened our front door. Lying on our enclosed porch was a long, rectangular box addressed to me. I was surprised at its lightness.

"What is this?" I asked, holding the phone with my shoulder and cheek as I grabbed the box, pulled it inside, and closed the door.

"Open it and see."

TJ was right. He already had me smiling.

I pulled the box into the kitchen and took a pair of scissors from the junk drawer. TJ continued to talk to me about how this was an incredible gift, and everyone would soon want one.

I cut through the tape and took out the plastic-wrapped spongy package. I cut the plastic off, and the gift inflated a little, then quickly doubled in size and length until fully expanded.

"Oh, my God," I laughed, examining my new present.

"Well?" he asked, waiting for my response.

It was a body pillow with TJ's entire form printed on it. His arms at his sides, beautiful blue eyes, a sweet smile on his face. He wore a soft-looking gray T-shirt, camo shorts, and white crew socks.

"This is adorable," I giggled.

"See? You're smiling."

I turned it around to the back. TJ had on comfy-looking shorts and a plain white T-shirt with no socks, but his eyes were closed, and he was still smiling.

I started laughing again.

"What?" he laughed.

"Okay, tell me about the backside."

"So, that's my 'sleeping side.'"

"But," I paused, still giggling. "You're smiling. With your eyes closed."

"Right. I'm next to you and probably dreaming of you. Of course, I'm smiling."

"Oh, my goodness, TJ. This is hilarious."

"So, now, when you miss me, you can hold me."

"This may be the best gift I've ever gotten," I said wholeheartedly, blinking back laughter-tears.

"Told you. Make sure you send your family and friends the QR code so they can order one, too."

"I will look into that," I chuckled again and held the pillow tighter against me.

"Sweet dreams, Beck and TJ Pillow."

Journal Entry #33 ~ Doorstep

After three weeks without any contact from my Rebecca, my heart wanted to collapse in on itself. I just wanted her home. She had made it clear that she didn't want to see or talk to me again because of my actions. I hated myself for pushing her away.

As much as I longed to make peace with her, I was paralyzed by my stubbornness, afraid she would reject me further. I resolved to give her space to come around when she was ready. Yet, she hadn't.

Robert offered to go to Eastern and speak with her. He was Rebecca's favorite, after all. Part of me knew the injustice of that. I was the one who had spent my days with her, raising her. Robert had barely been around. I had been busy keeping the household up and running. I had driven her to swim lessons and gymnastics practice. Huddled in blankets, sat on folding canvas chairs, I had watched her performances at meets and soccer games. I had ensured she was dressed, fed, and provided with anything she needed, except the most important thing: affection. Robert gave her that. Rebecca had his heart, and he had hers. That, of course, won out over everything else. That's what made me even more envious of the two of them. He couldn't help it. He was lovable and darling, whereas I was not.

Robert was finally home for a weekend, with no golf excursions or business trips. We had just gone over the plans for our primary bath remodel when I heard two quick knocks on the door.

I was not prepared for who I was about to see.

Rebecca was standing at our door like a fantasy. She looked so grown-up with her shoulders back and determined expression, but her eyes were weary. I was the reason for that. I stared into her shining hazel eyes with every bit of Robert's gold, green, and brown flecks. I could see him in her eyes, and in that moment of stunned surprise, I was never more grateful that she had more of him in her than me. I should've leaped toward her and grabbed her, pleading for forgiveness and thanking her for coming home. I didn't care then about her screaming and running from me. I just wanted to drink her in for as long as she'd let me.

"Hi, Mrs. Winslow. May we come in, please?" a deep voice broke through my stunned silence.

It wasn't Rebecca.

I shifted my sight to the person standing beside her and nearly fainted. The ghost of John Lawson stood on my doorstep.

I gaped at him, glad I didn't faint or cry out. Then I knew, as I should've, that it was Tommy. Rebecca's TJ, not John. He had his eyes, height, body structure, and blond hair, although John's hair had been more white-blonde than Tommy's golden hue.

I processed what he'd said. "May 'we' come in, please?" The "we" is what threw me. They were here together, in real life, not a decade ago when the Lawsons left town. I moved my eyes down to their hands, noticing they were folded together as a couple. It was happening. I backed away in slow motion, still in a trance, alarmed at their locked hands. I just moved aside, so they could step into the house.

The racing beat of my heart thundered in my chest. What is going on? Am I still being punished? It was as if God himself had placed Tommy there on my doorstep to remind me of my sins. I was desperate for an adult Rachel to be there and take me in her arms to tell me I was overreacting.

"Suzanne? Who is it?" Robert called, but I had lost the ability to speak. It was too much all at once for me to wrap my head around. I looked at Robert, grinning at the end of the hallway, his arms stretched wide, waiting to embrace them both.

He made it look so easy with his warm smile and extended arms. He had no qualms about the two of them side by side in our foyer. Robert was elated that they were here—together.

"Hey, Mr. Winslow. If it's ar-right with you, we'd like to talk for a little bit," Tommy announced after hugging Robert back. He glanced at me, and my stomach dropped further.

"Yes, that's a good idea," Robert declared, skimming his eyes over me.

Rebecca still hadn't spoken to me. She hadn't even looked at me. It was clear she had once again chosen Tommy over me. This time, it felt like a forever decision.

I needed to sit down, or I would pass out. I glanced at the front room and gestured to a couple of chairs. I took a breath and said with prayerful control, "Why don't we sit over here?" I kept my composure and put everything I had into my posture on that seat. I wanted to collapse but kept it together. I sat on the edge with my legs crossed. My hands were shaking, so I kept fidgeting with them in my lap.

I stole a glance at Tommy. He looked so much like his father; it was more than unnerving. He had my daughter's hand in his and sat beside her on the loveseat like they had never been apart.

When Tommy began speaking it took a few seconds to focus on his words. I forced some sort of pleasant expression on my face. My head was spinning, and my insides were swirling. I couldn't imagine all they wanted to discuss. Did Rebecca know I had kept him away from her after they moved? Did she know how much I had hoped his sudden reappearance would turn into nothing, and Tommy would just disappear again?

I caught a sense that Tommy's politeness was wilting; he was here for a reason.

"Here's the thing …" I heard him say, his tone harsh. Harsher than expected. I met his blazing blue eyes and felt his judgment. I was certain he thought I was a terrible mother and a terrible example for my Rebecca. My pulse quickened, and my stomach flipped. I moved in my seat and shifted my legs, wringing my hands together, praying that this would all just be over.

"I love your daughter, and there's nothing I wouldn't do for her."

I blinked to stop tears from slipping out. Of course, he loved Rebecca. He had always loved her. There she sat, leaning on him so tenderly. She was so full of love for him, too. It hurt so badly to see her take comfort in him, yet I understood it all.

"I know she's unhappy with how things are right now between the two of you. So, Mrs. Winslow, I was hoping you could help me out here and take some of this uneasiness from my girl." Then, he smiled at me.

How could I return his smile? I was sick to my stomach that I was in this situation again, thinking I had seen the last of the Lawsons. I forced my lips to twitch up in what I hoped was an expression of acceptance. My heart wasn't in it. "My girl," Tommy had said. She'd been his girl for as long as she'd known him. It was fitting.

I couldn't say anything. I just sat there with my frozen, plastered face, grief-stricken and writhing internally at the situation. Then, Rebecca asked to walk with me.

I took a long breath and responded, "Fine."

I was so grateful to be out of that room and away from Tommy. We walked a while on the trail, and my heart rate slowed a little, but deep *down, I felt broken.*

We talked on the surface. How could I open up to her in just these few moments? I had been hiding from my daughter my whole life. I never wanted her to see inside me, yet here she was, making the mature choice to speak with me. Again, I was thankful for that piece of Robert coming through.

I still didn't make it easy for her.

She mentioned phrases like, "I don't feel like you notice me ... the real me." She may have been right on that. I saw her as being so much greater than she saw herself. I was terrible at showing it. And I wished I could explain why it killed me to see her with Tommy. I wished I could confess how much she meant to me. A coward's answer that held some truth finally bubbled from my lips.

"We're different people, Rebecca. We see things differently."

"I know that, but how do we get past it?"

That was the problem. I didn't know how to move forward, or let her in. I wanted to be involved and hear her speak to me. I wanted her to be around and confide in me.

And then a shocking revelation: Rebecca said, with a quiver in her voice, "I'm never going to be Rachel, Mom."

I was stunned, so horribly stunned it hurt. What had I been doing? She was crying, in pain. I couldn't believe I had caused her to think she wasn't enough and that I wanted her to be Rachel. Yet, of course, I had. It's what had happened to me my whole upbringing. When you turn your back on a child, they feel as though they are not enough or that you need them to be someone else.

A crack in my heart, like a wall collapsing, rendered me only able to exhale, "Of course."

All I could do was grab onto Rebecca's hand. I hated myself for keeping her at bay and not spending every second touching her and giving in to my love for her. How stupid I was to think it would help me feel less— that it would relieve some of my constant agony. I looked at our hands together—just fingers hanging on—but that little connection gave me so much love.

CHAPTER 32

Discovery

I spent a few more nights rereading parts of my mom's journal and trying to figure out what was between the lines. My stomach turned sour as I thought of the timeline and what part could've been missing. I had a hunch about what may have happened; now, I was desperate to find the missing pages. There's no way she would've kept them. Right? If it were something bad, regrettable, probably secret, she wouldn't want anyone to know. She would have shredded or destroyed them.

I would've.

A strange intuition told me the pages were somewhere in the house. Especially if my mother liked to punish herself, which I knew she did.

My dad was at his office. My mom was at Colleen's for a bit. Aunt Colleen thought it would be good for my mom to get a change of scenery for the afternoon.

I had been in the art studio, working on a painting. When I wrapped up and was putting some extra canvases back in the closet, I noticed several boxes of files on the shelf above my head. The box was labeled "Tax Returns, Insurance Bills, and Statements." My mind spun that maybe the missing pages could be here. I spent almost an hour digging through folders, files, and random papers but didn't find anything.

I took down another box labeled "Health Insurance." Once I opened the box, I was stunned to see it filled with pictures and framed portraits of Rachel. Pictures I'd never seen. I couldn't believe what I'd found. That these ever existed. Why hadn't my parents shared these with Ryan and me? Rachel and I looked more alike than I thought.

Our hair and eyes differed, but she and I had the same chin, nose, and facial structure.

I sat on the floor and stared at one photo after the next, unable to take my eyes off them. All at once, I missed my sister. As my eyes welled up with tears, I traced her smile with my finger. I wished I knew her. My life would be so different if she were here.

I kept scanning the pictures in the box. It was big and bulky. I lifted it onto my lap and continued to sort through the photos.

"Ah!" I yelped and pulled my finger away, noticing I'd sliced it on a broken frame. I set the box down and went to my mom's bathroom for a first-aid wipe and a Band-Aid.

I rummaged through the boxes in the front of the cabinet and pulled out a Band-Aid. Then, I noticed an old, rose-colored box at the back. It didn't look like anything belonging to my mother.

Even though it was worn and drab, I was drawn to it. I grabbed the box and set it on my lap. I swabbed my finger with the wipe, peeled the Band-Aid from the wrapper, and secured it over the cut. The box was filled with old makeup and perfumes. My brow furrowed as I tried to understand what was in there. It smelled like powder and strong floral perfume. *Was this my grandma's? Why does she have this?* I sifted through some of the eyeshadows and uncovered a thick, folded wad of paper, then jerked my hand away like the paper was a flame. My breath caught at what I'd found. I unfolded the paper from the ancient makeup case.

It was the same paper as the journal with the ripped-out pages. The same off-white pages and light gold lines. This folded bit of paper had an identical tear at the top, just like the one in the journal. Part of me wanted to set it back. Just tuck it back into this case, set it down, and forget about it. I could spend the rest of my life without knowing why my mother hated the Lawsons.

But I was in too deep. I had to know. I tucked the pages into my shirt and placed everything back. I would wait until nightfall and see what she was too afraid to face.

Journal Entry #19 ~ Regret

THE MISSING PAGES

Janet flew to Nashville for her cousin's thirtieth birthday. Robert was in Singapore while I was at home, stewing in loss again. He was traveling so much that it was becoming a huge burden on me. Yes, he brought love and energy to the house and always took care of me, even when I pushed him away, but when he was on a trip, I was lost.

I had just dropped Ryan at a friend's house for a sleepover. Rebecca had been over at the Lawsons for hours. I couldn't get ahold of anyone over there, not John or even Tommy. It shouldn't have been alarming that my kid was playing at someone else's house, but John Lawson's flighty behavior made me nervous. How was he not at least answering the phone? My face flushed with worry. It was exhausting. All I could think was is Rebecca okay? What is she doing over there?

I decided not to sit at home and panic.

I drove the short way to the Lawsons, parked on the street, got out, and rang the doorbell. Nothing. Then I heard giggling and playful yelling out back. I walked down the porch steps, avoiding the scattered toys, and opened the gate to the backyard. The sun was sinking lower in the clouded sky, casting a softened pink glow over their expansive yard.

John, Rebecca, and Tommy were working at a table in the back corner of the yard where John had created a self-made carpentry area. The kids were taking turns hitting wood with hammers and laughing. I stopped moving and clenched my hands into fists. Of course, they were outside, playing with tools. What in God's name?

John noticed me then and waved. "Sue!" he called. "Come over here."

I was irritated that my five-year-old daughter was playing with a hammer nearly at dusk. More than irritated. I was angry.

John thought nothing of it, as if he were invincible.

Rebecca had a big smile on her face, but it fell the moment she saw me. Her reaction quickly spun my anger into sorrow. I always got that response from her. She was never happy to see me anymore, like I was a real-life buzzkill.

"Hey," John said again happily. I moved closer to their area now. But I was not happy, far from it, and I was so tired of pretending. Rebecca seemed unharmed, joyful even. But I didn't trust him.

"I couldn't get ahold of anyone," I said to the tabletop.

"My bad. We're making birdhouses. Right guys?"

"Right!" TJ piped up.

Katie squealed, and my eyes drifted to her sitting on a patch of grass, holding clumps of dirt, picking up tuft after tuft and throwing them in the air. She wore a little yellow top with a matching pompom in her tiny ponytail. A vision of Rachel as a baby surfaced, with her big dimples and sunny tops and dresses. How she would throw so much passion into everything she loved. Like Katie banging dolls or staring at bubbles with awe.

"Sue, are you okay?" John said in a low tone.

Every emotion must've read clearly on my face. I just stood there, lost in his little girl, wanting to go back to Rachel at that age.

"Okay, guys! Hammers down," John said. "Go get some chalk. TJ, you and Beck color these wood pieces for me, alright?"

The next thing I knew, John came around the table to stand before me. "Sue," he said quietly.

My face was frozen in emptiness as I tried to meet his eyes.

"Let's have a chat."

John disappeared into the house and came out with a bottle of bourbon and two shot glasses. He forced me to sit at the picnic table. "I see your worries are stuck. Let's air 'em out." He poured the brown liquid into the shot glasses and threw his back.

"That's what Janet would say," I said as I swirled the liquid around and around in the shot glass.

"Well, she is the brains in this family," John declared.

Rather than getting into the troubles I was wearing on my face, John confessed his woes. He and Janet were living paycheck to paycheck. He had been working odd jobs, side jobs, anything he could find. They had already purchased the campground, but he didn't know if he could afford it. Actually, he knew he couldn't afford it. It was a dream to own a campground. He had convinced Janet too easily about that. It hadn't been that hard since they all loved being outside. His family just wanted this dream to work.

I sipped at the rim of the shot, working up the courage to swallow it down. Maybe it would help. Nothing else really did.

Thunder cracked through the sky from the north, and John rushed us all inside.

John was completely self-sufficient, making pigs in a blanket for the kids to eat, along with setting out fresh blueberries. He cut Katie's meal into tiny bites and plopped her right on top of the table to eat from a paper plate.

"Should she be up here?" I asked, my words groggy on my tongue as the alcohol took effect.

"Yep, Katie's not a wanderer."

It amazed and startled me at the same time.

Shortly after their meal, Tommy ran up from playing in the front room to beg for a sleepover.

"Please, Dad! I'll go right to sleep."

"It's not up to me, TJ," he said. "That's Mrs. Winslow's answer." John pointed to me as he poured various liquids into two tall glasses.

"Puh-lease!" Tommy whined.

"I don't think so," I said flatly, my head cloudy.

"Here, you kids snuggle up, and I'll throw on a movie," John said. "And I'm making you a Long Island iced tea," he indicated to me.

He really was a jack of all trades. Changing diapers, wiping counters, nuking Pop Secret for the kids who were shoulder to shoulder, watching a Disney movie on the TV in his and Janet's bedroom. John never missed a beat or seemed bothered.

We sat at his kitchen table, and he told me about being from a small town. Sure, he loved it, but he wanted more adventure than just running the family farm. He wanted to prove himself. So far, he hadn't. John didn't ask me about anything. He probably assumed I would close down and storm away if he did. He was right.

"It's getting late," I said quietly.

"What do you guys have going on? Nothing," he asked and answered for me. "Bob's on a trip. Kids are watching shows."

"No, I should get going," I insisted, adjusting myself in my chair, about to rise.

"Just stay 'til the storm's over." John got up and moved to the hallway then peered into his bedroom. His face lit up in a huge grin. "Look at these kids, Sue. Come here." He waved me over. The three little ones, side by side by side on their queen-sized bed, all had their eyes closed sweetly, their mouths open in soft snores. It was pretty adorable.

John soon had me drinking a second one of his homemade Long Island iced teas.

"You really don't drink?" John asked.

"No. Not usually," I said, studying the brown liquid in my glass. "My father was an alcoholic," I said, startling myself. I never talked about my father. Not to Janet or my friends from Julian's. I had barely told Robert about him.

The easy expression dropped off John's face. "Well, shit," he said. "Does it bother you that I have a drink? I can put it down."

"No. I just don't want to resort to that."

He was on his third Long Island while I was still finishing the second. I barely drank alcohol. I had seen enough abuse in my earlier years with my father. This time, the liquor hit me, and instead of making me chipper or slapstick, it knocked me solemn.

I sat on his kitchen chair, assessing the drink in my hand.

"You ever tell Robert about all this hurt rolling around inside you?"

"He sees it all the time."

"I'm no therapist, Sue, but you look like you need to get rid of something. Southerners are good listeners. We run on our own clocks."

"I'm tired of feeling like this. When will I be able to cope?" I asked aloud, not expecting an answer.

John worked his closed mouth, like he was searching for something to say.

"Maybe just a little every day?"

"It's my fault," I confessed and unsheathed that knife in my heart. I had never said it to anyone.

"What is?"

"The reason Rachel's gone."

He didn't react. Just waited until I explained more. "I should've seen the signs. She had asthma. Anytime she was sick, I took extra care with her. It was Christmas, and I didn't want to ruin the day for Ryan and Rebecca. They'd had colds a week or more before that and were fine. They recovered with no problems. But Rachel was sick more than they ever were." The words poured out. "I left her with Robert to go to my sister's with the kids for a party instead of staying with her. I never should've left her. She just kept going downhill. We waited in urgent care, and I knew it was worse than they said. I should've insisted she be admitted to the hospital to monitor her. I never knew how to fight back. The medicine didn't do anything. She was so sick. I didn't know what to do. I should've made sure she had her flu shot; I should've insisted everything else was checked. Then, she was intubated in the hospital, and she never recovered. We never even had a service for her. I couldn't do it. The guilt is suffocating." My barely-held-back tears wracked my body in shivers. "It's all my ..."

"Stop it," John scolded. He put his glass down and rose from his seat,

gently lifting my elbow to get me to stand up. His blue-green eyes were liquor-filled but serious. "Nobody's judging you. You cared for your daughter. Shit, I've seen enough of you to know you probably knew everything that kid did the second she did it. Sometimes, it's just in God's hands, Sue." He wrapped his strong arms around me and pressed my head onto his shoulder.

I stared at the floor, wobbling a little, my eyes blurring in and out from the alcohol and tears.

"It never stops hurting. I'm so tired of this hurt," I cried into his T-shirt. John held me closer and swayed with me.

After a while, I felt as if I had expelled poison. The guilt of Rachel seeped out of me and left me feeling weak. I pulled my head up and peered at John, suddenly grateful for this talk. Why could I finally tell it to him, of all people? He was so insignificant in my world.

His light stubble and dazzling blue eyes were intoxicating. In that moment, washed over by alcohol, pain, and longing to be soothed, I stared too long.

A different emotion surged through me. For months, it had only been sorrow, fleeting smiles, and forced, attempted laughter that was never constant.

Finally, after months of only feeling misery, of only feeling gutted, something new and intriguing took me over. The warmth from his arms mixed with the unfamiliarity of him. A low rumble started inside me, and I parted my lips, my face flushed with liquor and heat.

Through the alcohol, I saw him recognize what was brewing inside me. His hands slowly rubbed my back as his eyes narrowed. He licked his lips and glided his hands down my arms, his fingertips tracing my skin.

His eyes didn't leave mine. They stayed and deepened. His mouth opened as his chest rose and fell faster. I moved involuntarily closer. This new ache was taking over, and I was letting it. I didn't have a single other thought going through my head.

John pressed up to me, and I could feel the length of him under his drawstring shorts. His eyes burned into me as if he would devour me. It was making me lightheaded. His hands came around my shoulders and down the edges of my chest. I let out a strangled breath, and my eyes closed momentarily.

John raised his hands to my face and cupped my cheeks. He lowered his lips to mine. His open mouth was slow and deep, tainted with stark liquor and cool, sweet lemon as I opened my mouth to invite him for more. His tongue licked at mine in heady fire, slow and deep. I melted from the inside out with need, moving my tongue over his and scraping his shoulders. A soft moan escaped my throat.

John released my face, then bent quickly, his hands on my hips, yanking me up and onto his waist. I wrapped myself around him, keeping my tongue in his mouth the whole time as he moved us to a different space, still kissing me, while the other hand closed and locked the hallway restroom door. He set me on the counter, frantically kissing and biting at my neck.

I grabbed his T-shirt, and sensing my urgency, John pulled it off in one swift movement, tossing it on the tile. His chest was solid but tender at the same time. He lifted my shirt and released my bra with a practiced move. Then his mouth was all over me. I was panting, desperate.

I fumbled for his shorts, but he moved his hands quickly and lowered them.

I scooted one way and the next to strip off my shorts and panties. Then I was exposed, fully spread with lust. John made some unintelligible sound, quickly dropped to his knees, and, with rough, calloused hands, pushed my thighs further apart. He dragged his tongue in soft, slow, torturous circles along the inside of my thighs, my breathing coming faster and faster in exquisite relief. I dug my nails into the back of his hair as his mouth set my whole body on fire. Just as I thought I could take no more, he stood up, grabbed my hips, and pushed himself deep inside me.

We both let out a yelp of pleasure. I called out again and again as he stood before me, charging in and out of my wrecked body. I strained to hold my legs out, squeezing his sides, grasping the edge of the counter with one hand to hold me against each drive of his hips.

His pace quickened as my moans got higher and faster. Then, I was completely undone with release as he shuddered inside me. It was everything I needed in that moment.

After, we were mirrors of hot breaths and rising chests.

Then, the gravity of our actions hit us like a punch in the stomach. Within the span of a few moments, I had gone from bliss to panic. All that was left in place of hunger, need, and passion was humiliation. That, and massive regret. It was all over his face when he finally managed to look at me.

Our mouths were still open, our lips dry from breathing hard. But there was no heat now. It had been replaced with cold fear.

Those beautiful, almost turquoise eyes were suddenly afraid with a question … What have we done?

John backed away, swaying and pulling up his shorts, his eyes fixed on mine, riveting through me as if looking for some way out of this.

I hopped off the counter and threw on my bra. I whipped my shirt over my head and pulled my panties and shorts on gruffly.

"I can't. I can't do this," I choked on the words as my eyes glued to the floor. I rushed out of the bathroom, darted into the kitchen, grabbed my purse from the table, and flung the strap over my head and shoulder.

"Sue …" John tried to get in my way. His voice echoed a tone I had never heard in him before. Despair.

I pushed past him and rushed to the bedroom. Their bedroom. The bedroom he shared with Janet, my closest friend. I shook my head, expelling that thought, or it would paralyze me. I pulled Rebecca up from sleep and lay her over my shoulder, biting back tears as I quickly walked to the front door. My feet fiddled with my shoes until I could step into them.

Then, I saw John's feet in front of me, yet I didn't look up at him.

I didn't know it at the time, but I would never set eyes on John Lawson again.

"Sue," his voice was thick. "I'm sorry. I'm so fucking sorry." He was crying now.

I barreled past him out to my car to get to my house. The house I shared with Robert, my husband. I opened the back seat with one hand and carefully laid Rebecca on the seat. She stirred a little. "Ma," she whined, rubbing her eyes.

I closed the door and folded myself into the driver's side, where I finally broke down, sobbing. I started the car and tore down the street. A wave of nausea from the liquor and at what I'd done hit me so hard that I screeched to a halt on the deserted street, thrust the car into park, threw open the door, and heaved right there, choking and gagging on shameful tears.

Rebecca woke up fully then with a cry. "Mom! Mom! Stop! What are you doing?"

I couldn't respond. After a few more moments, the lowest of my life, I wiped off my mouth with the back of my hand and closed the door. Then, I drove us back home.

They can never know. They can never know. I repeated the mantra to myself like a crazed person. In the days to come, I would say it over and over again. Right then, with their home in my rearview mirror, I vowed never to set foot in the Lawson house again.

CHAPTER 33

Disbelief

I slumped down to the floor against the side of my bed and wept. I didn't know what to think. Other than *how? How could they?* The shame in my heart built as I sobbed. *Did Janet know? If my mom ripped these pages out, why are they still here? Does she want to be found out? What do I do? How can I keep this from TJ? From Janet? From my dad?* I battled the same nausea my mother had all those years ago.

So many pieces were falling into place. Horrific realities filling in the unknowns like a puzzle I'd been trying to unlock my whole life. *This was why she couldn't talk to Janet.* I gripped my hair, ready to rip it from the roots, as I struggled to catch my breath.

Suddenly, a spasm clenched my gut as I saw my mother's words flash across my mind: "I didn't know it at the time, but I would never set eyes on John Lawson again."

"No," I whispered, frantic to read on and learn the worst of it.

Journal Entry #20 ~ Lies and Darkness

I was numb. I had avoided Janet for an entire week. I wouldn't see or speak to her, although she kept trying. She'd leave me text messages and voicemails:

"Want to go for a jog?"

"Hey, I'm taking the kids to the zoo. Would Becky like to tag along?"

"I've got the sprinkler running. Drop the kids over."

I ignored all requests.

One thought stayed with me daily: I don't know how to do this.

Robert needed an explanation. One moment, Janet and I were the best of friends, and then she was out of my life. I had to dig deep for the lie that would be the answer.

I told him that Janet was pressuring me. (Lie.) She kept giving me parenting advice. (Lie.) Their home seemed unsafe. (Lie.) There were saws in the backyard. (Truth, but they were put away.) The kids were always dirty. (Truth, but it didn't bother me deeply.) Rebecca caught a cold from Tommy a few weeks ago. (Lie. Rebecca caught a virus, but the Lawson's weren't sick.) I told him John was a drunk. (Lie.) That Janet confided in me that John drank all the time. (More lies.) I cried hard as I told him this, confessing that John reminded me of my alcoholic father, and he made me sick. (Lie.) I told him how my father used to hit my mother when he'd been drinking. (Lie. Yes, my father was no good, but he abused my mother with his words, never physically.)

There was no end to the lies spewing out of me. I told Robert I saw that same look in John's eyes when he drank. That it was the crazed expression my abusive father had had. (Lie. John's eyes were a gorgeous green-blue filled with humor and compassion.) How he scares me. (Truth. The thought of John Lawson scared me. He could be the end of my family and stability. He would be the face of betrayal I would see when I looked at Robert. More than anything, I was afraid of myself—that I was so loosely tethered I could just throw it all away in a vulnerable moment. I had to be better for Robert and for all of us.) I was crying so hard I almost hyperventilated. Robert reached out and cradled me in his arms, rocking me. He believed me—even though I had just committed another sin.

***

Ten days went by. I had not contacted Janet. She had been texting me less, but I quickly deleted any messages when I heard my phone ping. Rebecca was still whining about seeing her "TJ." I was coming up short on what to tell her. I signed her and Ryan up for various summer camps.

They would be swimming, crafting, and doing all sorts of activities. I hoped it would help keep her mind off him.

Tommy was too little to come this way alone, and I couldn't imagine Janet would bring him here without being invited. I hadn't been friendly. I couldn't think about it, or it would break me down. She deserved better.

Then, the phone call from Robert.

It was early afternoon, which signaled alarm bells immediately. He never called at that time. From the second the phone rang, my heart dropped. My hands shook as I picked up his call.

Robert was in his car. I could tell from the ding of the seatbelt reminder and the background noise.

"Suzanne," the tone of his voice cut through me like a blade of ice.

"What's wrong?"

"Janet just called me."

My throat tightened at this. He knows, was my first thought. My second was, oh, God, please don't let it be Tommy. Please, not Tommy.

"John's been killed."

All at once, my sidelines swirled to black, and everything turned into slow motion as I fumbled to grab the back of the dining room chair. I doubled over it.

I had yet to respond to Robert.

"Suzanne?" he asked roughly.

"Oh my, God," I forced myself to answer, covering my mouth from the cry desperate to escape.

"I don't have all the details. I'm running over there now. I'll call you soon." He hung up.

My mind swam with questions and instant grief. Why is this happening?

Hours later, Robert staggered into the house. His posture and face reminded me of the weeks that followed Rachel's death, as if a hole had opened up and everything was falling into it, while Robert could only watch in agony.

Rebecca ran over and tried to jump up on Robert. When he held onto her too long, she pulled away, concern shadowing her face. He set her down in front of him.

I was standing, legs locked in one spot in the kitchen, frozen with fear. Anticipating details I didn't want to think about kept me from rushing over to hug him. It should've hurt worse that Robert didn't come to me to hold me and tell me more.

Ryan must've sensed a problem. It was too quiet in the house. He came down the stairs from his bedroom and walked closer to Robert.

"What's wrong, Dad?"

Robert simply looked at Rebecca and turned her shoulders, squaring her to his line of sight.

"We got some bad news today."

She blinked up at him, her eyebrows crunched together in confusion.

"Mr. Lawson was in a really bad car accident, and he didn't survive," Robert's voice was carefully quiet as if he had been practicing this exchange for hours.

Ryan's mouth parted wide. Rebecca's head dropped as she processed the news more slowly. When she raised her face up to Robert, tears filled her eyes.

"I'm sorry to tell you this." Robert's jaw flexed. He was trying hard to be strong in this moment.

"TJ's dad?" Rebecca asked, her tiny voice breaking.

"Yes, honey," Robert whispered, then picked her up and held her for a long time.

Ryan just looked at me as tears ran down my face. He seemed for a second like he wanted to come over and cling to me, but he didn't. He'd learned by then that I was broken and didn't hug them anymore. That knowledge made me splinter apart even further. Ryan turned to Robert, who then switched to holding Rebecca on one arm, and rubbing Ryan's back with the other.

My mind pulled up an image of Janet, now alone with those two kids.

Katie was so young that she wouldn't have any memory of her dad. It was like Rebecca not remembering Rachel.

Robert comforted the kids for a while, then explained in a firm voice, "When Mrs. Lawson comes back up from their grandma's in a few weeks, it's our job to make sure we include them and make the kids comfortable. Rebecca and Ryan, you have my permission to go to and from Tommy's house on your bikes. Their neighbor, Helen, will be watching Katie, but Tommy is welcome here any time. Everybody understand?"

He didn't have to look my way to make me understand that this included me, too. His words were intentional. We have now been secured to the Lawsons for a very long time.

When the kids were finally asleep, Robert sat at the end of our bed with his head in his hands and gave me more disturbing news.

"He was down south visiting his family. A semi smashed into them."

"Them?" I gasped.

Robert realized he left something out.

"No, Janet and the kids are fine. They weren't there. Although his cousin Luke and his wife, Abigail, were in the car, too. All three of them died. I guess his cousin has a son about Tommy's age, and Abigail was pregnant with their second."

My mouth went dry.

"Janet said she and John were having some issues, and he went down there to help them get some space and get through things. God, it's just awful." Robert rose from the bed, walked into the bathroom, and closed the door behind him.

I stepped back and leaned against the bedroom wall, sliding down it, the tears coming in streams now. I had done this. I was responsible for his death. First Rachel, now John. He left because of me, and now, he would never come back. Then I thought of Tommy and Robert's promise to our kids about looking after him. Tommy would be here often. I turned cold, knowing I would see John's face almost every day in the form of his six-year-old son. It was to be the karma for my sins.

I didn't sleep at all that night as my mind filled with my own personal terror. I waited until Robert was sound asleep and crept across our bedroom floor. I opened the door to the hallway and walked out, inching down the steps and over to the patio doors. I went out to our backyard, cloaked in darkness except for the streetlight at the corner. I crossed the yard and climbed up the steps of our deck, feeling the chilled, textured wood beneath my bare feet. Night air prickled my arms.

I moved to the edge of the water and looked at my reflection, unable to recognize the broken woman staring up at me. Distorted by night, destroyed by my choices and my losses. I got down on my knees and pushed my face closer to the water. I wanted to see Rachel. More than anything else, I wanted to be with her.

Quiet tears rolled down my face again, and I dove gently into the water. It was shockingly cool, but I kept my body under, just wanting to sink lower, for it all to be over. I imagined Rachel's face pulling me closer. Her thin arms reaching out to me below her dark brown hair and dimpled cheeks. I saw her hooked up to machines, simulating her breathing. Her little hand, lying on that hospital bed, flinching as I grabbed it.

My body shook from lack of air, but I kept hold of Rachel's hand. I looked again, trying to see her face in my mind, but instead, I saw Rebecca's. It jarred me. I pushed up to the surface and coughed, sputtering air and water. Clinging to the ladder, with my head against the edge of the pool, my mind filled with Rebecca's angelic face, and it pulled me back to life.

Minutes later, I was dripping wet in our bedroom, touching Robert's arm with icy fingers as he startled awake. He shot up and stared at me in horror.

My eyes found his in desperation as I panted a whisper, "I need help."

CHAPTER 34

Shattered Heart

I don't know how long I sat there, holding the pages of my mother's desperation. It seemed an eternity.

I read it all again, crying throughout the whole confession on those pages. I had never known the details of her losing Rachel, and now I couldn't unsee it. Her loss rattled me to my core. I thought of Tana and couldn't imagine Jenna or Mason handling life without that precious girl.

Finally, I reread the part where my mom learned that John had died, and she wanted to die, too. Until my face. She saw *my face* in that cold water, and I was the reason she got out. It was too much to process.

My heart broke that she'd had to go through so much trauma. And now she was waiting for death to take her. For this cancer to consume her. I would protect her for the last bit of her life. I had to be here for her and give her some peace. And so, knowing my next step, my heart splintered even more.

***

I asked TJ to meet me at Lake Katherine. It wasn't exactly a halfway point, but it helped.

Although weak and a little out of it, my mom knew I was keeping something from her. My dad was home for a few days. I told them there was an in-person meeting for an art class, and I had to submit my work and pick up new materials. Dad seemed to know I was on the verge of breaking but was unsure how to help me. I kept it together enough to make it to my car on the driveway.

But in my car, with just me and my thoughts and my mother's secrets, I couldn't stop crying. I tried. I just couldn't.

Everything was shattered. I didn't know how TJ and I could get past this.

I parked near our camping spot, and when I saw him, I could not hide my expression. He approached me cautiously, and I put my hand up to stop him. He stumbled, and his lips parted, his emotions moving his throat up and down like he was swallowing something stuck halfway.

I hated this. Every single thing about it. But it would be harder to convey my message if he was touching me.

"I found out something important about my mom."

The slightest wrinkle appeared in the center of his forehead.

"Remember I asked you if you knew our parents were friends?"

One nod.

"Well, they were. Really good friends. My mom wrote about it in a journal. I've been reading it for weeks now." I chanced a glimpse at his guarded expression. "I found pages and pages of memories. Which has been great on one hand because I never really knew her well, and now," my voice quavered. "Now, I know a lot. How your mom was like a savior for us and how she helped my mom through her grief. And then there was a section missing. But I found those pages. And now I know why she's acted like she's hated you."

TJ's mouth opened like he wanted to say something but was unsure where I was going.

"But really, she just hated herself the most." I twisted my fingers together. "And I don't know how to tell you this. But I just have to."

TJ was clenching his jaw now, like he had an idea where I was heading. His nostrils flared. "Beck," he said cautiously as if his voice was a safety net he was trying to spread beneath us.

"No. Please. It's necessary." My chin betrayed my strength and quivered uncontrollably. "She wrote about this night I was over with you and Katie, and she and your dad were drinking and … "

I couldn't say the rest. I just let the silence break with my tears.

I took a second to look up at TJ. He'd gone pale, his eyes wide and mouth gaping.

"And then your dad went to Carlyle and drove with Mason's parents and … never returned." I couldn't meet his eyes now. I was talking faster. "It wasn't an affair. There was nothing there. She never wrote about him much at all. One night, they were drinking, just her and him, and she was so upset about losing Rachel, so they talked about her, and she blamed herself for Rachel's illness, and they … "

TJ's hands raked through his hair as he backed up to the hood of his truck for balance, breathing hard.

"She won't ever forgive herself. Ever. It was a terrible mistake. And she feels like she sent him away because of their mess. And that she's killed him. It all makes sense now. Every time she sees you," I cried. "She's reminded of this infidelity and his death."

He trusted me and didn't stop to question me, to say that I must be mistaken or confused. He believed me wholeheartedly, and it said everything about him. His love for me was endless. That's why this next part would nearly kill us both.

"I love you, TJ. I will love you forever. I promise you that above all. You are the only one for me. I know this so deep in my heart." I was bawling now.

"But I can't love you right now," I expelled the words as if they were toxic. The guttural noise in my throat churned inside me like I was drowning.

It was the only time he looked desperate. I was grateful for that flash in his eyes. That even though I'd delivered the worst news of my life, of his life, he'd still choose me. I was so thankful for who TJ is.

"My mom has lived with this guilt for decades, and it's killing her. She's wanted to die my whole life. And now she is. She's dying. I have to choose her while she's still here. I can't be with you while she's still alive." I was steadfast in this resolve, although I wanted him desperately. I couldn't have him now.

"I'm so sorry."

"I ..." TJ tried. "I don't." He swallowed again and tented his hands over his brows.

I found my legs and started toward my car, where I pulled the door open and almost didn't look back, but I had to.

TJ's face was panicked, pleading. "Beck," he fumbled in a voice that didn't sound anything like him.

"I love you. I'm so sorry," I choked out.

Then, I lowered myself into my car and drove off.

Fixing This

Rebecca refused to tell me what was wrong. After she went to Eastern for a class meeting, she came back completely drained. She was so attentive and helpful with me but won't give us any information to explain her demeanor. I was sure she hadn't slept, and her face was puffy and red each time I saw her. I barely noticed her on her phone. As far as I knew, she was not talking to Tommy. He hadn't called her either.

Battling sleep one afternoon, unable to get comfortable, I sat up on the side of my bed. Rebecca and Robert thought I was sleeping. Their voices carried from the kitchen. I edged my way over to the door and stood beside it, listening.

"Honey, you're not yourself. I just want to know how to help you. Can you please tell me what's wrong?" Robert pleaded.

"It won't change anything, Dad!" she cried.

Robert was quiet for a beat. "Is this about Tommy?" he asked gently.

I couldn't tell what was happening, but it sounded like Rebecca was sobbing.

"Sweetheart," Robert cooed. "What is it?"

"I just can't be with him," she said in a voice so quiet I almost didn't hear her.

"Oh, honey," Robert replied. "Did he break up with you?"

"No. I can't. Not now. I can't talk about it, Dad."

"You can tell me anything," Robert pleaded.

"I wish," she paused. "I wish things were different."

"I know, honey."

"No. You don't know, Dad. I'm gonna go for a run. Okay?"

A chair scraped across the floor. My heart shuddered, and I quietly worked my way back to the bed. I crept in, pulled the covers over my shoulder, and closed my eyes. I could hear soft footsteps outside the room, as if Robert were at the door, looking in on me. Then the door closed softly, and the footsteps drew farther away. I waited a few moments until I heard the television blast from the great room. I waited another beat before sitting up and looking at my bedside table drawer, Rebecca's voice echoing in my head, "No. You don't know, Dad." Something struck me about those words.

I leaned over, opened my nightstand drawer, and searched under the jewelry catalogs for my journal—missing.

"Oh no," I whispered, staring at the empty space and thinking of all it implied.

Then my stomach dropped while my mind landed on the pages under my bathroom cabinet. She couldn't have found those.

I got up off the bed and staggered into the bathroom. I squatted down and dug through the back of the cabinet. I pulled out my mother's old makeup case. That was the only thing she'd left behind besides Colleen and me. I couldn't stop my hands from shaking as I opened the lid. My fingers roamed through it, finding nothing. Frantic, I dumped the contents out onto the floor. The pages I had torn out were gone. I covered my mouth as a scream gurgled its way up my throat.

The blood leached down from my face as I bent forward, trying to breathe, my head on the panel of the cabinet.

My mind thumped out a beat in rhythm with my heart: Rebecca knows.

And she has ended things with Tommy because of me.

I wanted her to end things with Tommy, yet now ...

Now, my heart was broken in a whole new way. I feared the worst, that I was turning her into me, into this person who hid and broke away from love. This was worse than the surgeries, worse than the chemo, worse than grasping clumps of my hair in my hands as it thinned and shed, worse than watching my frame turn frail, and my bones jut out from my body, worse than knowing she loves him. I was certain she would choose Tommy over me.

Yet that was not my new reality. Rebecca was showing me her love and loyalty, and now I only wanted everything for her, like I never had. I swallowed hard, searching for a new strength inside me.

I scooped up the makeup, brushes, and trinkets, shoved them all back into the case, and tossed them under the cabinet. My body began protesting at all this effort, making me light-headed. I made it back to my bed and picked up my phone. I didn't have Tommy's number, but I had Lindsay's. I hit the call button. She picked up on the third ring.

"Hello? Mrs. Winslow?"

"Lindsay, yes. I need your help." I knew I sounded out of breath. I pushed my hand on the bed and closed my eyes.

"Oh my God, of course. Whatever you need. Are you okay? I mean, what can I do? Is it Rebecca?"

"Lindsay," I said, trying to catch my breath and slow her down.

"Sorry," she breathed.

"I need you to give me Tommy's number."

Long pause.

"Tommy, as in Tommy Lawson?"

"Yes, Lindsay."

"Are you sure there isn't something that I can help with?" Lindsay was a doll, but she ran her life with feelings, not facts.

"Lindsay," I repeated as calmly as I could. "Tommy's number. Please."

"Yes, right. I'm so sorry, Mrs. Winslow. Hang on a sec. I hope everything is okay. Let me know, won't you?"

Then she rattled off the digits. I found some paper and a pen in my bedside drawer and wrote them down.

"Thank you. Please do not tell Rebecca I called about this."

"Really?" Now, she seemed more panicked. "Is there anything you'd like me to tell Tommy ahead of time?" Lindsay's jittery voice confirmed my assumption that they'd discussed my dislike of Rebecca's relationship with Tommy.

"No, sweetheart. He doesn't need to worry."

I hung up with Lindsay, holding the paper in my hands. I'd been pushing my feelings back for so long. How am I going to do this? I gave myself a second to cry over the note I had scribbled with his contact information.

Fate had defied me, slapping me in the face. All the distance, the lack of acknowledgment, changing our address and phone numbers, finding someone worthy for Rebecca to love, and it still brought me here.

With trembling fingers, I tapped the digits on my phone.

"Hello?" a man's voice answered on the second ring. I was slightly startled he wouldn't let an unknown number go directly to voicemail, but I was certain he was grieving in his own way and wanting a lifeline.

"Is someone there? Hello?" Tommy didn't sound the same. There was no vibrancy in this voice. I realized I hadn't spoken.

Just as I thought he would hang up, I breathed out, "Tommy, this is Suzanne Winslow. I was hoping to talk to you." I tried to speak without emotion, but I collapsed into painful tears that had built up for decades.

I could hear him breathe in. "Mrs. Winslow." He cleared his throat.

He was probably struggling with what to say to me. I didn't deserve his forgiveness, but I had to get through my thoughts quickly.

"I ..." I tried again. "I would like you and ..."

After a raspy breath, the coughing started, doubling me over. I pulled up a pillow and covered my cough with it so that Robert wouldn't come to investigate. My chest rattled, and tears seeped from my eyes. I squeezed the pillow tighter and coughed violently into it. When I pulled it away, I almost expected to see blood soaking into the cloth, but thankfully, there was none. I took in a strained breath.

When I put the phone back up to my ear Tommy was addressing me, his voice heightened. "Mrs. Winslow, is anyone with you? Where's Beck? Should I call an ambulance for you?" He sounded as though he'd moved into a different space; it was louder there.

"No," I got out, barely able to catch my breath. I clutched at my chest, feeling the ache that Rachel must've felt while struggling for breath. I had to keep trying. "Please," I breathed. "I would like for you and Janet to please come see me. There's a lot to be said. Please." I glanced at the door, hoping I had a few more seconds before Robert came to check on me.

Tommy was quiet for what felt like a full minute. I wondered if I'd lost the connection. I heard the creak of our hall floorboards and was about to end the call. Then, his low voice, "Ar-right. Just tell me when."

CHAPTER 35

Perfect Timing

Two weeks after confronting TJ, I had a peaceful afternoon of warmth and sunlight, which evaporated my tense mood. I was weeding the garden and planting flowers in pots along the front of the house and on the edges of the patio in the backyard.

Why hadn't I enjoyed a task like this more often? It really suited me. And it suited my mom. Quiet in the sun. Nothing but flowers and fresh scents in my proximity. It was therapeutic. I needed that. It was better than crying alone in my bedroom or in my car or in the shower. I was still waiting for a sign that TJ and I would be okay. We would make it through this, right?

The "we" part was the difficult word now. If the "we" was me and TJ, then I wasn't certain. How could he forgive my mom? How could he ever want to be part of my family? How could he ever look at me and not think of this stain connecting our families? Yet, I felt like I knew the answer because it was TJ. I knew he would still choose me. He had the whole of my heart, and being without him for two weeks, without even a text to him, was awful. But, without him, indefinitely was death. I'd been dreaming about seeing his sweet face turn up in some unexpected place. My arms wrapping around him. It was painful without him. As painful as these days had been watching my mother's cancer torment her, it was equally awful not having TJ here.

If the "we" related to me and my mom, it was beyond our control. I felt her become weaker. The deep brown of her eyes looked almost black now. As if the cancer itself had taken over the color of her irises. She was uncomfortable all the time and made these little moaning sounds that I feared would be the last sounds she uttered.

When I watched her fitfully sleeping, I could see the struggle for survival and the pull of peace.

I'd seen a change in her attitude toward me for a few weeks. She wouldn't fight me on anything. She complied with all my requests and wanted me around constantly, like she was buttering me up for something.

She had given in to me partly about sharing her life stories. With my only chance of getting to know her before she was gone growing slimmer, I did my best to get her talking. Our connection intensified; I knew her better than I ever had. It still didn't help. Because although she was making time for me, she was still choosing death. Living with her guilt has killed her slowly over the years. Living with the daily grief of losing a daughter she hasn't let go of has aged her, too.

I couldn't give her the forgiveness she was desperately seeking. That she had to give herself and get from my dad and the Lawsons. But it didn't appear she would ever forgive herself.

Lindsay called me, and I opened up as much as possible about what was happening with me. She was already back working at the daycare in Naperville for the summer in between interviews for full-time teaching jobs. One interview went incredibly well, and she wanted to take me to dinner to celebrate and complain about the daycare. I opened my mouth to voice my hesitancy at leaving my mom, but she said she had already talked to my dad, who would be home to care for my mom so I could take her to the Cheesecake Factory. She really needed a giant slice of turtle cheesecake after the week she'd had with her group of pre-K kids at the daycare. The cheesecake would be good luck for her job chances. Lindsay was such an adorable and predictable friend. Our relationship grounded me. She was so full of life and energy that she barely came up for air when she told her stories. I couldn't lie. I needed that.

Lindsay drove us to the Cheesecake Factory. Once we had sat down and placed our order, she turned on her comedy act, which was just Lindsay being herself.

"In case you were wondering if I had my first pee-er, it's a yes! A big, damp-panties 'yes' from me!" Lindsay practically shouted.

I covered my face with my hands and tried to smother my laughter.

"Oh, and not a discreet little, 'Hey, Miss Kelso, I just leaked in my underwear a little. Can I go to the potty?' But a river of piss sitting on the little plastic seat, dripping onto the floor and soaking into tight, pink leggings!"

"Oh no." By now, I was open-mouth smiling. "That's not good."

"No, it is not. Tell me why I wanted to work with children again?" She probed my face for an answer.

"I really don't remember. Summers off?" I guessed.

"No, definitely the parent conferences and the money. For sure." She put her head on the table dramatically.

"Of course, I'm teasing. You are the sweetest, Linds. You are warm and fun and super good with kids. You will be the best teacher. You will absolutely get a call back about your interview. Just think of the good stories you'll have now! And I thought the teaching gig was getting better?" I asked.

"That was student teaching in a school. A controlled setting. Now, I've realized I'm working with kids who are too young. I need, like, third graders. They wipe their own noses, read their own stories, tie their own shoes, and go to the bathroom in an actual bathroom. You know? But I'll still get coloring pages about how much they love me." Lindsay wiggled her shoulders confidently. "I have to get this job so I can quit the daycare."

"Because," Lindsay continued, "the puking and peeing and these little people can't walk down a freaking hallway without molesting the walls. Literally. There's like one kid, Rebecca. When we walk down the hall at the daycare to go to the playground, she's in the front of the line with her cute little pointer finger pressed against her lips and walking like a normal person. Everyone else is a turd. Wall hugging, running in the hallway with scissors, turning around and slapping each other, and stepping on other kids' feet. Turds. Ugh. I hate everything," she whined.

I raised my glass to toast her. "Same," I said, trying to keep the mood light. Then, I took a sip of my wine.

But Lindsay knew me too well. "Oh, crap ... " Her eyes clouded over, trying to avoid the emotion surfacing on the table between us. "I don't know what to say."

I studied the stem of my glass, thinking I didn't know what to say, either. I hadn't graduated alongside my best friends, I didn't know when or how I would continue my education to get a degree, and I'd basically told the love of my life I couldn't choose him until my mom was dead. Either way, my life was in ruins.

"I think there's still hope. Somehow, right? And I don't hate everything. I don't hate you."

"I don't hate you, Linds. I'm so grateful for you."

"Damn it." She raised her glass to her lips and started to cry.

***

When we arrived back at my parents' house from Lindsay's dinner date, I was nearly overcome with shock. TJ's truck was parked along the street in front, glowing in the setting sun's light.

"Oh, my God," I uttered, my eyes glued to TJ's truck. My stomach fell a foot at once. *What is happening?* I scanned the windows of his truck, but he wasn't inside. *Is he here to talk to my parents? When did he get here? What is happening inside my house?* I was frantic.

My breaths came out in little puffs as I stole a glance at Lindsay, thinking she had to be stunned as well. But she was sitting cool as could be, thin lips upturned.

"Wait." I gawked at her. "What's going on? Did you know he would be here?" My eyes popped in amazement.

"I'm a teacher. It's my job to know a lot," she proclaimed with a confident smirk.

My mind was playing catch up to my heart. *He's here. Did my mom know he was coming? Is she falling apart in there? Did he know I was out of the house when he got here?*

I was still lost, but it didn't matter. TJ was here. My desperation to see him was so great that I was about to crawl out of my skin. I shot Lindsay an expression asking if I could bolt from her car.

"So, the dinner?" I asked, my hand resting on the door handle.

"A delightful and somehow perfectly timed meal. Wouldn't you say?" Lindsay scrunched her forehead, purposely not looking my way.

"What is going on?" I asked, my heart fluttering in my chest.

"My part is over," Linds admitted, smiling at me. "Go. It's all okay. I promise. You'll call me later. Love you!"

I flung open the passenger door and bounded up the front walk.

I stood just outside the door and paused for a second. TJ and I had had some intense moments not that long ago. Not a car-buying moment or an I-just-signed-up-for-fall-semester moment. How does one move on from life-altering news? *My mother had sex with your father, and because of that, he left town and was killed in a horrific accident.* Of course, she didn't cause the car crash directly, but that event put him on that path.

I couldn't think any more about that. If TJ was here, and Linds was in on something, it had to be good for me. Lindsay wouldn't have been so calm. She was terrible at hiding anguish.

The thought of him in there talking with my mother was alarming. I had no way to prepare her or my dad for this. God, how I wished so badly that TJ would be himself. Not unhappy. Not regretting hearing about his dad. I hoped he'd still found a way to see his dad in the light that he always had: fun-loving, energetic, devoted. I hoped so desperately that it didn't derail him from being himself. I wanted him to be fully who he always was and crazy in love with me. I sent that last thought into the universe. Then, I took a deep breath and opened the door.

CHAPTER 36

Invitation

Nothing was amiss immediately. I didn't hear any shouting, not that I would guess that. Yet, I could make out voices from the living room past the foyer and to the right. My feet were heavier now. I crept toward the voices—soft, no laughter.

I had just planted my foot into the living room when TJ turned around from a chair that had been placed to face my mother. My dad was sitting on the arm of the couch beside my mom. Mrs. Lawson sat on the other side of my mom, and my mother was sitting up and wide awake for once.

That was my observation in an instant. My mouth opened and my eyes almost failed me as TJ rose from his chair, a panicked, hopeless expression and something else on his face. Desperation, maybe?

"Beck," he breathed and then cracked a barely-smile.

"Hey," I answered back, stealing a glance at my mom. She didn't look surprised to see TJ or me.

TJ all but raced toward me and wrapped his arms around me. In an instant, everything was peace. Just TJ. That was all I needed. The scent of him, the warmth of his soft skin on his firm body. His hair dangling lightly over my left ear as we clung to each other. He told me everything I needed to know in that one embrace.

His breathing steadied, and we swayed together to the pace of it. He repositioned his arms, making them tighter around me. I wasn't sure who made a noise outside our embrace, but when we pulled back a little, I could see TJ's gorgeous blue eyes hooked on mine.

"I love you so much. Nothing's ever going to change that." He put his hands on either side of my face. "I'm sorry if I didn't make you realize that. Even for a second."

"I love you," I gasped as he stared at my lips. "No sorries, please. Are *we* alright?" I willed him to know how much I needed us to be okay.

"We're better than ar-right Beck." Then he bent down to kiss me once on the lips.

TJ let go of my face and stepped back, his lips twitching in a brief smile as the rest of the world stirred, and we realized we were not alone.

A moment of silence echoed in the room. TJ took my hand, and as if explaining what was happening, he walked me over to the living room and the ominous hospital tray covered with water bottles, tissues, pill cases, and an ice pack. Extra bedding and blankets mounded in a basket next to the tray. Mrs. Lawson came over to us with a tight grin but true warmth in her eyes.

"Becky, sweetie," she said, wrapping me in an embrace for so long it seemed we would start dancing.

When she finally did let go, I thought I'd see her teary-eyed, but she just inhaled deeply. My eyes flitted to my mom. Her expression had changed. Something new was under the surface.

"Did you have a good dinner, honey?" my dad asked in a tired but cheerful voice. He pushed off the side of the couch and walked over to hug me, too.

"It was great," I said, a lilt in my mood. "Lindsay is entertaining."

My dad gave a snuff of a laugh, "She's a wonderful friend."

The stillness in the room closed in on me as uneasy questions bounced around in my head. *Why are they all here? What is going on?* An intervention was about to begin. Or maybe had already happened. All the cards were on the table now. In a moment of horror, I half expected to see my mom's journal splayed out in front of everyone.

"What's exactly … " I started.

But then my dad said, "Tommy, let's leave these gals to have some time together." He motioned to TJ to head back through the foyer with him.

TJ nodded, kissed my cheek, and followed my dad into the hall. I watched him walk away as my dad put an arm around his shoulder. I loved the look of the two of them together.

I turned back toward my mom and Mrs. Lawson.

"Mom?" I asked. So much was implied from that one word, spoken like a plea.

"Your mom asked us to come up here. Tommy and me," Mrs. Lawson began.

I stared at Mrs. Lawson, sure, I'd heard wrong. "What? How? I ... I don't understand."

Mrs. Lawson glanced at my mom.

"You know why," my mom whispered. Shame clouded her eyes. "I asked Janet and Tommy for forgiveness. I asked your dad for forgiveness as soon as I could."

"You ... ? Dad knew?" I asked, not believing.

"Yes. He's known for a long time."

A huge weight slid off my shoulders.

"And we talked and hugged and ... " Mrs. Lawson added, then closed her mouth to stave off her tears. "John and I talked before the car accident. All was forgiven then. I forgave you both years ago, Suzanne. And it's alright now, Becky." Mrs. Lawson grabbed my hand and my mom's hand.

I was trying to put the pieces together. My mom had reached out to them. She somehow knew I'd found the journal pages; that was the only explanation. And she'd asked them for forgiveness.

I swallowed back my tears as I took in her face.

"Rebecca, I'm sorry for all of this. And I'm so sorry to you, Janet. You deserved a much better friend than you got," she told us both in the softest voice. She was so depleted as her eyes softened into a lazy stare. A new worry that time was running out hit me.

"Mom?" I asked, with no question in mind.

"I think she needs to rest a bit, right, Suzanne?" Mrs. Lawson cut in.

"Yes."

"Why don't you and Tommy catch up, sweetie?" Mrs. Lawson winked at me. "I'm gonna keep my long-lost friend company."

My mom gave us the briefest smile and put her head back onto the couch cushion.

CHAPTER 37

An Answer

"Come with me. I've got something to show you." TJ grinned mischievously. Knowing him, it was probably something weird or completely normal, like a plate of crackers and cheese he had arranged for me, and he was just trying to be funny and grab my attention. I took his warm hand and followed him out the patio doors. By now, the sun had set and the few lights circling the lake set off a soft, yellow glow. A cozy fire crackled in our fire pit, surrounded by the plush patio furniture.

"Oh, this is great." I nodded toward the fire and put my arm through his.

"It gets better," TJ smirked as he moved us past the fire pit onto the wide expanse of the yard.

"What? Marshmallows, too?" I asked playfully.

"A little better than that," he admitted.

Then he clicked a button on a small remote I hadn't realized he'd fished from his pocket, and at once, his favorite tent was illuminated on the side of our yard in beautiful white, twinkling lights.

I stopped moving as my mouth hit the ground in awe. TJ jogged a few more steps ahead but turned to see my shocked face. He didn't say anything.

"Oh, my God." I smiled.

"Pretty cool, huh?" TJ nudged his head toward the tent.

"Really cool. You are so adorable." My eyes found his, and sweet love poured out. I strolled closer to him and draped my arms around his neck. I kissed him softly at first, then deeper. He opened his mouth to mine and pulled me closer to his body. We kissed like that for a few moments until he broke away and studied me.

"Are you ar-right with everything in there?" TJ tilted his head toward the house. His eyes burned through mine.

It was all moving so quickly. I barely had time to process things. But yes. I was so grateful that the Lawsons were reconnecting with my mom. I felt relief for her that this terrible secret was finally cast out from her memory and into the reality of those willing to forgive it.

I nodded at TJ, then fought to find what I needed to see in his eyes. He took in a deep breath. "Are you?" I asked the loaded question: *Are you able to really forgive her for everything? Forgive your dad, too?*

"It'll be ar-right now," he said quietly. Then his mouth found mine again. That kiss was a promise in itself. TJ kissed my forehead. "There's still a better surprise." He shyly smiled at me and motioned toward the tent.

"I don't know if *that* will be a surprise. A treat, maybe." I raised my eyebrows at him.

"No, you'll see."

He had the two sides of the front zipper rolled up and fastened in loops, presented like a gift. He grabbed my hand, let me crawl into our childhood tent, and then crawled in after me.

Inside the cozy interior TJ had somehow fit a soft, thin mattress. It was covered with the most comfortable plush cotton sheets and blankets ever, like a luxury hotel bed.

"This is awesome," I cooed gleefully, moving slowly along the blankets toward the back edge of the tent, where king-sized pillows in soft white linens padded the tent wall. It was easy to navigate because of the dim light coming through the tent fabric from the outside lights

TJ had strung up. I was about to lie back when TJ said, "Hold on. There's one more surprise, but sit still for a sec." I turned to face him as he fidgeted.

"Okay." I smiled, settling myself to face him.

TJ took a breath and clicked another button, extinguishing the lights on the outside of the tent. We sat in darkness for a moment until I heard another click. Fewer lights flickered, this time on the inside of the tent at the peak and on the edges of the clear, plastic dome that showed the sky.

I smiled up at the lights, imagining his efforts to get every detail just right. How he'd tried so hard to make this reconnecting time so special for us. So sweet. Then, my eyes adjusted to the dim lighting, and another shape came into view. One small string of lights dangled directly from the center of the tent. I followed the length of it to the end, and my eyes caught on an object as my lips parted in stunned silence.

A diamond ring.

I stared at it.

Just stared at it. It had to be at least a two-carat round, brilliant stone on a band of white gold and an eternity band of tiny round diamonds. I couldn't breathe. I looked back at him, unable to read his expression right away.

"So, I was thinking," he started, then shifted his weight on the mattress. "That if I had to envision my life from now on, in any moment, I see you in it."

Impossibly, my mouth dropped open ever further. Now, at least, my head was catching up, and my heart was starting to understand this moment. He was proposing to me. *TJ is proposing to me. In his tent. In our tent.* I didn't want to ruin the moment by crying, but tears were brimming on my eyelids, so I closed my mouth tightly, thinking that somehow that would help to trap the tears inside.

"I had this really awful moment when I understood what you told me about my dad. It scared me to think that I may not have explained how strong my love is for you. Scared that I hadn't genuinely shown you what I meant. Beck, I will *never* give up on us." He took my hands, and I couldn't hold the tears in anymore. I opened my mouth and let out the breath I was keeping in.

"I have loved you since I ran into you on the sidewalk when I was five years old." He smiled slightly. "I have never stopped loving you and *only* you. No matter what, I will never stop feeling this love for you." He squeezed my hands a little, and I blinked some tears away as I lost myself in his impossibly blue eyes.

TJ let go of my hands and sat up on his knees to reach up toward the ring. My heart kept pounding in disbelief.

"This doesn't have to be now, this year, next year, or in three years, but I'm absolutely sure about you." He smiled big. "You are bright and patient and passionate and gorgeous and sweet and lovable and talented beyond belief and so strong. You are exactly what forever looks like, Beck."

I let out a teary gasp and touched my lips with my fingertips. Then I leaned forward and kissed him once. He touched his forehead to mine and we both took in a breath.

"So, I have a question for you." He backed up again and searched my eyes. "Will you marry me?" I didn't even reply; I just crushed his mouth with a kiss and wrapped my hands around the back of his head, pulling at the tufts of his soft hair and pushing hard kisses onto his lips.

TJ pulled away and brought the ring closer to me, so it sparkled between us. He was momentarily lost for words, his mouth working, swallowing.

"I had a little help selecting the ring," he whispered.

My whole body froze. My mouth hung agape, and my eyes were a heart-wrenching question. TJ's jaw clenched to keep his emotions in check.

"I know she wants to see it on your hand before ... " his voice trailed off, and he cast his eyes down, inhaling deeply.

Then, I was limp with emotion. I gave a shuddering cry and threw my arms around him, sobbing onto his shoulder. It was the most meaningful moment of my life. What had he done to finally win her over? How had they both kept this from me? The overwhelming sense of love was astounding. *My mother helped him with my ring. My engagement ring to TJ. Giving her approval in a way I didn't know she could or would ever do.* It was perfect.

TJ held me like a fragile piece of art. Gentle and protective. He kissed the top of my head, and I tried so hard to stop bawling on him. But it hit me that I had finally made progress with her. And now she was checking out. I couldn't let this happen. I had to convince her to keep going.

"Ar-right. So, do you think I could get an answer sometime?" TJ asked sweetly.

I laughed into his shoulder, then dabbed my eyes with the end of my sleeve before pulling back enough to say with all my heart, "Yes, TJ. I will absolutely marry you."

He gave me the proudest smile and kissed me again. Then he slid the exquisite ring onto my finger with a satisfied sigh.

CHAPTER 38

Fight for Me

After I composed myself to the best of my ability, TJ and I crawled out of the tent. The lights from inside reflected on my new, favorite piece of jewelry, decorating my finger. I had a feeling I wouldn't be able to tear my eyes off it for a while.

We entered the great room and found my dad and Janet talking quietly.

Janet grabbed a tissue from a box on the end table. She dabbed at her eyes and cheeks.

My dad was the first to notice me. His bright smile was all the confirmation I needed to know he was happy with our engagement. As I imagined, he quietly walked over and hugged the both of us for so long that it brought my tears right back up to the surface.

He took a tiny step back and, with a knowing smile and glistening eyes, turned to me first, then TJ. My new fiancé smiled so sweetly at my dad.

"Congratulations," Dad said. He kissed my cheek and hugged TJ again.

"Thanks, Mr. Winslow."

Mrs. Lawson rose from the sofa and put her hands over her mouth.

"Ah," she cried softly and hustled over to us. She had no words but was a complete mess of tears. TJ actually shook his head at her, softly laughing. She kissed him about ten times and then squeezed me. She rocked us side to side repeatedly, then grabbed my left hand for confirmation and squeezed me again.

"Love you," she said to the both of us and patted TJ's face.

"Love you," TJ said.

"Love you," I said.

I looked at the couch, but my mom wasn't sitting there.

My dad saw my eyes sweep the room. "She's lying down in bed," he clarified.

I knew she needed rest, but I needed to see her and have her be part of this moment. I walked down the hall, touching my ring the whole way. I gently pushed the door open and entered my parent's bedroom.

She wasn't sleeping, but her body was so completely calm in a way I'd never seen before, like a lifetime of regret had lifted off her shoulders. Seeing me, my mom suddenly gave me a tear-filled smile. I rushed to her.

"Mom," I breathed out, leaning over her. It was an answered prayer as it released from my lips. This was the first time she felt truly like the mom I'd always hoped she'd be. I carefully placed my head on her blanketed chest as I cried into the duvet.

She petted my hair with one trembling hand while the other cradled my left hand, fingering the ring. "It's beautiful," she commented.

I pulled my face up to meet hers.

"Thank you for your blessing. Thank you. It's all I wanted." And I knew in these words, it was not just about TJ. It was as if she finally saw me.

"I love you, Rebecca. And you're right. This is best for you. I'm so sorry I've been so awful to Tommy." She looked at me earnestly. "I'm so sorry. Do you forgive me?"

"I do. If you forgive yourself."

She stared at me.

"Mom, you messed up. You did. And it was a horrible lapse in judgment from a grieving mother with her heart torn to shreds, just trying to exist. But you didn't kill John. And you didn't kill Rachel. I'm sorry that happened. I am. And I'm sorry that you couldn't give me your whole heart. But I'm sorrier that you are giving up and killing yourself. When are you going to finally forgive yourself? Because we all do. Except you. Can you forgive yourself, finally?"

She appeared to stare through me, thinking of all this question implied.

"Okay," she said at last.

My mom attempted a smile, but I saw something else on her face that made my pulse spike. She was giving up. That's what the peace was. I sat up and took both her hands in mine.

"Good. I have one more thing I need from you. Fight. Fight for me." I flared my nostrils and made my eyes power through the tears.

She pulled in her lip and closed her eyes.

"What is it going to take, Mom, for you to fight for me? Don't you get it? I want you here. I finally need you here. Rachel's had you all this time. You haven't been alive for me, but I want you here now. You aren't checking out, not when we've come farther in the last few months than the last twenty years, Mom. I'm not letting you choose this path. We are going to figure this out. There are treatments. Experimental trials. Other chemo. There are options."

She looked up at the ceiling as if battling between Heaven and Hell.

"I need you." I tugged her sleeve a little. My voice was breaking, but I kept going.

"I need you to *want* to fight for me. Rachel is just going to have to wait longer," I cried as she shuddered in grief. "I will do anything you need to help you, but you aren't giving up." I shook my head as if that would obliterate the idea.

"It might be too late," she whispered, trying to impart the truth into my eyes. "I don't think I can do this."

I heard what she said, but I was so confident then that anything could be mended. This lifetime of hurt between Janet and my mom was healing. My dad, who had never stopped loving my mom for a second despite everything, had forgiven her. And TJ. He was still here to love me beyond all this. That and she had me. I wasn't giving up.

"I don't think it's too late. And we're going to fight together and find out."

Epilogue

Six months later, the January winter is upon us again. I am standing at the podium next to Ryan, who is wearing his best suit. I am in a yellow dress with a navy sweater covering my shoulders. We are just about to start. My eyes take in the scene before us. Pictures cover every square inch on the wall in this funeral parlor. Pictures of Rachel, Ryan, me, my dad, and my mom.

Aunt Colleen is here with Jim, Carly, and Jeremy. My dad's sisters and their kids have made long treks for this occasion. Pilar's and Ryan's co-workers are here. My mom's jewelry friends are here. Lindsay and her whole family are looking at pictures around this space. Amy is sitting in the back with Trevor and Cassie. Taylor and her girlfriend are here. The art friends I've become close with these past months are here, too. Along with Professor Bahnimin and my art professor from my new college, the University of Chicago.

All the Lawsons are here: Janet and Howard, Grandma, Katie, and Sarah. Mason is here holding Tana on his lap with Jenna beside them.

But the most important attendant is sitting directly in front of me in a yellow cardigan sweater with a floral scarf tied loosely around her head. She is flanked by my dad, her right hand linked in his, and TJ, who is holding her left arm securely.

My mom.

At the front of the parlor is a huge, painted canvas of Rachel—a painting I made for my sister's memorial service.

My mom has a strange, peaceful look on her face. I think about how far we've come. I've never been prouder of her than in this moment.

I am so proud of myself, too. About how I worked so hard to get to this point. I am proud to be Rachel's little sister. I feel a connection to my sister that I never had. I am proud of how I convinced my mom to tell me everything about Rachel over the past six months. How my dad and Aunt Colleen have told me so many stories. They shared videos. They searched for every single photo of her. And we printed all of them.

Ryan and I explained to our parents that Rachel needed a funeral. That she deserved to be celebrated, remembered, and properly put to rest. That Ryan and I deserved to pay respects to our sister. That was one more thing my mother needed to forgive of herself.

"Before we begin, Ryan and I would like to thank you all who have made time for this celebration of life today. We appreciate each one of you for being here. Some of you have traveled a long way (my eyes slid to my father's side of the family and TJ and his family), and some have been close all along (I winked at Lindsay). Thank you for your help with this tribute," I said.

"We are here to celebrate and honor the life of our sister, Rachel James Winslow," Ryan said in a dignified voice.

"Eighteen years ago, was a horrific day for our family when Rachel passed away. She had asthma and a compromised immune system. She caught influenza, and that destroyed her body, leading to pneumonia and, ultimately, her death. Our family was so broken at the loss of this energetic and charismatic girl that we never quite coped with it. We never paid her the tribute she deserved. It was too soon and too hard. And it's still hard, especially for my parents. That loss will always resonate in their hearts. But, we have now come together as a family to showcase her."

"Rachel was feisty," I said. "She was opinionated and independent. She loved to sing. Usually at the top of her lungs. She was into Disney princesses and loved girly things like Barbies and colors like yellow, light pink, hot pink, purple, teal, and silver. Pretty much every color, but definitely yellow."

"She had my dad's dimples and my mom's eyes, but her smile was all her own. You usually had to work to get it, though. She didn't give it out easily," Ryan said.

"She loved shopping with Aunt Colleen and loved jewelry most of all. She would sneak into my mom's closet, put on every necklace and bracelet, and then walk around in my mom's heels like she was on a runway," I said.

"She made friends easily. Probably because she was so bossy," I explained. "She forced everyone to be friends with her. She loved being part of her dance school and was a leader in the class. Rachel danced all the time. She would make up routines and perform them for her stuffed animals."

Ryan continued, "She was oddly afraid of puppets. Especially Muppets like Kermit. The eyes creeped her out or something." Soft laughter resounded at this. "She was terrible with pets. She killed three fish within days of receiving them. She wanted a guinea pig until she realized how much they pooped and then didn't want one and returned it." The crowd collectively chuckled at this. "She loved being a big sister. She preferred me over Rebecca," Ryan said and side-eyed me with a grin as I shook my head. "She used to read to us on her bed with me on the right and Rebecca on her left, closer to the wall so that she wouldn't fall off. She liked taking care of others."

"She was gone too soon. But she is not forgotten," I said. "We have given everyone a bracelet for attending. These are the bracelets my mom and I spent weeks assembling. Each comes with a poem and the lyrics to Rachel's favorite recital song. One lesson we have all learned as a family is that life is precious. We don't know the path or the reasons. We can't dwell on those what-ifs." I gave TJ a look as he held me up in pride. "But we know to leave ourselves open to loving each other and loving ourselves. We will see you again, Rachel. But please be patient. Our work down here isn't done yet. Right, mom?" I eyed her meaningfully.

She beamed at me from her seat.

My mom has been on an experimental treatment for over five months now. The tumors are stable. They are not shrinking, but they are not growing. There have been no new tumors for months. My mother has no hair, no eyebrows, and no eyelashes. Her breasts have been removed. She's thin and frail and has an odd brown tinge to her complexion. Her eyes are darker than they used to be, but somehow, a miracle has happened. In spite of that darkness, her eyes are alive with hope. She is more beautiful today than ever.

The quality of her life has improved. She looks like someone trying to beat this. Like she is content to be herself. Like she is finally willing to fight again. She looks like my mom.

THE END

Author's Note

Writing is such a personal journey. In one aspect, you can create a whole world of fiction with ideas from the edges of your imagination. You can pull readers into a fantasy, feed them lies, and make them into believers. On the other hand, I find it impossible to write a story completely void of my experiences, my path, and my people. And for this story, I especially thought of my mom.

My mom, Barb Sansone, passed away in 2018 from renal cell cancer after living most of my life with cancer. She was diagnosed when I was eight years old, had surgery to remove her kidney (which was encased in a tumor), and lived another fourteen years before the same cells were found in her lungs. My mom endured twenty more years with that cancer in her body before it eventually spread to her brain and, at last, took her from us.

We found out my mom's cancer had spread when I was 22 years old—roughly the same age as Beck in this story. It was important to me to give Beck more time with her mom, so that she could know this other side of Suzanne, the vulnerable, motherly side.

When I was a child, I think I was largely overlooked. I had two older brothers and an older sister, who all got good grades in school and seemed to please my mom at every turn. But I was the baby. I don't think I had the same expectations set before me. I didn't perform as well in school and sort of marched to the beat of my own drum. I knew I was loved and taken care of. I just didn't ever feel that I impressed my mom, as my siblings did.

I also don't recall knowing my mom that well as a child. I think about my children and what they must've thought of me when they were so young. If they thought of me at all. At four years old, my son literally told his preschool teacher that I was a "dishwasher" (rather than a classroom teacher) because of how often he witnessed me cleaning and cooking and doing dishes each night. He didn't see all that I was. He was just a boy who noticed his mom was tired each night from parenting, teaching, being everything. I didn't see certain pieces of my mom when I was young. I never inquired about her life, her goals, her hardships.

As I grew to be an adult, my relationship with my mom grew as well. When I got my first teaching job, I could feel all the love and pride she had for me in a new way. My mom became my biggest cheerleader. She offered to be my teacher's assistant every Friday in my elementary school classroom. She baked homemade sugar cookies, chocolate chip cookies, oatmeal raisin cookies, brownies, Rice Krispie Treats, and kolaches, and made JELL-O jigglers for my students and the school staff. She helped to run my little classroom store, teaching the kids to count their Mrs. Janes' money and even giving advice about when to save for something better. She showed up for our dinosaur museum when some of my students had no one in attendance for them. My mom was the devoted and loving grandparent for my students who didn't have a stable family life.

That time in my classroom was so incredibly special for us. After years of living in the shadows of my older siblings, I could finally show my mom that I excelled in my own right as a teacher, and I got the opportunity to see her in a different light, too. We worked so well together in the classroom and rotated student stations, so the kids would get teacher check-ins with Mrs. Janes and time at the store with Mrs. Barb.

Every August, she made time for me to cut up laminated projects and stickers so I could give them to my students as rewards. She helped me decorate my classroom and grade my papers. She came to my little classroom play productions and boasted to everyone we knew how wonderful her little Margie, "the teacher," was doing at that school.

Another huge blessing came from seeing my mom as a grandma. She made each interaction with my kids special. She turned her basement into a playground for riding in big, foot-pedaled cars or bouncing on giant exercise balls. She thrilled my kids with fort-building and would crawl along under blankets and cushions with them. She and my dad would set up Jenga blocks in long winding paths and let the kids knock them down like dominos. She played Barbie dolls, cars, and dress-up. She ordered fake food from my kids at their little toy kitchen. They played Uno together, read books, colored pictures, played with stickers, and watched cute children's shows like *Super Why* on PBS.

All of these adult interactions I had with my mom happened as she battled cancer. And she never complained.

My mom fought cancer for 20 years after they discovered it had spread from her kidney to her lungs. She is the strongest woman I've ever known. She put her faith, family, and friends before her pain and discomfort, and God blessed us with another twenty years of Barb Sansone.

My adult years with my mom were so important to me.

My mom was an old soul and a classic in her own right. She literally never used a computer. She never sent a single text message. And although she didn't have a Facebook account, over 1,000 people showed up at her wake to pay their respects and honor her life. In a world of fake friends, pretenses online, and living for "likes," my mom was truly authentic.

This story is dedicated to you, Mom, the beloved Mrs. Barb, and Grandma Chino. I love you, and I miss you so much. I hope I'm making you proud.

If you or someone you love is battling cancer and
you need help, contact *CancerCare* at
1-800-813-HOPE (4673).

If you or someone you love is suffering from grief
and loss, please contact *Grief Share* at
1-800-395-5755.

If you or someone you love is battling depression
or having thoughts of self-harm, there is hope.
Contact *Pathlight the Mood & Anxiety Center* at
1-866-619-9298.

Acknowledgments

This book would not have been possible without a collection of people who are so dear to me.

Hilary, Book Goddess, and Word Nerd. You never cease to amaze me with your insight, brilliance, and endless positive influence. Thank you for taking on another project with me. I am so grateful for your time and efforts. I know that working with you will always result in the best version of what my heart strives to compose. Thank you for believing in me and for loving my stories.

Thank you to the entire Bookmark Publishing House team. Kirby and Mats, you have been visionaries for me. Your time, efforts, and expertise are much appreciated. I am so fortunate to work with both of you.

I am very grateful to Renee and Kelly for their help with the research. I appreciate the time you took to speak with me and problem-solve some sensitive matters in this story.

I am once again so thankful for Jean Lachat Photography and her gorgeous photos. Jean, I appreciate your time and professionalism. Thanks for being there to see this project through, from the first photos to the blog and this latest photoshoot. I am so grateful for your support.

Thanks to Gigi for bringing Beck to life AGAIN on this second cover. I am honored to have you be a huge part of this process. Thank you to Brooke and Vivi for the gorgeous images you gave me. It was a true joy to have you light up this cover the way only a mother and daughter could do. Thank you.

A big thanks goes out to my advance readers, Stacie, Stephanie, Mike, Katherine, Karen, and Carey. I am grateful for your assistance, sharp eyes, collaboration, and suggestions. Thank you for helping to make this story better. And thank you to Katie for helping me realize that, yes, a sequel did exist; I just had to unlock that.

This time around I have to give a huge thank you to the Bookstagram friends who have embraced me as an author and helped in some way to get the word out about my books. Thank you Katie (@nose.stuck.in.abook), Kelsey (@Kelseysbooked), Victoria (@vlanigan.f.off.im.reading), Heather (@_lifewithheather_), Christine (@behappyreadbooks), and Sarah (@bookmarked_by_sarah) for the posts, stories, ratings, reviews, and book love for *True Companion* and *True Promise*. I am so happy to have discovered this fun and supportive world of book lovers. Thank you!

I hoped, in some way, that this story would honor my parents. Dad, thank you for your endless, unconditional love and for taking such good care of Mom for all those years. I can't imagine a better example of faithfulness and care from a father or a husband to his family. I love you so much. And thanks for being such a supportive cheerleader for me. You are the sweetest, and we are so blessed to have you.

Billy, Haley, and Hunter, you are my world. I love you so much and thank God for you. Nothing in my life happens without the thought of you all behind it. Thank you for giving me so much inspiration and love. Thank you for being my everything.

The older I become, the more I understand how important girlfriends and sisters are in this life. As I wrote situations with Janet, Lindsay, and Amy, I realized how fulfilling my life is because of my own friendships. My EIU girls, my girls' trip girls, book club friends, my teacher friends. You ladies keep the smile on my face and give me a sense of belonging. When I wrote about Colleen in this book, I felt that sister bond. I am blessed to have my sister, Sue, who is so encouraging and so giving of her time. Sue has become my stand-in at any moment when I need to talk to my mom. She's not replacing my mom, but she's become more than a sister to me. I know we will always have each other's backs in any situation. It's amazing to have that connection. I love you, Suesh. Thank you for everything. Some friends become sisters, like

Michele and Marisa, of course. I know that we will always be there for each other. Whatever heartache or joy we will encounter, we will experience it together without question. I am beyond grateful for you both. Colleen and Janet are my tributes to you.

Last, but not least, to you, dear reader. If you are reading this section of my book, then YOU are the most important thank you I could give. Thank you, reader, for choosing this story. Thank you for going on this emotional rollercoaster with Beck and TJ. Thank you for giving me an audience. I can't tell you how much it means to me to have you absorb the words I have poured into this story, so you can keep them and make this story yours. You have an essential part in TJ and Beck's love story. I hope you enjoyed *True Companion* and *True Promise*. If you did, please share your thoughts about them, post about these stories, and rate and review them. Please tag me in your comments if your experience was a positive one. I am so very grateful to have captured your attention with my stories for a brief time in this hectic world. Thank you, thank you, thank you!

About the Author

Margie Janes is an Amazon best-selling author and the 3x first-place winner of The BookFest Awards for her debut, new adult romance *True Companion*. Margie grew up in the suburbs of Chicago and graduated from Eastern Illinois University, where she met her husband, Bill, before earning a master's degree from Olivet Nazarene University. Now an elementary school teacher, she is fortunate to spend her days teaching, connecting with, learning from, and entertaining a room full of 9-year-olds. Margie began writing *True Companion* at the age of thirteen after being inspired by Phil Colin's 1990 music video "Do You Remember?" featuring a girl and boy who instantly connect and become friends until an unexpected event separates them. *True Promise* is the continuation of *True Companion* and picks up where Beck and TJ's story left off. Margie loves reading, writing, watching movies, spending time with family and friends, cheering at her kids' sporting activities, and playing with her rescue pup, Skyler.

Book Club Discussion Questions

1. How has Beck changed over the course of Book 1 and Book 2?

2. What if anything surprised you in this book? Why?

3. In the bridge painting scene, who do you think Suzanne is leaving behind, Beck or Rachel? Why do you think this?

4. How could you connect the art space and TJ's church? What do these spaces have in common, and how do these areas help to move the story forward?

5. If you could hang out with any female character in this story, who would it be and why?

6. If you could hang out with any male character in this story, who would it be and why?

7. What was your favorite scene and why?

8. Is there any part of this story that made you nostalgic for your younger years? If so, which scene and why?

9. Where do you see this story going after the epilogue? What happens next?